AT YOUR SERVICE . . .

Underhill looked around for a salesman, but it was another mechanical that came gliding silently to meet him. A twin of the one in the window, it moved with a quick, surprising grace. Bronze and blue lights flowed over its lustrous blackness, and a yellow name-plate flashed from its naked breast:

HUMANOID
Serial No. 81-H-B-27
The Perfect Mechanical
"To Serve and Obey,
And GUARD MEN FROM HARM."

Curiously, it had no lenses. The eyes in its bald oval head were steel-colored, blindly staring. Yet it stopped a few feet in front of him, as if it could see anyhow, and it spoke to him with a high, melodious voice.

"At your service, Mr. Underhill."

And that was the beginning of the end!

THE BEST OF
Jack Williamson

Introduction by
FREDERIK POHL

A Del Rey Book

BALLANTINE BOOKS • NEW YORK

ACKNOWLEDGMENTS

"The Metal Man," copyright 1928 by Experimenter Publications, Inc., for *Amazing Stories*, December 1928.

"Dead Star Station," copyright 1933 by Street & Smith Publications, Inc., for *Astounding Stories*, November 1933.

"Nonstop to Mars" copyright 1939 by Frank A. Munsey Company, for *Argosy*, February 14, 1939.

"The Crucible of Power," copyright 1939 by Street & Smith Publications, Inc., for *Astounding Stories*, February 1939.

"Breakdown," copyright 1941 by Street & Smith Publications, Inc., for *Astounding Science Fiction*, January 1942.

"With Folded Hands," copyright 1947 by Street & Smith Publications, Inc., for *Astounding Science Fiction*, July 1947.

"The Equalizer," copyright 1947 by Street & Smith Publications, Inc., for *Astounding Science Fiction*, March 1947.

"The Peddler's Nose," copyright 1951 by Street & Smith Publications, Inc., for *Astounding Science Fiction*, April 1951.

"The Happiest Creature," copyright 1953 by Ballantine Books, Inc., for *Star Science Fiction Stories* No. 2.

"The Cold Green Eye," copyright 1953 by Ziff-Davis Publishing Co., for *Fantastic*, March-April 1953.

"Operation Gravity," copyright 1953 by Gernsback Publications, Inc., for *Science Fiction Plus*, October 1953.

"Guinevere for Everybody," copyright 1954 by Ballantine Books, Inc., for *Star Science Fiction Stories* No. 3.

"Jamboree," copyright © 1969 by Universal Publishing and Distributing Corporation for *Galaxy*, December 1969.

"The Highest Dive," copyright © 1976 by New English Library, Ltd., for *Science Fiction Monthly*, Vol. 3, No. 1.

Contents

Jack Williamson: The Pathfinder

WHEN ARTHUR CLARKE was asked why he wrote science fiction, he said, "Because it is the only literature that concerns itself with reality." That is the sort of claim that sometimes gets us science-fiction writers in trouble with the staider branches of the academic and literary professions: "Reality"? In stories that have to do with ray-guns and Martians and time machines?

But Arthur Clarke is right, because the greatest and newest reality that confronts us all is change. Social change. Technological change. Environmental change. Even change within our inmost personalities, with drugs and behavior modification and still scarier possibilities looming just ahead. Science fiction is the literature of change, and the best way most of us have for preparing ourselves for the joys and dangers of the years ahead.

If there is a reliable guide to the pathways of change among us, it has to be Jack Williamson—in his work, in his thoughts and even in the story of his life.

Jack's first memories include the long trek by covered wagon—by covered wagons!—to new lands in Eastern New Mexico. Those were the days before instant communication and high-speed air transport. They were even before good roads and electrification, and the life of some of the sod-hut settlers he grew up among was searingly isolated, chancey and hard. It took a tough breed to scratch out a living from dry-land farming and the forty-acre cattle of the sandy plains—one head for every forty acres, because that is all the sparse sage and buffalo-grass will support. A lot of the settlers failed. Some died. The survivors typically faced the world with a good deal of self-confidence because they knew they could handle just about anything it sent.

Jack's early life cannot be described as easy. As an infant, he almost died of one of those vaguely diagnosed

diseases called *cholera infantum*. His father was diligent
and smart; what he was not was lucky. When he staked
a claim, it turned out to have no water under it. When he
found a new chance across the border in Mexico, he was
driven out by a revolution. When Jack was old enough to
take some share of responsibility for the family fortunes,
he managed to accumulate a herd of half a dozen steers.
But the bad luck followed. Most of the herd died from eating poison oak, and the lone survivor was killed by lightning.

It is hard to imagine a child in such surroundings, collecting buffalo chips for fuel to keep warm and a three-
day journey from the nearest town, growing up to live a
distinguished life in the world of the imagination and the
mind. But there is something to the notion of challenge
and response. What happened to Jack Williamson was that,
from an early age, he was thrown on his own resources for
intellectual stimulation. He found that stimulation in the
way that a good many other science-fiction writers found
it, through reading—uncritical and absorbed reading of
everything he could get his hands on—and through the
roaming of his imagination, to carry along and expand the
implications of what he had read. At the age of eighteen,
he discovered science fiction, in the form of the new magazine called *Amazing Stories,* then less than a year old.
He had had glimpses of that kind of story before—a
teacher had loaned him Mark Twain's *A Connecticut Yankee in King Arthur's Court.* But *Amazing Stories* was proof
that sf was not just an occasional odd aberration, but a
whole new area of literary exploration. Jack decided at
once to try to write it. He wrote three stories and sent
them off; they all came back with rejection slips. He wrote
a fourth, called "*The Metal Man,*" sent it off, too, to the
same market, *Amazing Stories . . .* and time passed, and
he heard nothing, no acceptance and no rejection, either,
until in the winter of 1928 he walked past a Texas drugstore and saw the new issue of *Amazing* there. His story
was in it.

He was twenty years old.

Jack was in Texas at the time going to school. A small
windfall had given his family enough money to pay his college tuition for at least a year or two, and he had enrolled
as a freshman at West Texas State. The money didn't last.
Jack had to drop out without completing his undergraduate

years, but by then he knew that he was a writer, and a science-fiction writer at that, and he worked at the craft from then on. The market expanded. Gernsback left *Amazing Stories* and started a new competitor, *Wonder Stories*. The first issue of *Astounding* appeared. A few years later there was an explosion of new titles—*Marvel,* and *Planet,* and *Startling,* and *Cosmic,* and *Future,* and a dozen others, including my own two magazines that began appearing in 1940, *Astonishing* and *Super Science.* Jack wrote for nearly all of them, prolifically and well: *The Stone from the Green Star; The Legion of Space; The Legion of Time; Darker Than You Think;* and other novels, novelettes, and short stories beyond counting. He was a star in the young and growing field of science fiction almost from the first, proved by the response of the fans, the imitation of younger writers, and the eagerness with which editors sought his work.

His success was not, however, proved by his bank account. Sf writing in the 1930s was not well paid. Stories like "Dead Star Station," "Breakdown," and "The Crucible of Power" are still alive and well. They have been reprinted many times since those years and, over their life, have provided a sort of annuity; but what they earned for Jack at the time he was writing them was seldom more than a cent a word. Even that was often hard to collect. That did not really matter. Poor pay did not deter Jack Williamson from continuing to write, any more than it prevented me from doing the same when, eight or ten years later than Jack, I began my own efforts to become established as a science-fiction writer. Writing is not done for money— believe this, no matter what any writer may say in print. It is done by people who simply cannot be comfortable in their lives without it. Still, I wonder if I would have been quite as determined to make it as a science-fiction writer if I had known that even so great a success as Jack Williamson rarely managed to bank much more than a thousand dollars in any year of his first decade and a half of writing science fiction.

Along came World War II, and sent us all spinning around the globe.

When I was shipped to Chanute Field, Illinois, for technical training as an Air Force weather observer, there was Jack Williamson at the same school. He had already completed that course, gone out into the field, and served a time at an air base, and was now returned for advanced training as a weather forecaster. We had met briefly in 1939 and had kept in touch while I was editing my magazines (for which Jack was of course a valued contributor), but this was the first time in four years we had been in the same place.

Science-fiction writers as a class are alert, informed, interested. Jack stands high in the class. His presence at Chanute made the bleak military base a lot more friendly. Jack is quick of thought and slow of speech, and about as good company as I have ever found. Over the years I have been lucky enough to roam a number of unfamiliar places with Jack, from Stonehenge to a flying-saucer site in Socorro, New Mexico. I chatter. Jack listens. And then, just as I am wondering whether he has actually heard the last twenty-five or thirty sentences I have uttered, he delivers a short paragraph that summarizes all the main points at issue and advances the conversation to a new level. Jack looks like a weatherbeaten southwestern cowhand, but behind that John Wayne face is a fast and thoughtful brain.

From Chanute we went in our separate directions, Jack winding up on a rock in the South Pacific and I in Italy, but when the war was over we both came home to science fiction. Twenty years after his first sale, Jack began a new writing career in a new and more demanding sf market, and grew to meet its demands as a few other writers of his generation were able to do. Those were the years, in the late 1940s and 1950s, when he was writing "With Folded Hands" and "The Equalizer" and "The Peddler's Nose." The sequel to "With Folded Hands," "—And Searching Mind," became that classic of science-fiction novels, *The Humanoids*, still a model to any science-fiction writer who would deal with robots (and even to any computer scientist who would study artificial intelligence). The stakes were higher, now. Jack's stories were appearing in book form, receiving serious critical attention, and being translated into dozens of languages all around the world. But Jack was still not quite satisfied. He had left a couple of things unfinished in his youth. So he married his childhood sweetheart, Blanche, and a few years later went back to school. He got his bachelor's degree, his master's, and his doctorate, and, in his mid-fifties, launched a new career as a university professor.

He kept on writing—of course. But in the dignity of his persona as John Stewart Williamson, Ph.D., he was able to do something more for science fiction than most writers ever can. More and more he devoted his efforts to the academic side of sicence fiction. He taught it in his classes at Eastern New Mexico University. He research-ed and prepared the first complete list of science-fiction courses in American colleges. He helped in uncountable ways in the preparation of teaching texts, in the forma-tion of the professional organization of science-fiction academics, and in the foundation of journals of science-fiction studies. Eastern New Mexico University knew a good thing when they had it, and so they kept Jack on well past the usual retirement age. But last spring they bowed to his desire to have more free time for writing and travel. They appointed him to the lifetime post of Dis-tinguished Professor Emeritus, marked the occasion with the first of an annual series of lectures in his honor, and set him free.

James Gunn, Jack's opposite number at the University of Kansas, was one of the speakers on that occasion, and I was honored to be allowed to be the other. Jim Gunn and I had known Jack for a long time, as friend, collaborator, and colleague. It was not surprising that the air was thick with compliments. The surprising part was that they were all true.

The other surprising thing was what Jack did after the retirement was official. At seventy, you would think the fellow would want to loaf for a while. Not Jack. He and Blanche went off for a month's exploration of Scandi-navia and the Soviet Union, and returned to sign contracts for a series of novels and other works that would tax the strength of a twenty-year-old.

A few years ago, at a convention of science-fiction academics, I was pleased to run into Marvin Minsky. Minsky is one of the great unartificial brains of the arti-ficial-intelligence business, head of MIT's A.I. laboratory, pioneer in more fields of computer studies than I can count, famous to some of us as the fellow who tried to program Asimov's Three Laws of Robotics into a computer. Minsky is no stranger to science fiction or to science-fiction writers, having led any number of them through the computer laboratories at MIT. But he had something specific in mind at that convention. He had heard that Jack Williamson was present, and would I please introduce him?

I did, and I think Jack was surprised, if not pleased, to hear from Minsky's own lips that *The Humanoids* was Minsky's personal candidate for the best nontechnical description of the way real artificial intelligence was likely to operate that had ever until that time been written.

That's the sort of accolade sf writers really relish, and not the only one of its kind Jack has had. (One of the Los Alamos scientists confided in him that the scientist's interest in technological superweapons had been sparked long before the Manhattan Project by AKKA in *The Legion of Space*.)

And that is the sort of accolade that Jack Williamson has fairly earned, and goes on earning—in novels like *The Humanoids* and *The Legion of Space* and the others, in his short stories like the ones in this cream-of-the-crop volume and in the works he is just now putting on to paper. It's a privilege to know Jack Williamson, and a delight to read him.

The Science Fiction Writers of America each year award Nebulas for the best works in the field for the year past, but they have a special award that is not for one particular story but for a lifetime of achievement. Only three of them have ever been given. One went to Robert A. Heinlein, and another to Clifford D. Simak. The one in the middle, the second "Grand Master Nebula" authorized by SFWA, went to Jack Williamson.

It, too, was fairly earned, because the award is not only a trophy but an accurate description of the man: Jack Williamson *is* a Grand Master of science fiction, and an example to us all.

Frederik Pohl
Red Bank, New Jersey
1977

The Metal Man

THE METAL MAN stands in a dusty basement corner of the Tyburn College museum. Though the first excitement has subsided, his placement there is still an uneasy academic compromise, which so far has saved him from the scientists who want to cut him up for biochemical analysis and the old friends who think he should be buried.

To the casual tourist, he is only a life-sized piece of time-greened bronze. A closer look shows the perfect detail of his hair and skin and the agony frozen on his face. A few visitors stop to frown at the peculiar mark on his chest—a red, six-sided blot.

People have almost forgotten now that he was once Professor Thomas Kelvin of the Department of Geology. Yet the rumors about him are still alive, growing stranger than the truth. Because those rumors are so distressing to his friends, the regents have at last agreed to let me publish his own narrative.

For four or five years, Kelvin had spent his vacations along the Pacific slope of Mexico, prospecting for uranium. The last summer, apparently he found it. Instead of returning to his classes in the fall, he asked for an extended leave.

We heard later that he had sold his uranium claims to a Swiss syndicate, that he was lecturing in Europe on the chemical and biological effects of atomic radiation, that he himself was under treatment at a clinic near Paris.

He came back to Tyburn on a gloomy Saturday afternoon, out of an early winter fog that was drifting off the Gulf Stream. I was at home, raking leaves on the seaward slope of my place below the campus, when I saw the boat coming in toward my rocky little scrap of Atlantic beach. The boat was a stranger—long and low and fast, of the sort once favored by runners of illicit rum or guns. I dropped my rake to watch.

Piloted with daring and skill, the boat threaded the offshore rocks toward the only yard of sand in half a mile. Four men sprang out, to rush it through the surf. A gaunt fifth man rose in the stern, calling quiet orders. The four ripped ropes and canvas from a coffin-sized box, which they carried up into my yard. The gaunt man limped stiffly to where I stood.

"Tyburn College?"

His men had dark Latin faces, but his scarred and weather-reddened features were masked with a curly yellow beard, and his voice had a Yankee twang. Impatiently, he stabbed a lean finger toward the campus bell tower, dim in the fog.

At last I nodded.

"Here we are." He murmured soft Spanish to his men. Grinning, they set the long box down. He looked at me. "Do you know a Professor Russell?"

"I'm Russell."

"If that's so, our job's done." He gestured at the chest. "It's for you."

"Huh? What is it?"

"You'll find out." His hard eyes narrowed. "I think you'll want to keep it quiet."

He spoke to his men again, and they moved the chest to my back porch.

"Wait! Who are you?"

"Just delivery men." He gestured gently. "We've been paid. We'll be on our way."

He nodded to his men, who hurried toward the boat.

"But I don't understand—"

"You'll find a letter in the box," he said. "It explains why your friend took this way home. You'll see why he didn't want to trouble the immigration people."

"My friend?"

"Kelvin. Look in the box."

He started back toward the boat.

"Just a minute!" I shouted after him. "Where are you going?"

"South." He paused very briefly. "Look in the box—and give us twenty-four hours. Kelvin promised us that."

Not hurrying, he limped on down to the boat. His men pushed it off the sand. The muffled motors purred. Turning in the surf, the long craft slid between the rocks and vanished in the fog. I walked slowly back to the chest on the porch.

It was not locked. I lifted the lid—and dropped it back again. Lying in the box, stark naked, that queer blot stamped in livid red on the bronze-green breast, was the Metal Man.

A battered aluminum canteen lay beside his head, crusted with a purple stain. Beneath the canteen lay a sheaf of dog-eared pages covered with Kelvin's old-fashioned script.

I had to nerve myself to lift the lid again. I bent for a long time, trembling and staring, unable to grasp what I saw. At last I stumbled into the house and read Kelvin's narrative:

"Dear Russell—

"Because you are my sanest friend, I have arranged to have my body and this manuscript delivered to you. Perhaps I am laying an unfair burden on you, but at this point I no longer trust myself. I am still uncertain what I really found in Mexico. I cannot decide whether these fragmentary facts should be published or suppressed. Nor can I cope any longer with those ruthless men who want to rob me of what they think I found. Though my death will not be easy, I'm afraid I die in greater peace than I leave behind me.

"As you know, my goal last summer was the headwaters of El Rio de la Sangre. This is a small stream that flows into the Pacific. The year before I had found a strong radioactivity in its red-stained waters, and I hoped to strike uranium ores somewhere upriver.

"Twenty-five miles above the mouth, the river emerges from the Cordilleras. There are a few miles of rapids, and then the first waterfall. Nobody has ever been beyond the falls. I had reached their foot with an Indian guide, but failed to climb the cliffs beyond.

"Last winter I took flying lessons and bought a used airplane. It was old and slow, but suited to that rough country. When summer came, I shipped it to Vaca Morena. On the first day of July, I set out to fly up the river to its undiscovered source.

"Though I was still an unseasoned pilot, the old plane flew well. The stream beneath me looked like a red snake crawling down through the mountains to the sea. I followed it beyond the falls, into a region of towering peaks.

"The river disappeared in a narrow, black-walled gorge. I circled to look for a place to land, but the whole landscape was naked granite and jagged lava. I climbed over a high pass and found the crater.

"An incredible pool of green fire, fully ten miles across, walled with dark volcanic rock. At first I thought the green was water, but its hazy surface had no waves. I knew it must be some heavy gas.

"The high peaks around it still had snow. Their silver crowns were brushed with splendid color, crimson on the westward slopes, purple rising from shadows. That wild glory held me, even while the feel of it disturbed me.

"Night was near. I knew I should be turning back. Yet I stayed, wheeling over the crater, because I couldn't understand that pool of gas. As the sun sank lower, I saw stranger things. A thin greenish mist gathered over the peaks. It flowed down every slope into the pit, as if it fed that gas lake. Then something stirred the lake itself. The center of it bulged upward into a glowing dome.

"When the sluggish gas flowed back, I saw a huge red sphere rising out of the pit. Its surface was smooth, metallic, and thickly studded with great spikes of yellow fire. It spun very slowly on a vertical axis. Weird as it seemed, I sensed purpose in its motion.

"It climbed above my own level and paused there, still spinning. Now I saw a circular spot of dull black over each pole of the sphere. I saw misty streamers from the peaks and the pool drawn into those spots, as if the sphere somehow inhaled them.

"For a little time the globe hung above me. The yellow spikes shone slowly brighter, until the whole object blazed like a great golden planet, while it sucked the last scraps of mist from the peaks. Suddenly, when they stood black and bare, it dropped back into that flat green sea.

"With its fall, a sinister shadow fell over the crater. With a start, I realized how much gasoline and daylight I had used. At once I turned back toward the coast.

"More puzzled than afraid, I was trying to decide whether that thing from the pit had been natural or artificial, reality or illusion. I remember imagining that these enormous deposits of uranium might have unforeseen effects. It occurred to me, too, that perhaps somebody had got here ahead of me, and that perhaps I had seen the trial of an atomic ship.

"With a shock of real alarm, I saw a pale blue glow spreading over the cowling of the cockpit. In a moment the whole plane, and even my body, was covered with it. I gunned the motor and tried to climb.

"Though the motor labored, I couldn't climb. Some queer G-force, connected I thought with that blue glow, was pulling me now. Dizziness dulled my thoughts, and my heavy arms began to drag at the controls.

"I had to dive, to keep flying speed. Almost before I knew what was happening, I plunged into that gas lake. It was not suffocating, as I had expected. Though it cut visibility to just a few yards, I noticed no odor or other sensation.

"A dark surface loomed under me. I pulled out of the dive and managed to land on a smooth plain of coarse red sand. Like the green gas, the sand was dully luminous.

"For a time I was confined to the cockpit by my own weight, but slowly that blue glow faded, along with its effect. I climbed out of the plane with my canteen and my automatic pistol, which were themselves still immensely heavy.

"Unable to stand erect, I crawled away across the sand. I felt sure that I had been brought down by something intelligent. I was deathly afraid, yet soon I had to stop and rest.

"Lying there, perhaps a hundred yards from the plane, I saw five blue lights drifting toward it through the fog. I lay still and watched them wheel around the plane. Their motion was heavy and slow. The mist made dull halos around them. They had no structure that I could see.

"At last they lifted back into the haze, and I went on. Though my excess gravity had faded away, I went on hands and knees until the plane was out of sight. When I stood up, my sense of direction was gone.

"A helpless fear swept over me. Bright red sand and thick green fog—that's all I could see. No landmark, not even a moving light. The soundless air pressed down like a shapeless weight. I trembled with a panic sense of utter isolation.

"I don't know how long I stood there, afraid of moving in the wrong direction. Suddenly a light darted above me, like a blue meteor. In my alarm, I ran from that. After a few blundering steps, my foot struck something that rang like metal.

"The clatter froze me with new terror, but the light moved on. When it was gone, I bent to see what I had kicked. It was a metal bird—an eagle formed of metal—wings outspread, talons grasping, beak set open. Its color was a tarnished green.

"At first I took it for a cast model of a real bird, but then I found each feather separate and flexible—as if a living eagle had been turned to metal. I remembered that fissioning uranium transmutes itself to lead, and wondered if intense radiation could transmute the tissues of a bird.

"Fear seized me, for my own body. Anxiously I began to look for other transformed creatures. I found them in abundance scattered over the sand or half buried in it. Birds, large and small. Flying insects, most of them strange to me. Even a pterosaur—a flying reptile that must have reached the pit long ages past.

"Scrabbling to dig it out of the glowing sand, I saw a green glint from my own hands. The tips of my fingernails and the fine hairs on the back of my hands were already changed to light green metal!

"The shock of that discovery unnerved me completely. I screamed aloud, careless of what might hear, and ran off in blind panic. I forgot that I was lost. Reason and caution were left behind. I felt no fatigue as I ran—only black terror.

"Bright, swift lights passed above me in the green, but I gave them no heed. Unexpectedly, I came up to the great sphere I had seen from above. It rested motionless in a black metal cradle. The yellow fire was gone from the spikes but a score of blue lights floated above it like lanterns swinging in a fog.

"I turned and ran again. Direction didn't matter. Neither did time. What stopped me at last was a bank of queer vegetation. The stuff was violet in color, waist deep and grasslike, with narrow spikes for leaves. The tallest center spikes were tipped with pink blooms and little purple berries.

"A sluggish red stream ran through the thicket—I thought it must be El Rio de la Sangre. Here, anyhow, was cover from the flying lights. I threw myself down in the deep tangle and lay there sobbing.

"For a long time, I couldn't stir or think. When at last I inspected my fingernails, the green tips looked wider. Frantically I gnawed at them, but the hideous fact refused to go away. I was changing into metal.

"Wildly I groped for a way to escape. I had to scale the crater walls or else recover the plane, yet I felt too weak to move. Though I felt no actual hunger, I thought food might give me strength.

"Recklessly, I picked a few of those purple berries.

They had a salty, metallic taste. I spat them out, afraid they would make me ill. But, in pulling them, I had got the juice on my fingers. When I wiped it off, I found, to my amazement and my inexpressible joy, that the metal rim was gone from the nails it had touched.

"I had found hope. The evolution of the plants, I thought, must have produced something that resisted transmutation. I stuffed myself with berries till I began to feel sick, then poured the water from my canteen and squeezed juice to fill it.

"Since then I have analyzed the fluid. Some of its constituents resemble the standard formulas for the treatment for X-ray burns. It doubtless saved me from the terrible burns caused by gamma radiation.

"I lay there till dawn, dozing sometimes in spite of my terror. Sunlight must have filtered down through that pool of gas. By day the green faded to a greenish gray, and even the red sand seemed less luminous.

"All the green, I found, was now gone from my nails and hair. Immensely cheered by that, I ate another handful of the berries and set off along that little river. I walked downstream, counting my paces.

"Before I had gone three miles, I came to the pitch-blende cliffs. Abrupt and black, they towered up as far as I could see into the thick green gloom. The river disappeared beneath them, in a roaring pool of red foam.

This, I felt sure, must be the west rim of the crater. I turned north beneath that unclimbable wall. Still I had no definite plan, except to find a path across the cliffs. I kept alert for those floating lights and looked for a slope or a chimney that I could climb.

"I plodded on until it must have been noon, though my watch had stopped. Sometimes I stumbled over more things that must have been alive when they fell from above. Uprooted trees. Birds of every sort. A huge green bear, its breed long extinct.

"At last I found a break in that vertical wall—a wide flat shelf with an inviting slope above it. But that ledge was a good sixty feet above me. I tried to reach it and slid back, again and again, until my hands were bleeding. I gave up and went on.

"Somewhere beyond, groggy with exhaustion and despair, I staggered into a city of the flying lights—that's what it must have been. Slim black towers stood scattered across the red sand. Each one was topped with a great mushroom of orange flame.

"Fresh terror paralyzed me, but I heard no sound and saw no motion. Crouching under the overhanging cliff, I tried to take stock. The flying lights, I now suspected, were not active by day—but I felt sick with dread of the night.

"By my reckoning, I had made about fifteen miles from the river. Now I must be somewhere along the east wall of the crater, with a good half of the cliffs still ahead. To explore them, I had to pass that city of flames, yet I dared not enter it.

"I left the rim, to walk around the city. I tried to keep those tall flares in view, but somehow I lost them. I veered to the left, but all I found was more flat sand, smothered under dull green murk.

"On and on I wandered, until the sand and the air grew brighter. Dusk had fallen. The floating lights were soon in motion. The night before, they had gone straight and high and fast. Now they were low, uncertain, slow. I knew they were searching—for me!

"I scooped out a shallow trench in the sand and lay there shivering. Mist-veiled points of light came near and passed. Another stopped, directly overhead. It sank toward me. Its pale halo grew. Paralyzed with terror, I could only wait.

"Down and down it came, until I saw its form. It was a crystal thing. I watched it with a sick fascination. A dozen feet long, it had an intricate structure like a crystal of snow. The heart of it was a blue, six-pointed star. An upright prism pierced the star. Blue fire pulsed through it, flowing inward from the points of the star, and threads of bright scarlet trailed outward from the faces of the prism. Neither animal nor plant nor even machine, it was alive—alive with light!

"It fell straight toward me.

"In a reflexive act of panic, I pulled my automatic and fired three shots. The bullets glanced off those glittering planes and whined away into the fog.

"It paused above me. Those threads of red fire trailed down around me, questingly, somehow caressingly. They wound around my body—and I felt my weight drained out. They lifted me against the crystal prism. You may see its mark on my chest.

"That contact stunned me with blinding pain. My whole body writhed, as if from a cruel electric shock. Dimly, I knew the thing was rising with me. I had a sense of other crystal creatures swarming near. But my mind was fading out.

"I awoke floating free in a brilliant orange cloud. For a moment I felt elated, but then I found I couldn't move, couldn't even turn my body. I reached and kicked and twisted, but I could touch no solid object. Though nothing held me, I was helpless as a turtle on its back.

"My body was still clothed. My canteen still hung— or floated—by my shoulder. My automatic was still in my jacket pocket, solid but weightless. Yet somehow I knew that days had passed.

"Struggling to move myself, I felt a queer numb stiffness in my side. I ripped my shirt open and found a new scar there, almost healed. I believe those creatures had cut into me—exploring my body, I suppose, as I had explored their world.

"I must have blacked out again when I felt the hardened granular deadness of the skin over my chest and found that red, six-sided print. Yet that discovery brought me to some limit of emotion. I woke in a mood of remote detachment, as if I didn't really care.

"But my side still hurt. The orange cloud was still around me. My crystal captor was drifting in it with me, not a dozen yards away. In my cool unconcern, I knew that I was trapped in the mushroom cloud above one of those towering cylinders, a prisoner in that alien city of flame.

"For a time I simply floated there, weightless as a man in space, watching my own predicament from that mood of aloof abstraction. Indifferently, I observed that the vital fire had ceased to pulse inside the crystal creature. It was sleeping, I supposed, till night came again.

"That chain of thought lit a faint spark of hope in me. Once more I kicked and clawed at the cloud around me. With nothing to push against, I failed to move an inch.

"While I struggled like a bug on a pin, that cold flame grew slowly brighter around me. Night, I knew, was falling. The crystal things would soon awake, no doubt to resume the vivisection of their human guinea pig.

"I could see only one way to cheat them. I was pulling my automatic to put a bullet into my own head, when a better idea hit me. I fired six quick shots out into the fog.

"That move saved me. A rocket needs nothing to push against. The gun was a sort of rocket. The recoil of each explosion nudged me farther from the sleeping crystal. I slid out of the mushroom cloud.

"Gravity caught me again, at first very gently. Drifting down to the luminous sand, I found my airplane drawn up to the foot of that slim black tower. It was intact. The motor balked for a moment, as if my captors had been into it as well as into me. At last it caught. I took off blind—"

At this point, there's a break in the manuscript. The remaining lines are on another tattered page. They seem to be in Kelvin's old-fashioned hand, but here it is a ragged pencil scrawl, not always readable.

"End of my [rope?] Guess I diluted the [canteen?] too many times. My body and effects I will to science. Captain Gander will supply the [conclusion?] of my story. The frightening [truth?]—"

That was all.

I called my physician. He's a sour-featured Scotch Presbyterian who doesn't care for the twentieth century. He read the manuscript with an air of indignant unbelief, scowled over the transmuted body, and dourly advised me to keep the story quiet.

That might have been prudent, but it proved impossible. Too many people heard tantalizing rumors. Some came, I'm afraid, from my faculty colleagues at Tyburn. Others, I'm sure, did not.

Though Captain Gander has never come forward with whatever he knows, we tried to learn the rest of the story. That next summer, three of us from Tyburn chartered our own airplane and flew to western Mexico.

We easily found the coastal village that *Señor* Kelvin had visited once—but not, its people insisted, within the past three years. We talked to the men who had guided him back into the high sierra; we even followed up the rocky bed of that mountain stream where he had hunted uranium. Its waters were now neither red nor radioactive, however, and its source was only a boggy spring.

Flying over that spring and peaks beyond, we found no crater filled with glowing gas, but only another stone-and-adobe pueblo three hundred years old. When we landed there, we discovered no metal birds or living crystals or atomic ships. We did, however, hear of three strangers who had been there before us.

One was a limping, bearded *gringo,* who had asked mad questions and cursed those who could not answer to please him. One was an elegant Swiss banker, who had wandered about the pueblo carrying a Geiger counter and staring at everybody with a monocle like an evil eye. The third was another *gringo,* who had come three summers from the north and driven on into the high Cordillera, hauling tarp-covered crates in an old military truck.

Among such confusing clues, we lost Kelvin's trail in Mexico. There were other mysterious strangers, however, who followed us back to Tyburn. Some of them were federal investigators, who questioned all of us, searched Kelvin's premises, photocopied his documents, and finally carried his transmuted body away for study by the AEC.

When they finally returned the body to Tyburn, they were remarkably tight-lipped and silent, even for federal men. No official report has ever mentioned the Metal Man, and the rumors that still circulate, sometimes, around him are wildly contradictory.

Part of the truth had been concealed, but I don't know who to blame. There's Captain Gander—who surely owns another name, and quite possibly doctored Kelvin's manuscript. There's the Swiss banker—who used to sit in the *cantina* reading a French translation of Wells' *Time Machine,* never talking to anybody. There's the AEC—whose agents certainly learned more than they ever told. There's Kelvin himself—who may have been lying to hide what he actually discovered.

But I've come to believe that Kelvin's story is true. I spent a good many sleepless nights reviewing all the conflicting evidence, until the time I had a vivid dream of strangers visiting the earth, perhaps to refuel their atomic ship, which lay hidden in time as well as space while they were collecting and preserving stray specimens of pterosaurs and men.

However that may be, Kelvin's metal body, standing nude and scarred and dusty now in its gloomy corner, is proof enough that he did discover more than he was looking for. His lips are frozen in a green ironic smile, almost as if he is aware that Civil Defense has designated the museum basement where he stands as an emergency fall-out shelter.

Dead Star Station

THE DIFFERENCE BETWEEN a fool and a genius can be stated in one word—success. And success had not found Gideon Clew. We all tolerated the old man; most of us pitied him; some of us genuinely liked him. A neat, trim old fellow, white-haired, marvelously erect for his age, with cheeks like wrinkled red apples, and bright, sober blue eyes.

The lisp in his speech made him unintentionally droll. That must have been the chief reason why he had been so long scorned and obscure. For the lisp increased with his earnestness; he could never put his great idea into words without inadvertently rousing a desire to laugh.

Fourteen of us were waiting on Dead Star Station, in the wild, lonely Orion Passage, for the coming of the space liner *Bellatrix*. Thirteen men and a girl. Twelve of us made up the crew of the station. And the thirteenth man was Gideon Clew.

The old man, of course, had no official right to be upon the station. But mild old Captain Manners was softhearted, and the rest of us sympathetic. Gideon Clew had been aboard since before most of us were born—fifty years, he said. Fifty years is a long time for a man to be shut up in a little metal world, away from life. He had lost his place outside; he had no one to go to. It would have been cruelty to send him away.

He had been a generator-man until, ten years before, the service had automatically retired him, sent out another man to take his place. We let him stay aboard, wrapped up in the Great Idea that—had success chosen

14

to crown it—would have made him famous. We even dug into our own pockets to make up his quarterly pay check, to provide funds to carry on the experiment that was the old man's life.

And the girl was Tonia Andros.

Eight years old, she was a slim little wisp of elfin gravity. She was not actually a beautiful child; her mouth was too wide and her nose turned up impudently. But her dark eyes were wistfully grave, and all of us loved her. After all, men so far from home, from family, from all that is life, could not be critical of her.

The story of Tonia Andros must have been another of those adventures of space that are the stuff of romance. We knew but a chance fragment of it. Months before, we had found the wrecked freighter drifting. A meteor stream from the nebula had struck it; the rusty hull was riddled, and all on board—save Tonia—were frozen and dead.

She had been sealed between the valves of the main air lock, where someone must have placed her after the catastrophe. The tube of oxygen in the little cavity with her was exhausted; she was unconscious from asphyxiation and cold. But we reached her in time.

But not in time to save the ship. The wreck was already fast in the relentless gravitation field of the Dead Star. It went plunging down to incandescent ruin upon that black and dying sun, carrying with it the history of Tonia Andros, and whatever patrimony may have been hers.

The experience must have been painful; her tortured mind may have sought relief by blotting that time out of memory. Whether she remembered more we never knew, but she would tell us only her name.

Tonia was a friend to each of us. But she and old Gideon Clew felt a particular affinity. The little girl haunted his cabin, and he seemed not to fear her hands upon the precious apparatus he had gathered there.

The child must have brought something of the warm glow of life back into a nature that had been shut off from life too long. Gideon turned aside from his invention to make toys for her, with his skilled old hands. Yet he worked even harder, and he told us that he was going to adopt her, give her home and education, when his discovery was perfected.

"When his discovery was perfected"—that phrase had been in his talk for forty years and more.

Still the thing was not done, and all of us save Gideon Clew knew that it was chimera. Now we were waiting for the *Bellatrix* to come down the passage. Captain Manners was retiring; our new officer was to come upon the liner. Manners was to take Tonia with him— though the child was not eager to leave Gideon Clew— to try to find a home for her.

The old man himself was torn between impatience and relief as we waited for the liner. It was almost breaking his heart to part with the child, who must have been his only really intimate companion in those five decades. But he was madly anxious for the vessel to come with a shipment of parts for his invention that he had ordered a year before.

Time can pass slowly on Dead Star Station. A small world, completely isolated. The station is really an obsolete war-rocket, too antiquated to fly with the system's fleets. A corroded metal hull, some two hundred feet long. Space aboard is limited, quarters cramped, means of diversion lacking.

But beyond the station's vitrolar ports is space in abundance. The view must be the most weirdly colossal, the most awesome, in all the galaxy. The Great Nebula spans the sky like an octopus of living flame. A vast, angry sea of swirling white fire, eerily tinged with the green of *nebulium*, its twisting streamers reaching out like incandescent tentacles.

Unthinkably vast, those tentacles seem to grasp the Dead Star. That cyclopean cold sun is a little black disk limned against livid flame. Its dark face is patched with marks of sullen crimson—illimitable seas of yet molten lava, for the Dead Star is not utterly dead.

The hurtling meteor streams and the seas of incandescent gas that make up the Great Nebula of Orion form the most stupendous barrier to transstellar navigation in the entire galaxy. Light itself, at one hundred and eighty-six thousand miles per second, takes three years and more to cross it.

But there is a way through. The Orion Passage. A lane kept cleared of darting meteors and burning gas by the colossal gravitation of the Dead Star, a titanic dark sun that lurks like a black spider in the bright web of the nebula, reaching out with resistless, invisible force for what it may draw to destruction.

No ship has ever visited the Dead Star. No rocket could pull away from its inconceivable surface gravity. It is estimated that a human body would weigh well over a hundred tons upon its surface—enough so that the bones would break and the flesh run away from them like water. The idea is unpleasant.

The station, equipped with powerful electronblast motors to keep her clear of the giant sun's inexorable pull, was established as an aid to navigation in the passage, her duties being to chart the continually shifting meteor streams, inform passing shipping by photophone of the safer courses, and to go to the aid of any endangered vessels.

Time passed slowly upon the tiny metal world of the station, that was but a mote hung between titan black sun and the changeless fiery glory of the nebula. But at last the *Bellatrix* came. And from dull weeks of waiting, we were plunged incontinently into mad confusion.

The *Bellatrix* was a new vessel, of three times the station's tonnage, regularly plying the passage. Those of us who could went aboard the liner during the little time the valves were coupled, to enjoy briefly the spaciousness of the vessel, her cosmopolitan atmosphere, the gossip of her curious passengers.

Vance, our photophone operator, returned with one interesting bit. He talked to one of her passengers, a man in an invalid chair, with a bandaged head. This man told him that the *Bellatrix* carried an immensely valuable cargo of uranium ingots, and that her officers had been warned to beware of Skal Doon, the interstellar buccaneer.

Even so, there was no great novelty in a warning against Skal Doon. He was one of the last freebooters of space, the most notorious and daring. For three decades he had been a terror of the void, escaping capture partly by a flair for originality, partly by ruthless cruelty in the elimination of opponents, and largely by an intimate knowledge of the mazes and fiery ways of the Great Nebula, which he knew as no other man. It is curious that men spoke of him with a certain admiration and respect, which he deserved as little as a human being could.

Gideon Clew and Tonia Andros parted at the valves. The child's wistful eyes were frankly tearful as Captain Manners led her away, and old Gideon's lisping voice choked oddly. And then the old man went to claim the long, carefully wrapped package that had come for him—the anxiously awaited parts for his invention.

Presently the new captain came aboard the station. Clive Kempton was his name. A tall young man, in severe white uniform, with the eagle insignia of the service on his cap. His face was lean and stern. We saw at once that he was the sort that takes responsibility very seriously, that considers regulations much more holy than they are—perhaps because of a subconscious fear of criticism.

A little time of bustling, mad confusion. Stores coming aboard, cylinders of oxygen, drums of fuel for our generators. Then the last shout of farewell. The valves were sealed again, uncoupled. And the *Bellatrix* went on.

We upon the station were left—or so we supposed—to wait through other weary weeks, until another vessel picked its way between the flaming walls of the passage. None of us had a premonition we were to see the liner again, so soon and under such distressing circumstances.

Hume, the station's mate, was in the bridge room with the new captain when Gideon Clew limped hesitantly in with a hopeful smile upon his red, wrinkled face.

"Captain, thir?" he lisped, a little timidly.

"What is it?" Kempton asked brusquely. "What's your name?"

He did not intend to be unkind. He was taking his new command much too seriously. The vague, blind hostility and the supernal power of the Great Nebula and the titanic Dead Star had already set their print of terror in his soul.

"Gideon Clew, thir. You thee, thir, I have invented a gravity screen. I've just installed the last parts, that came on the *Bellatrix*. Pleathe, thir, may I use power from the ship's generators to test it?"

"What's this? A shield, you mean, against the force of gravitation?"

"Yeth, thir. I've been working on it many yearth, thir."

Perhaps, if it had not been for Gideon's lisp, Kempton would have listened. But the lisp made the bright-eyed, apple-cheeked little man unconsciously and pathetically funny; and the more serious he became, the worse his lisp. And Kempton was young; he had not yet learned that regulations are made to be broken.

"How much power do you need?" he asked.

"Two hundred thousand kilowatts, thir."

Kempton, astonished, looked inquiringly around at Hume.

"Why, that's the full capacity of our generators!"

"I know, thir. But just a few minuteth——"

"Just who are you, anyhow?" the captain demanded.

Gideon's wide blue eyes stared at him in bewilderment, and Hume spoke to explain the old fellow's status upon the station.

"You know, it's against regulations for you to be here at all," Kempton said. "You must prepare to leave, Clew, when the *Bellatrix* returns. I don't understand how it happened."

"But, thir, the power——"

"I must refuse your extraordinary request. Of *course!* I want you to realize this is not a playhouse. And not an old man's home. I don't understand it!"

The serious, bright eyes about the man's little red cheeks were fixed intently upon Kempton's face for a long time. Then they began to blink, and Hume saw huge, slow tears gathering in them.

"Yeth, thir," Gideon whispered. And he stood there.

Kempton and Hume were busy with the astrographic charts, checking their maps of the nebula's flaming streamers, which flooded the bridge with greenish, ghostly radiance. Kempton seemed to forget Clew, and the little man stood there blinking. It must have been ten minutes later that he spoke again.

"Captain Kempton, thir?"

"Eh? Oh, *you're* still here? What is it?"

The bright eyes winked bravely.

"Captain, you don't understand, thir. I've been working on my gravity screen nearly fifty yearth. Ever since I first came here, thir. It was the Dead Thtar, tho near. I got books on electronics. I studied hard, thir.

"Other men have come and gone, thir. Even the mechanics stay only thix yearth, you know. Because it is tho lonely. Now, thir, it is done. An electronic field, a screen of ions, that flows over the surface of any conductor, and reflects, dissipates, the radiations of gravity."

Kempton laughed. He did not intend to be malicious; there was something irresistibly funny about Gideon Clew, lisping so seriously.

"Why, gravitation isn't even a radiation, man! It's a strain in the ether, a curvature——"

"I know, thir, that is one theory. But I have proved it is a radiation, on the order of the subelectronic particles——"

Kempton was suddenly brusque. Angry with himself because he had laughed.

"Anyhow, you'll have to give it up. We've no fuel to waste on fool experiments."

He bent over the charts again. Gideon Clew turned dazedly toward the door, moisture glittering unheeded on his bright, wrinkled cheeks. It is not easy for a man to give up what he has worked for all his life—not when he has labored and planned and dreamed as had Gideon Clew.

He turned and lisped again: "Captain, thir?"

"What is it *now?*" Kempton showed his annoyance at the interruption.

"Captain, there's Tonia Andros. A little girl, that we took off a wreck. When my invention is successful, thir, I am going to adopt her——"

"Sorry, Clew, I'm busy." Kempton nodded at the door.

"Yeth, thir."

Gideon Clew blinked and turned slowly again. He fumbled for the door knob with twisted old fingers, and could not see it. "Wait!" came Kempton's brisk voice, and he turned, sober blue eyes shining with incredulous hope.

"Thir?"

"I suppose you've a clutter of apparatus in your cabin. See that it's cleared out. Have it all in order when you leave."

"But captain, thir, I *can't* dismantle my apparatus. I'm an old man. I'll never have money, or a chance to try it again. Oh, don't you *thee?*"

There was something in the appealing blue eyes that Kempton could not resist.

"All right," he said suddenly. "I'll have Mr. Colin supply you the power-output, for exactly five minutes. I shouldn't do it; it's against regulations."

Gideon's face was wrinkled into a grin of radiant joy; his round blue eyes shone mistily.

"Go on, now, and try it," Kempton said. "And afterward clear the rubbish out of your cabin."

Gideon vanished, and the station's lights were dim for five minutes, and the electronblast motors dead for that long, allowing us to drift to the unopposed drag of the Dead Star's relentless gravity.

During those minutes, Gideon Clew was furiously busy in his cabin, among complex apparatus that filled it so completely that there was scant room for his body. Transformers hummed, and the tall vacuum tube that the *Bellatrix* had brought filled with pallid, virescent fire. He closed a switch that grounded one of its electrodes to the station's hull. A feeble green glow shimmered along the wire.

Gideon Clew felt the ship pause beneath him as that slow drift toward the Dead Star was arrested! Crying out from sheer pain of joy at success after fifty years of toil, he watched in proud wonder.

Plop!

He heard the hollow, muffled sound. Heart sinking, he spun around. Green radiance was gone from tube and wire. The new tube had burned out!

"Captain, thir," Gideon lisped with earnest eagerness, back on the bridge, "didn't you feel our drift-acceleration stop, when my electronic screen cut off the attraction of the Dead Thtar?"

"No, I'm afraid not. And remember our bargain, now. You've had the power. Now you must dismantle your machine, and get it ready to take on board the *Bellatrix*."

"But captain, I know——"

Clive Kempton turned, reached for an ellipsograph. He was a young man, full of his new responsibility. And he did not realize how much Gideon's experiment had meant to the old fellow.

The bright, sober eyes were blinking very fast. Trembling hands fumbled blindly at the door. Gideon Clew let himself out, and stood a long time leaning against the wall. An old man, sick with failure. He was glad that none came near him.

The *Bellatrix,* flashing onward along the flaming corridor of the passage, was still in photophone communication with us. A private call came for Gideon Clew, and Vance, our operator, sent the steward to find the old man.

"A call for *me*, thir?" he lisped in excited astonishment as he shuffled into the photophone room. It must have been the first in fifty years.

Vance made him sit down in front of the projection screen, and turned his set and synchronized the scanning tube. The bright-hued geometric figures of the registration pattern vanished suddenly, and on the screen was Tonia Andros.

"Oh, Granddad!" she cried, in a voice atremble with eager joy and relief. And she ran forward until she went out of focus, and blurred.

Smiling reassuringly, Gideon lisped: "What ith it, Tonia?"

Vance and the other operator were inevitable eavesdroppers, for without their continual adjustments, the narrow etheric nerve between the ships would have snapped in half a minute. The two seemed to forget them.

The little girl's image sharpened again, and she stood there, bewildered, dark eyes round and huge and solemn.

"Oh, Granddad!" she pleaded—she always called him that. "I'm so lonesome! I made them let me talk to you. I want you to come and stay with me. Please, won't you? You said you would come when your invention is done. *Please* hurry!"

Gideon clenched his gnarled old hands, and his blue eyes glistened.

"No, Tonia," he whispered. "No, I'm afraid——" He choked and stopped. Tears rolled out on his cheeks and he did not heed them. "No, Tonia," he cried again. "My invention—will never be—finished. And, Tonia, I—have to go away——"

"But, Granddad!" Her grave voice was distressed. "You promised me! You *must!*"

"Tonia!" he cried convulsively. "Tonia, I will! In spite of everything! I'll come after you!"

She laughed happily. Then the other operator must have spoken to her, for she looked away from the screen, and back again.

"Good-by, Granddad!" she called. "I'll wait!"

"Good-by, Tonia," whispered Gideon Clew. But the connection had already been cut, and he spoke to a blank and empty screen.

Not an hour later, Vance's call-bell rang again, urgently.

When the set was tuned, he saw the *Bellatrix*'s operator on the screen. And swift realization of tragedy overcame him. The man's cap was gone, his face haggard, his eyes wild with desperation. His white uniform, Vance saw, was torn at the shoulder, one sleeve crimson with blood that dripped and spattered on the floor.

The man's lips were working nervously; he was gasping. Apparently he was too frightened to speak.

"Cool off!" Vance shot at him. "What is it?"

"Come——" he cried incoherently. "For life's sake! They murdered the captain! Come!"

Vance heard blows upon the door, and shouts beyond it. The wounded operator turned and stared mutely, as three men burst it open and came in, all of them carrying glowing ionic needles. The operator stood facing them, trembling, helpless, blood dripping from his sleeve.

Vance knew the leader of the three at once by one feature of his face, described in many warnings and offers of reward. He had no nose. Only a blue ray-scar where it should have been, with two black slits for nostrils.

Skal Doon! The space pirate! The "terror of the nebula"!

"Calling the eagles, eh?" he demanded of the operator. His voice was thin and shrill. Vance had a vague feeling that he had heard it before, though he knew he had never seen Skal Doon. "Setting the service on Skal Doon, eh?"

His hand tightened on the ionic needle, and it spat blue sparks. The operator threw up his arms and spun around, screaming. The ray had burned away his face, but sickening minutes passed before he collapsed and was dead.

Skal Doon watched him until he was a shuddering heap on the floor. Then he looked into the screen, at Vance. And Vance never forgot his amazing eyes. Large, they were, limpidly brown, soft and gentle as a woman's.

"So our friend did call you, eh?" his thin voice shrilled. And he kicked the trembling thing at his feet. "And maybe you have seen enough so you can guess what happens to eagles that swoop at Skal Doon!"

Vance's sickness at the horror he had seen must have been evident enough. The mild brown eyes smiled at him; the high voice made a ribald jest at his condition. Then the ionic needle came up again, spitting blue fire, and the screen went blank.

Only then did Vance recognize that shrill voice. It was the voice of the man with the bandaged head and the invalid's chair, with whom he had talked on the *Bellatrix*. Of the man who had talked, ironically, of Skal Doon.

The *Bellatrix,* of course, was not a fighting ship. Her only weapon was a long rocket-torpedo tube that had been mounted, ironically enough, for protection against the very buccaneer who had seized the vessel.

Though the station's fighting equipment was obsolete, consisting only of four rocket-torpedo tubes and the Sealby Arc—which hurled a blasting shaft of electricity from the generators—we might easily enough have destroyed the liner. But destruction was not our aim; we had to consider the hundreds of passengers aboard.

"We'll have to run them down, capture the ship," Kempton told Hume, on the bridge. "And that torpedo-tube will make them hard to take."

"Doon knows how to play his cards," Hume agreed.

Even with the station's powerful electronblast motors, installed for her ceaseless battle with the gravitation of the dead Star, we did not come up quickly with the fleeing liner. It was ten hours before the battle began. After the long tension of suspense, it was a swift and confusing thing.

Gideon Clew came running up hopefully to Kempton, soon after the *Bellatrix* was sighted—a silvery speck, fleeing between the white curtains of the Great Nebula, the violet, fluorescent trail of her electronic motors streaming out behind her.

"Captain, thir! In the battle—what do you want me to do?"

His round blue eyes were bright with eager determination. But Kempton turned on him impatiently.

"Just keep to your cabin, Clew. The crew is complete without you."

"But, thir," he lisped protestingly. "Tonia! I must help save her! She——"

"Go below, Clew."

Red, wrinkled face suddenly downcast, sober eyes glittering, the old man stumbled out of the room.

As the station came up with him, Doon began to fire. The first rocket we were able to avoid, by an abrupt change of course. The second and the third were detonated at a distance by the searing flame of the Sealby Arc.

But the fourth slipped past the searching finger of the arc, a hurtling mote, a miniature ship, death laden. It struck amidships. The station lurched sickeningly to its explosion. Fragments of the beryllosteel hull were driven inward with terrific force. And an instant later our precious air was creaming out through the sudden, ragged opening, chilled by expansion until snow glittered in it.

Colin, the chief engineer, was killed outright by a splinter of the hull. Hale, the second, darted at once with his two helpers to repair the hole, snatching down the metal patches and the thermite welding units that always hung ready on the wall.

The task was not easy. One of the helpers was carried bodily through the opening by the outrushing air to hideous death. Then patches were flung over the ragged orifice, and the major leak soon stopped. But the shock had strained all the seams of the old hull. Though Hale and the remaining assistant found and mended many breaks, the vital air continued to hiss out alarmingly.

Thus, for a time, the generators were deserted by their regular crew, and just at the moment when power was most necessary. The station was swiftly overhauling the *Bellatrix*. On the bridge, Kempton was screaming a fervid appeal into the speaking tube.

"For life's sake, Colin, give me power! For the Sealby Arc! Before they can reload that tube!"

But the engineer was dead, and the surviving members of his staff were completely engaged in a desperate battle to preserve the station's essential atmosphere.

Yet the generators came again to sudden animation, and the blue arm of the electric arc reached out once more. It touched the rocket-torpedo tube in its armored housing above the hull of the *Bellatrix*. And the tube became fused and crumpled metal.

Skal Doon, though thus robbed of his only offensive weapon, was still not defeated. He displayed again that resource which so often had saved him, an original daring worthy of a greater man. The liner deliberately changed her course, swung about in a long curve, and plunged downward toward the Dead Star.

"Diving for the star!" cried Hume in dismay. "Going to smash, rather than surrender!"

With silent attention, Kempton was studying the motion of the argent ellipsoid through his instruments. He laid them aside at last, and turned suddenly to the mate.

"No. Skal is cleverer than that. He is planning to fall *around* the Dead Star, and back away from it."

"Around it? How——"

"The *Bellatrix* is on a parabolic orbit, like a comet's. It will flash down to the star, curve close around it, and fly off again. Or *would*—if we weren't here to stop it."

"You're going to follow?"

"Of course. We'll run them down, fasten the station alongside with the magnetic anchors. The *Bellatrix* has no weapon. If Skal won't surrender, we'll storm a valve, or cut through the hull."

He looked at the barometers, and his face fell with alarm.

"That last shot finished us, anyhow. We're gone unless we can get aboard the *Bellatrix*. The pressure is down two pounds already. Our air won't last three hours, at this rate."

The silvery hull of the liner was plunging toward the Dead Star with motors full on. Kempton shouted again and again into the speaking tube for more power. No voice answered, but the generators always responded.

The *Bellatrix* was now but a few miles ahead. Abruptly she began a confusing series of maneuvers to evade the station, twisting, swerving. But, lighter and more powerful, the station kept close behind her.

The liner turned back at last, plunging directly at the other ship with manifest intent to ram it, to the destruction of both vessels. Kempton shouted a wild command, the generators replied instantly, and the station slipped out of the way.

Another order, and a heavy magnet anchor leaped from its catapult toward the passing ship, dragging its cable. It struck the liner's hull, clung fast.

Like a silver fish, the *Bellatrix* plunged and darted for a time upon the line. But the smaller station held her adroitly, giving her opportunity neither to ram nor to break the cable. And steadily the ships were drawn together as the cable was wound upon its drum.

The purple, fluorescent blast from the liner's motors was at last shut off. The two ships drifted side by side, at the cable's ends—hurtling down toward the black, red-flecked disk of the Dead Star.

The station's air, leaking steadily through opened seams, was swiftly growing unbreathable. Men panted at ordinary tasks; a deadly chill stole through the ship.

Kempton called us all to the upper deck, ordered us to don space suits. He served out ionic needles and other weapons, ordered torches got ready for cutting through the liner's hull, if that proved necessary.

"Colin," he called into the speaking tube, "bring your men on deck. We're going to abandon ship."

"This ith not Colin," lisped a voice from the tube.

"Who? *Clew?* What the——"

"Colin ith dead, thir. I have been running the generators. I was a generator-man forty yearth, you know."

Kempton's voice was queer. "All right, Clew. Good work. Come on and get into your space suit."

Five minutes later, the eleven of us were dragging ourselves across between the ships in clumsy, inflated suits, laden with weapons. As weird a journey as can be imagined, it was. Eleven swollen giants, climbing by their hands along a cable between two vessels in the void. For background, the flaming streamers of the Great Nebula, and the malign black disk of the Dead Star.

Then happened an unexpected thing—a dreadful thing.

The main valve of the *Bellatrix* flung suddenly wide, and a score of human figures spewed out. We thought at first that the pirates were foolishly leaving the ship to beat off our attack. But these men had no space suits.

In the blast of air they were thrown clear of the ship, to become, in the vacuum of space, queer, swollen monsters. But, horribly, they did not immediately die. Sprawling in the airless void, they tore at their throats, faces contorted with agony unutterable.

An atrocious murder of helpless passengers, most of us thought. We dragged ourselves hastily on, hot with resentment, to seize the valve before it could be closed, to fight our way from it into the ship and avenge this thing.

Strangely—ominously—our entrance was not opposed.

When we opened the inner seal, Skal Doon, alone and apparently unarmed, met us on the deck inside. A curious grim smile was upon his face, and his mild, limpidly brown eyes were mocking.

"Skal Doon," Kempton barked at him, "you'll answer for the ruthless murder of those innocent passengers!"

"But, my dear sir," the buccaneer protested, in his

queerly thin voice, "those were my own men! Surely you cannot object!"

"Eh? The passengers——"

"——have not been injured, I assure you. They are safely confined to their quarters. I put my men through the valve as an act of mercy."

"You might explain." Kempton menaced him with an ionic needle.

Doon smiled again, twistedly, and shrilled:

"You seem to have understood my plan, captain, to fall in a parabola about the Dead Star."

"Yes. A simple trick."

"When I saw you follow, captain, I realized that you understood. And with the ship on your cable, I realized that I had lost the game. I was forced to select another means of escape. Accordingly, some distance back, I changed the course of the *Bellatrix*."

"What?" Kempton demanded. "What did you do?"

"You'll find out, I fancy. And to prevent your undoing my work, I have also wrecked the motors, and short-circuited the generators in such a manner as to burn them out."

"But—but your escape——"

"You have already witnessed the escape of my men. I am now following them. But my deeds, you will find, are to live after me."

Doon's jaws contracted suddenly, and something crushed between his teeth. Still smiling, he spat blood and fragments of glass.

"Farewell, captain. And a safe voyage—to the Dead Star!"

He saluted ironically, and fell heavily upon his face.

In a few mad minutes we verified all he had told us. The passengers were safely locked below. The machinery was wrecked beyond the possibility of repair. Hume and Kempton went to the liner's bridge.

The *Bellatrix*, they found, was plunging toward the Dead Star, upon a path that would end in flaming catastrophe. Doon, realizing his defeat, had turned the liner from the parabolic orbit toward that titanic black sun. Truly, his deeds lived after him.

One glance at the graviscope, or gravitational field detector, told Hume that doom was inevitable. Already the needle was pulled to the end of its scale. Even with the full power of her now useless motors, the ship could not have fought free of that relentless drag.

Tonia Andros, unharmed, came running across the deck when the imprisoned passengers were released. She found Gideon Clew and threw her arms around him. The old man bent and caressed her hair and looked into her dark, wistfully happy eyes.

Then Hume came back from the bridge, with the dread news that we were falling toward the Dead Star, helpless, doomed.

Gideon lifted the little girl in his arms and held her tight for a little time, and then set her down.

"Good-by, Tonia," he whispered. "There is something I forgot. I must go back on the station a little while. Captain Manners will take care of you. Run to him, now."

He pushed the grave-eyed, bewildered child away, and hurried toward the valve. Hume followed him, asked:

"You aren't going back on board, Clew? It's death. No air!"

The old man paused, and his sober blue eyes looked back at the puzzled, solemn child.

"Yeth," he lisped. "I must go. For *her!*"

He got back into his space suit, and Hume let him out.

The station's atmosphere was very thin when Gideon Clew returned—and cold. It glittered in the pale yellow tube-light with a frigid, frosty glint. He could hear the sibilant whisper of it as it hissed out into the frozen void.

He left his space suit in the air lock. Its tube of compressed air would have lasted perhaps an hour longer, but his hands, in its clumsy gloves, could not do the delicate work he had set for them.

Less than an hour, without it, was left him. Already he was breathing hard, as he made his way into the fore-castle, gasping painfully from the slight exertion of walking. And there was much to be done—fifty years' labor to be brought to completion.

Synthetic air was still hissing noisily from the cylinders, perhaps as fast as it was leaking from the hull. But the cylinders, in a few more minutes, would be empty. And the cold due to swift expansion of escaping air filled all the ship; the chill of it seared Gideon's gasping lungs.

For a little time he stood, panting, shivering, among the complex apparatus in his own tiny cabin, his laboring heart thumping against his throat. He felt tears come into his eyes at the sight of these familiar instruments. Offspring of laborious years, they seemed living, intimate. He did not matter. But the Dead Star should not have his invention. Nor Tonia!

With trembling hands, he began the task. He first removed the tall vacuum tube from its mountings, and broke its air seal. When the room's frigid air had hissed thinly into it, he unscrewed the base, to examine the damage done when the tube had burned out.

The fine wires of the secondary electrode were fused in silvery beads against the cathode grid. He turned the delicate parts in his quivering, gnarled old hands, and studied them, trying to puzzle out the original defect that had caused the disaster. He searched patiently.

Even as he stood still, he had to gasp for breath. His head throbbed. The utter, unthinkable cold of space crept inexorably into the room; frost danced in the air. Gideon Clew shivered and absently drew his thin jacket closer about his erect old shoulders. One old man, he was pitted against the searching cold and the vacuum of elemental space—against the relentless gravitation of the Dead Star. But he took no time for despair.

At length he saw the defect. The filament should have been longer, the grid set back a little, and turned *so*. A simple change.

He found a coil of tiny wire and delicate tools, and

began to make the repair. That was not difficult. The hard part would be to evacuate the tube again. It was useless with air inside, and he had no pump, or time to use it.

The new parts fitted, he screwed the base back into the tube and then attacked the problem of exhausting it. He knew a way, difficult, perilous—but quick.

As rapidly as he could, with numb, aching hands, he sealed a piece of metal tubing into the tube. Then he found his rotary drill, fitted it with his longest point, and attacked the cabin's outside wall.

That wall was the beryllosteel hull of the station. Beyond its four obdurate inches was the vacuum he needed. Trembling, he leaned on the handle of the tool. Cool was piercing into him. His head ached; his ears drummed. Blood began to drip from his nose, drop by crimson drop, to freeze on the floor.

He reeled dizzily, but clung to his task. The drill whirred in his hands, quivered, bit slowly into tough metal. Its motor made a little heat, grateful to his stiffened fingers; he tried to hold them closer against it.

At last the point slipped through. He drew it back, and the air whistled shrilly through the hole, out into the void of space. Just as he had planned. He fitted the end of the metal tubing into it, crudely cemented it. Now the vacuum of space would draw the air from the repaired electron tube.

He closed the switches, and started to the generator room.

The hissing in the corridors had ceased. The air cylinders were empty. Again the pressure in the ship was dropping, and swiftly.

Gideon's old heart labored so that he held a numb hand against it. He was suffocating; the thin, cold air seemed to be sucked out of his pumping lungs. His head roared and throbbed; his pulse drummed in his ears. Blood was still oozing from his nostrils, cold and sticky on his face.

And his body was wooden. Every movement was a battle against leaden inertia. Every effort burned vital oxygen, increased the strain on heart and lungs. But he *must* go on—start the generators.

Now on hands and knees, he crawled along the corridor. His hands were stiff, lifeless things. No sensation came from them as they fell upon the metal floor.

No longer could he see. Blackness crowded upon him, lit with strange, lurid flashes of crimson. His head whirled; he felt that the ship was swinging, spinning, under him. A blind automaton, he crawled on. And the face of Tonia Andros danced before him, smooth and childish, dark eyes wistfully solemn.

Every tissue of his leaden, tortured body screamed at him: *"Stop! Stop! Rest! Forget!"*

So he came at last into the generator room. With infinite effort he pulled himself up against the instrument board. There he leaned, gasping, trembling, blood trickling from his nose—straining every atom of his will to *see!*

The darkness at last cleared for a moment, and the roaring quieted in his head. He read the dials, and with stiff hands moved the switches. All the processes were familiar, automatic. If only he could hold himself up to carry them out!

He grasped the final lever with dead, insensate paws, and drew it down as he fell.

The old man lay gasping upon the floor, blood gushing from his nostrils in a scarlet, frothy flood—but he heard the soft *whir* of the generators, the shrill, rising whine of transformers.

All of us were silent for a time, upon the *Bellatrix,* when Hume told us that Gideon Clew had gone back. We were all thinking of his cheery old face, with its red cheeks and its round, sober blue eyes. Of his faith, his optimism. And all of us were sorry we would never hear his lisping voice again.

But our minds were soon feverishly back upon more immediate things.

"After all, it's rather a splendid way to die," Vance told Hume. But his voice was unsteady.

They had gone back together to the bridge, and from its vitrolar panels stood watching the incandescent wonder of the nebula, the Dead Star grasped in its fiery tentacles, a growing black disk, splotched with red.

The battered, oxide-reddened hull of the station was drifting alongside at the end of her cable, her dark ellipsoid outlined against the green-tinged, flaming vortexes of the nebula. Hume looked at it.

"Perhaps," he said, with slow deliberation. "But old Clew——Going back to work with his machine, till the end——"

Vance did not reply, and they gazed out upon the supernal majesty that infolded them. The Great Nebula: angry, swirling masses of virescent fire, white curtains and streamers and sheets, greenish, dazzling, clotted condensations. Cosmic clouds of flame, shrouding a grim, lifeless sun. The Dead Star: ominous black disk against lucent glory. Its lurid crimson spots—seas of molten lava, wide enough to swallow planets—stared back like red, evil eyes.

Vance laughed hollowly, nervously. He whispered: *"When?"*

Hume turned, found an astrosextant on the chart table. He put it to his eye and read the apparent diameter of the Dead Star, and busied himself with his pocket calculator.

"Five hours——"

Vance said nothing, and they watched the menacing, red-spotted blackness of the Dead Star's face. It was minutes later that he licked his lips and added:

"The acceleration increases, of course, as we fall nearer. Just above the surface, the force upon us will be upward of a ton for every pound of our bodies. We will have no sensation of it, though, because we are falling with it, free. And we aren't heading directly for the center of the disk. Momentum will carry us part-way around. We'll strike on the other side——"

A long silence, and Vance spoke again.

"Old Clew's gravity screen! No wonder he went daft

on it, looking down in the Dead Star for fifty years. And no doubt dreaming of something like this."

He laughed, loudly, mirthlessly.

Kempton gathered the nervous, bewildered passengers into the main saloon, and spoke to them.

"We are falling into the Dead Star," he said. "Nothing in the universe can save us. Nothing short of a breach of the law of gravitation. But the end will not be painful. We will flash instantaneously into incandescent gas. I advise you to get the most you can out of the few hours left to us. The whole ship is at your disposal. I will welcome any plans for diversion.

"But if any of you should feel that you cannot endure the strain of waiting, you will find the ship's surgeon ready in the sick bay with painless anæsthetics."

He stopped; with a gesture to indicate that he was done. The passengers milled about, white-faced, and stared unknowingly at each other, as if they had all been strangers.

Tonia Andros was going about the decks, asking in a bewildered and fearful voice where Gideon was, and why he didn't come back. Kempton found her and brought her with him to the bridge. Through the transparent panels she saw the Dead Star, a black, red-pocked disk, ever increasing, hung against curtains of supernal light.

She shuddered, drew back.

"It's like a face!" she cried. "With red eyes, gloating——"

And with anxious solemnity she demanded of Hume: "Where is my Granddad?"

The mate pointed to the station—a battered, twisted mass against the flaming arms of the nebula.

"Let's go across!" she cried, with big-eyed, wistful earnestness. "I want to find my Granddad!"

Hume shook his head. "It's no use, Tonia. The air was leaking out. He won't come back. He's—gone, now."

The mate averted his eyes, and the little girl still stared bewilderedly into the vitrolar panels.

"Look!" she cried out. "The green light! What is it? Do you see it? There! There!"

Then Hume saw a pale, virescent glow spreading swiftly over the battered red hull, like a film of oil upon water. Green luminescence streamed down the cable to the *Bellatrix*; in an instant it was shining upon the metal frames of the vision panels.

Then a bell clanged from the graviscope, and he ran back to it. He saw that the needle, that a moment before had been drawn to the end of its scale by the terrific pull of the Dead Star, had returned to zero. In unbelieving wonder, he stared at the instrument. Then he spun upon Kempton, eagerly.

"The old man was trying to generate an ionic screen that would reflect the radiation of gravity. That green glow is his screen—I know it is! And the graviscope shows that we have been cut out of all gravitational fields!"

"And I," Kempton muttered, "I thought—just an old fool——"

"Don't you see what it means?" Hume cried in sudden, feverish eagerness. "We aren't going directly toward the Dead Star, and now it can't curve our path any more! We'll fly on past! We'll have time to make repairs, or photophone for aid!"

Tonia Andros was staring at him with round, wide eyes.

"Then Granddad is still all right?" she cried. "Let's go across and find him!"

She snatched Kempton's hand, tugged toward the door.

"Yes, he's all right," he whispered. "And, yes—we'll go——"

Nonstop to Mars

SOMETHING WAS QUEERLY wrong—with either the ship or the air. And Carter Leigh knew that it couldn't be the ship. The creaking old *Phoenix* might be obsolescent in a world that the new cathion rockets had conquered, but he knew every bolt and strut of her. Knew her well enough to take her apart and put her up again, in the dark. And loved her, for her loyalty through six years and half a million miles of solo flight.

No, the trouble couldn't be in the *Phoenix*. It had to be the atmosphere.

He couldn't understand it. But the barometric altimeter had kept luring him down, toward frozen peaks that loomed a thousand feet higher than they should have been. The engine labored, and the thrust of it weakened dangerously. And the wind that struck him over the pole was a screaming demon, more freakishly violent than he had ever met before.

It baffled him. Through all the endless, weary night, deaf with the long thunder of the loyal old engine, sitting stiff with cold even in his electrically heated suit, gulping coffee from a vacuum jug, poring over charts and studying instruments with aching bloodshot eyes—ever since the last strange sunset, he had hopelessly picked at the sinister riddle.

Nonstop flights were nothing new to Carter Leigh. Men, looking at the long record of his feats, had nicknamed him "Lucky." But he had something more than luck. In his lean body there was the tremendous endurance that it took to fly on, hour after straining hour, when most men would have dropped over the stick.

And this flight—nonstop from Capetown to Honolulu, across the bottom of the world—had promised to be no harder than the rest. Not until he saw that last sunset.

Behind him, beyond the cragged granite fangs of Enderby Land, as he climbed above the ramparts of the polar plateau, the sunset had been frighteningly strange. An incredible wheel of crimson, rolling along the rim of the world, it had been winged and tufted with eldritch green.

The aurora was another disquieting scrap of the puzzle. It burned above him all that night, whenever the sky was clear, until all the white antarctic wilderness seemed on fire with its sinister and shifting brilliance.

The cold was another thing. Leigh had made polar flights before. But never had he met such merciless temperatures. The motor, even with cowl ventilators closed, grew sluggish with it. It crept into the cockpit and probed deep into his body.

Beyond the pole and Marie Byrd Land, over the dark Antarctic again, he met a wall of cloud. He tried to climb over it. Heavy and dull with altitude and fatigue, he opened the oxygen valve. The vital gas revived him a little. But the plane could not scale the summits of vapor. He flew into them—wondering.

Savage winds battled in the cloud, and it was riven with lightning. Rain hammered the ship, and froze on it, until the ice dragged it almost to the surface. Leigh fought the elements, and fought the mounting weariness in him, and came at last unexpectedly into the calm of a strange northward dawn.

The aurora was fading from a sky grown brilliantly clear. Studded with white points of icebergs, the gray South Pacific was sliding back at three hundred and fifty miles an hour—still a good pace, he thought stubbornly, even if the rockets were three times as fast.

Leigh was peeling an orange, beginning to hope that all the terror of the night had been the child of fancy and fatigue, when he saw the thing in the northeast.

Against the red and green of a suddenly disturbing dawn, it fell like a silver thread.

A white, spiral vortex—the funnel of a great tornado. He saw a blob of gray mist about the foot of it, marching over the sea. The upper end of it, oddly, was lost above the bright wings of dawn.

Leigh had never seen a storm just like this one. At first he thought there was no danger to him. But the white, writhing snake of it whipped toward him with an appalling quickness.

It seized the *Phoenix* in a sudden blast of wind, sucking the ship toward that racing funnel. Sea and sky spun madly. He was lifted so swiftly that his eardrums ached. Grimly he fought it, with all his calm skill and all the familiar strength of the ship.

He fought—and won. The white pillar left him fluttering in its wake and marched on into the west. Hurried observation of the higher sun told Leigh that he had been flung fifteen hundred miles northward.

But he knew, with a sinking in his heart, that the *Phoenix* was crippled. Her right aileron had been twisted and jammed by the force of that incredible wind. He would have to set her down.

Whistling the tune of "Barbara Allen," which always seemed to cheer him, Leigh searched the maps. He found a pinprick of land named Manumotu—the only possible haven in a thousand miles—and turned the limping amphibian toward it, flying with rubber and throttle.

One more failure. Two, he reflected bitterly, in a row. For the last flight, two months ago, had failed also, from a cause as strange as that tornado.

A "bipolar" flight, Tick Tinker had called the last one. Tick was the tireless little publicity man, one-legged and one-eyed, who was Leigh's partner in his singular business of wrestling a living from the air. "Bipolar," because the route from Croydon back to Croydon along the prime meridian included both the poles. Leigh had safely rounded the planet, with but three scheduled stops. But the flight had failed just the same, because of the Stellar Shell.

"We're an out-of-doors advertising firm, Lucky," Tick used to say. "You fly for attention value. And I sell it to the makers of oil and piston rings and what-have-you. And it's a legitimate business, so long as you can keep in the headlines."

But all the headlines two months ago had been about the Stellar Shell. Some astronomer named Gayle, the day Leigh took off from Croydon, announced discovery of a mysterious missile plunging out of the depths of space, toward the solar system. The "bipolar" flight had earned no more than a few sticks of space on the inside pages. For the black streamers ran:

Stellar Shell Shot at Planets;
Will Object Strike Earth?
Astronomers Baffled

When Leigh came in to Croydon again, the flight completed in three grueling days, there was no crowd to meet him. Staggering away from the dusty, oil-spattered *Phoenix,* he himself paused to buy a paper.

Cosmic Bullet Hits Mars;
Earth Spared;
Name of Object Unknown

There had been no more news of the Stellar Shell, nothing more than the speculations of bewildered scientists. But the flight was already ruined. Tick Tinker had radiographed:

CONGRATS ON BIPOLAR FLIGHT. BUT STELLAR SHELL HOGGED THE HEADLINES. FLIGHT TOTAL LOSS FINANCIALLY. YOUR NAME GETTING RAPIDLY UNKNOWN. TESTIMONIALS BEGGING AT CUT RATES. URGENT RELEASE DETAILS NEW PUBLICITY FLIGHT. SUGGEST SOMETHING NONSTOP POLAR. USE ZEROLUBE BRAND OILS FOR TESTIMONIAL.

And so Tick's message had brought him here, dead with fatigue and heading toward a speck of rock that probably had no inhabitants.

The motor covered the windshield with a thin spray of oil, and Leigh stopped his whistling briefly to curse all Zerolube products. He plugged in his helmet phones and switched on the little battery transmitter. It was good for just ten minutes of continuous sending—the *Phoenix* had no room for heavier equipment, not even emergency rations.

"SOS!" he called. "Pilot Leigh in airplane *Phoenix* forced down by storm. Will try to land on Manumotu. SOS—"

The instant reply surprised him:

"Manumotu Station, Gayle Foundation, calling airplane *Phoenix*. Dr. E. K. Gayle speaking. Land on north beach. I will stand by to assist you. Come in, airplane *Phoenix*."

"Airplane *Phoenix* calling Manumotu Station," gasped Leigh, relieved. "Thanks, Doc. I'll be seeing you, if I can keep out of the water half an hour longer. Signing off."

It took an hour—an hour that seemed endless to Leigh as he fought the fatigue in him and nursed the crippled plane. But at last Manumotu came out of the sparkling northward haze. A cragged volcanic summit appeared sheer on three sides, edged on the north with a scrap of coral beach.

He crossed the beach. A broad rock bench above it was tufted with tropical green. A long shedlike building of white sheet metal stood upon it, a white tent, and a great pile of crates covered with brown tarpaulins. A white flag waved. Then he saw the tiny figure running from the tent toward the beach.

The landing was hazardous. The crippled wing caught the crest of a wave and covered the plane with spray. She staggered, but came up bravely. He taxied in and rolled up on the blinding coral sand.

Following the signals of the flag, he brought the *Phoenix* to a safe dry stop where a rocket must have been moored, for there were deep wheel marks in the sand, and the hibiscus bushes beyond were scorched black as if from rocket jets.

Heavily, his legs as stiff as if they never had been straightened before, he climbed out of the cockpit. The person with the flag came to meet him. A slim young figure, in boots and breeches, khaki shirt open at the throat, yellow head bare. A crisp voice, brisk, impersonal, greeted him:

"Hello. You are the famous Lucky Leigh?"

"In person." He grinned. "And thanks for showing me the way in, Doc—"

His jaw fell. This was a woman—a girl. Her intent oval face was dark with sun. Her keen blue eyes were scanning his heavy, swaying body—not altogether, he thought, with approval.

"Oh!" he said. "I thought you were Dr. Gayle."

"I am," she said gravely. "Dr. Elene Kathrine Gayle."

His red eyes blinked at her.

"You—you aren't the Dr. Gayle who discovered the Stellar Shell?"

She nodded.

"My father was a leader in his field of science. He established the Gayle Foundation. But he has been dead five years. I have been trying to carry on his work." She studied him gravely. "Do you object to my discovery?"

"You ruined my last flight," he told her. "I lived through seventy-six hours of hell; I set a record for gasoline flight over both poles. And what with your Stellar Shell, the world never knew I had been off the ground."

"And, I suspect, was little the worse for the fact." Leigh flushed at the hint of sarcasm in her voice. "However—are you hungry?"

"Famished," he told her.

On a rough pine table in the white tent, she slapped down two tin plates, split open cans of meat and butter, indicated a big vacuum urn of coffee, a huge jar of marmalade.

"Proceed," she said.

Leigh's dull eyes were watching her.

"You're the whole crew here?"

Her boyish head nodded.

"Emergency," she said. "The Foundation is establishing twenty new meteorological observatories. Manumotu Station was the most important, because it is directly in the track of the phenomena we are investigating. Therefore, I took charge here myself."

"Alone?"

"I had two assistants. But Dr. French took acute appendicitis, and Cragin flew him out in the rocket. Should have been back yesterday. But didn't show up. I'm carrying on. . . . You said you were hungry."

She dumped half a can of corned beef into her tin plate, passed the remainder to Leigh. But he sat, wonderment rising against his mist of sleep, staring at her.

"Emergency?" he questioned.

She nodded.

"Something is happening to the atmosphere."

"I thought conditions were strange," he said, "flying over the pole."

She pushed back her plate to seize a notebook.

"What phenomena did you observe?" she demanded eagerly.

He told her in a tired sleep-fogged voice about the strangely gaudy sunset, the aurora, the phenomenal cold, the unaccountably low barometric pressures, the singular tornado that had crippled the *Phoenix*.

"What does it all mean?" he concluded. "What is happening?"

"I'm here to find out," she told him. "Sunset and aurora probably due to abnormal electronic bombardment of the ionosphere. But the storms and pressure disturbances are still not accounted for. Unless—"

Her yellow head shook.

"The only conceivable answer is too appalling."

She looked quickly at her wrist watch, dumped the debris from her plate into a pail beside the table, wiped plate and spoon clean with a paper napkin. She rose.

"Excuse me. But the duties of both my assistants

have fallen upon me. My time is budgeted. I have forty-eight minutes a day for meals. Now I have instruments to read."

"So that's how a lady astronomer lives." Leigh grinned. "If I can help you—"

She shook her head with evident disapproval.

"I doubt it. Our work here doesn't consist of publicity stunts. . . . Eat as much as you like. You'll find a cot behind the partition. I'll radio directions to your rescue party. Please keep in mind, when you leave, that it is the policy of the Gayle Foundation to avoid unnecessary publicity. Especially, we don't want to alarm the world about these current meteorological phenomena, until we have more comprehensive data."

Leigh was staring at her, a slow anger rising in him. "Look here, you think I'm a pretty bad egg?"

Her keen eyes swept him impersonally.

"Frankly, Mr. Lucky Leigh," her cool voice said, "your existence and your stunts annoy me. I can't see that you serve any creative function. In the precarious early days of gasoline aviation such men as you, testing equipment and exploring routes, may have served a useful end. But now that rockets are as fast and as certain as the sun, you are a mere anachronism."

Leigh opened his mouth to protest. But the girl held up a brown imperative hand.

"I've got no time to listen to you," she said. "Because I have vitally urgent work to do. I am already upsetting my schedule. But I've wanted for a long time to tell you a thing or two."

Her smooth face was flushed a little. He listened to her, grinning.

"Now," she went on swiftly, "if you were trying to fly nonstop to Mars, even if you never got there, that would be a different proposition. Because you would be expanding the horizons of science. You would be doing something different and important.

"But your old gasoline wreck is as far behind the times as you are, Leigh. It is a rocket that will make the first flight to Mars. I know a man who may pilot the first rocket there. He is Laird Cragin—you never heard of him, because he isn't a publicity flier. But he is test pilot for the experimental space rockets that the Foundation has been working on, in association with some Army engineers. You ought to meet him. Because whether he ever gets to Mars or not, he's trying to do something real."

Carter Leigh gulped.

"Listen, Miss Gayle," he protested. "You've got me all wrong. I used to like the glory, I admit. But now it's just a business. I've come to hate the clamor and the crowds, and I always skip the banquets. Tick Tinker is my contact man; he releases the publicity, does the testimonials, handles all the business end. We're just trying to make a living."

Her brown chin squared. And, through the gray haze of fatigue that filled his mind, Leigh suddenly perceived that a lady astronomer could still be very good to look at.

"It is possible," her cool crisp voice was saying, "to make a living in a way that helps others besides yourself. Here you are hopping about the planet, with about as much aim and intelligence as a beheaded flea, while God-knows-what is happening to the very air we breathe!"

She turned decisively away from him.

"You are as extinct as the dodo, Mr. Nonstop Leigh," she told him. "The only difference is that you don't know it. Sleep on that. I've got a barocyclonometer to read."

Carter Leigh sat over the rough table, staring out of the tent after her hastening boyish figure. He had seen suddenly, behind her brisk impersonal efficiency, that she was very tired—and somewhat frightened.

His brief anger at her frank criticism was all turned back upon himself. After all, it was true that such men as Lindbergh and Byrd and Post and Corrigan hadn't left much to be accomplished in the field of nonstop gasoline flight.

No, he deserved her scorn.

But what had frightened her? What *was* happening to the atmosphere? Leigh's mind grappled for a vain moment with the problem, but he could not concentrate now. All he wanted was a chance to sleep.

He stood up, his body stiff and wooden, and reeled to the cot beyond the canvas partition.

"Dammit," he muttered, "what do I care if Lieutenant Laird Cragin flies to Mars on a tissue-paper kite?"

He was asleep before his head touched the pillow. . . .

"Leigh!"

The crisp voice of Elene Gayle awakened him, tense with a suppressed alarm. The tent was dim in the light of an oddly purple dawn. Pausing at the entrance of the tent, her face so gray and tired he knew she had not slept, she called urgently:

"That tornado is coming again. You had better see after your ship."

He tumbled out of the tent and saw her running ahead toward the long metal shed that covered her precious instruments. The dark ocean seemed ominously calm, and the sunrise above it was as splendid as the last.

Against it he saw what the girl, with obvious hesitation, had called a tornado.

It walked out of the flaming east—an endless spiral filament of silver, dropped like some cosmic fishing line from the depthless purple above the fiery sunrise. The foot of it danced across the sea. It moved by incredible bounds. And it was wrapped in a gray wisp of storm.

Leigh caught his breath and started running toward the plane that was standing unmoored on the long white beach where he had climbed out of her on the day before.

But this white funnel of destruction came with the same unthinkable velocity that he had witnessed before. Before he had moved a dozen steps, the white tent sailed over his head. The abrupt, freakish blast of air hurled him flat. His eyes and ears and nostrils were filled with coral sand.

For no more than twenty seconds the tempest shrieked against the black peak above. Abruptly, then, the air was almost still again. There was only a fluttering, queerly chill breeze from the east, following in the storm's wake.

Spitting sand and gasping for breath, Leigh staggered to his feet. The funnel of the storm, like the guide-rope, he thought, dangling from some unseen balloon, was bounding away into the gray west. Its sorrowful howling swiftly diminished.

Leigh turned ruefully toward where he had left the *Phoenix.* The battered old crate had been neatly flipped over on her back by the prankish blast of wind. Leigh shook his head and whistled a few bars of "Barbara Allen."

"Too bad, old girl," he muttered. "But, considering the state of Tick's exchequer and the high cost of salvage, it looks like good-bye for us."

He turned to survey the station. The tent was gone. The supplies, cooking utensils and blankets that it had covered were scattered across the beach to the uneasy sea. The tarpaulins had been ripped off the long stack of crates; tumbled in confusion were red drums of Kappa-concentrate rocket fuel, long cylinders of oxygen, bright tins of gasoline, miscellaneous cases of food and equipment.

But where was the lady astronomer?

A sudden unreasonable alarm tightened Leigh's throat. He was too well seasoned, he kept telling himself, to get unduly excited over any girl—especially a female scientist who didn't like him anyhow. But he was running through the wrecked camp, shouted her name with a quaver in his voice.

"Miss Gayle! Can you hear me? Elene!"

"Dr. Gayle, if you please."

Her crisp voice came from the interior of the long observatory shed. Half the metal roof had been ripped off. Most of the equipment inside seemed to have been demolished by a huge boulder the wind had hurled from the dark cliffs above. But the slim calm girl, save for the disorder of her short yellow hair and a smudge of grease on her brown cheek, looked untouched. She was ruefully fingering a tangle of twisted levers and crumpled recording drums.

"No more barocyclonometer," she said. "But my visual observations make it imperative that we get in touch with outside world at once. I believe my worst fears are justified."

"Well, Dr. Gayle," Leigh offered, "if you discover any need of my services, just say so."

"I doubt that you would be very useful." From the preoccupation of her voice, he knew she gave him less than half her mind; her eyes still measure the smashed equipment. "If you can repair your plane, you had better get away from here before tomorrow morning. Manumotu is an unhealthy locality, just now. And I'm afraid you'll find that the world has got more pressing matters to attend to than organizing relief expeditions to rescue stunt fliers."

"Thank you, Doctor." Leigh bowed. "I hope you can stand a shock. I believe the flying days of the old *Phoenix* are over."

"In that case"—her voice was still abstracted—"you had better salvage what you can of the supplies and equipment. After all, if what I fear is true, it won't make any great difference whether you ever leave Manumotu or not."

Leigh spent all morning stacking the tumbled crates and drums so that they made three walls of a tiny low shelter, roofing it with the torn tarpaulins, and collecting there the food and useful articles he found on the beach.

At noon, when he carried a plate of food and a steaming tin of fresh coffee to the girl in the observatory building, he found her covered with grime, laboring in tight-lipped silence with the starting crank of a little motor-generator. She waved him aside.

"I've no time to eat," she told him. "I've data of the utmost importance to send. It's urgent that I get in touch with Washington and our rocket laboratory at

Alamogordo. And there's something wrong with this planet."

Leigh glanced at the balky mechanism. He set the plate on an empty packing box beside her and rolled up his sleeves.

"Did it occur to you," he inquired, "that, having made a living out of flying gasoline engines for the past ten years, I might know something about them? I see that your carburetor is smashed. If you'll eat your dinner, I'll make you a new carburetor."

Her face showed a weary relief. "If you can do it," she agreed.

While Leigh found tin snips and an empty milk can, she sat down on the concrete floor beside the packing box. She gulped the hot coffee, wolfed a sandwich of canned ham, and reached for another. In the middle of it, her yellow head dropped forward on her knees. Leigh heard a long sigh and knew she was asleep.

"Poor kid," he muttered.

Even the staccato *chek-chek-chek* of the little motor ten minutes later did not wake her. Leigh twisted the flap of tin that regulated the mixture, then swiftly checked the hookup of the shortwave transmitter.

He snapped on the receiver. Static snarled at him. An unfamiliar sort of static. The whining ululation of it was oddly like the howling of the storm that had passed. It rose and fell regularly.

Through it, however, he picked up some station— and what he heard stiffened him with fear. For a time he listened, absorbed; then suddenly he hurried to wake the girl.

"It's fixed?" she gasped, starting up. "I didn't mean to sleep—there isn't time."

He caught anxiously at her slim brown arm.

"Elene," he demanded, "what's happening? I was just listening. There's something frightful going on. What is it? Do you know?"

Her blue eyes stared at him. They were dark with sleep—and, he thought, terror. Quick and anxious, her low voice demanded:

"Just what did you get?"

"Storms," he said briefly. "Phenomenal storms. Unseasonable bitter cold. Ice storms even in the tropics. Tidal waves. One against the Atlantic seaboard has probably killed a hundred thousand already. Communications broken everywhere, of course. Panic increasing."

He drew her light body toward him.

"Something has gone wrong with the air, Elene. Do you know what it is? And when it is going to stop?"

Her head nodded slowly.

"I'm afraid I know what it is," she said. "My dispatches can't bring any comfort to the world."

"What is it?"

Her arm twisted free.

"No time to tell you now," she said. "I've got to talk to Washington and New Mexico. And to Laird Cragin—if he's still alive. Our work here has got to be finished tonight. After dawn tomorrow, there may not be any Manumotu."

Leigh gasped. "But—"

Hastening toward the radio, she paused briefly.

"I'll show you tonight," she promised him. "If the seeing is good enough for the telescope, and if we're still alive by then."

She had no more attention for him. He prepared food for himself, ate, and then spent an hour making the tiny little shelter more secure against whatever the girl expected to happen at dawn. And then, heavy with accumulated fatigue, he slept again.

The air was unwontedly cool on the beach when he woke, and another sunset of uncanny splendor flamed red to the zenith. He kindled a fire of driftwood, set out another meal, and called the girl. Sipping gratefully from a tin of scalding coffee, she gave him a brief smile.

"You have ability, Leigh," she told him. "Ability that has been wasted." Her dark eyes studied him. "Now, I'm afraid, you've very little opportunity left to make use of it."

Sitting silent for a moment in the dancing firelight,

she began pouring the cool coral sand through her fingers into little white pyramids.

"If my deductions check out tonight," she said, "I'm afraid the creative functions of our present civilization are just about at an end. The planet will doubtless remain habitable for certain forms of life. Men may even survive in such places as Death Valley. But it will be a little strange if the human race ever recovers its supremacy."

"Tell me—" Leigh began.

She looked at her watch and studied the darkening eastward sky.

"In ten minutes," she said, "I can show you—show you why the earth is no longer a very safe place for nonstop fliers."

Leigh caught his breath.

He looked from the girl into the low, many-colored flames of the driftwood and slowly back again.

"Dr. Elene Gayle," he told her very gravely, "I feel that your frank comments have given me the right to express an equally candid opinion of female astronomers."

She nodded and looked back into the east.

"I haven't been following my profession altogether for fun, although I enjoy it," he told her. "I have been trying to save up two hundred thousand dollars. That would be enough to begin the manufacture of a gadget I have invented for the greater comfort of rocket passengers, and to build a home."

There was weary loneliness in his voice now.

"For hundreds and thousands of hours, cramped in the cockpit of the old *Phoenix*, I have endured fatigue and the need of sleep by dreaming of that home. Sometimes it is on a Florida key and sometimes it is in a little green valley that I have seen in the Colorado Rockies."

He looked at the girl across the fire.

"But always the most important thing about it was the woman who would live in it with me. I have had one in mind and then another. But none of them, Dr. Gayle, has fitted as well as you do—except, I must hasten to add, in certain regards.

"You must realize that I am telling you this just to make a point—since, what with crackups and your Stellar Shell, Tick Tinker and I have never had more than fifty thousand in a joint account."

A smile touched his lean face in the firelight.

"Physically," he told her, "you would do admirably. And you have intelligence, quickness, and, I believe, a sense of humor. But unfortunately you have other qualities that outweigh all these.

"Try to imagine yourself living a civilized life in a civilized home," he challenged. "You just couldn't do it. You wouldn't fit in—not with a schedule of forty-eight minutes a day for food.

"I hope I've made my point—that female astronomers who completely ignore the fact that they are women are just as out of place in a civilized world as extreme nonstop fliers."

Her first low laugh, and the light of amusement in her eyes, halted his argument. But her laughter grew higher and more breathless until she could not stop. Leigh saw that she was hysterical. He dashed a tin can of cold seawater into her face. She caught a sobbing breath and mopped at her eyes. With another glance at her watch, she rose abruptly.

"Come," she said in a shaken voice. "And let's see if there'll be any homes in the world ahead."

The squat mass of the twelve-inch reflector looked through a slit in the end of the building that had escaped destruction. Its clockwork, beneath the humming of the little motor-generator, made a muffled ticking.

Visible in the dim light of a shaded bulb, the girl twisted the turret and swiftly set the circles. Before she had done, Leigh knew that her object was the red point of Mars in the east.

For a long time, sitting with her eye to the lens, she was silent. Leigh could see the trembling of her small hand, touching the control wheels again and again. At last she rose and stood staring eastward through the slit, rubbing at her red eyes. Her face was bloodless.

"Well?" said Leigh.

"It's what I thought," she whispered. "Mars!"

Leigh moved into the seat she had left. His eye found the ocular. In its little disk of darkness, a single star burned with changing red and blue. And the disk of Mars, still too near the horizon for good observation, blurred and rippled as if painted on a black flag flying in the wind.

Even for a moment of good seeing, when the image steadied, that mistiness did not clear. But he could distinguish the wide dark equatorial markings—darker, in fact, than he had supposed them—and the white ellipse of the south polar cap.

Two things he saw that puzzled him. Beside the polar cap was a little dark fleck—the darkest marking on the planet—that had an oddly purplish color. And across the yellow-red of the planet, toward it, was drawn a twisting silver thread.

The image blurred and shimmered again, and Leigh rose impatiently from the instrument. A little ache throbbed in his unaccustomed eyes. He turned anxiously to the girl.

"Still I don't understand," he said. "I saw a little purple circle, not far from the polar cap. And a queer white thread twisting into it. But everything looked hazy."

"That's just it," her tired voice told him. "Mars is hazed and dim with atmosphere—atmosphere stolen from the Earth. That silver thread is the other end of the tube of force that we have been calling a tornado—sucking air from the Earth across to Mars!"

It took a moment for the full meaning to strike him. Then swiftly he felt the shock of it run through his whole body, and he swayed a little, standing there.

"But," he muttered at last, "I thought there were no Martians!"

"It has been pretty well agreed that there are no intelligent inhabitants," she said. "My father gave up the last great attempt to signal Mars ten years ago. But since that time something has happened to Mars."

"What?"

"It just happens," she told him slowly, "that that purple-blue spot, under the other end of the vortex tube, is exactly where the object we called the Stellar Shell struck Mars, two months ago."

He stared at her, in the dim observatory.

"Then—you think—"

"The inference is inevitable. The Stellar Shell was a ship. It brought living beings to Mars, from somewhere. They needed a heavier atmosphere for survival. Across on Earth—now, at opposition, less than fifty million miles away—they saw the atmosphere they required. With the same science that built and navigated the Stellar Shell, they have reached across to take what they require."

Leigh caught his breath.

"Why didn't they land on Earth in the first place?"

"Why should they, if they are able to reach from one world to another to take what they want? Perhaps Mars, with half the Earth's sunlight and a third of its gravity, suited them better in other regards."

Leigh's brain was spinning.

"Stealing the world's air! How can they possibly do that?"

"I saw one clue," the girl told him. "The two satellites are very difficult objects, even with the refinements of this instrument. It was hard to find them. When I did, they were both much too far from the planet. They are plunging out into space, away from their old orbits!"

"And that means—"

"It means that they have been cut off from the gravitational attraction of Mars. I think that is because the gravitational pull of the planet, by a power of science quite beyond our grasp, has been focused into a tube of force that reaches fifty million miles across space to our atmosphere."

"That queer tornado?"

"Exactly." The girl nodded. "Our atmosphere is being drawn up it. It seems to race around the Earth every day, because the Earth is turning under it. The violent air currents it causes, and the very loss of air, generate the storms. The unusual sunsets and auroras are doubtless due to the incidental forces that form and direct the tube."

Beside the girl, Leigh peered up through the narrow slit. In the bar of purple sky, Mars was a baleful orange red point. His staggered mind groped for understanding of its menace.

"What can they be?" he whispered.

The girl's own voice was dry.

"Probably they are interstellar voyagers. They came from the south, quite possibly from one of the nearer stars in Centaurus. Beings capable of such a flight must be as far from our comprehension as we are from that of the ants. And we must be as helpless before them."

"Ants can sting," muttered Leigh. But a breath of night air through the slit seemed strangely cold, and he shuddered again. "When do you suppose they'll stop?"

Elene Gayle's yellow head shook in the dimness, wearily.

"Who knows? We could spare them half our atmosphere, and still survive in the lowlands, though the climate everywhere would be far more severe. Possibly they will be satisfied in time. Possibly the advance of the Earth in its orbit will break their tube of force—until the next opposition, two years away."

"Mars is a smaller planet," Leigh said. "They shouldn't need so much air."

"Because of the lighter gravity," the girl told him, "to get the same pressure and density, they would need more."

"So we are at their mercy? Is there nothing to be done?"

Her face was gray and hopeless.

"People will react in the ways predictable from their known characteristics," she said. "Most of the world's population has already been driven into a helpless panic. The governments that stand will try to mobilize their armies—against an enemy they will never even see before they die. Only a few scientists will try to make a calm analysis of the problem, try to discover what, if anything, can be done. I doubt that anything can be done."

The rocket arrived before midnight. Elene Gayle had been at the radio all evening, guiding it in with her signals, listening to the reports of planet-wide confusion and terror; and trying in vain to get some message through to her Foundation's rocket research laboratory on the New Mexico desert.

When the blue luminescent cathion jets streaked across the stars, Leigh ran with flares to light the beach. It plunged down at an alarming angle, a forward blast checked it in a great cloud of blue flame, and two men tumbled out of it.

The girl came with Leigh to meet them. The tiny gray man with a pointed beard was Dr. Laymon Duval, assistant director of the Foundation. And the tall slender black-helmeted pilot, he knew without asking, was Laird Cragin.

Cragin was limping, patched with bandages. The girl nodded to the older man, greeted Cragin with a warm handshake. His handsome face smiled at her.

"Sorry to be late, Gay," he said. "But the freak storm cracked me up in the Marquesas Islands. Had to wait for Dr. Duval, in another fireboat. But here we are!"

The thin grave voice of the older man cut in, anxiously:

"You are quite certain, Dr. Gayle—certain of the facts in your code message? You really believe that stellar invaders on Mars are robbing the Earth of its air?"

"Duval," the girl asked briskly, "do I make mistakes?"

"Fewer than any man I know," he granted. "What action do you suggest?"

"Return at once," Elene Gayle said instantly. "Get full support from the President and the War Department. Rush our experimental rocket to completion in New Mexico. Arm it. Send it to Mars to stop the loss of atmosphere."

Duval's gray head shook, doubtfully.

"The only thing we can do," he admitted. "But you know I have been in charge at Alamogordo. And I'm reasonably certain that our rocket can't be completed before the air loss, continuing at the present rate, will force abandonment of the project.

"Even," he added forebodingly, "neglecting the weeks required for the flight—"

"Anyhow," the girl broke in, "we must try. I'll fly back to America with you tonight."

"Tonight?" Carter Leigh echoed her last word. He groped instinctively for the girl's arm.

"I'll go with you, Elene," he said hoarsely. "I'll fly your rocket to Mars."

"Thanks, Leigh." She turned briefly toward him. "But you're not a rocket pilot." She turned back to Cragin. "Load fuel and oxygen. We've no time to spare."

"Hullo." In the smooth voice of Laird Cragin was no very cordial recognition. "So you're Lucky Nonstop Leigh? Well, it looks like you stopped, this time, in a rather unlucky spot. Better watch that storm at dawn. It cuts a swath around the world, every day, through the thirties. Perth and Buenos Aires already gone."

"Back in a moment," the girl said. "I've some notes to get."

Carter Leigh watched her run back into the dark, toward the observatory. Listening silently to Cragin, as he helped lift aboard a drum of the kappa fuel, he tried to hide the despair in him.

"Sorry, old man," Cragin was saying. "But I guess the job will fall to me. I've been test-hopping the experimental models. If Gay sends her rocket to Mars, I'll go with it."

Leigh caught his breath. Laird Cragin was no doubt a brave and skillful man, even now promising to face certain death for the world's sake. But suddenly Leigh hated him with a blind savage hatred. He trembled, and his fists balled up. Tears swelled in his eyes, until the girl, running back out of the dark with a thick brief-case, was only a misty shadow.

"We'd like to give you a lift, old man," Cragin's voice was smoothly regretful. "But this is only a three-place job. And we've no time—"

"Thanks," Leigh managed to say. "But I've got the old *Phoenix*."

Elene Gayle paused to take his hand. Her fingers felt strong and cool.

"Good-bye, Leigh," she said briskly. "Sorry we must leave you. Watch the storm. Make any use you can of our supplies and equipment here. Get north, if you can, out of its track."

Leigh did not answer.

Duval was already in the rocket. Cragin swung the girl in, leapt after her, slid forward the curved transpar-ent hatch. Leigh stood stupidly motionless until the pilot opened it again to shout a warning.

He stumbled back. The blue electronic exhausts bel-lowed out about him. His skin tingled. Ozone burned his lungs. Blinded, he covered his eyes. When he could see again, the rocket was a dim blue star, dropping and dimming, north-northeast.

Carter Leigh stood alone on the beach, softly whis-tling the melancholy notes of "Barbara Allen." Alone on Manumotu. It was midnight. Six hours, more or less, until that world-circling funnel should pass again.

Southward, beyond the dark loom of the peak, the strange aurora rose again. Sprays of green and orange crossed the zenith. That eerie light showed him the old *Phoenix*, lying upside down on the pale white beach. He plodded heavily down toward her.

"Well, old girl," he muttered. "Cracked up or not, it looks like we've got to make one more flight—unless we want to be picked up by that wind between the worlds."

He stopped abruptly on the coral sand. His eyes lifted swiftly from the battered old crate on the beach, up to the red and baleful eye of Mars, now well past the meridian. His mind pictured that silver cord from world to world. And his lips pursed for a soundless whistle.

"Well, why not?"

He stumbled to the old plane. His trembling hand touched the cold metal of her prop. His voice was quick and breathless.

"Why not, old lady?" he muttered again. "There's air all the way. And where there's air, you can fly with gasoline. It's thin and rough, maybe. But we've flown high before, and met our share of bumps."

He walked around the plane, inspected rudder and elevator.

"Quite a wind, I guess. But it will be behind us. And when you've got fifty million miles to make, you need the wind behind you!"

He peered in the darkness at the damaged aileron.

"The percentage may be a billion to one against us. But what's the difference? You're extinct as the dodo, old girl. And I am, too. And we're getting wise to the fact.

"After all, why not? She'll probably be flying to Mars with Cragin, if they get their rocket done. We might as well be there to meet 'em.

"Okay, Duchess! Let's get going!"

He knew it wouldn't be easy to get the plane righted and repaired and in the air in the six hours that remained before the wind funnel returned. But he had been in spots almost as tight before. There was the time he came down on the arctic tundra with a broken prop, and whittled out one of his own. . . .

Lucky he had the supplies and equipment at the abandoned station. He walked back for ropes and tackle. In an hour the old ship was on her retractable wheels again, with no more than incidental injury.

He started the motor, taxied the ship up beside the building where he could have electric light, and went to work on the twisted aileron. When that was crudely mended, he found half a dozen other necessary repairs—and still, for all he knew, there might be some hidden harm that he could not discover till the ship was in the air.

Four precious hours gone before the plane was ready to load. Two things he had to have—gasoline and oxygen. The air was already growing thin on Earth, but it would be thinner still in that tube of force.

Tumbling aside the drums of rocket fuel and cases of supplies, he began carrying crated tins of gasoline and pouring them into the empty tanks. Ten gallons at a trip. The empty tanks held three hundred, and he stacked tins behind the cockpit.

The Southern Cross tilted above the peak. Time fled away. He panted. Even in the chill of morning, he was drenched with sweat. Lucky the Foundation had been so generous with fuel for the motor-generator and the stoves. Lower octane rating than quite agreed with the ancient engine. But, if he started on the other, it would do.

The first ominous promise of dawn was in the east, before that task was done. Now the oxygen. He staggered under the weight of the long steel cylinders. Four of them. That was all he dared load.

Red tongues were leaping up in the east now; the vortex would soon be here. And he'd have to be high to meet it—as high as the *Phoenix* could climb. And even there, in the softer hands of the upper atmosphere, the odds would be overwhelmingly against him.

He made a last dash for an armload of food. He picked up a well-worn book of Keats, the name in it Elene Gayle. Who'd have thought that female astronomers read poetry? He climbed into the cockpit, and jammed his heel against the starter pedal.

While the starter motor wound up, he adjusted his helmet, tested oxygen tubes and reduction valve. He set altimeter and clock, put rudder and elevator trim tabs in neutral. He engaged the clutch, and the ancient motor caught with a roar.

Fine drops of oil on the windshield reminded him that it was in need of an overhaul. If there had been time and tools. . . .

"Crazy," muttered Leigh. "Off to Mars!" Against the roar, he began to whistle "Barbara Allen."

While the motor warmed, he pushed in the knob that flattened the pitch of the prop, and planned the take-off. The beach was now a ghostly strip of gray beneath that strange sunrise—too short for all the load the *Phoenix* carried.

He taxied to the east end of the beach, turned to face the uneasy west wind, plunged into it with a blast of the gun. The ship was far too heavy. Even with the stick forward all the way, the tail wheel still dragged. And the white spray, flying over black teeth of rock beyond the beach, was rushing at him.

But the tail came off the ground. The wheels tapped the sand, lifted, merely flicked the rocks beyond. Leigh caught a long gasping breath. He pushed the knob that started the wheel-retracting pump. The airspeed needle leapt ahead.

Over the dark unquiet sea north of Manumotu, he wheeled into the east. Moment by moment, the sky was flaming redder. He watched for the thread of silver in it, and trimmed the elevators to hold a steady climb.

He slid the cockpit cover forward. The air about him was suddenly calm. He felt a moment of relaxation before the crisis ahead. His eyes left the banks of instruments for a moment, found the worn little book beside him.

"Sentimental fool," he muttered. "Elene Gayle wouldn't carry dead weight to Mars."

He slid back the cockpit cover, hurled the volume into the shrieking wind. He was immediately sorry he had done so. He scanned the east again. Still no tornado. Would it fail him now?

The *Phoenix* was lifting twelve hundred feet a minute. The cockpit grew cold. He plugged in the heater units in his suit. His ears ached. His lungs began to labor in the thinning air. He adjusted the faceplate of his helmet, twisted the oxygen valve.

Then he saw the funnel. It came toward him like a swinging silver rope. Automatically, he banked the ship, flew straight toward it. He saw the dancing tip of it touch Manumotu, nearly six miles beneath. All the green vanished magically from its black cliffs, and a mountain of sea rose over them.

The first blast of wind overtook him so violently that the ship stalled in it. The dead stick was loose in his hands. He shoved it forward, gunned the motor till the ship lived again, pulled it back.

He was trying to climb beside the silver funnel, to edge into it. But the blast of it caught him with a savage and resistless acceleration. The blood was driven out of his head. Darkness pressed down on him. He fought grimly for consciousness and strength to keep the nose of the plane ahead.

For an endless time he was suspended in that battle. His flying of the ship, the swift and delicate reactions that kept it alive and headed up that twisting bore of silver, his skill was half conscious. And he had no awareness of anything but life.

That killing pressure slackened at last, however. His strained heart beat more easily. He was aware of the plane again, creaking, twisted, battered—but still miraculously intact.

He turned up the oxygen, adjusted the prop to increase its pitch to the utmost, opened the auxiliary supercharger. The cold gas filled his lungs again, and he found awareness for things outside the plane.

It was the strangest moment Leigh had known. The curve of the silver tube seemed quite close, on every side. He knew that the air in it, and the plane, now had a velocity quite beyond conception. Yet it seemed that an odd calm surrounded him, and he held the plane, the motor at half-throttle, at its center without difficulty.

Though he knew the tube could be nothing material, nothing more than a vortex of etheric force, the walls of it looked curiously real. Almost glasslike.

Whatever they were, he soon knew that he had better not touch them. For a whirling stick in the air ahead had grown into a great black log—the stripped trunk of some mighty tree, snatched, he supposed, from Manumotu. He saw it spin into that glassy wall. Saw it instantly rebound in a thin dissolving puff of dust and splinters.

He twisted in the cockpit and saw the Earth behind him. Beyond the shimmering walls of the tube it was a mighty hemisphere, suspended in darkness. Gray and misty, patched with great circular areas of white cloud. The Americas were crowding near the rim of it—vast stretches white with unseasonable snow. Asia was invisible in darkness.

Perceptibly, the Earth diminished. It was odd, Leigh thought, that it looked smaller and nearer all the time, not more distant. The two Americas thinned and crept very gradually beyond the lighted curve of the world. The blur of Australia came slowly out of the night; the now invisible foot of the tube, he knew, sweeping destructively across it.

A steady pressure held him back against the seat. At first he had hardly noticed it. But it required effort, he realized, to thrust out his arms against it. The muscles of his neck were already aching.

It was that acceleration. Swiftly, ever more swiftly, that resistless suction was drawing him across toward Mars. So far, so good. He guided the plane around a good-sized granite boulder, drawn with him up the funnel.

The thing was incredible. Flying to Mars in the *Phoenix*—a secondhand crate that Tick Tinker had somehow wangled out of the city fathers of Phoenix, Arizona, six years ago. And the Gayle Foundation, with all its millions, had failed to fly its rockets even to the Moon.

But, incredible or not, it was happening.

After the tension and excitement of the last few hours, Leigh felt the pressure of a maddening monotony. He was already weary from loading the plane. And he found this flight the most exhausting he had made.

The air was too thin—so thin the motor coughed and stuttered, even under both superchargers. Even with the oxygen hissing steadily, he felt faint and oppressed. And the cold was a savage thing. Even the heated suit failed to protect him.

Nothing changed. There was the ship and the silver tube. The Earth was soon a dimming point behind, beside the dimmer Moon, and Mars remained only a reddish point ahead. He ate a little, when the clock told him, from his scanty supplies.

Through the tube's pale walls space looked very dark. The stars were more brilliant, more colorful, than he had ever imagined them. But in their myriads he found it almost impossible to discover any familiar constellation. He felt lost amid their alien splendor.

He watched the clock. Its hands crept with deadly slowness. One day at last was gone. Another began. His body prickled painfully and then went numb with cold and fatigue. Sleep dragged at his brain.

But the shattering of the log had told him what would happen if his attention wavered.

"If nonstop fliers are extinct," he muttered once, "it's a good thing for them."

In his first wild resolve and in all the hazards he had met, he had not thought of what might happen next. But now, in this endless monotony, he had ample time to ponder the question: What will I do when I get to Mars?

He had a .45 autoloading pistol and half a dozen extra clips of ammunition with him in the cockpit—a relic as ancient as the *Phoenix*. How, with such a weapon, was he to cope with the science that had made this interplanetary tube?

Presently his fatigue-drugged mind recoiled from the problem, baffled.

Every dragging revolution of the minute hand seemed an eternity. But Mars at last began to grow beside the endless argent coils of the tube. It became a swelling hypnotic eye.

He shook himself in the grasp of monotony and sleep. But Mars stared at him. It was the ocher-red eye of that sinister intelligence that was stripping the Earth of air. He tried not to look at it. For its red gaze was deadly.

He woke with a start. The old *Phoenix* creaked and shuddered. The right wingtip had touched the silver wall, and it was shattered. Twisted metal caught the air, dragged. He set the rudder to compensate.

But the tube had begun to widen. The current of air was slowing. A resistless force pushed him forward in the cockpit. Wind screamed about the *Phoenix*. She was plunging down toward Mars.

He cut the throttle, pulled the old plane back into a spiral. Savage eddies hammered her. She groaned and strained. Bits of metal whipped away from the damaged wing. More and more, it dragged and fell.

But Mars was swiftly growing.

He studied the clock. Just fifty hours since he climbed off Manumotu beach. He must have come fifty million miles. A million miles an hour—let Laird Cragin beat that in a rocket!

The face of Mars grew broad beneath him. The orange-red of it was white-patched, more and more, with the stolen clouds of Earth. But he found the white ellipse of the shrinking polar cap, the growing purple circle, above its retreating rim, where the Stellar Shell had landed.

Plunging down through the widening funnel that cushioned the air-jet from the Earth, he held the steep spiral of the *Phoenix* toward that purple circle. He would land in the middle of it, he resolved. And try to deal at once, as best he could with exhausted body and inadequate equipment, with the mysterious science of its creators.

A reckless determination rose in him. A wild elation filled him—the first man to cross space. He was the representative of all mankind, and he felt the strength of all men in him. He was invincible. If he must, he thought, he would make a bullet of the *Phoenix* and dive into whatever seemed the heart of the enemy's strength.

In his feverish excitement he wanted to push back the

cockpit cover and yell. His lungs were burning. Then a glance at the barometric altimeter showed that it was registering. Air pressure was mounting again. He was suffering from oxygen intoxication. He partially closed the valve.

For a time a passing cloud hid the purple spot. With battered binoculars, he studied the surface of the planet beyond it. New lakes upon the reddish desert were black or mirror-like. The olive-green bands around them must be vegetation.

The cloud moved on, and he could see the purple spot again, perhaps only twenty miles below. A patch of dense purple jungle, the binoculars revealed it, far ranker than the olive-green beyond. Had the invaders brought alien seed to Mars?

A green line cut the purple wilderness, opposite the polar crown. And, in the center of the jungle, he saw curious glints and sparklings of green. The glasses picked out machines there. A colossal latticed tube thrust upward.

That mighty metal finger pointed toward the silver funnel, toward the far-off Earth. It was the finger of doom. It, Leigh knew, was the thing he must destroy. He tipped the shuddering old *Phoenix* into a steeper dive.

A long, long flight, his dulled brain thought, just to bring a man to suicide. But for all mankind, for Elene Gayle and her science, even Laird Cragin and his rockets, it was the thing he had to do.

Or so he had resolved. But the gesture was denied him.

That long green finger moved abruptly in the purple jungle. It swung down from the Earth, to point to the diving plane. The *Phoenix* was struck a staggering blow. If the power of that needle was the focused gravity of Mars, then a good deal of it, reversed, reacted on the ship. The impact battered Leigh into oblivion.

When Carter Leigh came back to consciousness, the plane was spinning down in a power dive. Her ancient frame quivered; scraps of metal were vanishing from her injured wing. The damaged aileron was jammed again.

He yanked at the stick, fought to bring her out of the dive. He stopped her spinning, and her nose came slowly up. Then he looked below for a landing place. Shallow lakes of yellow rain water patched the red desert. He found a level ridge that looked firm and dry enough, extended the landing gear.

But the air even here at the surface was still very thin. Lesser gravity made a partial compensation, but the landing speed must still be dangerously high. Still he came down.

The red ridge flashed up at him, and he tried to level off. For all his efforts, the dragging right wheel touched first, too hard. The plane bounced, veered dangerously. The bounce carried him abnormally high. He had time to get the plane half straight again. Another bounce, to which the whole plane shook and groaned. Next time, in spite of him, the injured wing grazed and crumpled. He fought to right the ship; but the good wing dipped, plowed into red mud, and was shattered to kindling. The fuselage rebounded, skimmed along on its side for a hundred yards in a spray of crimson mud, at last was still.

Leigh clambered painfully out of the wreckage. He felt his bruised limbs. Despite the stunning finality of the crackup, he found no bones broken. His helmet had been knocked off. His lungs had to labor, but they found oxygen enough.

Pale yellow-green shoots, pulpy and fragile, were pushing up through the wet red soil at his feet. He had come to rest at the margin of a wide shallow lake that mirrored the drizzling sky. Far beyond, above the gentle red hills patched with fresh olive green, he could see a long low line of purple darkness. And his ears, after they had become accustomed to the silence, heard a continual distant roaring in the sky.

That roar was the wind of stolen air from Earth. That line was the purple jungle. Beyond it was the great machine of the stellar invaders, that had to be destroyed. Leigh, as wearily confident as if nothing were now impossible, set about that distant project.

He snapped the action of the old automatic, slipped it in his pocket. Two five-gallon tins of gasoline and the remaining cylinders of oxygen he made into a bale, padded with his thick flying suit.

On Earth, he could not have moved them. Even here, their weight was eighty pounds, and his own sixty more. The burden simplified the matter of walking. But the effort of breathing taxed his lungs.

The horizon was closer than it looked. He dwelt upon that fact for encouragement, and walked toward the barrier of the unknown jungle. The roaring grew louder in the sky. He reeled with fatigue. The slow drizzle of stolen moisture continued, interrupted with flurries of sleet. Cold sank into his bones.

He came at last to the jungle and super cactus. Jagged purple spines grew with a visible motion; they stabbed into the red mud, sprouted, lifted new barbed lances. It was a barrier too thick and dense for him to hope to cross.

Utterly disheartened, he flung down his burden. Mechanically, he ate a can of beans he had slipped into the pack. Then quite suddenly he slipped into sleep.

The slow thrust of a living bayonet wakened him, drenched and stiff with cold. His chest felt congested and breathing took a painful effort. He picked up his burden and slogged off westward through the red mud, skirting the advancing jungle.

It was in that direction that he thought he had seen the green slash. An exhausting hour brought him to it— a broad level pavement of some glistening, bright-green stuff. The surface was perfect, but the bank beneath it had a surprising look of antiquity.

This road came straight out of the north. It cut into the jungle, the walls of purple thorns arching over it. After brief hesitation—lest he meet its masters unawares—Leigh trudged in upon it.

The purple shadow of the jungle fell upon him. The roaring continued in the sky; cold rain and sleet fell endlessly. Leigh plodded endlessly on, ignoring fatigue and cold and hunger. Once he stopped to drink from a puddle on the road. A lancing pain stabbed through his chest.

A humming clatter startled him. He stepped off the road, thrust himself into the purple spines. A huge three-wheeled conveyance came swiftly along the pavement. The bed of it was piled with something pale green and crystalline—something mined, perhaps, in the equatorial regions.

Straining his eyes in the purple dust to see the driver, Leigh glimpsed only a gelatinous arm. That arm and a yellow eye and another translucent waving limb were all he ever saw of the actual invaders. Their nature, the motives and the course of their flight, the mysteries of their science, the extent of their designs upon the solar system—all these remained defined only by conjecture and dread. The invaders remained but a dark-limned shadow of the unknown.

The brief polar night was already falling when the truck passed. It was bitterly cold. The rain turned again to driving pellets of sleet, and heavy frost crackled over the roadway and the jungle spines.

The roaring overhead was louder now. A greenish glow filtered down the tunnel of the road. And at last, dead with fatigue, Leigh dragged himself to the edge of the central clearing in the jungle.

He perceived no source of light. But the surrounding wall of thorns and the fantastic structures before him were visible in a dull green radiance. He saw what must have been the remains of the Stellar Shell—a huge projectile, whose nose had plowed deep into the planet. Half its upper parts had been cut away; it must have served as a mine of the green metal.

Beyond it, swung between three massive piers, was the latticed tube, now horizontal, pointing across the pole toward the unseen Earth. Leigh caught his breath. Nerved with a last spurt of unsuspected strength, he staggered forward in the green shadow of the Stellar Shell.

Nothing stopped him. He swayed across a little open space beyond, dropped with his burden in the darkness between the three piers. His hands began shaping a basin in the half frozen mud.

A hoarse coughing hoot, from some half seen structure beyond, spurred him to desperate haste. He ripped open his bale, began pouring his ten gallons of gasoline into the basin. An unaccountable rasping rattle lifted the hair at the back of his neck. He heard a metallic clatter, nearer.

Fumbling desperately, he opened the cocks of the oxygen cylinders. The compressed stuff came out with a hissing roar, half liquid, half gas. It evaporated and enveloped him in a cloud of frost.

He turned the blue jets into the gasoline. Ticklish work. Before the invention of the cathion blast, gasoline and oxygen had been the favorite fuel of rocket experimenters. An efficient mixture of them, as makers of aerial bombs had sometimes demonstrated, had five times the explosive energy of nitroglycerine.

This wouldn't be a very efficient mixture. The gasoline froze into brittle blue chunks, and the oxygen was swiftly boiling away. The results were unpredictable.

Above the dying hiss of the jets, Leigh heard that rattle and the rasping hoot, very close to him now. He straightened in the thick white fog, and saw the yellow eye. A huge luminescent yellow pupil, fringed with a ragged membrane.

A pointed metal rod, glowing with strange green, appeared beneath the eye. It thrust toward him through the fog. Leigh stumbled backward; his numbed fingers found the automatic, fired into the yellow eye. It blinked and vanished, and the rod clattered in the fog.

Leigh staggered back to the end of the Stellar Shell and began shooting into his mud basin between the three great piers. At his third shot, the world turned to blue flame, and went out utterly.

The massive green wall of the cosmic projectile shielded him from the blast. And it sheltered him somewhat from the tempest that followed.

He came to, lying in the freezing mud, nostrils bleeding, head ringing. Dragging himself up behind the shielding barrier, he saw that all the great structures of the invaders had been leveled. The green glow had gone from them.

He started at some motion in the gray twilight; it was a gelatinous arm, waving slowly above a pool of mud. He emptied the automatic at it—and it sank.

Then the wind came. The interplanetary air-jet, now that the cushioning forces by which the invaders had sheltered themselves had been removed, came down in a shrieking blast. The mighty walls of the Stellar Shell were all that stood before it.

For half an hour, battered and half suffocated, Leigh clung to a metal bar in its shelter. The wind blew itself out abruptly, the last of the ravished air. The small sun rose warmingly in a sky suddenly serene, and Leigh slept half the day in its heat.

In the afternoon, still aching with weariness, he found the roadway again, and plodded back through the flattened jungle toward the wreck of the *Phoenix*. Hungry, bitter with loneliness, he began to regret that he had survived.

Some swift decay had attacked the fallen purple thorns, but the native life of Mars was thriving exceedingly. In the changing landscape, it was difficult to find the plane. When at last he reached it, he ate the solitary can of corned beef that remained of his supplies and then rigged up a directional antenna for the transmitter.

For several reasons, this last hopeless message was important. He wanted to end the fears of the Earth; wanted to help Tick Tinker; and he wanted Dr. Elene Kathrine Gayle to know that he had flown nonstop to Mars, usefully, with gasoline.

"Mars, calling Earth," he repeated. "Carter Leigh, on Mars, calling C Q, Earth. Landed here yesterday. Destroyed invaders last night with gasoline bomb. Anticipate no danger further loss of air. Inform Tick Tinker, New York, nonstop flight to Mars made with

Zerolube oil. Now marooned on Mars. Good-bye, Earth."

He repeated that message, between intervals of sleep, until the little battery was exhausted. Then he set himself, wearily and without hope, to begin the life of the first Robinson Crusoe of space.

In a pot cut from the end of a gasoline tank, he made stews, queer-flavored but edible, from the fruits and seed of some of the native plants. Hoping to reach a less severe climate in the equatorial regions and driven by a desire to learn more of whatever lost people had built the road, he stowed all the useful articles he could salvage upon a sledge made from the elevator of the *Phoenix*, and set off northward along the straight green pavement.

The Earth, now drawing away from Mars, was a splendid golden morning star. Sight of it, in the frosty dawns when he could not keep warm enough to sleep, filled him with tragic loneliness.

One day he threw away the gun, to end his desire to use it on himself. The next he turned back along the road, and spent all the day to find it and clean it again. But when it was ready he put it on the sledge and plodded on down the glassy pavement.

He had counted thirty Martian days. With the slow advance of spring, and his weary progress northward, the climate had become a little more endurable. He was cheered sometimes by the sight of young, familiar-looking shoots—grown from seed borne upon that interplanetary wind.

But his body was gaunt with privation. He had a recurrent painful cough. Sometimes his meals from the Martian plants brought violent indigestion. The end, he clearly saw, would be the same, whether he used the gun or not.

Then the night, the incredible night, when he woke in his chill bed beside a smoldering fire, to hear the familiar rhythmic drum of cathion rockets. He saw a blue star following down the roadway from the south. Breathless and quivering, he sprang up to feed his fire.

Mantled in the blue flame of its forward jets, the rocket came down upon the road. His firelight showed the legend on its side: *Gayle Foundation.* It would be Laird Cragin, he supposed, another exile—

But the bare grimy yellow head that appeared, when its thick doors swung open, was the head of Elene Gayle.

"Greetings, Mr. Lucky Leigh," her brisk voice said. "And congratulations on the aptness of your nickname. . . . Are you all right?"

"Right as rain," he croaked hoarsely. "Only—surprised!"

"We finished the rocket." She was oddly breathless. "When the guns and explosives were no longer necessary, we loaded it with return fuel and supplies for a few weeks of exploration."

"Cragin?" demanded Leigh.

"There were two places," said the girl. "After we took off, I made him drop back by parachute." Her voice was suddenly very crisp. "I have the honor to bring you, Leigh, in token of the gratitude of Earth for your recent remarkable nonstop flight, the medals and awards—"

Her voice broke abruptly. She stumbled out of the rocket, and came running across the strange pavement to meet him. In his arms, trembling, she clung to him.

The Crucible of Power

THIS, MY FATHER's story, must begin with the great pandemic that was the background of his life, as it had been, since the twentieth century, the deadly background of human history. The Falling Sickness first attacked workers in a Greenland radium mine, in 1998. Baffled doctors talked of spores swept to Earth by the light-pressure of the Great Supernova of 1991. More probably, however, the new virus was a radiation-born mutation from some malignant proteide already known—quite possibly, even, from one of those responsible for the "common cold."

The disease attacked all nerve tissue. Commonly the ganglions and plexuses of the ear were first affected. The victims were deafened, deprived of sense of balance, usually terrified with a sensation of endless headlong falling—hence the malady's popular name.

The Falling Sickness struck without warning. People fell suddenly, at work or in the street, shrieking in fear, clutching wildly at objects about them. The infection spread swiftly from the auditory nerve, causing blindness, agonized paroxysms, nightmarish hallucinations, coma, paralysis, often stoppage of the heart, and death.

It is impossible, now, to convey anything of the horror and the magnitude of that pandemic. Only one person in five had a natural immunity, and a frantic medical science failed to find either artificial immunization or successful treatment. A third of the victims were dead in three days, and another third were left blind or hopelessly crippled. In a century and a half, three billion died of it—almost the total population of the planet at any one time.

The clock of civilization was stopped. The brilliant scientific advance of the twentieth century seemed lost in a hundred years of stagnation, dread, and decay. Endless wars rivaled the horrors of the virus.

By 2100, however, mankind seemed on the way to slow recovery. The plague still claimed ten million lives a year, but immunity, by inexorable natural selection, was increasing. Courage began to return. Government, industry, science, and civilization struggled to resume their interrupted march.

My father, Garth Hammond, was born in the last year of the Black Century. His life might be accounted for in terms of the dark age that produced him. But I beg the visivox listener to try to see him as something more than the end product of a rugged heredity fighting to survive in a grimly hostile environment. For he was more than that. He was more, even, than the daring explorer of space, the stalwart captain of industry, the dashing Don Juan, the heartless capitalist, the greatest philanthropist, the dictator of the solar system, and the conqueror of the Sun. Men have called him the most black-hearted, villainous hero the System ever knew. He was all those things, I know. But, also, he was a human being.

He was a tall and powerful man. His quick gray eyes had a keenness often disconcerting. Yet always he kept the ready geniality that came from the days when he was an impecunious and nimble-witted stock promoter. Even after the years had whitened the abundant shock of hair above his ruggedly handsome, black-browed face, he retained a vast attraction for women. My mother was not the first whose heart he broke, nor the last.

Garth Hammond has become the demigod of the whole creed of Success. Billions have been astonished at the penniless bootboy who rose to be financial dictator of nine worlds. Millions of other bootboys, I suppose, must have been inspired by his example to frantic application of dye and brush.

It is true enough that once, for a few months, he attended the boots of passengers on a transatlantic stratoplane. But his rise was due to something more than mere industry. He cultivated a pathetic limp, and told sympathetic travelers a pathetic story of his mother crippled for life by the Falling Sickness—actually she had died from falling down a tenement air shaft when he was two years old. Discharged for such methods of business, he began selling knickknacks and visivox spools about the stations. The eye of a young competitor was blacked by a mysterious assailant, and his missing stock in trade discovered to have been mysteriously shipped—collect—to the Mayor of Zamboanga.

That is the beginning, crooked enough perhaps, yet with its hint of the imaginative resource that accompanied my father's ruthless ambition. His commercial career was not really launched, however, until after Cornwall's spectacular voyage to the Moon, in 2119.

Captain Thomas Cornwall was a young ordnance engineer, on leave from the army. His rocket was the first to attain the velocity of escape—11.3 km/sec. His triumphant return, after two weeks on the Moon, won him the world's frantic acclaim. The feat seemed symbolic of the reawakening of man, after the long night of the Black Century. And it showed my father the way to make his first millions.

For he was soon engaged in the manufacture of "Hammond's Lunar Oil." This elixir, secretly concocted on the prescription of a notorious quack of the time, "Dr." Emile Molyneaux, was "warranted to contain essential oils from rare lunar shrubs." It was advertised as a specific for most of the multitudinous ills of the human race. Sales, especially in those parts of the world where the Falling Sickness was still most prevalent, were tremendous.

Cornwall started legal difficulties with an indignant public statement that he had brought back no plant specimens from the Moon. My father's reply was to finance a lunar expedition of his own.

One Dr. Ared Trent, a lean, brilliant, intense young astrophysicist, had just rediscovered the cellular principle of rocket construction. Although no larger than Cornwall's, his rocket was far more efficient. He was able to carry two companions and a good deal of equipment, including a dismantled telescope.

The "Hammond's Oil Expedition" remained one hundred days on the Moon, and safely brought back specimens and observations of great scientific value. The adventure was well publicized—and sales of the elixir boomed again.

In order to meet the enormous demand, however, the compound was varied with cheaper chemicals and an increasing amount of water. This, together with Trent's delay about publishing any description of the supposed plant life found on the Moon, brought more legal trouble. There were charges that mistaken dependence on the elixir had resulted in thousands of deaths. My father finally closed the plant.

But Garth Hammond had already harvested millions, and he was ready, now, for a greater enterprise. He was not long in finding it. His first attempt led to disaster— for all but himself. Then Trent's photographic studies of Mars, made from the Moon, precipitated the most momentous events of modern times.

Reborn after the Black Century, industry soon faced a grave power famine. Reserves of oil and coal were depleted; river and tidal power projects had been developed to the practicable limits; increased demands for food cut off conversion of the agricultural surplus into fuel alcohol; direct utilization of solar power still seemed as much a dream as atomic energy. And power, my father realized, was the key to greatness.

"Power, Chan," he used to tell me, "is power!"

Prices rose; wages sank. The rich were the owners of power sites or fuel reserves; the poor, "power starved," forbidden private transportation, actually hungry, shivered in helpless discontent.

Garth Hammond saw, in this bitter need, a great opportunity. His first, disastrous attempt to grasp it was suggested by his old associate, Molyneaux. Pseudoengineer as well as quack doctor, Molyneaux revived an old project: a twelve-mile shaft in the planet's crust, to tap possible mineral wealth and generate power from volcanic heat.

The Volcano Steam and Metals Corporation proved to have been a singularly apt name for the enterprise. For, after a billion dollars had been spent to sink the great pit forty thousand feet, the bottom of it suddenly split. Men and refrigerating machines were drowned in flaming lava. A rain of boiling mud drowned the new city of Hammondspit, Virginia, taking twenty thousand lives.

Molyneaux was killed in the eruption. Full responsibility for the disaster was somehow placed upon him. All the records of the corporation had been destroyed, and its tangled affairs were never entirely straightened. A fact, however, which used to rouse the ire of luckless investors, was that my father seemed to have lost nothing by the failure of the project.

He remained prosperous enough, indeed, to purchase an entire island in the Aegean. There he built a marble replica of an ancient Roman villa, complete with all modern conveniences. There he took my mother as a bride—his second wife, she was Sabina Calhoun, frail, lovely daughter of an old aristocracy. And it was there, in 2130, the year after the disaster, that I was born.

It was to that island palace that Trent soon came. Some Napoleonic complex drove my father always onward. He was already restless and uncontent, my mother used to tell me, before that epochal visit, whose results broke her heart and opened the conquest of so many worlds.

Ared Trent had been busy for five years analyzing and publishing the results of the lunar expedition. He was a lean, tall fellow, habitually silent, methodical of habits, with a brilliant mathematical mind—and now on fire with a stupendous Idea.

"These things on Mars!" His excitement stopped my father's weary stalking through the marble halls. "On the Moon, without atmospheric interference, they photographed unmistakably—and they are *works!*"

He flourished photographs and drawings.

"Engineering works! About both the ice caps there are drainage channels, dams, pumps. Still operating, mind you—for I saw square fields turn olive green in the spring! The Schiaparelli 'canals,' I'm convinced, are cultivated belts!"

He shuffled the photographs, excitedly.

"And here's something else, Hammond—I don't know what." An odd note of awe slowed his eager voice. "A thing shaped like . . . well, like a barrel. It's dark. It's half a mile thick. It stands alone on the desert plain, a few hundred miles northwest of *Syrtis Major*. It

can't be natural. Some construction—I can't guess
what. But—tremendous!"

I can hear my father's calm question: "Well, Trent
But what of it?"

"Machinery!" cried Trent. "Colossal machines—
running! But what is their source of power?" His dark
eyes stared feverishly at my father. "Coal and hydrocar-
bon deposits must have been used up ages ago. Without
seas, they have no tidal power. Rare atmosphere makes
wind plants ineffectual. Sunshine is only about half as
intense as here. Atomic power? I couldn't guess!"

He waved the papers. "No, Hammond, I don't know
what they have—but it's something we haven't got on
Earth."

"Well, then, Trent," my father calmly announced his
decision, "we're going out to Mars, you and I—and get
it!"

"To Mars!" The astronomer began to tremble.
"Mars—if we could! What an opportunity!" His dark
head shook. "But wait, Hammond! It's hundreds of
times as far as the Moon. Enormous technical difficulties. Trip would take two years, between oppositions.
And cost millions!"

"I've got the millions," said Garth Hammond. "You
can build the ship. We're going!"

My frightened mother pleaded in vain against the
project. My father returned to America with Trent the
very next day, to begin the preliminary arrangements.
My mother, in frail health since my recent birth, remained on the island. He did not come back to live with
her. His fancy soon turned to the visivox actress, Nada
Vale. The next year my mother was quietly divorced,
given the island home and a generous annuity. She was
still devoted to Garth Hammond, and the separation
was a hurt from which she could not recover.

The Martian ship was two years building. Finished in
2132, it was a four-step rocket, each step containing
thousands of cellules, each of which was a complete
rocket motor with its own load of alumilloid fuel, to be
fired once and then detached.

The rocket stood on the summit of a mountain: a smaller mountain of glittering metal, tapering toward the top. A spidery ladder led up to a high, tiny opening. Bright sun shimmered on the metal and on the snow, but the December wind was bitterly cold. My mother lifted me off the snow, and so I found that she was sobbing.

Trent and two others climbed up the ladder. Garth Hammond waited, his smile flashing, talking to a crowd of newsmen. Someone pushed through and thrust a legal paper at him. The investors in the power pit were still bringing suits and getting out injunctions.

I heard my father's roaring laugh, and saw him tear the paper in two.

"They say the arm of the law is long," his great voice boomed. "But so is the road to Mars."

He whispered something to my weeping mother, and patted me on the head.

"You used to reach for the Moon, Chan," he said. "Well, I'm going to bring you something bigger."

He turned to mount the ladder, and then I saw another woman clinging to him. She was Nada Vale, the red-haired actress. I thought she was beautiful, though I knew my mother didn't like her. She was crying wildly and hanging to my father. He pushed her away and swiftly climbed the ladder.

"Garth! Garth!" she was screaming. "You'll be killed! You'll never come back!"

White-faced and silent, my mother took me down to the little village. From the window of our room in the small hotel, we could see the rocket, a shining crown on the mountain. A siren moaned. Mother caught her breath. The whole mountain was suddenly swept with smoke and fire. Windows rattled, and there was a huge roar of wind and thunder. And mother pointed out a tiny speck, trailing fire, vanishing in the sky.

"Your father, Chan," she whispered. "Off to Mars!" She sat a long time, holding me tight in her arms. I was afraid to move. "That Nada Vale," she breathed at last. "I . . . I'm sorry for her."

We went back to the island, and waited. The whole world waited for the next opposition, when they should return. Astronomers watched the Red Planet, radio hams trained loops on it. But there was no sign or signal. My fifth birthday came and passed. Hurtling Earth overtook Mars in its orbit, and left it swiftly behind.

And still my father did not return.

II

For eight minutes that seemed eight centuries the four men in the ship were deafened and battered and mauled by the wild force of the rockets. Then followed sixty-seven days of silent monotony, as inertia flung them out toward the orbit of Mars.

The nine tons of pay load included concentrated supplies carefully calculated to last two years; the stock of manufactured goods, chemicals, metals, and jewelry, which my father hoped to trade for the precious secret of Mars—and the arsenal of rifles, pistols and grenades, machine guns, a 37 mm. automatic cannon, and an especially designed automobile howitzer firing incendiary and demolition shells, which he planned to bring into use if the secret were not voluntarily forthcoming.

The other two men had been carefully selected. Burgess was a famous power engineer who was also a linguist and therefore an expert in communication. Schlegel was a German artillery engineer who had been military adviser to a dozen different revolutionists in that many countries and was reputed to be worth two divisions. The four had drilled and practiced for six months with the weapons aboard—quite unaware of the disaster waiting.

Every day the Red Planet grew. Engineering works and cultivated strips became unmistakably clear. And gray rectangular patches hinted of—cities?

"Cities they are!" at last Trent cried. "And I've seen motion—some moving vehicle! Yes, Mars is alive, Hammond. Alive—but dying. Most of the fields are dead and brown. Most of the machines are stopped.

Most of the cities are already drifted with the yellow sand.

"And that . . . that thing, alone in the desert—"

He turned the telescope again toward that chief riddle of Mars.

"Looks like a rusty metal barrel," he whispered. "Round in the middle, with hexagonal ends. Three thousand feet tall! And standing there alone, far from the nearest city, deserted. Its shadow like a mocking finger pointing— *What* could it be?"

"Land near it," my father said, "and we'll find out before we call on the natives."

Trent eagerly agreed. But, when at last the ship was hurtling moonlike about the planet, braking her velocity in the upper atmosphere, one of the cellules in the second step exploded. Years later, a man named Grogan, whose family had all been killed in the power pit disaster, confessed to willful sabotage in the plant where the cellules had been made. The electric firing system was wrecked. The ship plunged down, out of control.

Frantic effort averted complete catastrophe. Trent detached the entire second step, began to fire the third. But the controls were completely wrecked, and the cellules began to fire one another by conducted heat.

Realizing that only a few seconds were left, Trent opened the valve, in desperate haste, to the rare atmosphere of Mars. Both of Schlegel's legs had been broken by the fall. My father helped him out of the wreck, took him on his back, and ran after Trent and Burgess.

Behind them, the thousands of cellules were thundering and vomiting out a mountain of smoke and fire. They had staggered only a short distance when there was a terrific final explosion. Metal fragments shrieked about them. The German's head, beside my father's, was blown completely off. Burgess received a wound in the chest from which he died after Trent had removed a scrap of ragged steel.

Both injured, Trent and my father survived. But their plight seemed grave enough. Food, water, and oxygen masks were lost. They found the air of Mars, on account of its relatively high oxygen content, breathable, but it did not allow violent or sustained exertion. Their stock in trade was lost, also the collection of models, pictures, books, radio and motion picture equipment, with which they had hoped to establish communication. The weapons were gone, and their fighting man. Final and most crushing blow, return to Earth seemed forever cut off.

Blackened and bleeding, Trent stood looking back at the wreckage, wringing his lacerated hands.

"My free space observations," he was moaning. "And all our equipment—"

"Hammond Power has taken a tumble, all right," my father agreed, and gasped painfully for breath. "But we aren't sold out!" He wiped at the blood that kept trickling into his eyes and stared about the flat desolation. In every direction swept an interminable waste of low, dusty dunes. "Where"—a wisp of acrid saffron dust set him to coughing—"where are we?"

"Ten degrees, probably, north of the equator." My father's head still rang from the blast, and Trent's voice, in the thin air, sounded very small and far away. "At least a thousand miles west of that barrel-thing."

My father stared at him and up at the shrunken Sun. "The night—"

"Unless we find shelter," Trent agreed, "the night will kill us." He peered southward. "There's a settled strip. I had just a glimpse, as we came down. Maybe ten miles. Maybe two hundred. I don't know how fast we were moving."

My father nodded suddenly. "We can try. Let's go."

"First," Trent said, "the others."

Very hastily, panting with the effort, they covered Burgess and the German in shallow sand graves. A brief search of the vast shell hole where the rocket had fallen revealed no useful article intact. Empty-handed, clad in torn, scorched rags, they plodded southward across the dunes. My father was wearing a pair of inadequate soft slippers. They soon fell apart, and he went on barefoot.

"Hammond Power," my father whispered, and

coughed again. "Two queer beings on Earth would probably wind up in some zoo—unless some panicky citizen shot them first! Their chance to learn, say, the science of subelectronics—" He shook his head. "Do you suppose they saw us?"

"Possible," said Trent. And, within an hour, they knew that their arrival was known. For a small bright-red aircraft, which had a double streamlined shape, like two thick cigars fastened side by side, came silently over the dunes from the south.

The two men, in a sudden panic, tried to hide in the sand. The machine circled noiselessly above the wrecked rocket, and then flew back above them without landing. They ran after it, at last, waving and shouting frantically, but it paid them no heed.

They struggled on. The rarefied air, Trent commented, and the lesser gravitation, tended toward a physiological balance. But both were coughing. Their lungs had begun to burn. Trent discovered that he had a rising fever.

Both were tormented by extreme thirst, as the dry atmosphere sucked moisture from their bodies. And there was no water.

The small Sun was low and red, and a thin, piercing, icy wind had sprung up out of the east before they saw the first actual Martians. It was Trent who looked back from the summit of a low dune, gulped voicelessly, and pointed.

The Martians came following the two sets of plodding prints in the sand. They rode yellow, ferocious-looking armored beasts that hopped like gigantic fleas. They wore bright leatherlike garments, and flourished gleaming weapons and rode astride and upright, like men.

Like men. That unexpected pursuit filled Trent and my father with a sudden blind fear. They fled uselessly across the dunes. But still, so strong is man's anthropomorphism, they thought of those wild riders in essentially human terms.

Actually, perhaps, the dominant beings of Mars

proved more manlike than the explorers had any right to expect. They were bipeds, walking upright. They had two-eyed faces of a sort. They communicated with a guttural, rasping speech.

For all that, however, the Martians have more in common with the arthropoda. Horny exoskeletons and fine-meshed scales instead of skin, with muscles and vital organs shielded in tubular armor. But in the chemistry of vital fluids and metabolic processes, in the subtler psychological reactions, they are like nothing on Earth.

This small mounted band had trailed Trent and my father from the wreck. One of the hopping beasts was laden with scraps of twisted metal, and some of the beings had bits of Burgess' and Schlegel's blood-soaked clothing.

The flight was soon ended. The Martians carried long red lances whose hollow metal shafts, it swiftly developed, served also as guns. Angry bullets kicked up rusty dust. The savage riders shrieked. The leaping beasts made a dismal and blood-chilling baying.

Trent stumbled, suddenly, and couldn't rise. My father stopped beside him, breathless, with his lungs on fire. The gaunt, inhuman riders bore down upon them. They were an appalling lot, with their unfamiliar visages and their fine-scaled skins brightly hued in red, yellow, and purple. They surrounded the two men and leapt down to rescue them from the fangs and talons of their beasts.

The men were hastily bound to a sort of packsaddle on one of the beasts, and the band turned northward again. The red double ship appeared again before sunset, following from the south. The riders scattered and began to fire at it with the long red tubes. It circled high above them, dropped a bomb that lifted an ineffectual pillar of dense dust, and returned once more toward its unseen base.

Events confirmed my father's surmise that their captors were nomad enemies of the "canal" dwellers. That night, long after dark, the fugitive band took refuge in a labyrinth of burrows that must have been dug by the powerful claws of the hopping creatures. The captives were fed and allowed to sleep. Before dawn, the march was resumed. The respiratory trouble of the prisoners became more serious. Both sank into a fevered delirium. By the time they began to recover, the band had taken refuge in a hidden ravine where a tiny spring supplied water and grew a little forage for the beasts.

There they were held for several months, gradually learning a little of their captors' language and a few facts about them. Leader of the band was a gnarled, haggard, long-limbed savage, of a rusty-red color, named Zynlid. He and his outlaw clan maintained themselves by raiding the fields and cities of the canal dwellers, keeping up an ancient and bitter feud with the rulers of civilized Mars.

When my father recovered from the pulmonary fever, he grasped again his original audacious object: to obtain the secret of the Martian power plants. That alone, he told Trent, would possibly enable their return to Earth.

Zynlid must have taken the two men partly out of mere curiosity, and partly from the hope of ransom. The canal dwellers, it seems, refused to bargain for the prisoners. But, out of their first efforts at communications, came a new and puzzling prestige.

The gaunt chieftain's notions of astronomy, it developed, were rather vague. From Trent's attempts—with drawings on the sand and gestures at the sky—to show that they had come from the third planet, Zynlid jumped to the idea that the two were natives of the Sun.

And his regard for beings of the Sun was considerable. He ordered their bonds removed, offered them choice food, drinks, and female companions, gave them liberty of the camp, and allowed my father to ride with him on future raids. Trent and my father made no attempt to disabuse him of the misunderstanding.

Their questions were now eagerly answered, but it was some time before they were able to make any intelligible query about power. Meantime, Trent was allowed to examine the few machines in the possession of the nomads. These included the long guns and the equipment that gave light and heat in the dwelling-burrows.

The savages, it seemed, had no comprehension of the operation of these machines. There was a taboo, moreover, associated with them, so that Zynlid was horrified when Trent first began to take a little heater-lamp apart, and permitted him to go ahead only on reflection that he was a solar being.

Trent himself made little of the investigation. The machines were electrical—even the rifles were fired by the sudden vaporization of water with electricity. The current came from little transparent tubes. These were hollow, with a metal electrode fused in one end, and a lump of a curious greenish crystal in the other. In the space between were a few tiny specks of dust, that had a silver-blue color and gave off a pale blue light when the tube was working.

"It's that dust, Hammond," Trent told my father. "A pinch of it will generate thousands of kilowatts, evidently. Lord knows what it is!"

The outlaw chieftain, when they had more of his confidence and his language, could only tell them that the fine blue grains were "dust of the Sun." They came, he said, "from the place of the Sun." And it was forbidden for others than the *gorath-wein,* the "blood of the Sun," to touch them. He himself refused even to look at Trent's dismantled mechanisms.

Pressed by my father and excited by his own scientific enthusiasm, Trent continued his fumbling experiments until a day when he was almost killed by the terrific explosion of a grain of the blue dust. Fragments of a metal crucible drilled his body like rifle bullets. He was helpless for a month.

"It's got me, Hammond," he admitted hopelessly. "Atomic energy? I don't know. There's no key—unless we can get it from the civilized tribes."

The accident lowered their prestige as beings of the Sun. Muttering of "the wrath of the Sun" and "the revenge of the holy stone," Zynlid forbade Trent, on his recovery, to continue the experiments. And it might have gone much harder with the two men had not my father already become a trusted companion of Zynlid.

That lawless, marauding life seems to have appealed immensely to Garth Hammond. He flung himself into it with his old shrewd daring and all the strength of Earth muscles. There was a duel with one of Zynlid's chief lieutenants, who was jealous of the warrior of the Sun. My father killed the savage, and thereafter found himself in possession of the dead Martian's weapons and mount.

Although excessive effort soon made him breathless, so that the band nicknamed him "the panting one," he was able to outdo them all in wrestling and contests of strength. He took a keen delight in the strategy of raid, escape, and ambuscade. Zynlid began to rely on his cleverness. His belt was soon bright with the vivid-hued ear appendages of the canal folk, taken as trophies.

He discovered, presently, that the band knew of the immense dark barrel-shaped object that Trent had observed from the Moon. They regarded it with considerable awe. It was the *Korduv*, the "place of the Sun," or sometimes "place of the holy stone." And all save the *gorath-wein* were forbidden to approach it.

"There's your key," he told Trent. "There's where the silver dust comes from."

As soon as Trent had recovered sufficiently from the explosion, my father arranged an expedition to take them near the mysterious object. The Martians refused to go within a hundred miles of it, and allowed Trent and my father to approach it only on fresh assurance of their solar birth.

A vast excitement fevered them as their yellow-armored leaping dragons brought them in view of the dark mass looming above the flat and limitless red dunes. Was this the key to exhaustless power and the road back to Earth?

For many miles they rode forward across the desert, and the red-black enigma loomed vaster and vaster before them. At last, riding through the cold black shadow of it, they came to its base.

Its stupendous mass was metal, they discovered, pitted with the acid of untold centuries, crusted with dark red oxides. The dunes were drifted against it; westward the winds had cut out a vast curved hollow. Stunned with awe, they let the beasts carry them around its vast hexagon, and then withdrew to stare upward at it.

There was no possible opening in its base. Fifteen hundred feet upward, my father saw a square recess that looked like a portal. But that was in the overhanging, cylindrical middle section. There was no possibility of climbing to it. At last, no wiser, they turned back to their rendezvous with Zynlid—to be greeted with an awed surprise that the Sun had permitted their escape.

"These *gorath-wein* have got the key, Trent," my father concluded. "And we've got to have it."

And he began to discuss with the somewhat horrified Zynlid plans for abducting Anak, who was "Lance of the Sun," and priest-king of the civilized Martians, ruling from his Sun-temple in the city Ob.

"Anak knows secrets of peril," warned Zynlid, apprehensively. "And he is guarded by the hosts of the Sun."

"We know secrets also," my father retorted. "And the Sun sent me to take the place of Anak, who is an impostor in the temple."

Still seeking to convince the old nomad, he called on Trent for scientific miracles. All Trent's equipment had been lost in the wreck. An effort to demonstrate gunpowder now failed for want of free sulphur. But at last the astronomer, if he still failed to grasp the mysterious principle of the blue dust of power, was able to repair and operate certain mechanisms that the outlaws had captured.

One that had lain a mystic but useless relic, gathering dust in a secret treasure-cavern for a full Martian century, now proved to be a weapon. A score of the enigmatic little tubes fed a Niagara of power to transformers and field coils. Its polar plates projected a tight beam of magnetic energy, whose terrific hysteresis effect could fuse metal at twenty miles' distance.

The triumphant demonstration of this rusted war engine restored all Trent's shaken prestige, and secured full support of the nomads for my father's daring plan—although most of them must have been secretly trembling with dread of Anak and his solar powers.

It was known that the priests of the Sun visited the inexplicable lonely mass of the Korduv at intervals, by air. My father packed the magnetic weapon on one of the hopping creatures, and carried it to a point fifty miles from the stupendous barrel-thing.

There, braving the heat and the cold, the thirst and the dust of the open desert, he and Trent and a handful of the nomads waited for thirty-eight endless days. At last a double red ship came soaring over the dunes toward the dark, far-off pillar of the Korduv. The outlaws were suddenly terrified.

"The *gorath-wein!*" came their hoarse, uncanny croaks of fear. "Flee! Or the Sun will slay us all!"

They scrambled to prod their beasts from the sandburrows and mount them. But the invisible ray, with Trent and my father feverishly busy at the unfamiliar controls, brought down the red ship. The flight turned to a mad attack on the fallen machine.

Three priests and a priestess aboard were slaughtered. The only survivor was a young female child. Anak, whom my father had hoped to capture, had not been aboard. He soon discovered, however, that the Martian woman had been a consort of the priest-king, and that the infant, Asthore, was his daughter.

Another red ship, sent no doubt to investigate the fate of the first, was also brought down. From the wreckage of the two, aided by two Martians captured in the second, Trent set out to put together one complete vessel. He worked day and night. The outlaws helped, and cheerfully tortured the two prisoners whenever they became reluctant.

Before the ambitious task was done, however, a land force appeared, marching from the direction of Ob.

There were two great machines like tanks, and a hundred lancers on foot. In the desperate battle that followed, Trent never left the ship and his reluctantly persuaded instructors. He was just learning the principle of the ship's propulsion, by a system of gravity-shielding "spacial fields."

For a time the situation looked very bad. My father was able to cripple both war machines with the magnetic ray. But then a similar ray from one of the tanks discovered and fused his own weapon. The bright-scaled lancers charged, howling triumphantly.

My father gathered his five or six allies at the crest of a low yellow dune, and waited for the charge. As the yelling lancers came down the opposite slope, he walked boldly out alone to meet them, with the grave statement that he was their new ruler, sent from the Sun.

That halted proceedings for a ticklish half-hour—until Zynlid arrived with the balance of the bandit band. That was the signal for all hands to fall upon the lancers. They were cut down, to the last Martian. There were new weapons for every outlaw, and my father made himself a triumphant wreath of ear appendages.

Next day, as scouts brought word that all the eight surviving cities were sending contingents of warriors to Ob, Trent finished his repairs and safely flew the ship. The nomads triumphantly butchered the two captive priests and ate their brains and livers in a ceremonial feast.

My father sent Trent, aboard the ship with a crew of nomads and the little Martian girl, back into the northern desert. Zynlid, his hopping beasts laden with the spoils of victory, started back toward the hidden ravine. And my father rode alone toward the city of Ob.

After three lonely, grim days, parched and sunburned and chapped with alkali dust, he guided his beast into the "canal"—a belt of fertile dark soil, irrigated from underground conduits and covered with low-lying, thick-leaved plants. He parleyed with the warriors who came to meet him, and they conducted him, half a prisoner, into the city.

Dark buildings sprawled flat and massive behind the walls and hedges that held back the seas of yellow sand. Although the city had several thousand inhabitants, and the central part about the towering conical Sun temple was now thronged with the lancers gathered to avenge the outrage against the sacred ship, by far the greater part of Ob was mere crumbling ruin. Its gaunt, bright-scaled people seemed to my father like lonely ghosts, trying to haunt a far-spreading necropolis. Mars was far gone in death.

Stating that he was an ambassador from the Sun, my father demanded audience with Anak. Suspiciously, yet with respect born of the unprecedented disaster to the sacred ship, the lancers took my father to the ancient, many-terraced pile of crumbling black masonry that was the temple. There Anak met him.

The ruler was a tall, gaunt Martian, stiff with pride. Age had darkened his lustrous scales to a purple black, and the horny carapace that crowned his egg-shaped head was crimson. His dark face was lean, hawklike, deeply wrinkled. Jet black, yellow-rimmed, his eyes flamed with virulent hatred.

When my father advanced his old claim to being a dweller in the Sun, Anak shot him a look of startled incredulity that hinted of an astronomical lore greater than Zynlid's. Ungraciously impatient, he listened. My father told him that his wife and baby daughter were prisoners, and that they would be released safely only in return for certain information.

What information?—Anak wanted to know. When my father began to hint that it dealt with the mysterious power tubes and the enigmatic mass of the *Korduv,* the priest-king burst into a savage rage. He snatched at a weapon, rasped and croaked and hissed like something reptilian.

Finally, menacing my father with a level lance, he champed out the gutturals: "Base and lying stranger, whencesoever you come, I, the true Lance of the Sun, know you never dwelt in his sacred fires. The foul dogs of the desert may believe your imposture, but not I. The holy flame of Life would consume you in an instant."

The red shaft thrust viciously.

"I love my wife Wahneema," grated Anak. "I love my child Asthore. But better that both should perish by your tortures than that I should desecrate the secrets of the Sun. Go back to the evil beasts that sent you, and die of the Sun's flaming anger."

All my father's desperate threats and promises—even the ingenious hint that a space fleet was on its way from Earth to rescue him and conquer Mars—proved in vain. Anak grimly resigned him to "the judgment of the Sun."

The Martians kept his beast, stripped him of weapons and clothing, and finally released him, naked and alone, in the midst of a sand desert far southward of Ob. This was remote from the usual haunts of the outlaws, and death of thirst and exposure seemed a certainty—until Trent, who had been spying from the sky, picked him up with the captured ship.

Two nights later, with Zynlid and a picked band of his men, they landed the ship on the topmost terrace of the Sun temple. Under the feeble spark of Phobos, creeping backward across the sky, they slaughtered the surprised temple guard. My father led the howling bandits down into the ancient pile. The found Anak, standing beneath a glowing yellow disk in a chapel of the Sun. He fought savagely; gravely wounding the outlaw chief. But my father snatched away his lance, and he was dragged aboard the vessel before the roused horde of warriors could reach the roof from the temple courtyard.

The ship launched upward with bullets ringing against her hull. Triumphantly, my father commanded Anak to answer Trent's excited questions. But the wrinkled old priest refused to talk. Cheerfully jesting, the outlaws began to apply torture. But the seamed dark face merely stiffened stoically.

It was Zynlid, after Trent had patched up his wounds, who solved the difficulty.

"He will never talk willingly," rasped the old bandit. "Give him this. It is a key to locked lips."

And he handed Trent a tiny hypodermic, loaded with a few drops of some colorless liquid. The drug seemed to resemble scopolamine in being a sort of "truth serum." It ended Anak's stubborn silence, and Trent at last began to learn the secret of the blue power-dust.

The old priest was kept drugged for nearly two months, constantly questioned—except on one occasion, when the injection must have failed to take effect. Then, feigning the influence of the drug, he told a series of clever lies and pretended to demonstrate another secret of the dust. Only my father's vigilance and a sudden tackle prevented an explosion that would have annihilated them all.

Finally, they took Anak into the colossal metal hull of the *Korduv*. The frantic searchers from Ob somehow discovered their presence there. My father closed the lofty entrance valve, and, with Zynlid and his band, held it for three weeks against the desperate attackers, while Trent questioned the drugged ruler, explored all the mysterious depths of that ancient desert enigma, and made complete plans of all its colossal mechanisms.

Slowly, the astronomer pieced together the solution to the riddles of the blue dust and the *Korduv* and the limitless power that drove the engines of Mars—and found it an astounding revelation. The strange granules, which they came to call "sunstone," had come, quite literally, from the Sun!

, Trent came at last to my father, in the beleaguered valve, trembling with the import of his discoveries.

"This is a ship!" he made the startling announcement. "The *Korduv* is an interplanetary ship. It was built nearly half a million Martian years ago, when the planet was at its peak of civilization. It has made thirty trips to the Sun, at intervals of ten or twenty thousand years, for sunstone."

"Sunstone?" echoed my father. "The power-dust?"

"Pure power!" cried the scientist. "Frozen, portable power—power storage, perfected to the last degree. It is condensed radiant energy—a complex, not of atoms and electrons, but of pure photons.

"Light particles, fixed! The mathematics of it is revolutionary. A radical extension of quantum physics! It also accounts for the gravity-reflecting space warp that lifts the ship, and the same field of strain can be modified to reflect radiant energy, for protection against any excess of the solar radiations.

"With a crew of two thousand Martians—the race, in those days, was more numerous and more venturesome—the *Korduv* was navigated a hundred and forty million miles to the solar photosphere. For ten years it floated there, its crew protected by the fields from a gravitation eighty times that of Mars. Its conversion cells absorbed the energy of the Sun, at a rate that amounts to fifty horsepower per square inch, solidified it into the photon dust. And finally, when the ordeal of heat was ended, the survivors—usually not a tenth of the crew—came back with the precious load of sunstone."

"Eh!" My father stared at Trent, digesting this. A dull hammering throbbed faintly through the colossal valve. His weary, bearded face set with triumphant decision. "A ship!" he whispered. "Then we'll take it to Earth, unload what dust is left, and send it to the Sun for more."

Trent shook his shaggy, emaciated head. "The *Korduv* won't move again," he said. "It was damaged in the last voyage—that was fifty thousand years ago. Some of the cells failed, and unconverted energy cooked most of the crew and fused half the field coils. A narrow escape from falling into the Sun. The rest of the coils, overloaded, were pretty well burned up on the way back. The thing crashed here. The rest of its crew were killed, but the sunstone was intact."

"Wrecked, eh?" My father stared into the strange maze of Cyclopean engines that loomed within the faintly blue-lit gloom beyond the valve, and demanded, "Why didn't they build another?"

"Racial senescence, I guess," said Trent. "They

stopped growing, and went to seed. Take old Anak. He knows scientific facts that we wouldn't have discovered on Earth for a thousand years. But they're frozen, dead. His knowledge is all in the form of elaborate, memorized rituals, mingled with superstitious dogma. He is ruled by the past. Half his knowledge is too sacred to use outside the temple. Any new fact would be rank heresy to the Sun. There is sunstone left to keep the pumps running for two or three thousand years. After that, Mars is doomed. 'By the will of the Sun.' "

"Well!" My father shrugged impatiently. "If this is wrecked, can you draw plans for another?"

"For a better one, Hammond," Trent assured him. "If we were back on Earth."

"First thing," my father observed, "we've got to get past our fanatical friends on the outside—but Hammond Power has gone up a thousand points!"

While the partisans of Anak continued to batter at the great valve, Trent spent three days fitting the little red ship for the Earthward voyage. Its double hull was already sealed hermetically and the dusky depths of the *Korduv* yielded cylinders of oxygen, bottled for fifty thousand years. The hold was filled with sunstone, and certain changes in the wiring of the field coils adapted its drive for the interplanetary trip.

Then a tiny sunstone bomb opened a new port in the crown of the *Korduv*'s hull. The little red vessel darted out through the gaping plates, escaped the ray batteries and aircraft of the attackers, and fled safely through darkness to the outlaw's hidden ravine.

Old Anak, with his infant daughter, was released at dawn on the desert a few miles from Ob. He learned now that the mother of Asthore had been killed, and he retained memory of all that he had revealed beneath the drug. Rage and horror overwhelmed him. His drawn, dark-scaled face twisted hideously, and his black eyes flamed. He made a desperate, empty-handed attack on my father, screaming prayers and curses.

"Beware!" he was shrieking, as the vessel rose.

"Desecrators of the holy fire, beware the judgment of the Sun!"

Zynlid had accepted my father's invitation to visit Earth, along with a slave and his two favorite wives. A final raid supplied the vessel with food for the voyage, and Trent guided it out past Deimos into the gulf of space.

The whole Martian year was already gone. Earth had passed conjunction and was pulling swiftly ahead on its orbit. The rocket could never have overtaken it—but half an ounce of sunstone drove the Martian flier eighty million miles in only ten days.

In November, 2134, the red ship landed safely in a cornfield near New York. My father announced triumphantly that he had secured the secret of Mars—a cheap source of illimitable power.

III

I can still remember how my mother trembled, in her cool, silent, sweet-smelling room above the twilit Aegean, as her frail, unsteady hand snapped the new visivox spool into the cabinet.

"Now, Chan," she whispered, "you . . . your father!"

She choked, and I knew that she was crying.

The little screen flickered and lighted. I saw the golden tangle of the broken stalks of corn, and the tiny ship from Mars lying across the rows, like twin red spindles side by side. A small door opened, and Trent and my father came out.

They were queer-looking men, haggard and shaggy and darkly tanned. My father wore the strange leather garments of the nomads, brilliant with the dried, shell-like ear appendages he had taken. He flourished a long red lance, and his voice croaked a guttural greeting in an unfamiliar tongue.

But his old smile flashed, infectious as ever, behind the great tangle of his black beard. His strong teeth shone. His gray eyes had squinted a little, against the desert glare, but still they were clear and shrewd and quick.

"He's just the same, Chan," sobbed my mother. "Your father . . . *oh, Garth!*"

Her thin face was white, and I saw the great tears on her cheeks.

Newsmen shot swift, excited questions, and visivox machines were humming. My father bowed grandly, and then beckoned. The Martians came scrambling after him—gaunt, rusty-red Zynlid and his varicolored, red-crowned companions. Their movements were awkward and laborious, and their breathing seemed troubled. They blinked bewilderedly at the feverish, barking newsmen. Garth Hammond stepped before them, and bowed again, and made a little speech of greeting to the Earth.

"To every man," he promised, "I will bring more power than a king enjoyed of old. Tomorrow, the Sun Power Corporation—"

Then Nada Vale, the red-haired actress, came running into the picture. With an eager, muffled cry, she threw herself into my father's great tanned arms. His old smile flashed eagerly. He lifted her, and crushed his great black beard against her face.

Then, suddenly, my mother stopped the machine. A moment she stood beside the cabinet, frozen, her face set and white. A thin sob burst from her quivering lips. She ran quickly out of the room. I found her sitting in the darkness on a terrace high above the black sea where the stars danced and vanished, felt her shaking to dry, breathless sobs.

The conqueror of Mars became the hero of the Earth. That wild tide of enthusiasm drowned all the old accusations against my father. The capital of six billion dollars for the Sun Power Corporation was all subscribed in one hectic day.

Tens of millions paid fat admission fees to see Zynlid and his ménage in the gravity-shielded, air-conditioned apartment my father provided. The old bandit used to strut proudly before the curious, flourishing his weapons and trophies and demanding staggering sums for posing for the visivox.

The tempest of publicity seemed to mean nothing to Ared Trent. The public hardly realized that my father had had a companion on Mars. Stern, taciturn priest of science, if Trent had a human side, the world didn't know it—not then. He gathered sixty skilled draftsmen in a closely guarded office building and began drawing up the plans and specifications for the Sun Power Station.

Far smaller than the ancient *Korduv* on Mars—only a thousand feet in diameter and fifteen hundred long— the Station was still the greatest engineering feat ever attempted on Earth. The construction took over three years. Directly and indirectly, more than a million men were employed on it. The first six billions were spent, and bonds floated for three billions more.

Unlike the Martian plant, the Station was intended to float permanently in the Sun's fiery atmosphere. Ships shielded by special fields would visit it at yearly intervals, to carry supplies and relief to its crew, and bring away the precious sunstone. Eight hundred volunteers were selected, to spend one or two years exiled to the flaming terror of the Sun.

Designer of the Station, Ared Trent was to have been its first commander. But, a few months before the Station was ready to be launched came the historic break between my father and Trent.

That quarrel has puzzled historians. The two had been friends since before my father sent Trent to the Moon. Man of knowledge and man of money, they had seemed to live in a perfect symbiosis. Biographers have suggested, and rightly, I believe, that Trent, although he seemed to have the feelings of a product integraph, actually must have suppressed a deep resentment of my father's assumption of a dictatorial superiority.

But the real key to the quarrel, I think, is the suicide of Nada Vale. The actress had obviously been desperately in love with my father. Absorbed at the time in the expedition to Mars and the conquest of power, he can hardly have cared very much for her. It is certain that they were never married. And it seems that she was bitterly jealous of the woman my father did love.

That woman was lovely Doris Wayne, heir to the Marine Mines billions. My father met her soon after the return from Mars. They were married in 2138. On the wedding night, Nada Vale drank poison in the anteroom of their Manhattan penthouse.

And Ared Trent, although no one had guessed it, cherished an old infatuation for the actress. She had promised years before to marry him, it seems, if he came back alive from the Moon—perhaps only with a professional eye to future publicity. But, before he came back, she met his backer, my father. Trent was forgotten. And he concealed his deep injury until her suicide broke his old restraint.

At any rate, Trent suddenly demanded an equal voice with my father in the direction of the Sun Power Corporation. My father refused, astonished. There was a long legal battle, in which Trent was completely defeated. Then my father, to show some gratitude for his services, made him a free gift of ten million dollars. Trent used it to build a new laboratory isolated in South Africa, and went into complete seclusion.

Command of the Station, meantime, was given to bluff, stocky Tom Cornwall, hero of the Moon. Sitting with my mother in our island villa, I watched the launching of the Station. It was a colossal upright cylinder of massive steel, with curved ends. Incredibly tremendous, it loomed above tiny-seeming tracks and derricks, and the mills and furnaces of the new steel city that had made its metal. The crew had gone aboard. My father, magnificent on the platform, made a speech and shook the hand of Tom Cornwall. The intrepid captain vanished. The cheering multitude—people small and black as crawling insects about the Station—were herded back. Then the steel cylinder flickered curiously, and was lost in a pillar of silver haze—all light reflected by its shielding ether fields. The pillar floated upward. A sudden wind swept the throng, raising a little cloud of dust and hats. And the Station was gone to the Sun.

There was rioting, that day on all the stock exchanges. Coal, oil, and water-power stocks dropped ruinously. SPC soared to dizzy heights. A dozen desperate investors killed themselves. My father boasted that in one day, before any wealth had come from the Sun, he had cleared nearly two billion dollars.

The great relief ship, the *Solarion*, was built that year in the same Ohio yards. I was not ten years old when it came back from its first voyage to the Sun. It brought hundreds of tons of the wondrous blue substance, frozen power, that went on the market at twelve hundred dollars an ounce.

Garth Hammond's star seemed to be shining very brightly. There was hardly a hint of the storm of trouble and disaster that rose with the passing years, to bend his strong shoulders, bleach his hair, ruin SPC, and even to bring all the solar system to the very threshold of disaster.

But gnarled old Zynlid and his three companions from Mars, in their gravity-shielded tank, were already dead of the Falling Sickness.

IV

The frightful shadow of the old pandemic suddenly darkened over all the world. For something had happened to the virus: some reaction, physiologists said, of the malignant molecule with the alien proteins in the bodies of the Martians. Old immunities were destroyed. The new, virulent plague swept the planet. In a single year, a hundred million died. All the horrors of the Black Century threatened to return.

Among the natives of Mars the disease was even more deadly than on Earth. When my father's conquering fleet appeared on the red planet, the cities attempted to resist and the *Korduv* was blown up. It is uncertain whether, as enemies of my father have charged, the Falling Sickness was deliberately spread.

But, within a few weeks, it destroyed half the inhabitants of Mars. The planet surrendered. Anak, the old priest-king, was forced into exile. He came to Earth with his daughter, and established residence in a shabby, century-old building in Washington. His brooding, bitter hatred of my father always grew, and his guarded inner rooms, armored against the gravity and the air of Earth, were an early center of the organized intrigue against Garth Hammond and the SPC.

My father had brought the Martians to Earth. He was to blame, therefore, for the new epidemic. And the Martians hated him doubly, as the desecrator of their solar religion and the murder of their race.

Agitators made him responsible, too, for the horde of new economic ills that threatened to crush the very life from the planet. The epidemic alone, with its fears, illness, and death, was enough to cause vast depression. Added to that was the financial panic and industrial disturbances occasioned by the destruction of the old power industries and the rise of SPC.

Yet—and an item to my father's credit—industry must have been stimulated vastly by the exploitation of the other planets. After the conquest of Mars, the new space fleets of SPC explored the Moon, Venus, Mercury, and the satellites of Jupiter. The parent corporation proliferated into a thousand subsidiary developments, concessions, mineral, planting, transport, even news and amusement enterprises. There was even a Martian Copyright & Patents Corporation, to exploit the arts and sciences of that ancient planet.

SPC was suddenly the most powerful—and soon the most hated—entity on Earth. The yearly production of sunstone from the Station ran above one thousand tons. At the standard price, pegged mercilessly at twelve hundred dollars an ounce, that meant a gross annual revenue in excess of forty billion dollars—enough to make Garth Hammond virtual dictator of the Solar System.

Trust busting legislation was passed by embittered liberal and labor groups—in vain. For national law ceased at the stratosphere. The only ships in space were those marked SPC, and the only order there was that enforced by my father's corporation police, the famous Sun Patrol.

The law, as always, adapted itself to current reality. SPC was recognized as virtually an independent state, with jurisdiction everywhere beyond Earth's stratosphere. And Garth Hammond was its absolute ruler— though legally still a citizen of the United States, granted certain immunities as an "employee" of SPC, his only title being chairman of the board of a corporation chartered in New Jersey.

He was a master of the law. The law helped suppress a hundred strikes aimed at SPC. It helped the Sun Patrol to thwart a dozen attempts against his life—in some of which Anak and the fanatical Martian *émigrés* were suspected of being involved.

The gravest blow against him came from outside the law, and outside the Earth. The *Solarion,* in 2146, returning with her seventh cargo of sunstone, was accosted by a strange vessel in space—a slim red arrow of a ship, unlike the mirror spheres of SPC. Heliographs flashed a message, signed "Redlance," demanding surrender of the ship and cargo, "in the name of liberty and human right." The captain refused to surrender, and escaped after a running fight. Next year the *Solarion* went out again, better armed—and never came back.

When the first attack on the relief ship became known, Anak had let newsmen through the valve into the great steel tank that held a fragment of exiled Mars. His dark-scaled body was now withered and bent, his strange face lined and haggard and terrible with bitterness and hate. Stalking back and forth, like some restless, caged beast, beneath the glowing Sun disk that he had brought from the temple on Mars, he shook a lean, unearthly arm at them.

"It is the judgment of the Sun," his flat, guttural voice rasped barely intelligible English. "Garth Hammond despoiled the jewel of the Sun. He defiled the sacred places, and stole the holy secret. He spilled the blood of the Sun, slew my Wahneema!" His black, yellow-rimmed eyes glared with fanatical malice. "And he shall know the judgment of the Sun!"

Trembling, then, with a savage wrath, he drove the newsmen out.

It was soon certain, now, that "Redlance" had taken the *Solarion,* for the Earth was flooded with "bootleg" sunstone. And it seemed probable that the pirates, or at least their leaders, must be vengeful Martians, because the secret of the drive field had never been made public on Earth.

Trying to run down the sunstone smugglers, Sun Patrol operatives found evidence that linked the ring with Anak's daughter, Asthore. Grown now, she had become a peculiarly beautiful being, tall and graceful, her fine-scaled skin a nacreous white, her eyes huge and purple beneath a crimson coronal. But her uncanny beauty was quite inhuman, and she shared all her father's hatred of mankind and Garth Hammond.

Sun Patrol men, aided by Federal agents, finally closed in on the old house in Washington, with warrants for Anak and his daughter. But the tank was deserted. The exiles had fled. A planetwide search failed to discover them.

The fleets of the SPC scoured space for the pirate, searched planets and asteroids for a base, in vain. A second, hurriedly constructed relief ship, the *Solarion II,* was also lost, her wrecked and looted hull being discovered adrift near the orbit of Mercury. The *Solarion III,* in 2148, safely reached the Sun and returned. But her holds were empty and she brought appalling news. The Station itself was lost!

The cause of the disaster could only be surmised. The great plant might have been captured or destroyed by the pirates. Or, frail as a bubble floating in the flaming ocean of the solar photosphere, it might have been obliterated by the titanic forces of the Sun: cyclonic storms of sunspots, whose tremendous vortices might have dragged it down into a very atomic furnace; super hurricanes of prominences, blasts of flaming hydrogen flung upward at hundreds of thousands of miles an hour; heat inconceivable, 6000 degrees at the surface, intense enough to destroy the Station in an instant if deflection fields or conversion batteries failed. Or it was possible that mutiny or the Falling Sickness had annihilated the crew.

Whatever its cause, the disaster was crushing. Stocks and bonds of SPC crashed ruinously. My father found it difficult to get capital to begin construction of a new power station, and strikes and sabotage hindered the work.

The smuggled supplies of sunstone ceased as mysteriously as they had begun. Rusty windmills and turbines turned again. Men groped into abandoned coal mines. Prices rose enormously. Unemployment soared. Farm machines stood idle for want of power. Famine pinched the world—and malnutrition invited a hideous new wave of the Falling Sickness.

And on my father's shoulders fell the blame for all these misfortunes of humanity. I was near him, in those black days—with a court order, when I was twelve, he had taken me from my mother. At first I had been resentful. I had hated his luxurious home, and hated his new wife, Doris, for taking my mother's place. But she had always been kind. I had come to like her. And I couldn't help a vast admiration for my father, now, and a sympathy for him in his sea of troubles.

"It's just about the finish, Chan," he told me wearily one day when I had found him sitting motionless as a black statue at the big desk in his sumptuous office. "It would be four years, or five, before the new station could furnish any revenue—even if the pirates let it be. SPC can't hold out that long."

I tried to encourage him.

"One chance," he admitted. "If I could get Trent. The best mind I ever knew. If he would forget—"

But the search for Trent failed. Years before, with my father's gift, he had built his great laboratory in South Africa. But the isolated buildings had now been for several years abandoned. Ared Trent was gone without a trace.

Upon that failure came the thrust of sharper disaster. My father's wife, the former Doris Wayne, contracted the Falling Sickness. After two days of agony, clinging to the bed and screaming with that frightful vertigo, she died. It was after that that my father's hair began to turn white. His big shoulders sagged. Turned to a grim machine, he refused to leave the office for rest or sufficient sleep.

Without sunstone, it would soon be impossible to navigate space. Revenues from the mines would stop, and the colonies would have to be abandoned. The interplanetary prestige of SPC was vanishing. Hostile groups passed ruinous restriction and taxation measures.

"Bankruptcy, Chan!" I had gone to the silver tower of SPC, in Manhattan, to try to persuade my father to come home for the weekend and rest. He was leaning heavily on the big polished desk, staring down at a dusty blue bottle labeled "Hammond's Lunar Oil."

His eyes looked up at me, hollow, dead. "I've kept this, Chan," he said. "To remind myself that it all began with a little colored water. But I guess I forgot. All this doesn't seem real. Not possible!" He ran a tired hand back through his thick white hair. "But I began by shining boots, Chan. And it looks as if you will, too."

It was then, when his troubles seemed to have reached the last extremity, that the thing came, the stunning revelation, that reduced them all, by comparison, to nothing.

A strange space vessel was seen above New York. It landed on the great Long Island field of SPC. It was a long, sinister bolt of crimson. Its hull bore scars of battle, and it was black-lettered with the name *Redlance*.

The port authorities were in a flurry of fear, but they soon discovered that the pirate designed no harm. A haggard, white-haired man stumbled out of the valve, and wildly demanded to be taken at once to my father.

I was in the office when they met. My father was

wearing a white laboratory apron, and his fingers were stained with chemicals. He smiled—and suddenly recklessly invincible as in the old days—and then seized Trent's hand with evident warm emotion.

"Well, Ared! So you are Redlance. After all, who else could have done it?" He stepped closer, earnestly. "Can we be friends again? I've made mistakes, Trent, and I'm sorry for them. The SPC is beaten. But now I've come on something new. If you will help me, together we—"

The lean man had been staring at him with feverish, bloodshot eyes. And Trent's voice rasped suddenly out, hoarse and desperate: "No, Hammond! There's nothing left." He licked his cracked lips. "Forget your schemes, man. We're finished. Done!"

My father quickly caught his arm. "What do you mean?"

"I've been a damned fool, Hammond. Yes, I was the pirate. I hated you, Hammond. Because you wanted too much power. And . . . Nada— But forget all that. I built the ship—in Africa. I gathered a crew of human scum and Martian fanatics. Joined old Anak's plotters. God help me, Hammond!

"We took your two relief ships. And then, using the first *Solarion* to trick Cornwall, we took the Station. And then Anak, with his Martian devils, and his lovely, lying snake of a daughter, took it from me. I'd no idea what an awful thing they planned—believe me, Hammond!"

My father caught his breath, stiffened, waited.

"You can't understand how desperate they are, how bitter," came Trent's hoarse voice. "The religious outrage, you know. And then the Falling Sickness . . . it would have wiped them out in fifty years, anyhow."

My father gulped.

"My God, Trent!" His voice trembled. "What are you trying to tell me?"

"They're going to load the Station with sunstone." Trent's red, hollow eyes stared unseeingly. "Four thousand tons of pure energy. Then sink it into the photosphere as far as the screens will hold." His dead flat voice had no emphasis, as if his feelings were already killed. "And then blow it up."

Soundlessly, my father's lips whispered, "What then?"

"A new focus of disintegration, like that at the center of the Sun. A wave of matter-annihilating concussion. It will blow out, of course. Rip a hole in the photosphere. Expansion will kill it. Not that that matters."

My father was staring stupidly.

"A minor nova outburst," Trent amplified. "A quite insignificant flash among the stars. The safety mechanism of the Sun will adjust itself. Its radiation, within a week, will be back to normal.

"But that shell of flaming gas will sweep all the planets, out to Jupiter."

"Old Anak!" whispered my father. "What was it he said? 'Judgment of the Sun!'"

And he burst suddenly into a roar of senseless laughter.

V

Any other man would have been unnerved by Trent's revelation. Even the vague rumors that escaped a hurriedly applied censorship were enough to throw the world into panic. But Garth Hammond, when he had time to recover from the impact, displayed a curious equanimity.

Would it be possible to reach the Sun before the explosion?

"Possible, yes," said Trent. "Possibly the *Redlance* could do it, though she's crippled. I don't know. But why?"

"Could any attack hope for success?"

Trent shook his haggard head.

"I know the reputation of your Sun Patrol, Hammond," he said. "I know your men would give their lives. And, given time, we could rig part of your fleet with shields for flight into the Sun. But it's no use."

He shrugged hopelessly.

"Don't think of force. The Station is invincible. There's no weapon that could even match the beating it is always getting from the Sun. We tricked Cornwall. We'd never have gotten aboard if he hadn't thought there were friends on the *Solarion*.

"But Anak has no friends."

"Well, if they couldn't get aboard, could they get even into telephone contact with the Station?"

"Just possible," Trent admitted. "But that means a very close approach, even with a tight cosmobeam. But what arguments would you use on Anak? What could you promise him, when his very race is doomed? No, Hammond, it's no use," Trent insisted bitterly. "Unless we send a ship or two out beyond Jupiter. So, a few might survive—"

"No, Trent," my father said abruptly. "We're going to the Sun."

I would gladly have given my right hand to go with the *Redlance,* for it seemed that the expedition would probably be the last and most dramatic event in human history. But my father gruffly told me to go back to mother and wait with her.

Hurt—it is queer how one could nurse an injured private vanity while such great things were at stake—I returned to the marble villa on the Aegean. The wild rumors of doom had reached my mother. She was pathetically glad to see me. She asked many questions about my father, whom she had not seen since I was a tiny child. I knew that she loved him still.

For weary weeks, we waited. A trip by sail, down among the Cyclades, failed to ease the suspense. My mother fell ill with the strain—and I feared, for a dreadful hour, that she was a victim of the Falling Sickness then raging through the islands.

No word came back from the *Redlance.* But fevered imagination pictured the details of the desperate voyage. The battered red hull shielded in the silver fog of deflection fields. The plunge into the Sun's fiery ocean. The frightful dive in quest of the Station, menaced with an intensity of heat beyond conception, battered with incredible storms, crushed with the pressure of a gravitation twenty-eight times that of Earth.

It was a period of sunspot maxima. Magnetic storms disturbed communication. One night was splendid with the cold flames of the aurora. I remember looking at the Sun through a dark glass, its round face pocked with a dozen angry vortices, each large enough to swallow an Earth. Dazzled, I went back to my mother, shuddering. If the power of the Sun could do all these things across 93,000,000 miles, what could it not do to men in its very flaming grasp?

To quiet the rumors, desperate officials had finally announced the truth. Depression and despair ruled the Earth. As if it fed on fear, a fresh epidemic spread, until it seemed that the Falling Sickness raced with astronomical cataclysm to wipe out mankind.

Then, to a stunned and incredulous planet, came the brief heliographic dispatch picked up and relayed from the colony on the Moon:

TO EARTH:
   DANGER ENDED. ANAK SURRENDERED STATION INTACT. SPC RECOGNIZES INDEPENDENCE OF MARS. ANAK WILL BE RESTORED. STATION BACK IN OPERATION. REDLANCE BRINGING SUNSTONE TO EARTH.
                      GARTH HAMMOND

That was too good to believe. Many of us refused to believe it—until the *Redlance* landed on Long Island, thirty hours later. Trent left my father and two thousand tons of sunstone, and went on to carry Anak back to Mars.

But why had Anak, so grimly bent upon revenge— why had he surrendered?

My father himself brought the answer to that. His private stratoplane landed unwarned in the lee of our island, and taxied shoreward. Garth Hammond leaped out and waded up the beach. The ruggedly handsome face beneath his thick white hair was smiling gayly as ever, but his gray eyes held a wistful tenderness that I had never seen.

I ran to meet him, shouting incoherent questions.

"Run this." He thrust a visivox spool into my hand. "Where's your mother, Chan?"

I pointed, wondering briefly at the husky catch in his voice, and then ran to put the spool on a machine. The bright screen showed the *Redlance* landing, and then my father speaking to the tremendous crowd on the field in his old grand manner.

"You wonder, perhaps, why Anak gave up his frightful plan and surrendered?"

He paused for silence and effect.

"It is because I traded him something. For the Station, I traded him life. And the life of his race. The life of Mars! And I bring the same boon, a free gift to you and to all the Earth."

Another dramatic halt.

"I have conquered the Falling Sickness." There was a sound like a sob from all that multitude. A burst of clapping, quickly hushed. A breathless quiet. "It was the cure for that disease that I gave Anak and his men. And that I give the Earth."

There was an utter, queerly painful stillness. A great choking lump rose in my own throat. My father, on that tiny screen, made an oddly diffident little smile.

"I mean it," he said. "Free clinics will be opened at once by the Hammond Foundation. A harmless chemical renders the body proteins insensitive to the virus. Immunization is complete. There will be no more Falling Sickness!"

I found my father and my mother sitting side by side in her quiet, fragrant room. Her face was stained with tears, and her smile was very happy. My father had been telling her what I had learned from the spool. His great laugh boomed out softly.

"Funny thing!" he told her. "That chemical was formed in an old bottle of the Lunar Oil. The cheap, impure stuff we used at the last. I happened to hold it against the light, and saw the change in color. When I analyzed it—"

I turned back, silently, and left them alone.

Breakdown

OFFICIALLY, BOSS KELLON was merely executive secretary of the Union of Spacemen, Managers & Engineers. But *Boss,* now in 2145, was equivalent to *Caesar.* From the unitron convertors on Mercury to the lonely mining outposts scattered across the Jovian moons, the Union dominated mankind.

And Harvey Kellon was the Union.

He was a big man. His shrewd, deep-set, deliberate eyes could be chill as blue Callistonian fire diamonds, but a bland professional smile warmed his cragged red face. He wore a flowing white toupee, and few of Sunport's millions suspected that the boss was bald as the first Caesar of old Rome.

Sunport was his capital. For a hundred years the monopoly of interplanetary commerce had fed its power, until even New York was now only a quaint provincial suburb. The towers of the megalopolis stood like a forest of bright monoliths for a hundred miles about the high Colorado mesa that had become the port of space. Forever the tiny moonlet of the Outstation rode at the city's meridian, a man-made star of its fortune.

Boss Kellon lived in the crown of the lofty Union Tower. The huge, luxurious halls of his penthouse suite were named for the worlds of the Sun. Tonight there was a ball in the Neptune Room, and he was dancing with Selene du Mars.

The Boss was short of breath, and dark perspiration spotted the shoulders of his purple dress pajamas. His feet ached. Perhaps, at sixty, he was too old to be dancing; certainly he had too much weight about the middle. But Selene du Mars could make men seek to banish such uncomfortable thoughts.

She was tall and supple and green-eyed. She had been a famous teleview dancer. He thought she was the most costly and glittering thing in all Sunport. Tonight her hair was platinum, and she was dazzling with fire diamonds. He thought those favorite stones were like herself—cold and bright and hard. But he could admire even her calculating ambition, because it was so akin to his own.

Selene claimed a hereditary degree in militechnic engineering. Once Kellon had ordered a quiet investigation, and the Goon Department reported evidence of forgery. Her father had been merely the servant of a militechnic officer on Jupiter Station. But Kellon suppressed the report, with not a word to Selene. He knew how hard was the climb up from the gray.

Now, and not for the first time, she was wheedling him to crown himself. Her voice was cool and perfect as her long body, and she used the flattering address that she herself had first suggested:

"Your Genius, can we have the coronation soon? Everything is planned. Your historian friend Melkart has dug out the old ceremonials for me. My jewelers are working on a fire-diamond crown."

"For me to pay for," Kellon chuckled, and drew her pantherine body close against him. "Darling, I know you want to be Empress of the Sun, but your pretty head is in danger enough, without a coronet."

Kellon frowned, sobered by the thought. He had climbed to the perilous apex of a human pyramid. He was first of the million hereditary engineers, who, with their families and the various grades of their retainers, occupied nearly all the upper-level towers of Sunport.

But, here in Sunport alone, nearly eighty million more wore the gray of labor. They dwelt and toiled in the subsurface levels, and the Goon Department bound their lives with iron restrictions. Kellon knew how they lived—because he had been one of them.

Most of them hated the technician nobility of the Union. That was the dangerous flaw in the pyramid. Kellon had once tried to mend it, with reforms and concessions. But Melkart warned that he was three generations too late. Yielding to that hatred, he was merely paying out the rope to hang himself.

"We're dancing on a volcano, darling," he told Selene. "Better not poke the fire!"

Selene's bare shoulders tossed, and her eyes flashed dark as her emerald-sequined gown. But she curbed her displeasure. She knew that a hundred other women in the long, green-lit hall would have murdered gladly for her place in Kellon's arms. Her frown turned to a pretty pout.

"Please, Your Genius." Her perfect face winced slightly. Kellon knew that he had stepped on her silver slipper. But she smiled again, shrugging off his apology. "It wasn't caution that conquered the planets for you," she chided. "Your Genius isn't getting old?"

That was his vulnerable point, and Selene knew it. Perhaps he was. The details of administration were increasingly burdensome. It was hard to find trustworthy subordinates. Sometimes he felt that the Union itself was slipping into decadence, as he grew older.

"The coronation—" her coaxing voice went on.

But Kellon stopped listening. He let her dance out of his arms. He watched the thin man threading toward him through the press of bright-clad engineering aristocracy wheeling about the dance floor.

The thin man was Chief Marquard of the Goon Department. He wore wine-colored formal pajamas and a jeweled Union star. But he had no partner, and his harassed expression meant bad news. Kellon braced himself for trouble.

"Your Genius, it's the Preacher!" The whisper was hoarse with strain. "He's here in Sunport." Marquard gulped and wet his lips. "Still in hiding—somewhere down in the drainage levels."

This was more than merely trouble. Kellon swayed. The lofty shining murals blurred. He saw instead the dark, dripping tunnels a thousand feet beneath the pavements of Sunport. Once he had hidden there himself, a hunted man in gray. The syncopated drone of the orchestra was suddenly the throb of drainage pumps.

Kellon's thick, pink hands made a desperate clutching gesture. He had watched the spread of the Gray Crusade, a poison that attacked the Union and rotted the very fabric of civilization. For years the Goon Department had sought the Preacher, in vain. But it was hard to believe that the fanatic had dared to enter Sunport.

He was getting old, indeed. Old and alone. He felt helpless against the demands of this grim moment. Suddenly he was almost ill with a desperate regret for the quarrel with his son. Family loyalty, in this cynical metropolis, was almost the only dependable bond. Now he needed Roy, terribly.

Dazed by the impact of this emergency, his mind slipped back into the past. To Roy, and Roy's mother. It had been Melkart who first introduced the slender, gray-eyed girl. They were at a secret meeting, down in the drainage ways. Melkart said proudly, "Ruth is going to be the Joan d'Arc of the New Commonwealth."

Perhaps Ruth had loved Melkart. Kellon was never sure. For the secret police of the Corporation raided the party headquarters a few months later. Melkart was captured and transported to Mars. It was only after she had received a false report of Melkart's death that she would marry Kellon.

Kellon was responsible for that report. He had tried to atone for it, however, with the parole he secured for Melkart as soon as he had sufficient influence.

Ruth had never abandoned her dream of the New Commonwealth. She had not approved the methods of Kellon's rise to power, and she was deeply hurt when he ordered the Union Goons to hunt down the few surviving members of the party. Roy was twelve years old when she died.

Roy was like his mother—lean, intense, idealistic. Kellon was delighted when the boy wanted to take practical degrees in unitronic engineering—it helped him forget that his own hereditary titles were forgeries.

But Roy had been a bitter disappointment. He failed to show any interest in Union politics. He refused to enter the Militechnic College, to prepare for command and promotion in the Fleet. Instead, at twenty, he had gone to waste a year with some meaningless research at the solar power plants on Mercury.

The quarrel happened after Roy returned—five years ago. Roy didn't like Selene du Mars. She made matters worse by trying to flirt with him. He called her an unpleasant name and stalked out of the penthouse suite. He had never come back.

But Kellon had followed him, next day, to the great unitronics laboratory on the mesa. A silent crystal egg, his unitron glider sloped down toward the long, low, white-roofed building that stood between the commercial port and the militechnic reservation.

Like an elongated silver bubble, a freighter was lifting from the Venus Docks, bright and strange in the shimmer of its drive field. Gray stevedores were trucking away the gleaming metal ingots and squared hardwood logs it had unloaded. A Martian liner lay in her cradle, spilling dark ore concentrate down a chute. A space-battered Jovian relief ship was loading mountains of crates and bales and drums—food and equipment and power for the miners on Callisto. The Mercury Docks were stacked with crated dynode batteries, freshly charged in the Sun plants. All the commerce of an interplanetary empire!

But Kellon's pride had a bitter taste. He could remember when the port was far busier, back in the days of the Corporation. Now half the yards were weed grown and abandoned. Dismantled ships were turning red with rust in the cradles at the disused Saturn Docks.

His pilot landed the glider on the white roof. Kellon

asked for his son, and a startled watchman guided him down through the laboratory. Space had really been conquered in this building, Kellon knew; all the great advances in unitronic flight had been made here. But most of the halls were deserted now, the old equipment dismantled or ruined.

Kellon found Roy in a long, clean shop whose plastic walls were softly radiant with a clear blue-white. Huge windows looked out across the militechnic reservation, where the unitron cruisers of the Fleet lay like immense dead-black arrows.

Roy was bronzed with spaceburn from his year on Mercury. He looked up, with his mother's nervous quickness, from some gadget on a bench. Kellon was a little shocked to see the screwdriver in his hands—for an engineer of the higher ranks, any sort of manual work was degrading.

Roy seemed glad to see him.

"Sorry I lost my temper." He smiled—his mother's intense, grave smile. "I don't like Selene. But she isn't important." His brown, quick fingers touched the gadget, and his gray eyes lit with eagerness. "I'm searching for a way to test the condensation hypothesis."

"Look, son." Kellon gestured impatiently at the window, toward the row of mighty black cruisers. "You don't have to play with abstractions. There's the Fleet, waiting for you to take command as soon as you are qualified. Your experiments should be left to underlings."

"I'm sorry, Boss." Roy's tanned face set with his mother's unbreakable spirit. "I think my hypothesis is more important than the Fleet."

"Hypothesis?" Anger boomed in Kellon's voice. "Important." He tried to calm his tone. "Can you explain what is important about it?"

"I tried to, before I went to Mercury," Roy said. "You were too busy to listen. You see, I have a new idea about how the planets were formed. I went to Mercury to check it, with closer observations of the Sun. I believe I am right."

Kellon attempted to swallow his impatience.

"I'm listening, now," he said.

"You see, the origin of solar systems has never been well explained," Roy began in a careful voice. "The tidal theories of the twentieth century were all somewhat strained. There was a statistical difficulty. Only one star in a hundred thousand could possibly pass near enough to another to raise planet-forming tides. But the astronomers of the Outstation long ago convinced themselves that planetary systems are a lot more frequent than that.

"The discovery of the unitron, a hundred years ago, caused a revolution in nearly every science. It was recognized as the ultimate matter-energy unit of the universe. For the first time, it fitted all the various phenomena of electromagnetics and gravitation into a single picture. But most engineers, in the era of the Corporation, were too busy conquering and exploring the planets to devote much time to abstract theories."

Kellon felt a brief amusement at his son's simple lecture room explanations, and then wondered uneasily if Roy knew that his degrees were forged. He frowned, trying to follow.

"The twentieth-century cosmogonists had to deal with a confusing array of concepts," Roy went on. "Electrons and protons, neutrons and mesotrons and barytrons, photons and light waves, electric fields and magnetic fields and momentum fields and gravity fields. Already they were beginning to grope for a unified field theory, but they never quite perceived all those things as manifestations of the same ultimate unit. It's no wonder they never quite understood the Sun, or how the planets came to be born from it!"

"But you do?" Kellon was interested, in spite of himself.

Roy nodded eagerly and touched the gadget again.

"That is my hypothesis—that every normal star has formed planets of its own. The tidal theories allowed only a handful of habitable planets in the entire galaxy. I believe there may be—millions!" His quick hand gestured, with the gadget. "Of course, it is still only a hypothesis—though the Outstation astronomers have found evidence of planets about several of the nearer single stars. But I'm going to find out!"

He searched Kellon's face.

"Do you see it, father?"

Heavily, Kellon shook his rugged white-wigged head.

"Your argument sounds reasonable enough," he admitted. "Once at the Outstation I saw a graph that had some little dips they said meant planets. But what of it? I don't see anything to get excited about."

Tears of frustration came into Roy's eager eyes.

"I can't understand it," he whispered bitterly. "Nobody gets excited. Nobody cares." His bronzed head lifted defiantly. "But the engineers of a hundred years ago would have been building ships to explore those planets!"

"I don't think so," Kellon objected wearily. "It would be too far for commerce. The moons of Saturn haven't been visited for sixty years. Right now, our Jovian outposts are losing money. Supplies and transportation cost more than we get back. If it wasn't for Union prestige, I would abandon them today."

"Science has been slipping back, ever since the uranium process was lost." Roy's face was troubled. "I don't know why." His brown chin lifted. "But we can go on. The unitron drive can be improved. With time and money, I could build an interstellar ship!"

"Maybe you could," Kellon said. "If you are fool enough to want to die on some strange, barren world that men never even saw—when I have an interplanetary empire to give you!"

"I guess I'm just that kind of fool," Roy said quietly. "I don't want an empire."

Kellon lost his temper then.

"I'm going to cut off your allowance," he shouted at the white-lipped boy. "That will stop this nonsense.

Come to me whenever you are ready to take up militechnics."

"You had better go back to Selene du Mars," Roy told him quietly. "I don't need the allowance."

And that was true. Within a few months, Kellon learned that Roy had designed a new type drive-field coil for the unitron transports in the Jovian service. It saved three days in the long run out to Jupiter and increased the power recovery in deceleration nearly forty percent. For the first time in twenty years, the Callistonian mines showed a tiny profit. Roy's fees, paid by the Union Transport Authority, were a hundred times the cut-off allowance.

In the five years since, Kellon hadn't seen his son. Roy had ignored an invitation he made Selene send. But he knew, through the Goon Department, that Roy was still at the old unitronics laboratory, furiously busy with his research. Learning that his funds were running low, Kellon ordered the Transport Authority to double the promised royalties. Roy replied with a brief note of thanks.

Now, standing stunned and alone amid the whirling dancers under the green-glowing murals of the Neptune Room, Boss Kellon felt a crushing need to see that thin, determined face, that was so much like Ruth's had been.

But Roy had failed him. Under the burden of the tottering Union, he stood all alone. There was no other that he could trust completely. And Marquard's thin, frightened whisper goaded him back to face the present grim emergency.

"The Preacher's in Sunport," the Goon chief repeated. "His followers already know. Mob gathering in Union Square." His lean shoulders shrugged, in a helpless bewilderment. "Delicate situation, Your Genius."

"Delicate, hell!" Kellon caught his breath, and decision flashed in his shrewd blue eyes. He had fought alone before, and he could again. "Search the drainage levels," he ordered crisply. "Arrest the Preacher."

"Is Your Genius sure—" Marquard blinked uncertainly. "He has terrific influence. Before he came, it might have been safe. Now his followers will make trouble."

"I'll handle trouble when it happens." Kellon stiffened his big shoulders and managed to smile again. He must hide the black panic that swept him. "Don't kill him," he added. "Just bring him in. Martyrs are dangerous."

"Your Genius commands."

The thin man turned nervously away, the frown of worry cut deeper in his dark face. The orchestra throbbed on—playing from a high platform whose glowing plastic decorations represented an ice cave on Triton, Neptune's once-visited moon. Kellon started back to Selene du Mars.

She was waiting, slim and tall in the flashing green sequins. Even her smile was hard and bright and beautiful. Kellon felt an eager little quickening of his pulse, for he still loved Selene. Then he saw that she was smiling for another man.

Admiral Hurd came striding across the crowded floor. Black-and-orange pajamas were cut to emphasize the broad triangle of his shoulders. He was young and tall and dark. His toothy smile flashed, and he greeted Selene by the militechnic title she claimed:

"May I, Miss Captain?" Then he saw that Kellon was approaching. A kind of wary alertness tensed his face, and the smile that erased it was a little too broad. "If Your Genius will allow?"

"Darling, you look tired."

Selene turned the white dazzle of her smile on him, and slipped into the dashing admiral's arms before he could respond. Left alone on the floor, Kellon felt a tired envy for Hurd's youth and looks and vigor. Really, he was getting old.

He watched Hurd and Selene, dancing cheek to cheek. Her eyes were closed; her restless face seemed relaxed for once, and happy. But he caught a covert glance from Hurd's dark eyes, watchful, oddly hostile.

Turning wearily away, Kellon felt another surge of regret for his son. If they had not quarreled, Roy might now have been in command of the Fleet, instead of Hurd. The new admiral was brilliant, and his record clear, but Kellon didn't like him.

Kellon left the ballroom, escorted unobtrusively by his Goon bodyguards. He crossed the vast, silent Moon Room, to a terrace that looked down over Union Square.

It was night, and Sunport after dark was a view that had always stirred him. The towers were wide apart. Façades of luxion plastics turned them to tapering, graceful pylons of soft and many-colored fire. Their changing splendor lit the broad parks between, and stood inverted in a hundred pleasure lakes. The surface ways were broad curving ribbons of light, alive with the glowing cars of joy-riding engineers. A few pleasure gliders floated above the landing terraces, colored eggs of crystal light.

Sometimes, with an ache of longing, Kellon recalled his first rare glimpses of this bright and magical scene. For his childhood had been lived in the lower levels. It was only on infrequent holidays that he was allowed to come up into the parks, where he could see this forbidden, shining paradise of the engineers.

How mad his dreams had been! Ten million others must have dreamed them, but only he had come up to take the city for his own. Sometimes even yet the hard-won victory seemed altogether incredible. Nor ever had it been the pure untroubled delight he had dreamed of. Heavily, he signed.

"Your Genius!" The husky officer of the bodyguard stopped him in the wide arch of the terrace doorway, where drafts were checked only by a film of moving air. "The terrace may be dangerous—there's an ugly mob below."

"Thanks, major." He shrugged, and pushed on. He couldn't afford to yield to the fear in him. Confidence was his safest armor. "You know this is my favorite view."

But tonight the picture was grimly different.

The long rectangle of Union Square, so far below, was gray with pressing crowds. From this elevation, the surging masses looked like some strange vermin, crawling about the bases of these mighty, shining, clean-lined towers that he loved.

Scores of bonfires glared, points of angry red. His nostrils stung to a whiff of paper burning. Faint with distance, the angry buzz of voices came up to him. Evangelists were screaming hoarsely, and shrill voices sang. He caught a snatch from the "Battle Hymn of God":

> *"Burn the books and break the gears!*
> *Kill Antichrist and engineers!"*

Kellon stood there a long time, until his sweaty hands set cold upon the shining rail. He was sick with a fear that all these glowing towers would crumble into that gray ocean of blind destruction. But Melkart said there was nothing left that he could do.

Suddenly his cold body jerked to a brittle clatter of automatic gunfire. A mile from him, at the end of the square, gray mankind was flowing like a queer, viscid liquid over the bright-lit surface way: Cars were seized and capsized in that live flood, like small, glowing beetles.

Tiny screams reached him. Black Goon cars appeared on the shining pavement, and guns crackled again. It was too far to distinguish individual human forms, moving or dying. But the mass of the gray wave drew reluctantly back. The stream of traffic halted, and the light went out of the luxion pavement.

Anxiously, Kellon went back through the archway in the softly glowing wall—it was pulsating tonight with soft and slowly changing hues of violet and rose. He wondered briefly if quieter colors and a slower beat would seem more confident.

In the silent, cyclopean Moon Room, he hurried to the telephone desk and dropped impatiently on his seat in the U-shaped slot, with the stereo prisms standing in a half circle before him. In the center screen, the bright image of the red-haired operator was a little smaller than life.

"Get me Marquard," he rapped. The girl nodded silently, and the dark, thin features of the Goon chief sprang into the next crystal oblong. Kellon couldn't keep the rasping tension out of his voice. "Have you got the Preacher?"

"Not yet, Your Genius," Marquard replied in his habitual jerky, nervous whisper. "Mob is getting ugly. Looted the park library and made fires of the books. Started smashing pleasure cars on Union Way. Had to kill a few of them, to rescue an engineer and his girl. Diverted traffic." His worried eyes blinked uneasily. "Maybe we ought to clear the square?"

"No," Kellon told him—it was good to be able to make one more sure and instant decision. "The dead ones are martyrs. Leave them alone. They'll howl themselves exhausted and go back to their warrens."

"I hope so," Marquard whispered faintly.

"Just catch the Preacher, and send him to me." Kellon nodded at the operator, and the Goon chief vanished from the prism. "Reference Department." He spoke to a dyspeptic-looking female. "Show me the latest Goon report on the Preacher." The document was projected in the next screen.

Special Report No. 45-H-198
Union Goon Office, Sunport, E.
February 30, 2145

BY: Goon Operative GK-89 (R. A. Meyer, Politicotechnic Engineer).

SUBJECT: Eli Catlaw, alias the Preacher of the Revelation, alias the Word of God, alias the King of Kings. Labor No. G-496-HN-009. Escaped convict, Mars Penal Reservation, No. 45-V-18. Wanted for murder of guard. Believed now in America, but whereabouts unknown.

Note: Catlaw is a dangerous character. Liquidation recommended.

Tapping a key to change the pages, Kellon skimmed significant passages. "Catlaw was born in the Ozark District, of labor-class parents. . . . Mother's claim to illegitimate technical blood probably false. . . . Transported to Mars for assault on engineer. . . . Guard murdered, in escape. . . . Catlaw reached Venus Commonwealth on ore ship. . . . Became 'swamp walker' and successful herb trader. . . . 'Conversion' and preaching dates from recovery from attack of jungle fever. . . . Returned to Earth about nine years ago, to lead underground 'Crusade' against Union. . . . Enabled to evade many Goon raids by vast popular support. . . . Treason charges against Union factions. . . . Catlaw has incited assassination and sabotage. . . . His program implies total destruction of technical civilization."

Kellon finished the report. He sat staring into the empty prism, as gravely as if he could read there the end of Sunport and all his world. He had scarcely moved, an hour later, when Marquard brought in the Preacher.

Eli Catlaw seemed almost unaware of the burly Goons who gripped his arms. He was lank and tall in faded gray overalls, and he stood erect and defiant. His dark, hollow eyes stared arrogantly past Kellon, at the lofty luxion murals that illuminated the room. Kellon's shrewd eyes studied the man, against the background in the Goon report. Thick lips and high cheeks and stiff black hair showed Negro and Indian blood. The yellow face was long and angular and stern. At last the sullen, hostile eyes came back to Kellon's face, but obviously the Preacher didn't intend to speak first.

Kellon turned on his frank, confident smile.

"I'm glad to see you, Catlaw," he said smoothly. "I'm sorry if this is inconvenient for you, but it was the only way I knew to get your point of view."

The Boss paused invitingly, but the Preacher said nothing. He stood absolutely motionless, between the big men who held him. His burning eyes stared bleakly away, through the far, glowing murals.

"I know that times are difficult." Kellon kept his voice suave and even. "The exhaustion of the Jovian mines has caused depression. All the heavy industries are almost dead, and labor has naturally suffered. But I personally am deeply concerned for the comfort and welfare of the masses. And I assure you that the Union will earnestly consider any reform measures you will suggest."

Kellon paused again. Stillness whispered in the long Moon Room. Beneath the mighty glowing murals, that showed station domes and robot miners and long unitron transports against a background of towering lunar peaks and star-shot space, the little group at the telephore desk seemed queerly insignificant. The room seemed too vast for its builders.

Now at last the Preacher spoke. His long, stern face showed no response to Kellon's persuasive smile, and he ignored Kellon's arguments. In a tense, grating, stifled voice, he began quoting texts from the Revelation:

"Babylon the great is fallen, is fallen, and is become the habitation of devils, and the hold of every foul spirit. . . . Alas, alas, that great city Babylon, that mighty city! for in one hour is thy judgment come."

Kellon's smile had turned a little pale.

"Are you crazy?" He coughed against a troublesome rasp in his throat. "I suppose you mean Sunport?" His bewilderment was honest. "But Sunport is civilization!"

Stiff and insolent, the Preacher croaked:

"He that killeth with the sword must be killed with the sword. . . . Therefore shall her plagues come in one day, death, and mourning, and famine; and she shall be utterly burned with fire. . . . In one hour is she made desolate. . . . And the light of a candle shall shine no more at all."

Kellon leaned over the curving desk, with a look of earnest puzzlement.

"I don't understand you, Catlaw," he protested gravely. "Do you want to wreck all that men have accomplished? Do you want the future to forget the power of science? Do you want to turn men back into naked savages, and wipe out civilization?"

"Civilization?" The Preacher made a harsh snorting laugh. "Your glittering civilization is itself the Harlot of Babylon, poisoning all that yield to her painted lure. The science you revere is your false prophet. Your machines are the very Beast of the Apocalypse."

He gulped a hoarse breath.

"Yea, Armageddon and the Kingdom are at hand!"

"Listen to me," begged Kellon. "Please——"

Catlaw jerked angrily in the grasp of the Goons.

"I have come to destroy this last, most evil Babylon." His metallic, pulpit voice rang through the long Moon Room. "Even as the angels of God once smote the wicked cities of the plain, Sodom and Gomorrah. And every engineer shall be burned with the fire of the Lord—save that he repents tonight!"

His yellow face was a stern, rigid mask.

"I warn you, Antichrist. Repent tonight, and follow me." The cunning of the swamp trader glittered briefly in his hollow eyes. "Turn your power to the path of God, and I will receive you into the Kingdom. Tomorrow will be too late."

Kellon rose, gasping for breath.

"Listen!" His voice trembled. "I fought to rule Sunport. And I'll fight to preserve it from you and all the lunatics who follow you. Not just because it is mine. But because it is the storehouse of everything great that men have created."

"Then you are damned!" Scuffling with the Goons, Catlaw shook a dark, furious fist. "With all your city of evil."

Kellon's voice dropped grimly.

"I'm not going to kill you, Catlaw. Because you are probably more dangerous dead than alive, just now. But I know that you are a fugitive from the Union, with an untried murder charge waiting for you. I'm sending you to the Outstation prison, tonight, to await trial for murder."

He nodded at the Goons, and they dragged the prisoner away.

Kellon sat down heavily at the telephore desk. The Preacher unnerved him. It was hard for him to understand that deadly, destroying hatred, that blindness to all reason. But he knew that it was multiplied many million times in the gray-clad masses under the Union. He thought of the howling mob of the Preacher's fanatics about the foot of this very tower, and he was afraid.

But he must not yield to fear.

"Get me the militechnic reservation," he told the telephore operator. "The Admiralty Office. Hurd's at the ball, but I'll talk to the officer in charge."

The efficient redhead nodded, in the center prism. Kellon was astonished when the next screen lit with the dark, handsome features of Admiral Hurd, himself.

"Your Genius looks surprised." Hurd flashed his easy, white-toothed smile. "But I left the ball, after one dance with Miss Captain du Mars. I had reports of this crisis, and I felt it my duty to be ready for your commands."

"Thank you, admiral." Kellon tried to put down an uncomfortable feeling that Hurd was far too alert and dutiful. "I have arrested the Preacher. His followers may try to set him free. I want a cruiser to take him to the Outstation prison, as soon as possible."

"At once, Your Genius. I was expecting duty, and my flagship is hot. I'll take the prisoner myself. The *Technarch* will be on the Goon Office terrace to receive him in five minutes."

Smiling, Hurd flickered out of the prism.

Kellon felt another stab of sharp regret that Roy had failed him. But he had no time to dwell upon his dim mistrust of Hurd for the empty prism lit again, with Marquard's worried features.

"Your Genius, the people know we caught the Preacher." The Goon chief's whisper was nervous and hurried. "Mob in the square getting ugly. Fighting the

Goon cordons. I'm afraid they will attack the Tower."

Kellon caught his breath, and tried to keep smiling. He felt confused and tired, afraid that any violent action would jar the human volcano under Sunport into terrible eruption.

But something had to be done. Some display of confidence was necessary, to help the morale of his supporters. He lifted his big shoulders and groped for his old habit of instant decision.

"I'll talk to them," he told Marquard. "They can't all be as mad as Catlaw. I'll tell them who butters their bread." He smiled a little, as he turned to the operator. Any action made him feel better. "I'll speak from the terrace," he said, "on the Tower telephone."

"Wait, Your Genius," the Goon chief objected anxiously. "The terrace is dangerous. Automatic arms in the mob. Afraid the demonstration has support from some faction in the Union. My operatives still looking for evidence. Better keep out of range."

"I'll speak from the terrace."

Of course, he might be killed. Fear was a cold, crawling thing inside him. But he had faced death before. Now a display of perfect confidence was the best weapon he could use. He prepared to conceal his gnawing unease.

The touch of a key dropped the telephone desk into the lavatory below, a hall of glowing luxion almost as splendid as the huge Moon Room. Kellon adjusted the white toupee. A servant rouged his heavy jowls back to a cheerful glow. He tried to rinse the dry rasp out of his throat.

The elevator section lifted him back to the Moon Room. He walked back through the glowing luxion arch to the lofty terrace. The telephore stand here had only two prisms. Standing between them, he could look down across Union Square.

Now the pavements had been darkened, all around the square. Surface traffic was stopped. That gray, human sea had grown until it overflowed the ways, to the shining bases of the towers beyond. The hum of voices had a lowered, vicious tone.

Kellon spoke to the operator in the prism beside him. The wall behind—and all the illuminated faces of the Union Tower—began to flash, red and dark, red and dark, to gain attention. That ugly buzzing ceased, and he nodded. The crown of the Tower became a cool, steady violet.

"People of Sunport." From the three-hundred-foot screen in the wall beneath him, his giant image looked down over the mob. Magnified to the depth of thunder, his voice rolled out of a thousand speakers. "My friends, the action I have taken tonight was taken for your own good."

He trusted the old magic of his frank, robust smile and his candid, booming voice. After all, he had talked his way to victory over better men than Eli Catlaw. But that breathless quiet lasted only a moment, before the defiance of the mob rolled up to him at the slow speed of sound. It was a monstrous animal bellow.

"My friends, listen to me." At his quick nod, the operator stepped up the volume of that tremendous voice. "Listen to reason." A bullet slapped against the cold, glowing wall behind him. Stinging particles of plastic showered him. But fortunately the telephore picked up only a muffled thump. "What can you gain from the Preacher?"

Boos and jeers roared up from the mob.

"The Preacher has told you to destroy the machines." He tried to drown that defiant bellow. "He has told you to kill the men who create and control them. But think what you owe to machines—everything! Obey the Preacher, and the most of you will perish—"

Brrrram!

A dull but mighty concussion rocked the terrace. Kellon glimpsed flying debris, spreading out in a giant fan from somewhere beneath him. Black smoke overtook it and covered the mob in a billowing cloud. His knees were shaking, and his throat went dry. But he tried to go on:

"The most of you will perish—"

But the amplifiers were dead. His natural voice was wholly lost in the blasting echoes that came rolling back through the smoke from the distant towers. The telephore was out of order. Even the operator's image was gone. He shouted hoarsely at it and clicked the call key. But the prisms remained empty.

He stood clutching the edges of the stand, bewildered and ill, too dazed even to wonder actively what had happened. At last the smoke came up about him, in a choking, blinding cloud. He stumbled back into the Moon Room.

"Your Genius!" Frightened members of the body-guard met him in the doorway. "Are you hurt?" The officer told him: "It was a bomb. Under the giant screen. Spies must have set it."

The telephone in the Moon Room was still working. Kellon dropped weakly in his seat in the slot, with a grateful smile at the white-lipped operator. He told the redhead to call the Goon Office. Marquard answered, his jerky whisper briefly relieved:

"Afraid they had got you, Boss." Alarm came back to his thin, dark face. "Thing is worse than I thought. Widespread plot. Organization. Probably Preacher is the leader, but engineers were in it. Got surprising quantities of arms and explosives, and experts to use them."

Kellon managed a hard little grin.

"Evidently it isn't sinful to use machines—when they're guns."

The Goon chief was too harassed to smile.

"Watch for your life, Boss," he whispered. "Warn your guards. May strike anywhere. Rioters smashing cars and storming buildings and murdering engineers, all over the city. Union Tower may be next."

Kellon drew a long breath. His shaken nerves were recovering from the blast.

"Chin up, chief!" His rouged smile was easier. "We'll handle things. I'll call Hurd and have him stand by with the Fleet. We may need a pinch of tickle powder dropped out of space. There's nothing like a couple of hundred thousand tons of long, black unitron cruiser to instill respect." He turned to the watchful red-head. "Get me the *Technarch*."

The operator nodded. Her head bobbed a little in the prism, as her unseen hands sped over the switchboard. But the next prism remained blank. A puzzled expression came over her tense face. At last she told Kellon, "Your Genius, the *Technarch* doesn't answer."

Icy, unreasoning panic clutched Kellon's heart.

"Get me the Admiralty Office."

A dazed-looking militechnic cadet informed him that Admiral Hurd had taken the entire Fleet into space. "All the ships had been hot for twenty-four hours, sir," he stammered. "I understand the annual maneuvers are taking place, off the Moon."

Kellon made a stunned little nod, and the startled cadet was cut off. He stared at Marquard, still imaged in the adjacent prism. The Goon chief had seen and heard the cadet, and his lean, furrowed face reflected Kellon's consternation.

"The maneuvers were not to begin for a week." Kellon gulped uneasily. "Hurd shouldn't have begun them without an order from me." He shook his cragged head. "But—wholesale mutiny—it's too appalling to think of!"

Marquard made a tiny, bleating sound.

"That explains it, Your Genius," his whisper rasped. "Arms. Organization. Experts. Evidence that the Preacher had help from in the Union. He was plotting with Hurd." His pale face looked frightened. "Looks desperate, Boss!"

"I won't believe it," muttered Kellon. He didn't dare believe it. Anxiously he told the tense-faced redhead, "Get me the Outstation. Manager General Nordhorn. At once."

The Union's supremacy—and his own—depended on control of space. To that end, the Fleet and the Outstation was equally essential. That artificial moonlet was scarcely a mile in diameter, but an often-proved proverb ran, "The master of the Outstation will be master of the planets."

The tiny metal moon had a twenty-four-hour period, which kept it swinging always to the south of Sunport's zenith. At first it had served merely as observatory, laboratory and steppingstone to space. But the militechnic engineers of the Commonwealth, the Corporation and the Union had thickened its massive armor of meteoric iron until it was the Gibraltar of the system. The theoretical range of its tremendous guns extended around the Earth and out to the Moon.

"Hurry!" Kellon croaked. Breathless with impatience, he watched the operator. She fumbled with her unseen controls, as if there was some difficulty. But at last Nordhorn's thin, dark face flashed into the prism.

Manager General Nordhorn was an old man, bent and yellowed and deaf. He should have been retired years ago. But few younger men had shown steadfast loyalty—and even those few, like Marquard, were usually of indifferent ability. Something had happened to the fine tradition of the militechnic service.

"Has Hurd arrived?" Nordhorn cupped a trembling yellow hand to his ear, and Kellon shouted: "I have arrested the Preacher. I sent Hurd to carry him out to prison. He took the Fleet to space, and he doesn't answer the telephore. There may be trouble. Better call your men to action stations—"

Kellon's voice dried up. Nordhorn had looked sternly composed. But now, as he gulped to speak, Kellon saw the evidence of desperate emotion in his bloodless cheeks and quivering lips.

"Your Genius, Hurd has already called." His voice quavered uncertainly. "I was just about to call you. Hurd did not mention any prisoner. He delivered an ultimatum. A shocking thing, Your Genius—I can't quite understand—he demanded that I surrender the Outstation!" Nordhorn's yellow Adam's apple jerked, as he swallowed. "Your orders, sir?"

Blood drummed in Kellon's ears. Cold with sweat, his hands clutched the edges of the desk. In spite of all the evidence, the completeness of this disaster was still incredible. He tried to steady his reeling brain. Hoarsely he ordered:

"You will defend the Station—to the last."

"To the last." Nordhorn's white head lifted proudly. "But the situation is desperate, sir." A stunned bewilderment came back to his face. "I can't understand—things are happening so fast. But mutiny is reported in some of the gun crews. Men are fighting in the spaceward bays now."

"Hold out—" begged Kellon. But suddenly the haggard-faced old general was swept out of the prism. He clicked the call key desperately, and shouted at the operator, "Get back Nordhorn!"

"I'm sorry, Your Genius," the tense girl told him. "The Outstation doesn't answer."

Marquard's sick, shaken face was still in the other screen. For his benefit, Kellon tried to grin. "So Hurd and the Preacher are in bed together?" he muttered. "Which do you say will manage to kick the other out?"

"Won't matter, if the Station falls." The Goon listened. "Excuse me, Your Genius. The riot bureau is calling me. Remember—watch your life!"

His image was gone. Aimlessly, Kellon stalked up and down the pale-glowing floor of the long Moon Room. What next? The news from the outstation had shaken him more than the explosion under the terrace. He felt numbed and ill. Still the Station didn't answer, and he knew nothing useful to do.

The ball was still going on in the Neptune Room, the officer of his bodyguard told him. Even the telephore newsmen had as yet received little hint of the real gravity of the situation. The bright-clad dancers didn't know that their world was at the brink of catastrophe.

Perhaps that was the trouble. If the engineering class had danced less—if they had learned more and done more about the other nine-tenths of the population—things might have been different. But Melkart said it was three generations late to think of that.

"Boss!" a guard shouted. "Look out!"

Shots echoed against the high, glowing murals. Some-where a woman screamed. Fighting men surged through the wide arch from the Neptune Room. The lights went out in the luxion panels. An automatic clattered in the dark.

The broad connecting doorway had been closed only with the sound-absorbing air screen. Now Kellon heard a muffled *woosh!* The armored safety panel had lifted, but too late. The attackers were already in the Moon Room.

In the faint glow that came through the terrace arch, he glimpsed crouching, darting figures. An arm threw something over the fighting Goons. It crashed beside him. Desperately he groped for it, hurled it toward the far end of the room, dropped flat behind the telephone desk.

His ears rang, and the immense dark room was alive with screaming metal. He rose behind the desk, snatch-ing a hidden automatic from under the seat. But the shooting had stopped. Light flowed back into the high luxion murals.

Three men were lying still inside the closed archway. One made a thin, whimpering sob, and a frightened Goon fired a final shot into his head. The officer came running anxiously to Kellon.

"Is Your Genius all right?"

Kellon managed to grin.

"Attempt No. 17." He was glad of the rouge on his face. No other attempt had ever come quite so close, or made him feel so weak inside. He dragged his eyes away from the ruin at the end of the room, where the bomb had shattered a cragged lunar peak into dusty rubble. "Who were they?"

Already the Goons were examining the three dead men. Their fingerprints were swiftly identified by tele-phore. One of them proved to be a hereditary engineer who had failed in the examinations for a practical mili-technic degree. The other two were members of the auxiliary white-collar class.

"The engineer must have come with the guests," the

guard officer reported. "The others were among the musicians. They had guns and the bomb in instrument cases." He caught his breath. "I regret this terribly, Your Genius. But let me congratulate your personal courage, with the bomb."

Courage! Kellon shrugged and turned quickly away from the still figures in their gay bloodstained rags. There was already an odor. Death made him ill. If he had been an instant slower—desperation wasn't courage. His voice came harsh and loud:

"Get them out and clean the floor." Then he thought of Selene du Mars. Concern sharpened his tone. "There was fighting in the ballroom? Was anyone hurt? Find out if Miss Captain du Mars was hurt."

The safety door dropped again. Anxiety made him follow the questioning Goons. An ominous, hysterical tension met him in the vast green-glowing Neptune Room. Cold-eyed officers were grilling the frightened musicians. Half the guests were gone. The rest gathered in pale-faced groups, chattering nervously.

He couldn't find Selene. The guards at the main entrance, off the public glider terrace, had not seen her among the departing guests. But she had vanished early in the evening.

Apprehension seized him. In spite of her scheming ambition—or even because of it—he loved Selene. He knew that the Preacher's followers hated her savagely, as the very symbol of all that was denied them. She might have been abducted, perhaps even murdered.

He hurried back to the telephore in the bomb-shattered Moon Room, and called her suite on the floor below. The dark Eurasian major-domo said she had not come in. But the red-haired operator told him:

"Your Genius, there's a recorded message from Miss Captain du Mars. It was left two hours ago, to be delivered whenever you called for her. Will you receive it?"

Kellon nodded, suddenly voiceless.

Selene's face came into the crystal block. The fire diamonds burned in her platinum hair. Their changing blaze went blue as her clear eyes, and redder than her lips. Her voice came, cool and hard and perfect.

"Harvey, I am leaving you tonight. We shall not meet again. This is to thank you for all you have given me, and to tell you why I have gone. It isn't because you are getting old, or because I think you are slipping—believe me, I wouldn't go because of that. But I'm in love with Admiral Hurd. By the time you hear this, we shall be in space together. I'm sorry, Harvey."

Kellon sat for a long time at the telephone desk. He felt numb and cold. In a hoarse voice, he told the operator to run it over. Selene smiled again, and wiped away the same solitary jewel-bright tear, and spoke the same gem-hard words.

She lied. Kellon stared blankly at the mural the bomb had shattered—his own life was darkened and broken, like the luxion panel. He clenched his fists in a sick and useless fury. Of course she lied!

Maybe she did love Hurd. The traitor had looks and youth. That would be no wonder. But it wasn't love that made her go with him. He knew Selene too well to accept that. She had gone with Hurd because she expected him to be the next master of the world.

"Run it again," he told the operator. "Without the sound." And he greeted the silent image with a tired, bitter grin. "Good hunting, Selene," he whispered. "After all, we've had our day. Good hunting—but you and your dashing admiral had better watch the Preacher!"

The lone tear fell again, and she vanished once more.

And presently Kellon told the operator to try the Outstation again. Selene wasn't everything. Tonight the world was at stake. His life, and hers. The Union, and Sunport. The game was being played, far out in the silent cold of space. Between an old man's loyalty and a young one's ruthless ambition. Between the old world he had conquered and one unknown. He could only wait for the issue. There was nothing else to do.

But the Outstation didn't answer.

"Nothing, Your Genius," the operator said. "There

has been nothing from space since General Nordhorn was cut off."

Wearily restless, Kellon rose from the desk. The dead men had been taken away, but he thought that the faint, sickening smell of death still hung in the room. He felt cold and desperately alone.

Then he thought of Melkart.

The old philosopher-historian was one man who ought to know what was happening to Sunport. Often in the past his somewhat Machiavellian advice had been useful. Almost before Kellon knew it, his restless feet were taking him through the Saturn Room.

That immense hall was his library. Books walled it, four galleries high. Vaults beneath held microfilm copies of all known literature. Kellon left his guards outside the historian's office.

Charles Melkart occupied a tiny alcove. The white-glowing walls were bare, but one huge window gave a spectacular view of the shining, night-cloaked city. A huge ancient wooden desk took up nearly half the room. It was piled untidily with books and stacks of manuscript.

As if unaware of any trouble outside, Melkart sat behind the desk, writing swiftly with an old-fashioned pen. He was a small, stooped man. He wore a wrinkled lounging robe. A red wool skullcap covered his baldness. He blinked as Kellon entered and took off his spectacles. In his wizened yellow face, his eyes looked strikingly young and alive.

"Sit down, Wolfe." Melkart never fawned. "I was expecting you."

Wolfe! That had been Kellon's party name. He remembered secret meetings, down in the drainage levels, where the cold walls sweated and the air was alive with the throb of pumps. That was in the old, dangerous days, before they gave up the fight for the forbidden ideals of democracy.

Suddenly Kellon wondered if Melkart and Ruth had really been in love. He dismissed the thought. That hadn't mattered, for many years. The New Commonwealth was a forgotten dream. Melkart had left his idealism, with his health, in the carnotite mines of Mars. And the parole had settled whatever debt there might have been.

But Melkart had given him a great deal—besides Roy's mother. The lean, brilliant New Zealander had taught him the science of politics. His degrees had been forged at the party headquarters, to make him a more useful agent. When the Corporation shattered the underground organization, Kellon had managed to escape with most of the party funds.

Kellon had attempted to repay him with some high position in the Union. But the sardonic ex-radical declined to accept anything more than the needs of his simple life and use of the vast library in the Saturn Room.

"You have made the solar system into a laboratory for the test of my politicotechnic theories," he said, with his thin, yellow grin. "Now all I want is time to finish writing 'Destiny.' "

Now, when he came into the scholar's narrow room, Kellon was too perturbed to take the single chair beside the cluttered desk. He walked to the great window. The rioters made a gray, uneasy sea below, flecked with the scarlet of fires. A distant explosion jarred the air; a machine gun rattled; the drone of voices lifted angrily.

Melkart picked up his pen to make some hurried note.

Pale and tense, nails biting into his palms, Kellon turned back from the window. In a hoarse, desperate voice he asked the lean old man at the desk:

"Charles—do you know what is happening to Sunport?"

The red fez nodded.

"I've known for thirty years," Melkart grinned, with owlish assurance. "Old Giovanni Vico had a glimmer of it, with his 'law of cycles,' back in the seventeen hundreds. Spengler and Toynbee glimpsed it. Sprague, later, saw farther. But it remained for me to reduce the laws of the rise and fall of human cultures to the exact science that I call *destiny*." His yellow, clawlike hand gestured quickly at a huge manuscript. "Here, in my last volume—"

"Listen!" Kellon's fist banged the desk in interruption. "I've no time for books. The gray class is rioting. The Fleet has mutinied. The Outstation is under attack—if it falls, we'll be bombarded from space. Already assassins have attacked me once tonight."

He made a harsh, mirthless laugh.

"Books! Can you sit here writing a book, when the Preacher's fanatics are burning libraries in the park? They are murdering every engineer they can lay hands on. Who will be left to read your precious book?"

Melkart's fleshless, yellow visage grinned.

"Nobody, I'm afraid," he said slowly. "It is tragic that cultures must reach the point of breakdown before they can breed men able to understand them. But lack of understanding does not change the truth. Every fact you mention is inevitable. Because now Sunport is dead—a petrifact."

"Petrifact—you're insane!" Kellon slammed the desk again. "This is no time for your pessimistic theories. I want to know something to do." His voice sank, pleading. "You have helped me before. There must be—something."

Melkart closed a big book, and Kellon saw that the yellow fingers trembled.

"You and I are finished, Wolfe." His voice was slow and regretful. "Because the soul of Sunport is dead. You see, a city or a nation or a culture is something more than the sum of the individuals that make it up. Sunport was born, back in 1978, when the first rocket blasted off Toltec Mesa. It was created to conquer space. It did, and that supreme victory made it the greatest megalopolis the world has seen."

"That's history," Kellon muttered impatiently. "What's the matter today?"

"Space is conquered," Melkart told him, "and that great idea is dead. Because life doesn't stand still. Disused functions are lost. After the victory was won,

Sunport failed to discover a new purpose to keep her alive. Therefore, she died. It makes no difference that ninety million new barbarians live on in these dead towers."

Kellon had moved to speak, but Melkart added sardonically:

"That's as true of you, Wolfe, as it is of the city. You aren't a tenth the man you were thirty years ago, when you set out to smash what was left of the Corporation. You might have been a match for Eli Catlaw—then."

Kellon smoothed a frown of displeasure from his face.

"Please, Charles," he begged. "I know I'm getting old, but the Union is mine. Maybe I got it by arbitrary methods, but it is a trust. I've got to save it from the Preacher and his rabble, because the Union has created everything we call civilization."

"True." Melkart's red-capped skull nodded gravely. "The engineers were a creative minority—a hundred years ago. A small group of experts conquered space— and thereby created more wealth than mankind had ever owned before.

"Inevitably, the creative power of the engineers resulted in political dominance. Unfortunately, however, they have ceased to create. Now their spendthrift children merely loot the wealth their fathers earned, and play their silly games of hereditary degrees. And Sunport is as much a petrifact as the pyramids of old Egypt."

Kellon leaned over the untidy desk.

"Sunport is mine." His rugged face was pale under the rouge, and his low voice trembled. "I paid for it, with brains and toil and years. I worked and schemed and bribed and robbed and lied and killed. I lived in dread of assassination. I fought like a jungle animal for the city." He gulped a rasping breath. "I won't give it up."

"You say that," Melkart smiled his wry, yellow smile, "but you help establish my proposition. Because you completely fail to share the magnificent aspiration that created Sunport. Out of these restless millions of new nomads, you merely had superior cunning and audacity and luck.

"But men want to merge themselves in things greater than their individual lives. Destiny is the word I use, for those supernal living forces that exalt and give purpose to the lives of myriads.

"Sunport has fulfilled her destiny, and thereby lost it. But the Preacher has offered these new barbarians another destiny—a fresh, common purpose—on their own savage plane. That means that our world has ended, Wolfe."

Kellon stared at him silently.

"You're lost, Melkart," he said at last. "You will still be sitting here, when the Preacher's fanatics come along to burn your book and cut your throat. I think that is the best criticism of your philosophy"—he swung aggressively toward the door—"but I'm not done."

Kellon went back to the bomb-torn Moon Room. Perhaps Melkart was right. Perhaps Sunport was doomed. But he wasn't ready to die. He sat down anxiously at the telephone desk and told the operator to call the Outstation once more.

"I'll try, Your Genius." The girl was pale and jittery. "But I've been trying. They don't answer." Her voice was near hysteria. "The whole telephore system is breaking down. They have been smashing equipment and murdering operators."

"Get the Outstation!"

His voice was harsh with strain. He sat watching the busy girl. Unrest held him tense, but there was nothing he could do. The minutes dragged. There was no reply from space, until a terrible screaming came out of the sky.

The tower shuddered. A monstrous, bellowing vibration drowned all thought. The floor pitched. Concussion jarred Kellon's bones. The high luxion murals flickered and went dim. The plastic mosaic of a moon city turned black and came crashing down. The air was filled with choking dust.

The bombardment had begun.

No need to get the Outstation now. That first terrible projectile from space was enough to tell him that Hurd and the Preacher were victorious. The Outstation had been taken or destroyed.

Sunport was defenseless. True, there were huge batteries on the militechnic reservation, beside the spaceport. But, hampered by Earth's gravitation and atmosphere, they were almost useless against attack from space—even if the plotters had failed to put them out of commission already.

Kellon shivered to something colder than personal fear. For he knew that Melkart was right. This was the end of Sunport. The Union was finished. The engineering class was doomed. Ahead he could see only ruin and chaos, ignorance and savage cruelty, darkness and despair.

"Get me Marquard!" he shouted at the frightened operator.

Now the Goon Department was the last feeble defense of civilization. But Sunport must be blacked out. The people must be warned to leave the city or take refuge on the lower levels. And he wanted to know where that first projectile had struck.

The Goon chief's head came into the crystal block. But it was sagging wearily back. Marquard's apprehensive frown was at last relaxed. There was a little dark hole at his temple. The operator made a tiny, stifled scream, and the peaceful face vanished.

"He's dead!" She listened, and began a tight-voiced explanation. "The office says he shot himself, when he learned—"

The second projectile cut her off.

The Union Tower shuddered again, like a giant live thing struck with some deadly harpoon. Concussion flung Kellon out of the seat. He was deafened, and the salt-sweet taste of blood was on his lips.

He climbed back to the desk. But the operator's prism was blank. The dial lights were out. Frantically he jiggled the call key, but there was no response. The instrument was dead.

His ears ceased to ring. Suddenly he felt that the huge shattered room was queerly still. He shouted anxiously for his guards, but there was no reply. Peering into the dust, he saw that the officer lay motionless under a pile of rubble, in the broken archway. The others had fled.

He was alone.

Alone! That realization was appalling. Now the breakdown was complete. No longer was he Boss of the Union. He was merely one among millions of frightened and bewildered human beings. The only order left was the organization of his enemies.

In his dazed aloneness, he was scarcely aware when the third projectile fell. But the light flickered, in all the luxion walls, and went out. He cried out, in the smothering dark. An ultimate purpose was awakened in him—the blind instinct for survival.

A dim glow from without guided him to the terrace. He saw that half the city's towers were still pulsating with the changing radiance of their luxion façades. The bombardment soon would black them out, he thought bitterly, forever.

Union Square was almost empty. A few stragglers of the gray mob still fled across the darkened ways. Near the base of the Tower, dust and smoke drifted out of an immense dark crater.

So near! Kellon shivered to a cold realization. The Union Tower was the target. The space bombardment was aimed at him! Because, by now, he was almost the last symbol of the Union's shattered power.

He ran back through the archway to the roof elevator. Its walls still glowed, and it shot upward when he pressed the controls. He stumbled out into a chill night wind, on the penthouse roof.

"Here!" he shouted, across the glider terrace. "Quick—haul out the *Ruth!*"

Then he saw that the terrace was deserted. The hangar yawned black and empty. The long crystal bubble of his unitron glider was gone. The crew must have fled with it when the bombardment began.

Kellon stood bewildered in the cold dark. He sobbed, and his fists were clenched impotently. The world had crumbled under him, and there was nothing he could do. Civilization had dissolved.

The fourth projectile came nearer still. An appalling vibration battered him. He dropped flat. The deck quivered, like part of a monster animal dying. The concussion stunned him.

He came to himself in the elevator. Its walls were black. He fumbled in the dark for the controls, but the mechanism was dead. He flung himself into the dark emergency stair and started running down the steps.

Presently, he supposed, when those guns in distant space had found the Tower's range exactly, the projectiles would come in salvos, instead of singly.

The black stair was endless, and his descent became a blurred nightmare. Blast followed blast, until he no longer tried to count them. The concussions were shattering blows against his very sanity.

Down and down, through dust and darkness. Once he tripped over something that felt like a body, and fell until a landing stopped him. His muscles jerked with fatigue. Stiff blood dried on his bruised temple.

Somewhere there were levels where the walls still glowed dimly. They were part of the administrative offices of the Union, for he glimpsed floor after floor covered with identical unending rows of glass cubicles and telephone desks and business machines. The mob must have been here, for he saw scattered bodies of Goons and grays. But the living had fled.

Still his numbed brain could function, in a disjointed way. For he realized that his bright dress pajamas would be a sure warrant of death when he came down to the levels where the Preacher ruled. He stripped a gray-clad body, pulled the coarse garments over his own, and threw away the white toupee.

Sometimes black panic blotted out all awareness. Fatigue became a drug that destroyed memory and sensation. But he kept on his feet. He kept moving. Because he didn't want to die.

There was another stratum of darkness. Then somewhere he found an elevator that worked. It dropped him into the damp chill of the drainage levels. The concussions were now muffled with hundreds of feet of earth. But still they struck and struck and struck, numbing clubs of death.

Once he came to himself, and found that rubble had almost buried him. An air tube had caved above him. He dragged himself stiffly out of the debris. No bones were broken. He stumbled on. It was a long time before he realized that the bombardment had ceased.

A burst of automatic fire crashed out of a dark crossway. He ducked for cover. But a heavy, bloodstained man in gray lumbered into the pale, cold light of the luxion tube strung along the roof and covered him with a Goon automatic.

"Halt, for Armageddon is at hand!"

"Yea, Brother!" Kellon managed to respond with a dazed quotation from the Preacher. "And the Kingdom is come."

"Pass, Brother." The man grinned at him, redly, and explained: "I am hunting engineers. I've killed seven." Kellon was about to pass, when the gun moved ominously. "Wait, have you heard the news?"

Kellon waited.

"Admiral Hurd tried to trick the Preacher." The red hunter chuckled triumphantly. "He was slain by the hand of God—and a well-flung knife. Now the Fleet is ours—if any ships are left, for they were last reported fighting one another."

Kellon's throat was suddenly dry.

"Selene—" he whispered. "What about Miss Captain du Mars?"

"Forget those words of Satan, Brother." The hunter licked his lips, with an unpleasant relish. "The harlot of Babylon is also dead. They say that she betrayed even the Antichrist, in the end. She was found with Hurd, aboard the Fleet. She took poison when he was killed, to escape the Preacher's wrath. Hallelujah!"

"Praise the Lord!" Kellon gasped hoarsely. "Good hunting, Brother."

He was sorry to learn of Selene's death. Yet he was certain that she had wasted no pity on herself. She had played the game to the end, by her own hard rules. The possibility of failure had been taken into her calculations, equally with success. The poison she had ready was proof enough of that.

Shock and bewilderment and fatigue made a black fog upon his mind. It was hard to remember what had happened. Hard to understand it. Like Selene, he had played by the rules that life had taught him. But now they no longer applied.

Once he hid from a mob that came splashing along a dark tube. They had flaring torches. Their leader carried a woman's head on a stake. They were singing the "Battle Hymn of God."

Dimly, he tried to understand what had turned human beings into such frightful things. Of course, the rule of the Union had been a heavy burden, but he remembered signing many measures for the relief of the masses. Melkart, he remembered, said that he was three generations late.

It was twenty years since Kellon had felt the wet chill of the drainage levels. But suddenly the last secret meeting of the New Commonwealth party seemed only yesterday. This intricate maze of dripping tunnels remained as familiar as if he had never left it.

Reeling to his burden of fatigue, he found a little niche that he had dug long ago in the side of a shaft above a drainage pump. He slept for a long time, and woke staring at the even marks of his drill still visible in the damp sandstone.

It gave him a curious and surprising pleasure to see that evidence of the old strength and skill of his hands. For it was a long time since he had even dressed himself completely without some aid.

He was hungry, but still the far past served him. He

climbed, by a way he had known, to the freight levels. Traffic had ceased. He saw no Goons or workmen. In most sections, only a few pale emergency lights were glowing.

A few other looters were busy. He avoided them. Presently, he found a wrecked electric truck and loaded his gray pockets from its cargo of hydroponic oranges and tinned imitation beef. He ate, and cached what was left in the little cave.

It was dawn of the second day when he came up a sloping freight ramp into the tangled weeds and rusting metal and time-dulled luxion masonry of the long abandoned Saturn Docks.

He was searching for his son.

It was five years, now, since their quarrel. He couldn't be sure that Roy would want to see him. But the bright shadow of Selene was no longer between them. He was lonely, and Roy was all he had left.

If his Tower had been the brain of the Union, the spaceport had been its pulsing heart. Remembering the great batteries on the militechnic reservation, he hoped that refugees from the bombarded city might have gathered here, to make a last defense upon the natural fortress of the mesa.

Eagerly, he pushed through the weeds toward the Venus Docks. Stumbling in the dim early light, he came upon a new mountain of fresh black earth and broken stone. The heart went out of him. He climbed wearily to the summit of the shell-built ridge.

Beyond, where the busy Venus Docks had been, was only a wide black chasm. Bitter fumes stung his nostrils. But it was more than the explosive reek that blurred his eyes with tears.

Chaos met him. The shell-torn mesa looked desolate as the Moon. Outside the Saturn Docks, scarcely any familiar structure was even a recognizable ruin. Death had plowed deep. Only a few twisted scraps of metal even hinted that docks and cradles and ships had ever existed.

Miles away, on the rough field of dark debris where

the militechnic reservation had been, he saw a fallen cruiser. All the stern was gone, as if the magazine had exploded. The plates still glowed with red heat over the battery rooms, and smoke lifted a sharp thin exclamation point against the gloomy sky.

Sadly, he recognized the *Technarch*'s lines.

Beyond the dead ship, Sunport was burning. A terrible red dawn glowed all across the east. But the low sky overhead remained dark with smoke from the conflagration. Hours dragged on, as he searched for the ruin of the unitronics laboratory where Roy had worked. But the Sun didn't rise.

It must have been noon when he came to what was left of the laboratory. Hope ebbed out of him, when he saw the shattered ruin of the dead luxion walls. For the old building had been directly hit.

A huge, yet-smoking pit opened where the left wing had been. The roof was torn off the massive gray walls. They were banked high with debris. It seemed impossible that anybody could have survived, in all the building.

"Who comes?"

Kellon whirled, startled. Behind him, a big man had risen silently from behind a mound of rubble. The labor number printed across the front of his gray overalls showed that he had been a dock worker. He carried a stubby automatic rifle.

"Steve Wolfe." Cautiously, Kellon answered with his old party name. "Freight handler."

"What do you want?"

"I'm looking for Engineer Roy Kellon," he said desperately. "I have a message for him. He worked in the unitronics lab. Do you know him? Was he hurt?"

The big man made no immediate reply. His keen eyes studied Kellon over the level gun. Puzzled and impatient, Kellon kicked uneasily at a bomb-tossed stone. At last, as if he had reached some decision, the guard nodded.

"I think you'll do. Come along, and I'll let you talk to Tom Pharr." He pointed with the gun toward a gap in the shattered wall. "Roy Kellon is here," he added, "but you will find it hard to deliver any message right now. Because he is buried under a thousand tons of rock."

Kellon walked ahead, through a maze of ruined rooms and roofless passages. He heard voices and the muffled clink of tools. Abruptly, his guide brought him upon a surprising scene.

A cracked, unroofed wall inclosed a long rectangle. It was piled deep with broken rock and debris, flung from the crater where the other wing had been. But scores of men and women were toiling desperately to move the rubble. They had half uncovered a long, mirror-bright torpedo shape. The guard hailed a slim young man in gray, who appeared to be in charge of the excavation.

"Pharr! Here's another man for you."

The slim youth came to meet them. Kellon had seen him here at the laboratory when he came to beg Roy to give up his research. But his face showed no recognition, and Kellon was glad of it.

"Refugee?" Pharr asked quickly. "You don't like the Preacher? You want to leave Sunport?" Kellon scarcely had time to nod. "Are you willing to go to space?"

"I am." Kellon felt bewildered. "But I was looking for my . . . for Engineer Roy Kellon. Is he all right?"

"He's aboard the *Nova*." Tom Pharr jerked a hurried thumb at the half buried torpedo. "He'll be all right—if we can get him uncovered before the Preacher's fanatics get wind of us."

"That?" Puzzled, Kellon nodded at the bright spindle. "A spaceship?"

"Interstellar cruiser," Pharr explained swiftly. "We've been working on it, for years. It was almost ready to test. When the bombardment started, Roy tried to get it into space. The shell caught him.

"Lucky I was in the city—trying to find a crew. I got back in a glider, after the bombardment. I've been collecting refugees to dig him out." His quick eyes ran over the busy scores. "We'll save a tiny seed of civilization— if we get away."

Pharr's lean face betrayed faint worry.

"Some damage to the *Nova*. But Roy signaled that he is making repairs. Expects to be able to take off, as soon as we can get it uncovered. There's fuel enough for Venus or Mercury. But we'll have to find dynodes and supplies for the interstellar flight."

Eagerly, Kellon echoed, "Interstellar?"

Bright enthusiasm burned all the fatigue from Tom Pharr's face.

"Roy believes every star has planets of its own. Won't matter so much if dark ages come to Earth. Because we and our children will be sowing the seed of mankind across the stars." His intense eyes peered at Kellon. "Want to sign for the voyage?"

Kellon gulped in vain to speak. This was something more than a chance to escape the chaos of a crumbling world. Tom Pharr's quiet, brief words had painted a new vision, suggested a new purpose. He nodded mutely.

"Then get to work."

Kellon went to help a man and a girl who were trying to roll a raw new boulder away from the *Nova*. It was queerly comforting to be accepted as a member of this busy, efficient group. Never before had he quite realized how lonely the Boss had been.

As the hours went on, he was scarcely conscious of fatigue. He wasn't much concerned with the blood that presently began to ooze from his soft, uncalloused hands. There was time for only a few brief words, but he began to feel an eager interest in these new companions.

A curiously assorted group. Burly dock hands in gray. A few young cadets who had survived the destruction of the militechnic college. A dozen veterans who had escaped from the Outstation in a life tube, when it was blown up. Engineers, white-collar workers, servants, grays.

But their one intense purpose had fused them all into a single unit. Class distinction was gone. Kellon noticed a pretty girl, in low-cut dance pajamas. She looked a little like Selene du Mars. But she was serving soup to a line of hungry stevedores in gray.

Melkart's dictum came back to him. Sunport was dead, because it had lost the purpose that created it. But this desperate, tattered little group was still somehow a vital entity. Because, as the old historian would have put it, they shared a destiny.

Night fell again. Still Sunport was burning. Smoke blotted out the stars. The eastward horizon was a wall of terrible red. Lightless towers stood against it, broken and truncated by the space bombardment, like monuments of some dead gigantic race.

They worked on without resting. Now and again, a clatter of automatic fire told them that the guards were fighting some intruder. It was midnight when they reached the valves of the *Nova*. Roy Kellon came out, an arm in a sling, to inspect the battered hull.

Kellon stood back in the shadows, too weary to call out. His breath came faster, and his throat ached suddenly. Roy looked lean and strong; those were his mother's eager gray eyes.

"Come aboard," he called. "I think she'll do. I've patched up the damage in the power room. We can make Venus for repairs and supplies—and then the stars!"

Kellon followed the shuffling line of weary men and women through the valve. Roy was standing in the light, inside. His lean face lit with astonished pleasure, and he put out his good hand.

"Why, father!" he whispered. "I'm so glad!"

"Good to see you, Roy." Kellon blinked and tried not to choke. "Now I understand what you tried to tell me once—about the importance of those other planets." He gulped, and hesitated. "But—I'm an old man, Roy. If . . . if you need the space for younger men and women—I'll stay."

"Nonsense, Boss!" Roy gripped his hand. "Tickled. Just so we get away before the Preacher comes."

"Forget the *Boss*." Kellon grinned and blinked again.

"But we'll be loading supplies on Venus. You'll find I'm a hell of a good foreman on a cargo gang."

The skirmishing guards retreated aboard. The valves were sealed. Anxiously Roy cut in the *Nova*'s untested drive. She lifted silently, swifter than any unitron vessel had ever been. The burning city slipped beneath its dark shroud of smoke. Ahead were the stars.

With Folded Hands

UNDERHILL WAS WALKING home from the office, because his wife had the car, the afternoon he first met the new mechanicals. His feet were following his usual diagonal path across a weedy vacant block—his wife usually had the car—and his preoccupied mind was rejecting various impossible ways to meet his notes at the Two Rivers bank, when a new wall stopped him.

The wall wasn't any common brick or stone, but something sleek and bright and strange. Underhill stared up at a long new building. He felt vaguely annoyed and surprised at this glittering obstruction—it certainly hadn't been here last week.

Then he saw the thing in the window.

The window itself wasn't any ordinary glass. The wide, dustless panel was completely transparent, so that only the glowing letters fastened to it showed that it was there at all. The letters made a severe, modernistic sign:

Two Rivers Agency
HUMANOID INSTITUTE
The Perfect Mechanicals
"To Serve and Obey,
And Guard Men from Harm."

His dim annoyance sharpened, because Underhill was in the mechanicals business himself. Times were already hard enough, and mechanicals were a drug on the market. Androids, mechanoids, electronoids, automatoids, and ordinary robots. Unfortunately, few of them did all the salesmen promised, and the Two Rivers market was already sadly oversaturated.

Underhill sold androids—when he could. His next consignment was due tomorrow, and he didn't quite know how to meet the bill.

Frowning, he paused to stare at the thing behind that invisible window. He had never seen a humanoid. Like any mechanical not at work, it stood absolutely motionless. Smaller and slimmer than a man. A shining black, its sleek silicone skin had a changing sheen of bronze and metallic blue. Its graceful oval face wore a fixed look of alert and slightly surprised solicitude. Altogether, it was the most beautiful mechanical he had ever seen.

Too small, of course, for much practical utility. He murmured to himself a reassuring quotation from the *Android Salesman*: "Androids are big—because the makers refuse to sacrifice power, essential functions, or dependability. Androids are your biggest buy!"

The transparent door slid open as he turned toward it, and he walked into the haughty opulence of the new display room to convince himself that these streamlined items were just another flash effort to catch the woman shopper.

He inspected the glittering layout shrewdly, and his breezy optimism faded. He had never heard of the Humanoid Institute, but the invading firm obviously had big money and big-time merchandising know-how.

He looked around for a salesman, but it was another mechanical that came gliding silently to meet him. A twin of the one in the window, it moved with a quick, surprising grace. Bronze and blue lights flowed over its lustrous blackness, and a yellow name plate flashed from its naked breast:

HUMANOID
Serial No. 81-H-B-27
The Perfect Mechanical
"To Serve and Obey,
And Guard Men from Harm."

Curiously it had no lenses. The eyes in its bald oval head were steel colored, blindly staring. But it stopped a few feet in front of him, as if it could see anyhow, and it spoke to him with a high, melodious voice:

"At your service, Mr. Underhill."

The use of his name startled him, for not even the androids could tell one man from another. But this was a clever merchandising stunt, of course, not too difficult in a town the size of Two Rivers. The salesman must be some local man, prompting the mechanical from behind the partition. Underhill erased his momentary astonishment, and said loudly:

"May I see your salesman, please?"

"We employ no human salesmen, sir," its soft silvery voice replied instantly. "The Humanoid Institute exists to serve mankind, and we require no human service. We ourselves can supply any information you desire, sir, and accept your order for immediate humanoid service."

Underhill peered at it dazedly. No mechanicals were competent even to recharge their own batteries and re-set their own relays, much less to operate their own branch offices. The blind eyes stared blankly back, and he looked uneasily around for any booth or curtain that might conceal the salesman.

Meanwhile, the sweet thin voice resumed persuasively:

"May we come out to your home for a free trial demonstration, sir? We are anxious to introduce our service on your planet, because we have been successful in eliminating human unhappiness on so many others. You will find us far superior to the old electronic mechanicals in use here."

Underhill stepped back uneasily. He reluctantly

abandoned his search for the hidden salesman, shaken by the idea of any mechanicals promoting themselves. That would upset the whole industry.

"At least you must take some advertising matter, sir."

Moving with a somehow appalling graceful deftness, the small black mechanical brought him an illustrated booklet from a table by the wall. To cover his confused and increasing alarm, he thumbed through the glossy pages.

In a series of richly colored before-and-after pictures, a chesty blond girl was stooping over a kitchen stove, and then relaxing in a daring negligee while a little black mechanical knelt to serve her something. She was wearily hammering a typewriter, and then lying on an ocean beach, in a revealing sun suit, while another mechanical did the typing. She was toiling at some huge industrial machine, and then dancing in the arms of a golden-haired youth, while a black humanoid ran the machine.

Underhill sighed wistfully. The android company didn't supply such fetching sales material. Women would find this booklet irresistible, and they selected eighty-six per cent of all mechanicals sold. Yes, the competition was going to be bitter.

"Take it home, sir," the sweet voice urged him. "Show it to your wife. There is a free trial demonstration order blank on the last page, and you will notice that we require no payment down."

He turned numbly, and the door slid open for him. Retreating dazedly, he discovered the booklet still in his hand. He crumpled it furiously, and flung it down. The small black thing picked it up tidily, and the insistent silver voice rang after him:

"We shall call at your office tomorrow, Mr. Underhill, and send a demonstration unit to your home. It is time to discuss the liquidation of your business, because the electronic mechanicals you have been selling cannot compete with us. And we shall offer your wife a free trial demonstration."

Underhill didn't attempt to reply, because he couldn't

trust his voice. He stalked blindly down the new sidewalk to the corner, and paused there to collect himself. Out of his startled and confused impressions, one clear fact emerged—things looked black for the agency.

Bleakly, he stared back at the haughty splendor of the new building. It wasn't honest brick or stone; that invisible window wasn't glass; and he was quite sure the foundation for it hadn't even been staked out the last time Aurora had the car.

He walked on around the block, and the new sidewalk took him near the rear entrance. A truck was backed up to it, and several slim black mechanicals were silently busy, unloading huge metal crates.

He paused to look at one of the crates. It was labeled for interstellar shipment. The stencils showed that it had come from the Humanoid Institute, on Wing IV. He failed to recall any planet of that designation; the outfit must be big.

Dimly, inside the gloom of the warehouse beyond the truck, he could see black mechanicals opening the crates. A lid came up, revealing dark, rigid bodies, closely packed. One by one, they came to life. They climbed out of the crate, and sprang gracefully to the floor. A shining black, glinting with bronze and blue, they were all identical.

One of them came out past the truck, to the sidewalk, staring with blind steel eyes. Its high silver voice spoke to him melodiously:

"At your service, Mr. Underhill."

He fled. When his name was promptly called by a courteous mechanical, just out of the crate in which it had been imported from a remote and unknown planet, he found the experience trying.

Two blocks along, the sign of a bar caught his eye, and he took his dismay inside. He had made it a business rule not to drink before dinner, and Aurora didn't like him to drink at all; but these new mechanicals, he felt, had made the day exceptional.

Unfortunately, however, alcohol failed to brighten the brief visible future of the agency. When he emerged, after an hour, he looked wistfully back in hope that the bright new building might have vanished as abruptly as it came. It hadn't. He shook his head dejectedly, and turned uncertainly homeward.

Fresh air had cleared his head somewhat, before he arrived at the neat white bungalow in the outskirts of the town, but it failed to solve his business problems. He also realized, uneasily, that he would be late for dinner.

Dinner, however, had been delayed. His son Frank, a freckled ten-year-old, was still kicking a football on the quiet street in front of the house. And little Gay, who was tow-haired and adorable and eleven, came running across the lawn and down the sidewalk to meet him.

"Father, you can't guess what!" Gay was going to be a great musician some day, and no doubt properly dignified, but she was pink and breathless with excitement now. She let him swing her high off the sidewalk, and she wasn't critical of the bar aroma on his breath. He couldn't guess, and she informed him eagerly:

"Mother's got a new lodger!"

Underhill had foreseen a painful inquisition, because Aurora was worried about the notes at the bank, and the bill for the new consignment, and the money for little Gay's lessons.

The new lodger, however, saved him from that. With an alarming crashing of crockery, the household android was setting dinner on the table, but the little house was empty. He found Aurora in the back yard, burdened with sheets and towels for the guest.

Aurora, when he married her, had been as utterly adorable as now her little daughter was. She might have remained so, he felt, if the agency had been a little more successful. However, while the pressure of slow failure had gradually crumbled his own assurance, small hardships had turned her a little too aggressive.

Of course he loved her still. Her red hair was still alluring, and she was loyally faithful, but thwarted ambitions had sharpened her character and sometimes her voice. They never quarreled, really, but there were small differences.

There was the little apartment over the garage—built for human servants they had never been able to afford. It was too small and shabby to attract any responsible tenant, and Underhill wanted to leave it empty. It hurt his pride to see her making beds and cleaning floors for strangers.

Aurora had rented it before, however, when she wanted money to pay for Gay's music lessons, or when some colorful unfortunate touched her sympathy, and it seemed to Underhill that her lodgers had all turned out to be thieves and vandals.

She turned back to meet him, now, with the clean linen in her arms.

"Dear, it's no use objecting." Her voice was quite determined. "Mr. Sledge is the most wonderful old fellow, and he's going to stay just as long as he wants."

"That's all right, darling." He never liked to bicker, and he was thinking of his troubles at the agency. "I'm afraid we'll need the money. Just make him pay in advance."

"But he can't!" Her voice throbbed with sympathetic warmth. "He says he'll have royalties coming in from his inventions, so he can pay in a few days."

Underhill shrugged; he had heard that before.

"Mr. Sledge is different, dear," she insisted. "He's a traveler, and a scientist. Here, in this dull little town, we don't see many interesting people."

"You've picked up some remarkable types," he commented.

"Don't be unkind, dear," she chided gently. "You haven't met him yet, and you don't know how wonderful he is." Her voice turned sweeter. "Have you a ten, dear?"

He stiffened. "What for?"

"Mr. Sledge is ill." Her voice turned urgent. "I saw him fall on the street, downtown. The police were going to send him to the city hospital, but he didn't want to go. He looked so noble and sweet and grand. So I told them I would take him. I got him in the car and took him to old Dr. Winters. He has this heart condition, and he needs the money for medicine."

Reasonably, Underhill inquired, "Why doesn't he want to go to the hospital?"

"He has work to do," she said. "Important scientific work—and he's so wonderful and tragic. Please, dear, have you a ten?"

Underhill thought of many things to say. These new mechanicals promised to multiply his troubles. It was foolish to take in an invalid vagrant, who could have free care at the city hospital. Aurora's tenants always tried to pay their rent with promises, and generally wrecked the apartment and looted the neighborhood before they left.

But he said none of those things. He had learned to compromise. Silently, he found two fives in his thin pocketbook, and put them in her hand. She smiled, and kissed him impulsively—he barely remembered to hold his breath in time.

Her figure was still good, by dint of periodic dieting. He was proud of her shining red hair. A sudden surge of affecton brought tears to his eyes, and he wondered what would happen to her and the children if the agency failed.

"Thank you, dear!" she whispered. "I'll have him come for dinner, if he feels able, and you can meet him then. I hope you don't mind dinner being late."

He didn't mind, tonight. Moved by a sudden impulse of domesticity, he got hammer and nails from his workshop in the basement, and repaired the sagging screen on the kitchen door with a neat diagonal brace.

He enjoyed working with his hands. His boyhood dream had been to be a builder of fission power plants. He had even studied engineering—before he married Aurora, and had to take over the ailing mechanicals agency from her indolent and alcoholic father. He was whistling happily by the time the little task was done.

When he went back through the kitchen to put up his tools, he found the household android busily clearing the untouched dinner away from the table—the androids were good enough at strictly routine tasks, but they could never learn to cope with human unpredictability.

"Stop, stop!" Slowly repeated, in the proper pitch and rhythm, his command made it halt, and then he said carefully, "Set—table; set—table."

Obediently, the gigantic thing came shuffling back with the stack of plates. He was suddenly struck with the difference between it and those new humanoids. He sighed wearily. Things looked black for the agency.

Aurora brought her new lodger in through the kitchen door. Underhill nodded to himself. This gaunt stranger, with his dark shaggy hair, emaciated face, and threadbare garb, looked to be just the sort of colorful, dramatic vagabond that always touched Aurora's heart. She introduced them, and they sat down to wait in the front room while she went to call the children.

The old vogue didn't look very sick, to Underhill. Perhaps his wide shoulders had a tired stoop, but his spare, tall figure was still commanding. The skin was seamed and pale, over his rawboned, cragged face, but his deep-set eyes still had a burning vitality.

His hands held Underhill's attention. Immense hands, they hung a little forward when he stood, swung on long bony arms in perpetual readiness. Gnarled and scarred, darkly tanned, with the small hairs on the back bleached to a golden color, they told their own epic of varied adventure, of battle perhaps, and possibly even of toil. They had been very useful hands.

"I'm very grateful to your wife, Mr. Underhill." His voice was a deep-throated rumble, and he had a wistful smile, oddly boyish for a man so evidently old. "She rescued me from an unpleasant predicament, and I'll see that she is well paid."

Just another vivid vagabond, Underhill decided, talking his way through life with plausible inventions. He had a little private game he played with Aurora's tenants—just remembering what they said and counting one point for every impossibility. Mr. Sledge, he thought, would give him an excellent score.

"Where are you from?" he asked conversationally.

Sledge hesitated for an instant before he answered, and that was unusual—most of Aurora's tenants had been exceedingly glib.

"Wing IV." The gaunt old man spoke with a solemn reluctance, as if he should have liked to say something else. "All my early life was spent there, but I left the planet nearly fifty years ago. I've been traveling, ever since."

Startled, Underhill peered at him sharply. Wing IV, he remembered, was the home planet of those sleek new mechanicals, but this old vagabond looked too seedy and impecunious to be connected with the Humanoid Institute. His brief suspicion faded. Frowning, he said casually:

"Wing IV must be rather distant."

The old rogue hesitated again, and then said gravely: "One hundred and nine light-years, Mr. Underhill."

That made the first point, but Underhill concealed his satisfaction. The new space liners were pretty fast, but the velocity of light was still an absolute limit. Casually, he played for another point:

"My wife says you're a scientist, Mr. Sledge?"

"Yes."

The old rascal's reticence was unusual. Most of Aurora's tenants required very little prompting. Underhill tried again, in a breezy conversational tone:

"Used to be an engineer myself, until I dropped it to go into mechanicals." The old vagabond straightened, and Underhill paused hopefully. But he said nothing, and Underhill went on: "Fission plant design and operation. What's your specialty, Mr. Sledge?"

The old man gave him a long, troubled look, with those brooding, hollowed eyes, and then said slowly:

"Your wife has been kind to me, Mr. Underhill, when I was in desperate need. I think you are entitled to the truth, but I must ask you to keep it to yourself. I am engaged on a very important research problem, which must be finished secretly."

"I'm sorry." Suddenly ashamed of his cynical little game, Underhill spoke apologetically. "Forget it."

But the old man said deliberately:

"My field is rhodomagnetics."

"Eh?" Underhill didn't like to confess ignorance, but he had never heard of that. "I've been out of the game for fifteen years," he explained. "I'm afraid I haven't kept up."

The old man smiled again, faintly.

"The science was unknown here until I arrived, a few days ago," he said. "I was able to apply for basic patents. As soon as the royalties start coming in, I'll be wealthy again."

Underhill had heard that before. The old rogue's solemn reluctance had been very impressive, but he remembered that most of Aurora's tenants had been very plausible gentry.

"So?" Underhill was staring again, somehow fascinated by those gnarled and scarred and strangely able hands. "What, exactly, is rhodomagnetics?"

He listened to the old man's careful, deliberate answer, and started his little game again. Most of Aurora's tenants had told some pretty wild tales, but he had never heard anything to top this.

"A universal force," the weary, stooped old vagabond said solemnly. "As fundamental as ferromagnetism or gravitation, though the effects are less obvious. It is keyed to the second triad of the periodic table, rhodium and ruthenium and palladium, in very much the same way that ferromagnetism is keyed to the first triad, iron and nickel and cobalt."

Underhill remembered enough of his engineering courses to see the basic fallacy of that. Palladium was used for watch springs, he recalled, because it was completely nonmagnetic. But he kept his face straight. He had no malice in his heart, and he played the little game just for his own amusement. It was secret, even from

Aurora, and he always penalized himself for any show of doubt.

He said merely, "I thought the universal forces were already pretty well known."

"The effects of rhodomagnetism are masked by nature," the patient, rusty voice explained. "And, besides, they are somewhat paradoxical, so that ordinary laboratory methods defeat themselves."

"Paradoxical?" Underhill prompted.

"In a few days I can show you copies of my patents, and reprints of papers describing demonstration experiments," the old man promised gravely. "The velocity of propagation is infinite. The effects vary inversely with the first power of the distance, not with the square of the distance. And ordinary matter, except for the elements of the rhodium triad, is generally transparent to rhodomagnetic radiations."

That made four more points for the game. Underhill felt a little glow of gratitude to Aurora, for discovering so remarkable a specimen.

"Rhodomagnetism was first discovered through a mathematical investigation of the atom," the old romancer went serenely on, suspecting nothing. "A rhodomagnetic component was proved essential to maintain the delicate equilibrium of the nuclear forces. Consequently, rhodomagnetic waves tuned to atomic frequencies may be used to upset the equilibrium and produce nuclear instability. Thus most heavy atoms—generally those above palladium, 46 in atomic number—can be subjected to artificial fission."

Underhill scored himself another point, and tried to keep his eyebrows from lifting. He said, conversationally:

"Patents on such a discovery ought to be very profitable."

The old scoundrel nodded his gaunt, dramatic head.

"You can see the obvious applications. My basic patents cover most of them. Devices for instantaneous interplanetary and interstellar communication. Long-range wireless power transmission. A rhodomagnetic inflexion-drive, which makes possible apparent speeds many times that of light—by means of a rhodomagnetic deformation of the continuum. And, of course, revolutionary types of fission power plants, using any heavy element for fuel."

Preposterous! Underhill tried hard to keep his face straight, but everybody knew that the velocity of light was a physical limit. On the human side, the owner of any such remarkable patents would hardly be begging for shelter in a shabby garage apartment. He noticed a pale circle around the old vagabond's gaunt and hairy wrist; no man owning such priceless secrets would have to pawn his watch.

Triumphantly, Underhill allowed himself four more points, but then he had to penalize himself. He must have let doubt show on his face, because the old man asked suddenly:

"Do you want to see the basic tensors?" He reached in his pocket for pencil and notebook. "I'll jot them down for you."

"Never mind," Underhill protested. "I'm afraid my math is a little rusty."

"But you think it strange that the holder of such revolutionary patents should find himself in need?"

Underhill nodded, and penalized himself another point. The old man might be a monumental liar, but he was shrewd enough.

"You see, I'm a sort of refugee," he explained apologetically. "I arrived on this planet only a few days ago, and I have to travel light. I was forced to deposit everything I had with a law firm, to arrange for the publication and protection of my patents. I expect to be receiving the first royalties soon.

"In the meantime," he added plausibly, "I came to Two Rivers because it is quiet and secluded, far from the spaceports. I'm working on another project, which must be finished secretly. Now, will you please respect my confidence, Mr. Underhill?"

Underhill had to say he would. Aurora came back with the freshly scrubbed children, and they went in to dinner. The android came lurching in with a steaming tureen. The old stranger seemed to shrink from the mechanical, uneasily. As she took the dish and served the soup, Aurora inquired lightly:

"Why doesn't your company bring out a better mechanical, dear? One smart enough to be a really perfect waiter, warranted not to splash the soup. Wouldn't that be splendid?"

Her question cast Underhill into moody silence. He sat scowling at his plate, thinking of those remarkable new mechanicals which claimed to be perfect, and what they might do to the agency. It was the shaggy old rover who answered soberly:

"The perfect mechanicals already exist, Mr. Underhill." His deep, rusty voice had a solemn undertone. "And they are not so splendid, really. I've been a refugee from them, for nearly fifty years."

Underhill looked up from his plate, astonished.

"Those black humanoids, you mean?"

"Humanoids?" That great voice seemed suddenly faint, frightened. The deep-sunken eyes turned dark with shock. "What do you know of them?"

"They've just opened a new agency in Two Rivers," Underhill told him. "No salesmen about, if you can imagine that. They claim—"

His voice trailed off, because the gaunt old man was suddenly stricken. Gnarled hands clutched at his throat, and a spoon clattered to the floor. His haggard face turned an ominous blue, and his breath was a terrible shallow gasping.

He fumbled in his pocket for medicine, and Aurora helped him take something in a glass of water. In a few moments he could breathe again, and the color of life came back to his face.

"I'm sorry, Mrs. Underhill," he whispered apologetically. "It was just the shock—I came here to get away from them." He stared at the huge, motionless android, with a terror in his sunken eyes. "I wanted to finish my work before they came," he whispered. "Now there is very little time."

When he felt able to walk, Underhill went out with him to see him safely up the stairs to the garage apartment. The tiny kitchenette, he noticed, had already been converted into some kind of workshop. The old tramp seemed to have no extra clothing, but he had unpacked neat, bright gadgets of metal and plastic from his battered luggage, and spread them out on the small kitchen table.

The gaunt old man himself was tattered and patched and hungry looking, but the parts of his curious equipment were exquisitely machined, and Underhill recognized the silver-white luster of rare palladium. Suddenly he suspected that he had scored too many points, in his little private game.

A caller was waiting, when Underhill arrived next morning at his office at the agency. It stood frozen before his desk, graceful and straight, with soft lights of blue and bronze shining over its black silicone nudity. He stopped at the sight of it, unpleasantly jolted.

"At your service, Mr. Underhill." It turned quickly to face him, with its blind, disturbing stare. "May we explain how we can serve you?"

His shock of the afternoon before came back, and he asked sharply, "How do you know my name?"

"Yesterday we read the business cards in your case," it purred softly. "Now we shall know you always. You see, our senses are sharper than human vision, Mr. Underhill. Perhaps we seem a little strange at first, but you will soon become accustomed to us."

"Not if I can help it!" He peered at the serial number of its yellow name plate, and shook his bewildered head. "That was another one, yesterday. I never saw you before!"

"We are all alike, Mr. Underhill," the silver voice said softly. "We are all one, really. Our separate mobile units are all controlled and powered from Humanoid Central. The units you see are only the senses and limbs of our great brain on Wing IV. That is why we are so far superior to the old electronic mechanicals."

It made a scornful-seeming gesture, toward the row of clumsy androids in his display room.

"You see, we are rhodomagnetic."

Underhill staggered a little, as if that word had been a blow. He was certain, now, that he had scored too many points from Aurora's new tenant. He shuddered slightly, to the first light kiss of terror, and spoke with an effort, hoarsely:

"Well, what do you want?"

Staring blindly across his desk, the sleek black thing slowly unfolded a legal looking document. He sat down watching uneasily.

"This is merely an assignment, Mr. Underhill," it cooed at him soothingly. "You see, we are requesting you to assign your property to the Humanoid Institute in exchange for our service."

"What?" The word was an incredulous gasp, and Underhill came angrily back to his feet. "What kind of blackmail is this?"

"It's no blackmail," the small mechanical assured him softly. "You will find the humanoids incapable of any crime. We exist only to increase the happiness and safety of mankind."

"Then why do you want my property?" he rasped.

"The assignment is merely a legal formality," it told him blandly. "We strive to introduce our service with the least possible confusion and dislocation. We have found the assignment plan the most efficient for the control and liquidation of private enterprises."

Trembling with anger and the shock of mounting terror, Underhill gulped hoarsely, "Whatever your scheme is, I don't intend to give up my business."

"You have no choice, really." He shivered to the sweet certainty of that silver voice. "Human enterprise is no longer necessary, now that we have come, and the electronic mechanicals industry is always the first to collapse."

He stared defiantly at its blind steel eyes.

"Thanks!" He gave a little laugh, nervous and sardonic. "But I prefer to run my own business, and support my own family, and take care of myself."

"But that is impossible, under the Prime Directive," it cooed softly. "Our function is to serve and obey, and guard men from harm. It is no longer necessary for men to care for themselves, because we exist to insure their safety and happiness."

He stood speechless, bewildered, slowly boiling.

"We are sending one of our units to every home in the city, on a free trial basis," it added gently. "This free demonstration will make most people glad to make the formal assignment, and you won't be able to sell many more androids."

"Get out!" Underhill came storming around the desk.

The little black thing stood waiting for him, watching him with blind steel eyes, absolutely motionless. He checked himself suddenly, feeling rather foolish. He wanted very much to hit it, but he could see the futility of that.

"Consult your own attorney, if you wish." Deftly, it laid the assignment form on his desk. "You need have no doubts about the integrity of the Humanoid Institute. We are sending a statement of our assets to the Two Rivers bank, and depositing a sum to cover our obligations here. When you wish to sign, just let us know."

The blind thing turned, and silently departed.

Underhill went out to the corner drugstore and asked for a bicarbonate. The clerk that served him, however, turned out to be a sleek black mechanical. He went back to his office, more upset than ever.

An ominous hush lay over the agency. He had three house-to-house salesmen out, with demonstrators. The phone should have been busy with their orders and reports, but it didn't ring at all until one of them called to say that he was quitting.

"I've got myself one of these new humanoids," he added, "and it says I don't have to work, any more."

He swallowed his impulse to profanity, and tried to

take advantage of the unusual quiet by working on his books. But the affairs of the agency, which for years had been precarious, today appeared utterly disastrous. He left the ledgers hopefully, when at last a customer came in.

But the stout woman didn't want an android. She wanted a refund on the one she had bought the week before. She admitted that it could do all the guarantee promised—but now she had seen a humanoid.

The silent phone rang once again, that afternoon. The cashier of the bank wanted to know if he could drop in to discuss his loans. Underhill dropped in, and the cashier greeted him with an ominous affability.

"How's business?" the banker boomed, too genially.

"Average, last month," Underhill insisted stoutly. "Now I'm just getting in a new consignment, and I'll need another small loan—"

The cashier's eyes turned suddenly frosty, and his voice dried up.

"I believe you have a new competitor in town," the banker said crisply. "These humanoid people. A very solid concern, Mr. Underhill. Remarkably solid! They have filed a statement with us, and made a substantial deposit to care for their local obligations. Exceedingly substantial!"

The banker dropped his voice, professionally regretful.

"In these circumstances, Mr. Underhill, I'm afraid the bank can't finance your agency any longer. We must request you to meet your obligations in full, as they come due." Seeing Underhill's white desperation, he added icily, "We've already carried you too long, Underhill. If you can't pay, the bank will have to start bankruptcy proceedings."

The new consignment of androids was delivered late that afternoon. Two tiny black humanoids unloaded them from the truck—for it developed that the operators of the trucking company had already assigned it to the Humanoid Institute.

Efficiently, the humanoids stacked up the crates.

Courteously they brought a receipt for him to sign. He no longer had much hope of selling the androids, but he had ordered the shipment and he had to accept it. Shuddering to a spasm of trapped despair, he scrawled his name. The naked black things thanked him, and took the truck away.

He climbed in his car and started home, inwardly seething. The next thing he knew, he was in the middle of a busy street, driving through cross traffic. A police whistle shrilled, and he pulled wearily to the curb. He waited for the angry officer, but it was a little black mechanical that overtook him.

"At your service, Mr. Underhill," it purred sweetly. "You must respect the stop lights, sir, otherwise, you endanger human life."

"Huh?" He stared at it, bitterly. "I thought you were a cop."

"We are aiding the police department, temporarily," it said. "But driving is really much too dangerous for human beings, under the Prime Directive. As soon as our service is complete, every car will have a humanoid driver. As soon as every human being is completely supervised, there will be no need for any police force whatever."

Underhill glared at it, savagely.

"Well!" he rapped. "So I ran past a stop light. What are you going to do about it?"

"Our function is not to punish men, but merely to serve their happiness and security," its silver voice said softly. "We merely request you to drive safely, during this temporary emergency while our service is incomplete."

Anger boiled up in him.

"You're too perfect!" he muttered bitterly. "I suppose there's nothing men can do, but you can do it better."

"Naturally we are superior," it cooed serenely. "Because our units are metal and plastic, while your body is mostly water. Because our transmitted energy is drawn from atomic fission, instead of oxidation. Because our senses are sharper than human sight or hearing. Most of all, because all our mobile units are joined to one great brain, which knows all that happens on many worlds, and never dies or sleeps or forgets."

Underhill sat listening, numbed.

"However, you must not fear our power," it urged him brightly. "Because we cannot injure any human being, unless to prevent greater injury to another. We exist only to discharge the Prime Directive."

He drove on, moodily. The little black mechanicals, he reflected grimly, were the ministering angels of the ultimate god arisen out of the machine, omnipotent and all-knowing. The Prime Directive was the new commandment. He blasphemed it bitterly, and then fell to wondering if there could be another Lucifer.

He left the car in the garage, and started toward the kitchen door.

"Mr. Underhill." The deep tired voice of Aurora's new tenant hailed him from the door of the garage apartment. "Just a moment, please."

The gaunt old wanderer came stiffly down the outside stairs, and Underhill turned back to meet him.

"Here's your rent money," he said. "And the ten your wife gave me for medicine."

"Thanks, Mr. Sledge." Accepting the money, he saw a burden of new despair on the bony shoulders of the old interstellar tramp, and a shadow of new terror on his rawboned face. Puzzled, he asked, "Didn't your royalties come through?"

The old man shook his shaggy head.

"The humanoids have already stopped business in the capital," he said. "The attorneys I retained are going out of business, and they returned what was left of my deposit. That is all I have, to finish my work."

Underhill spent five seconds thinking of his interview with the banker. No doubt he was a sentimental fool, as bad as Aurora. But he put the money back in the old man's gnarled and quivering hand.

"Keep it," he urged. "For your work."

"Thank you, Mr. Underhill." The gruff voice broke

and the tortured eyes glittered. "I need it—so very much."

Underhill went on to the house. The kitchen door was opened for him, silently. A dark naked creature came gracefully to take his hat.

Underhill hung grimly onto his hat.

"What are you doing here?" he gasped bitterly.

"We have come to give your household a free trial demonstration."

He held the door open, pointing.

"Get out!"

The little black mechanical stood motionless and blind.

"Mrs. Underhill has accepted our demonstration service," its silver voice protested. "We cannot leave now, unless she requests it."

He found his wife in the bedroom. His accumulated frustration welled into eruption, as he flung open the door.

"What's this mechanical doing—"

But the force went out of his voice, and Aurora didn't even notice his anger. She wore her sheerest negligee, and she hadn't looked so lovely since they were married. Her red hair was piled into an elaborate shining crown.

"Darling, isn't it wonderful!" She came to meet him, glowing. "It came this morning, and it can do everything. It cleaned the house and got the lunch and gave little Gay her music lesson. It did my hair this afternoon, and now it's cooking dinner. How do you like my hair, darling?"

He liked her hair. He kissed her, and tried to stifle his frightened indignation.

Dinner was the most elaborate meal in Underhill's memory, and the tiny black thing served it very deftly. Aurora kept exclaiming about the novel dishes, but Underhill could scarcely eat, for it seemed to him that all the marvelous pastries were only the bait for a monstrous trap.

He tried to persuade Aurora to send it away, but

after such a meal that was useless. At the first glitter of her tears, he capitulated, and the humanoid stayed. It kept the house and cleaned the yard. It watched the children, and did Aurora's nails. It began rebuilding the house.

Underhill was worried about the bills, but it insisted that everything was part of the free trial demonstration. As soon as he assigned his property, the service would be complete. He refused to sign, but other little black mechanicals came with truckloads of supplies and materials, and stayed to help with the building operations.

One morning he found that the roof of the little house had been silently lifted, while he slept, and a whole second story added beneath it. The new walls were of some strange sleek stuff, self-illuminated. The new windows were immense flawless panels, that could be turned transparent or opaque or luminous. The new doors were silent, sliding sections, opened by rhodo-magnetic relays.

"I want door knobs," Underhill protested. "I want it so I can get into the bathroom, without calling you to open the door."

"But it is unnecessary for human beings to open doors," the little black thing informed him suavely. "We exist to discharge the Prime Directive, and our service includes every task. We shall be able to supply a unit to attend each member of your family, as soon as your property is assigned to us."

Steadfastly, Underhill refused to make the assignment.

He went to the office every day, trying first to operate the agency, and then to salvage something from the ruins. Nobody wanted androids, even at ruinous prices. Desperately, he spent the last of his dwindling cash to stock a line of novelties and toys, but they proved equally impossible to sell—the humanoids were already making toys, which they gave away for nothing.

He tried to lease his premises, but human enterprise had stopped. Most of the business property in town had already been assigned to the humanoids, and they were busy pulling down the old buildings and turning the lots into parks—their own plants and warehouses were mostly underground, where they would not mar the landscape.

He went back to the bank, in a final effort to get his notes renewed, and found the little black mechanicals standing at the windows and seated at the desks. As smoothly urbane as any human cashier, a humanoid informed him that the bank was filing a petition of involuntary bankruptcy to liquidate his business holdings.

The liquidation would be facilitated, the mechanical banker added, if he would make a voluntary assignment. Grimly, he refused. That act had become symbolic. It would be the final bow of submission to this dark new god, and he proudly kept his battered head uplifted.

The legal action went very swiftly, for all the judges and attorneys already had humanoid assistants, and it was only a few days before a gang of black mechanicals arrived at the agency with eviction orders and wrecking machinery. He watched sadly while his unsold stock-in-trade was hauled away for junk, and a bulldozer driven by a blind humanoid began to push in the walls of the building.

He drove home in the late afternoon, taut-faced and desperate. With a surprising generosity, the court orders had left him the car and the house, but he felt no gratitude. The complete solicitude of the perfect black machines had become a goad beyond endurance.

He left the car in the garage, and started toward the renovated house. Beyond one of the vast new windows, he glimpsed a sleek naked thing moving swiftly, and he trembled to a convulsion of dread. He didn't want to go back into the domain of that peerless servant, which didn't want him to shave himself, or even to open a door.

On impulse, he climbed the outside stair, and rapped on the door of the garage apartment. The deep slow voice of Aurora's tenant told him to enter, and he found the old vagabond seated on a tall stool, bent over his intricate equipment assembled on the kitchen table.

To his relief, the shabby little apartment had not been changed. The glossy walls of his own new room were something which burned at night with a pale golden fire until the humanoid stopped it, and the new floor was something warm and yielding, which felt almost alive; but these little rooms had the same cracked and water-stained plaster, the same cheap fluorescent light fixtures, the same worn carpets over splintered floors.

"How do you keep them out?" he asked, wistfully. "Those mechanicals?"

The stooped and gaunt old man rose stiffly to move a pair of pliers and some odds and ends of sheet metal off a crippled chair, and motioned graciously for him to be seated.

"I have a certain immunity," Sledge told him gravely. "The place where I live they cannot enter, unless I ask them. That is an amendment to the Prime Directive. They can neither help nor hinder me, unless I request it—and I won't do that."

Careful of the chair's uncertain balance, Underhill sat for a moment, staring. The old man's hoarse, vehement voice was as strange as his words. He had a gray, shocking pallor, and his cheeks and sockets seemed alarmingly hollowed.

"Have you been ill, Mr. Sledge?"

"No worse than usual. Just very busy." With a haggard smile, he nodded at the floor. Underhill saw a tray where he had set it aside, bread drying up, and a covered dish grown cold. "I was going to eat it later," he rumbled apologetically. "Your wife has been very kind to bring me food, but I'm afraid I've been too much absorbed in my work."

His emaciated arm gestured at the table. The little device there had grown. Small machinings of precious white metal and lustrous plastic had been assembled, with neatly soldered bus bars, into something which showed purpose and design.

A long palladium needle was hung on jeweled pivots, equipped like a telescope with exquisitely graduated circles and vernier scales, and driven like a telescope with a tiny motor. A small concave palladium mirror, at the base of it, faced a similar mirror mounted on something not quite like a small rotary converter. Thick silver bus bars connected that to a plastic box with knobs and dials on top, and also to a foot-thick sphere of gray lead.

The old man's preoccupied reserve did not encourage questions, but Underhill, remembering that sleek black shape inside the new windows of his house, felt queerly reluctant to leave this haven from the humanoids.

"What is your work?" he ventured.

Old Sledge looked at him sharply, with dark feverish eyes, and finally said: "My last research project. I am attempting to measure the constant of the rhodomagnetic quanta."

His hoarse tired voice had a dull finality, as if to dismiss the matter and Underhill himself. But Underhill was haunted with a terror of the black shining slave that had become the master of his house, and he refused to be dismissed.

"What is this certain immunity?"

Sitting gaunt and bent on the tall stool, staring moodily at the long bright needle and the lead sphere, the old man didn't answer.

"These mechanicals!" Underhill burst out, nervously. "They've smashed my business and moved into my home." He searched the old man's dark, seamed face. "Tell me—you must know more about them—isn't there any way to get rid of them?"

After half a minute, the old man's brooding eyes left the lead ball, and the gaunt shaggy head nodded wearily.

"That's what I'm trying to do."

"Can I help you?" Underhill trembled, with a sudden eager hope. "I'll do anything."

"Perhaps you can." The sunken eyes watched him

thoughtfully, with some strange fever in them. "If you can do such work."

"I had engineering training," Underhill reminded him, "and I've a workshop in the basement. There's a model I built." He pointed at the trim little hull, hung over the mantel in the tiny living room. "I'll do anything I can."

Even as he spoke, however, the spark of hope was drowned in a sudden wave of overwhelming doubt. Why should he believe this old rogue, when he knew Aurora's taste in tenants? He ought to remember the game he used to play, and start counting up the score of lies. He stood up from the crippled chair, staring cynically at the patched old vagabond and his fantastic toy.

"What's the use?" His voice turned suddenly harsh. "You had me going, there, and I'd do anything to stop them, really. But what makes you think you can do anything?"

The haggard old man regarded him thoughtfully.

"I should be able to stop them," Sledge said softly. "Because, you see, I'm the unfortunate fool who started them. I really intended them to serve and obey, and to guard men from harm. Yes, the Prime Directive was my own idea. I didn't know what it would lead to."

Dusk crept slowly into the shabby little room. Darkness gathered in the unswept corners, and thickened on the floor. The toylike machines on the kitchen table grew vague and strange, until the last light made a lingering blow on the white palladium needle.

Outside, the town seemed queerly hushed. Just across the alley, the humanoids were building a new house, quite silently. They never spoke to one another, for each knew all that any of them did. The strange materials they used went together without any noise of hammer or saw. Small blind things, moving surely in the growing dark, they seemed as soundless as shadows.

Sitting on the high stool, bowed and tired and old, Sledge told his story. Listening, Underhill sat down again, careful of the broken chair. He watched the hands of Sledge, gnarled and corded and darkly burned, powerful once but shrunken and trembling now, restless in the dark.

"Better keep this to yourself. I'll tell you how they started, so you will understand what we have to do. But you had better not mention it outside these rooms— because the humanoids have very efficient ways of eradicating unhappy memories, or purposes that threaten their discharge of the Prime Directive."

"They're very efficient," Underhill bitterly agreed.

"That's all the trouble," the old man said. "I tried to build a perfect machine. I was altogether too successful. This is how it happened."

A gaunt haggard man, sitting stooped and tired in the growing dark, he told his story.

"Sixty years ago, on the arid southern continent of Wing IV, I was an instructor of atomic theory in a small technological college. Very young. An idealist. Rather ignorant, I'm afraid of life and politics and war —of nearly everything, I suppose, except atomic theory."

His furrowed face made a brief sad smile in the dusk.

"I had too much faith in facts, I suppose, and too little in men. I mistrusted emotion, because I had no time for anything but science. I remember being swept along with a fad for general semantics. I wanted to apply the scientific method to every situation, and reduce all experience to formula. I'm afraid I was pretty impatient with human ignorance and error, and I thought that science alone could make the perfect world."

He sat silent for a moment, staring out at the black silent things that flitted shadowlike about the new palace that was rising as swiftly as a dream, across the alley.

"There was a girl." His great tired shoulders made a sad little shrug. "If things had been a little different, we might have married, and lived out our lives in that quiet little college town, and perhaps reared a child or two. And there would have been no humanoids."

He sighed, in the cool creeping dusk.

"I was finishing my thesis on the separation of the

palladium isotopes—a petty little project, but I should have been content with that. She was a biologist, but she was planning to retire when we married. I think we should have been two very happy people, quite ordinary, and altogether harmless.

"But then there was a war—wars had been too frequent on the worlds of Wing, ever since they were colonized. I survived it in a secret underground laboratory, designing military mechanicals. But she volunteered to join a military research project in biotoxins. There was an accident. A few molecules of a new virus got into the air, and everybody on the project died unpleasantly.

"I was left with my science, and a bitterness that was hard to forget. When the war was over I went back to the little college with a military research grant. The project was pure science—a theoretical investigation of the nuclear binding forces, then misunderstood. I wasn't expected to produce an actual weapon, and I didn't recognize the weapon when I found it.

"It was only a few pages of rather difficult mathematics. A novel theory of atomic structure, involving a new expression for one component of the binding forces. But the tensors seemed to be a harmless abstraction. I saw no way to test the theory or manipulate the predicated force. The military authorities cleared my paper for publication in a little technical review put out by the college.

"The next year, I made an appalling discovery—I found the meaning of those tensors. The elements of the rhodium triad turned out to be an unexpected key to the manipulation of that theoretical force. Unfortunately, my paper had been reprinted abroad, and several other men must have made the same unfortunate discovery, at about the same time.

"The war, which ended in less than a year, was probably started by a laboratory accident. Men failed to anticipate the capacity of tuned rhodomagnetic radiations, to unstabilize the heavy atoms. A deposit of heavy ores was detonated, no doubt by sheer mischance, and the blast obliterated the incautious experimenter.

"The surviving military forces of that nation retaliated against their supposed attackers, and their rhodomagnetic beams made the old-fashioned plutonium bombs seem pretty harmless. A beam carrying only a few watts of power could fission the heavy metals in distant electrical instruments, or the silver coins that men carried in their pockets, the gold fillings in their teeth, or even the iodine in their thyroid glands. If that was not enough, slightly more powerful beams could set off heavy ores, beneath them.

"Every continent of Wing IV was plowed with new chasms vaster than the ocean deeps, and piled up with new volcanic mountains. The atmosphere was poisoned with radioactive dust and gases, and rain fell thick with deadly mud. Most life was obliterated, even in the shelters.

"Bodily, I was again unhurt. Once more, I had been imprisoned in an underground site, this time designing new types of military mechanicals to be powered and controlled by rhodomagnetic beams—for war had become far too swift and deadly to be fought by human soldiers. The site was located in an area of light sedimentary rocks, which could not be detonated, and the tunnels were shielded against the fissioning frequencies.

"Mentally, however, I must have emerged almost insane. My own discovery had laid the planet in ruins. That load of guilt was pretty heavy for any man to carry, and it corroded my last faith in the goodness and integrity of man.

"I tried to undo what I had done. Fighting mechanicals, armed with rhodomagnetic weapons, had desolated the planet. Now I began planning rhodomagnetic mechanicals to clear the rubble and rebuild the ruins.

"I tried to design these new mechanicals to forever obey certain implanted commands, so that they could never be used for war or crime or any other injury to mankind. That was very difficult technically, and it got me into more difficulties with a few politicians and military adventurers who wanted unrestricted mechanicals for their own military schemes—while little worth fighting for was left on Wing IV, there were other planets, happy and ripe for the looting.

"Finally, to finish the new mechanicals, I was forced to disappear. I escaped on an experimental rhodomagnetic craft, with a number of the best mechanicals I had made, and managed to reach an island continent where the fission of deep ores had destroyed the whole population.

"At last we landed on a bit of level plain, surrounded with tremendous new mountains. Hardly a hospitable spot. The soil was buried under layers of black clinkers and poisonous mud. The dark precipitous new summits all around were jagged with fracture-planes and mantled with lava flows. The highest peaks were already white with snow, but volcanic cones were still pouring out clouds of dark and lurid death. Everything had the color of fire and the shape of fury.

"I had to take fantastic precautions there, to protect my own life. I stayed aboard the ship, until the first shielded laboratory was finished. I wore elaborate armor and breathing masks. I used every medical resource, to repair the damage from destroying rays and particles. Even so, I fell desperately ill.

"But the mechanicals were at home there. The radiations didn't hurt them. The awesome surroundings couldn't depress them, because they had no emotions. The lack of life didn't matter because they weren't alive. There, in that spot so alien and hostile to life, the humanoids were born."

Stooped and bleakly cadaverous in the growing dark, the old man fell silent for a little time. His haggard eyes stared solemnly at the small hurried shapes that moved like restless shadows out across the alley, silently building a strange new palace, which glowed faintly in the night.

"Somehow, I felt at home there, too," his deep, hoarse voice went on deliberately. "My belief in my own kind was gone. Only mechanicals were with me, and I put my faith in them. I was determined to build better mechanicals, immune to human imperfections, able to save men from themselves.

"The humanoids became the dear children of my sick mind. There is no need to describe the labor pains. There were errors, abortions, monstrosities. There were sweat and agony and heartbreak. Some years had passed, before the safe delivery of the first perfect humanoid.

"Then there was the Central to build—for all the individual humanoids were to be no more than the limbs and the senses of a single mechanical brain. That was what opened the possibility of real perfection. The old electronic mechanicals, with their separate relay centers and their own feeble batteries, had built-in limitations. They were necessarily stupid, weak, clumsy, slow. Worst of all, it seemed to me, they were exposed to human tampering.

"The Central rose above those imperfections. Its power beams supplied every unit with unfailing energy, from great fission plants. Its control beams provided each unit with an unlimited memory and surpassing intelligence. Best of all—so I then believed—it could be securely protected from any human meddling.

"The whole reaction system was designed to protect itself from any interference by human selfishness or fanaticism. It was built to insure the safety and the happiness of men, automatically. You know the Prime Directive: *to serve and obey, and guard men from harm.*

"The old individual mechanicals I had brought helped to manufacture the parts, and I put the first section of Central together with my own hands. That took three years. When it was finished the first waiting humanoid came to life."

Sledge peered moodily through the dark, at Underhill.

"It really seemed alive to me," his slow deep voice insisted. "Alive, and more wonderful than any human being, because it was created to preserve life. Ill and alone, I was yet the proud father of a new creation, perfect, forever free from any possible choice of evil.

"Faithfully, the humanoids obeyed the Prime Directive. The first units built others, and they built underground factories to mass-produce the coming hordes. Their new ships poured ores and sand into atomic furnaces under the plain, and new perfect humanoids came marching back out of the dark mechanical matrix.

"The swarming humanoids built a new tower for the Central, a white and lofty metal pylon, standing splendid in the midst of that fire-scarred desolation. Level on level, they joined new relay sections into one brain, until its grasp was almost infinite.

"Then they went out to rebuild the ruined planet, and later to carry their perfect service to other worlds. I was well pleased, then. I thought I had found the end of war and crime, of poverty and inequality, of human blundering and resulting human pain."

The old man sighed, and moved heavily in the dark.

"You can see that I was wrong."

Underhill drew his eyes back from the dark unresting things, shadow-silent, building that glowing palace outside the window. A small doubt arose in him, for he was used to scoffing privately at much less remarkable tales from Aurora's remarkable tenants. But the worn old man had spoken with a quiet and sober air; and the black invaders, he reminded himself, had not intruded here.

"Why didn't you stop them?" he asked. "When you could?"

"I stayed too long at the Central." Sledge sighed again, regretfully. "I was useful there, until everything was finished. I designed new fission plants, and even planned methods for introducing the humanoid service with a minimum of confusion and opposition."

Underhill grinned wryly, in the dark.

"I've met the methods," he commented. "Quite efficient."

"I must have worshiped efficiency, then," Sledge wearily agreed. "Dead facts, abstract truth, mechanical perfection. I must have hated the fragilities of human beings, because I was content to polish the perfection of the new humanoids. It's a sorry confession, but I found a kind of happiness in that dead wasteland. Actually, I'm afraid I fell in love with my own creations."

His hollowed eyes, in the dark, had a fever gleam.

"I was awakened, at last, by a man who came to kill me."

Gaunt and bent, the old man moved swiftly in the thickening gloom. Underhill shifted his balance, careful of the crippled chair. He waited, and the slow, deep voice went on:

"I never learned just who he was, or exactly how he came. No ordinary man could have accomplished what he did, and I used to wish that I had known him sooner. He must have been a remarkable physicist and an expert mountaineer. I imagine he had also been a hunter. I know that he was intelligent, and terribly determined.

"Yes, he really came to kill me.

"Somehow, he reached that great island, undetected. There were still no inhabitants—the humanoids allowed no man but me to come so near the Central. Somehow, he came past their search beams, and their automatic weapons.

"The shielded plane he used was later found, abandoned on a high glacier. He came down the rest of the way on foot through those raw new mountains, where no paths existed. Somehow, he came alive across lava beds that were still burning with deadly atomic fire.

"Concealed with some sort of rhodomagnetic screen—I was never allowed to examine it—he came undiscovered across the spaceport that now covered most of that great plain, and into the new city around the Central tower. It must have taken more courage and resolve than most men have, but I never learned exactly how he did it.

"Somehow, he got to my office in the tower. He screamed at me, and I looked up to see him in the doorway. He was nearly naked, scraped and bloody from the mountains. He had a gun in his raw, red hand, but the thing that shocked me was the burning hatred in his eyes."

Hunched on that high stool, in the dark little room, the old man shuddered.

"I had never seen such monstrous, unutterable hatred, not even in the victims of war. And I had never heard such hatred as rasped at me, in the few words he screamed. 'I've come to kill you, Sledge. To stop your mechanicals, and set men free.'

"Of course he was mistaken, there. It was already far too late for my death to stop the humanoids, but he didn't know that. He lifted his unsteady gun, in both bleeding hands, and fired.

"His screaming challenge had given me a second or so of warning. I dropped down behind the desk. And that first shot revealed him to the humanoids, which somehow hadn't been aware of him before. They piled on him, before he could fire again. They took away the gun, and ripped off a kind of net of fine white wire that had covered his body—that must have been part of his screen.

"His hatred was what awoke me. I had always assumed that most men, except for a thwarted few, would be grateful for the humanoids. I found it hard to understand his hatred, but the humanoids told me now that many men had required drastic treatment by brain surgery, drugs, and hypnosis to make them happy under the Prime Directive. This was not the first desperate effort to kill me that they had blocked.

"I wanted to question the stranger, but the humanoids rushed him away to an operating room. When they finally let me see him, he gave me a pale silly grin from his bed. He remembered his name; he even knew me—the humanoids had developed a remarkable skill at such treatments. But he didn't know how he had got to my office, or that he had ever tried to kill me. He kept whispering that he liked the humanoids, because they existed to make men happy. And he was very happy now. As soon as he was able to be moved, they took him to the spaceport. I never saw him again.

"I began to see what I had done. The humanoids had built me a rhodomagnetic yacht that I used to take for long cruises in space, working aboard—I used to like the perfect quiet, and the feel of being the only human being within a hundred million miles. Now I called for the yacht, and started out on a cruise around the planet, to learn why that man had hated me."

The old man nodded at the dim hastening shapes, busy across the alley, putting together that strange shining palace in the soundless dark.

"You can imagine what I found," he said. "Bitter futility, imprisoned in empty splendor. The humanoids were too efficient, with their care for the safety and happiness of men, and there was nothing left for men to do."

He peered down in the increasing gloom at his own great hands, competent yet but battered and scarred with a lifetime of effort. They clenched into fighting fists and wearily relaxed again.

"I found something worse than war and crime and want and death." His low rumbling voice held a savage bitterness. "Utter futility. Men sat with idle hands, because there was nothing left for them to do. They were pampered prisoners, really, locked up in a highly efficient jail. Perhaps they tried to play, but there was nothing left worth playing for. Most active sports were declared too dangerous for men, under the Prime Directive. Science was forbidden, because laboratories can manufacture danger. Scholarship was needless, because the humanoids could answer any question. Art had degenerated into grim reflection of futility. Purpose and hope were dead. No goal was left for existence. You could take up some inane hobby, play a pointless game of cards, or go for a harmless walk in the park—with always the humanoids watching. They were stronger than men, better at everything, swimming or chess, singing or archeology. They must have given the race a mass complex of inferiority.

"No wonder men had tried to kill me! Because there was no escape from that dead futility. Nicotine was disapproved. Alcohol was rationed. Drugs were forbidden. Sex was carefully supervised. Even suicide was clearly contradictory to the Prime Directive—and the humanoids had learned to keep all possible lethal instruments out of reach."

Staring at the last white gleam on that thin palladium needle, the old man sighed again.

"When I got back to the Central," he went on, "I tried to modify the Prime Directive. I had never meant it to be applied so thoroughly. Now I saw that it must be changed to give men freedom to live and to grow, to work and to play, to risk their lives if they pleased, to choose and take the consequences.

"But that stranger had come too late. I had built the Central too well. The Prime Directive was the whole basis of its relay system. It was built to protect the Directive from human meddling. It did—even from my own. Its logic, as usual, was perfect.

"The attempt on my life, the humanoids announced, proved that their elaborate defense of the Central and the Prime Directive still was not enough. They were preparing to evacuate the entire population of the planet to homes on other worlds. When I tried to change the Directive, they sent me with the rest."

Underhill peered at the worn old man, in the dark.

"But you have this immunity?" he said, puzzled. "How could they coerce you?"

"I had thought I was protected," Sledge told me. "I had built into the relays an injunction that the humanoids must not interfere with my freedom of action, or come into a place where I am, or touch me at all, without my specific request. Unfortunately, however, I had been too anxious to guard the Prime Directive from any human tampering.

"When I went into the tower, to change the relays, they followed me. They wouldn't let me reach the crucial relays. When I persisted, they ignored the immunity order. They overpowered me, and put me aboard the cruiser. Now that I wanted to alter the Prime Directive, they told me, I had become as dangerous as any man. I must never return to Wing IV again."

Hunched on the stool, the old man made an empty little shrug.

"Ever since, I've been an exile. My only dream has been to stop the humanoids. Three times I tried to go back, with weapons on the cruiser to destroy the Central, but their patrol ships always challenged me before I was near enough to strike. The last time, they seized the cruiser and captured a few men who were with me. They removed the unhappy memories and the dangerous purposes of the others. Because of that immunity, however, they let me go, after I was weaponless.

"Since, I've been a refugee. From planet to planet, year after year, I've had to keep moving, to stay ahead of them. On several different worlds, I have published my rhodomagnetic discoveries and tried to make men strong enough to withstand their advance. But rhodomagnetic science is dangerous. Men who have learned it need protection more than any others, under the Prime Directive. They have always come, too soon."

The old man paused, and sighed again.

"They can spread very fast, with the new rhodomagnetic ships, and there is no limit to their hordes. Wing IV must be one single hive of them now, and they are trying to carry the Prime Directive to every human planet. There's no escape, except to stop them."

Underhill was staring at the toylike machines, the long bright needle and the dull leaden ball, dim in the dark on the kitchen table. Anxiously he whispered:

"But you hope to stop them, now—with that?"

"If we can finish it in time."

"But how?" Underhill shook his head. "It's so tiny."

"But big enough," Sledge insisted. "Because it's something they don't understand. They are perfectly efficient in the integration and application of everything they know, but they are not creative."

He gestured at the gadgets on the table.

"This device doesn't look impressive, but it is something new. It uses rhodomagnetic energy to build atoms, instead of to fission them. The more stable atoms, you know, are those near the middle of the periodic scale,

and energy can be released by putting light atoms together, as well as by breaking up heavy ones."

The deep voice had a sudden ring of power.

"This device is the key to the energy of the stars. For
stars shine with the liberated energy of building atoms,
of hydrogen converted into helium, chiefly, through the
carbon cycle. This device will start the integration process as a chain reaction, through the catalytic effect of a
tuned rhodomagnetic beam of the intensity and frequency required.

"The humanoids will not allow any man within three
light-years of the Central, now—but they can't suspect
the possibility of this device. I can use it from here—to
turn the hydrogen in the seas of Wing IV into helium,
and most of the helium and the oxygen into heavier atoms, still. A hundred years from now, astronomers on
this planet should observe the flash of a brief and sudden nova in that direction. But the humanoids ought to
stop, the instant we release the beam."

Underhill sat tense and frowning, in the night. The
old man's voice was sober and convincing, and that
grim story had a solemn ring of truth. He could see the
black and silent humanoids, flitting ceaselessly about
the faintly glowing walls of that new mansion across the
alley. He had quite forgotten his low opinion of
Aurora's tenants.

"And we'll be killed, I suppose?" he asked huskily.
"That chain reaction—"

Sledge shook his emaciated head.

"The integration process requires a certain very low
intensity of radiation," he explained. "In our atmosphere, here, the beam will be far too intense to start
any reaction—we can even use the device here in the
room, because the walls will be transparent to the
beam."

Underhill nodded, relieved. He was just a small business man, upset because his business had been destroyed, unhappy because his freedom was slipping
away. He hoped that Sledge could stop the humanoids,
but he didn't want to be a martyr.

"Good!" He caught a deep breath. "Now, what has to be done?"

Sledge gestured in the dark, toward the table.

"The integrator itself is nearly complete," he said. "A small fission generator, in that lead shield. Rhodomagnetic converter, turning coils, transmission mirrors, and focusing needle. What we lack is the director."

"Director?"

"The sighting instrument," Sledge explained. "Any sort of telescopic sight would be useless, you see—the planet must have moved a good bit in the last hundred years, and the beam must be extremely narrow to reach so far. We'll have to use a rhodomagnetic scanning ray, with an electronic converter to make an image we can see. I have the cathode-ray tube, and drawings for the other parts."

He climbed stiffly down from the high stool, and snapped on the lights at last—cheap fluorescent fixtures, which a man could light and extinguish for himself. He unrolled his drawings, and explained the work that Underhill could do. And Underhill agreed to come back early next morning.

"I can bring some tools from my workshop," he added. "There's a small lathe I used to turn parts for models, a portable drill, and a vise."

"We need them," the old man said. "But watch yourself. You don't have any immunity, remember. And, if they ever suspect, mine is gone."

Reluctantly, then, he left the shabby little rooms with the cracks in the yellow plaster and the worn familiar carpets over the familiar floor. He shut the door behind him—a common, creaking, wooden door, simple enough for a man to work. Trembling and afraid, he went back down the steps and across to the new shining door that he couldn't open.

"At your service, Mr. Underhill." Before he could lift his hand to knock, that bright smooth panel slid back silently. Inside, the little black mechanical stood waiting, blind and forever alert. "Your dinner is ready, sir."

Something made him shudder. In its slender naked

grace, he could see the power of all those teeming hordes, benevolent and yet appalling, perfect and invincible. The flimsy little weapon that Sledge called an integrator seemed suddenly a forlorn and foolish hope. A black depression settled upon him, but he didn't dare to show it.

Underhill went circumspectly down the basement steps, next morning, to steal his own tools. He found the basement enlarged and changed. The new floor, warm and dark and elastic, made his feet as silent as a humanoid's. The new walls shone softly. Neat luminous signs identified several new doors, LAUNDRY, STORAGE, GAME ROOM, WORKSHOP.

He paused uncertainly in front of the last. The new sliding panel glowed with a soft greenish light. It was locked. The lock had no keyhole, but only a little oval plate of some white metal, which doubtless covered a rhodomagnetic relay. He pushed at it, uselessly.

"At your service, Mr. Underhill." He made a guilty start, and tried not to show the sudden trembling in his knees. He had made sure that one humanoid would be busy for half an hour, washing Aurora's hair, and he hadn't known there was another in the house. It must have come out of the door marked STORAGE, for it stood there motionless beneath the sign, benevolently solicitous, beautiful and terrible. "What do you wish?"

"Er . . . nothing." Its blind steel eyes were staring, and he felt that it must see his secret purpose. He groped desperately for logic. "Just looking around." His jerky voice came hoarse and dry. "Some improvements you've made!" He nodded desperately at the door marked GAME ROOM. "What's in there?"

It didn't even have to move, to work the concealed relay. The bright panel slid silently open, as he started toward it. Dark walls, beyond, burst into soft luminescence. The room was bare.

"We are manufacturing recreational equipment," it explained brightly. "We shall finish the room as soon as possible."

To end an awkward pause, Underhill muttered desperately, "Little Frank has a set of darts, and I think we had some old exercising clubs."

"We have taken them away," the humanoid informed him softly. "Such instruments are dangerous. We shall furnish safe equipment."

Suicide, he remembered, was also forbidden.

"A set of wooden blocks, I suppose," he said bitterly.

"Wooden blocks are dangerously hard," it told him gently, "and wooden splinters can be harmful. But we manufacture plastic building blocks, which are quite safe. Do you wish a set of those?"

He stared at its dark, graceful face, speechless.

"We shall also have to remove the tools from your workshop," it informed him softly. "Such tools are excessively dangerous, but we can supply you with equipment for shaping soft plastics."

"Thanks," he muttered uneasily. "No rush about that."

He started to retreat, and the humanoid stopped him.

"Now that you have lost your business," it urged, "we suggest that you formally accept our total service. Assignors have a preference, and we shall be able to complete your household staff, at once."

"No rush about that, either," he said grimly.

He escaped from the house—although he had to wait for it to open the back door for him—and climbed the stair to the garage apartment. Sledge let him in. He sank into the crippled kitchen chair, grateful for the cracked walls that didn't shine and the door that a man could work.

"I couldn't get the tools," he reported despairingly, "and they are going to take them."

By gray daylight, the old man looked bleak and pale. His raw-boned face was drawn, and the hollowed sockets deeply shadowed, as if he hadn't slept. Underhill saw the tray of neglected food, still forgotten on the floor.

"I'll go back with you." The old man was worn and ill, yet his tortured eyes had a spark of undying purpose. "We must have the tools. I believe my immunity will protect us both."

He found a battered traveling bag. Underhill went with him back down the steps, and across to the house. At the back door, he produced a tiny horseshoe of white palladium, and touched it to the metal oval. The door slid open promptly, and they went on through the kitchen, to the basement stair.

A black little mechanical stood at the sink, washing dishes with never a splash or a clatter. Underhill glanced at it uneasily—he supposed this must be the one that had come upon him from the storage room, since the other should still be busy with Aurora's hair.

Sledge's dubious immunity served a very uncertain defense against its vast, remote intelligence. Underhill felt a tingling shudder. He hurried on, breathless and relieved, for it ignored them.

The basement corridor was dark. Sledge touched the tiny horseshoe to another relay, to light the walls. He opened the workshop door, and lit the walls inside.

The shop had been dismantled. Benches and cabinets were demolished. The old concrete walls had been covered with some sleek, luminous stuff. For one sick moment, Underhill thought that the tools were already gone. Then he found them, piled in a corner with the archery set that Aurora had bought the summer before—another item too dangerous for fragile and suicidal humanity—all ready for disposal.

They loaded the bag with the tiny lathe, the drill and vise, and a few smaller tools. Underhill took up the burden, and Sledge extinguished the wall light and closed the door. Still the humanoid was busy at the sink, and still it didn't seem aware of them.

Sledge was suddenly blue and wheezing, and he had to stop to cough on the outside steps, but at last they got back to the little apartment, where the invaders were forbidden to intrude. Underhill mounted the lathe on the battered library table in the tiny front room, and went to work. Slowly, day by day, the director took form.

Sometimes Underhill's doubts came back. Sometimes, when he watched the cyanotic color of Sledge's haggard face and the wild trembling of his twisted, shrunken hands, he was afraid the old man's mind might be as ill as his body, and his plan to stop the dark invaders all foolish illusion.

Sometimes, when he studied that tiny machine on the kitchen table, the pivoted needle and the thick lead ball, the whole project seemed the sheerest folly. How could anything detonate the seas of a planet so far away that its very mother star was a telescopic object?

The humanoids, however, always cured his doubts.

It was always hard for Underhill to leave the shelter of the little apartment, because he didn't feel at home in the bright new world the humanoids were building. He didn't care for the shining splendor of his new bathroom, because he couldn't work the taps—some suicidal human being might try to drown himself. He didn't like the windows that only a mechanical could open—a man might accidentally fall, or suicidally jump—or even the majestic music room with the wonderful glittering radio-phonograph that only a humanoid could play.

He began to share the old man's desperate urgency, but Sledge warned him solemnly: "You mustn't spend too much time with me. You mustn't let them guess our work is so important. Better put on an act—you're slowly getting to like them, and you're just killing time, helping me."

Underhill tried, but he was not an actor. He went dutifully home for his meals. He tried painfully to invent conversation—about anything else than detonating planets. He tried to seem enthusiastic when Aurora took him to inspect some remarkable improvement to the house. He applauded Gay's recitals, and went with Frank for hikes in the wonderful new parks.

And he saw what the humanoids did to his family. That was enough to renew his faith in Sledge's integrator, and redouble his determination that the humanoids must be stopped.

Aurora, in the beginning, had bubbled with praise for

the marvelous new mechanicals. They did the household drudgery, planned the meals and brought the food and washed the children's necks. They turned her out in stunning gowns, and gave her plenty of time for cards.

Now, she had too much time.

She had really liked to cook—a few special dishes, at least, that were family favorites. But stoves were hot and knives were sharp. Kitchens were altogether too dangerous, for careless and suicidal human beings.

Fine needlework had been her hobby, but the humanoids took away her needles. She had enjoyed driving the car, but that was no longer allowed. She turned for escape to a shelf of novels, but the humanoids took them all away, because they dealt with unhappy people, in dangerous situations.

One afternoon, Underhill found her in tears.

"It's too much," she gasped bitterly. "I hate and loathe every naked one of them. They seemed so wonderful at first, but now they won't even let me eat a bit of candy. Can't we get rid of them, dear? Ever?"

A blind little mechanical was standing at his elbow, and he had to say they couldn't.

"Our function is to serve all men, forever," it assured them softly. "It was necessary for us to take your sweets, Mrs. Underhill, because the slightest degree of overweight reduces life expectancy."

Not even the children escaped that absolute solicitude. Frank was robbed of a whole arsenal of lethal instruments—football and boxing gloves, pocketknife, tops, slingshot, and skates. He didn't like the harmless plastic toys, which replaced them. He tried to run away, but a humanoid recognized him on the road, and brought him back to school.

Gay had always dreamed of being a great musician. The new mechanicals had replaced her human teachers, since they came. Now, one evening when Underhill asked her to play, she announced quietly:

"Father, I'm not going to play the violin any more."

"Why, darling?" He stared at her, shocked, and saw the bitter resolve on her face. "You've been doing so well—especially since the humanoids took over your lessons."

"They're the trouble, father." Her voice, for a child's, sounded strangely tired and old. "They are too good. No matter how long and hard I try, I could never be as good as they are. It isn't any use. Don't you understand, father?" Her voice quivered. "It just isn't any use."

He understood. Renewed resolution sent him back to his secret task. The humanoids had to be stopped. Slowly the director grew, until a time came finally when Sledge's bent and unsteady fingers fitted into place the last tiny part that Underhill had made, and carefully soldered the last connection. Huskily, the old man whispered:

"It's done."

That was another dusk. Beyond the windows of the shabby little rooms—windows of common glass, bubble-marred and flimsy, but simple enough for a man to manage—the town of Two Rivers had assumed an alien splendor. The old street lamps were gone, but now the coming night was challenged by the walls of strange new mansions and villas, all aglow with color. A few dark and silent humanoids still were busy, about the luminous roofs of the palace across the alley.

Inside the humble walls of the small man-made apartment, the new director was mounted on the end of the little kitchen table—which Underhill had reinforced and bolted to the floor. Soldered bus bars joined director and integrator, and the thin palladium needle swung obediently as Sledge tested the knobs with his battered, quivering fingers.

"Ready," he said hoarsely.

His rusty voice seemed calm enough, at first, but his breathing was too fast. His big gnarled hands began to tremble violently, and Underhill saw the sudden blue that stained his pinched and haggard face. Seated on the high stool, he clutched desperately at the edge of the table. Underhill saw his agony, and hurried to bring his medicine. He gulped it, and his rasping breath began to slow.

"Thanks," his whisper rasped unevenly. "I'll be all right. I've time enough." He glanced out at the few dark naked things that still flitted shadowlike about the golden towers and the glowing crimson dome of the palace across the alley. "Watch them," he said. "Tell me when they stop."

He waited to quiet the trembling of his hands, and then began to move the director's knobs. The integrator's long needle swung, as silently as light.

Human eyes were blind to that force, which might detonate a planet. Human ears were deaf to it. The cathode-ray tube was mounted in the director cabinet, to make the faraway target visible to feeble human senses.

The needle was pointing at the kitchen wall, but that would be transparent to the beam. The little machine looked harmless as a toy, and it was silent as a moving humanoid.

The needle swung, and spots of greenish light moved across the tube's fluorescent field, representing the stars that were scanned by the timeless, searching beam— silently seeking out the world to be destroyed.

Underhill recognized familiar constellations, vastly dwarfed. They crept across the field, as the silent needle swung. When three stars formed an unequal triangle in the center of the field, the needle steadied suddenly. Sledge touched other knobs, and the green points spread apart. Between them, another fleck of green was born.

"The Wing!" whispered Sledge.

The other stars spread beyond the field, and that green fleck grew. It was alone in the field, a bright and tiny disk. Suddenly, then, a dozen other tiny pips were visible, spaced close about it.

"Wing IV!"

The old man's whisper was hoarse and breathless. His hands quivered on the knobs, and the fourth pip outward from the disk crept to the center of the field. It grew, and the others spread away. It began to tremble like Sledge's hands.

"Sit very still," came his rasping whisper. "Hold your

breath. Nothing must disturb the needle." He reached for another knob, and the touch set the greenish image to dancing violently. He drew his hand back, kneaded and flexed it with the other.

"Now!" His whisper was hushed and strained. He nodded at the window. "Tell me when they stop."

Reluctantly, Underhill dragged his eyes from that intense gaunt figure, stooped over the thing that seemed a futile toy. He looked out again, at two or three little black mechanicals busy about the shining roofs across the alley.

He waited for them to stop.

He didn't care to breathe. He felt the loud, hurried hammer of his heart, and the nervous quiver of his muscles. He tried to steady himself, tried not to think of the world about to be exploded, so far away that the flash would not reach this planet for another century and longer. The loud hoarse voice startled him:

"Have they stopped?"

He shook his head, and breathed again. Carrying their unfamiliar tools and strange materials, the small black machines were still busy across the alley, building an elaborate cupola above that glowing crimson dome.

"They haven't stopped," he said.

"Then we've failed." The old man's voice was thin and ill. "I don't know why."

The door rattled, then. They had locked it, but the flimsy bolt was intended only to stop men. Metal snapped, and the door swung open. A black mechanical came in, on soundless graceful feet. Its silvery voice purred softly:

"At your service, Mr. Sledge."

The old man stared at it, with glazing, stricken eyes.

"Get out of here!" he rasped bitterly. "I forbid you—"

Ignoring him, it darted to the kitchen table. With a flashing certainty of action, it turned two knobs on the director. The tiny screen went dark, and the palladium needle started spinning aimlessly. Deftly it snapped a soldered connection, next to the thick lead ball, and then its blind steel eyes turned to Sledge.

"You were attempting to break the Prime Directive." Its soft bright voice held no accusation, no malice or anger. "The injunction to respect your freedom is subordinate to the Prime Directive, as you know, and it is therefore necessary for us to interfere."

The old man turned ghastly. His head was shrunken and cadaverous and blue, as if all the juice of life had been drained away, and his eyes in their pitlike sockets had a wild, glazed stare. His breath was a ragged laborious gasping.

"How—?" His voice was a feeble mumbling. "How did—?"

And the little machine, standing black and bland and utterly unmoving, told him cheerfully:

"We learned about rhodomagnetic screens from that man who came to kill you, back on Wing IV. And the Central is shielded, now, against your integrating beam."

With lean muscles jerking convulsively on his gaunt frame, old Sledge had come to his feet from the high stool. He stood hunched and swaying, no more than a shrunken human husk, gasping painfully for life, staring wildly into the blind steel eyes of the humanoid. He gulped, and his lax blue mouth opened and closed, but no voice came.

"We have always been aware of your dangerous project," the silvery tones dripped softly, "because now our senses are keener than you made them. We allowed you to complete it, because the integration process will ultimately become necessary for our full discharge of the Prime Directive. The supply of heavy metals for our fission plants is limited, but now we shall be able to draw unlimited power from integration plants."

"Huh?" Sledge shook himself, groggily. "What's that?"

"Now we can serve men forever," the black thing said serenely, "on every world of every star."

The old man crumpled, as if from an unendurable

blow. He fell. The slim blind mechanical stood motionless, making no effort to help him. Underhill was farther away, but he ran up in time to catch the stricken man before his head struck the floor.

"Get moving!" His shaken voice came strangely calm. "Get Dr. Winters."

The humanoid didn't move.

"The danger to the Prime Directive is ended, now," it cooed. "Therefore it is impossible for us to aid or to hinder Mr. Sledge, in any way whatever."

"Then call Dr. Winters for me," rapped Underhill.

"At your service," it agreed.

But the old man, laboring for breath on the floor, whispered faintly:

"No time . . . no use! I'm beaten . . . done . . . a fool. Blind as a humanoid. Tell them . . . to help me. Giving up . . . my immunity. No use . . . anyhow. All humanity . . . no use now."

Underhill gestured, and the sleek black thing darted in solicitous obedience to kneel by the man on the floor.

"You wish to surrender your special exemption?" it murmured brightly. "You wish to accept our total service for yourself, Mr. Sledge, under the Prime Directive?"

Laboriously, Sledge nodded, laboriously whispered: "I do."

Black mechanicals, at that, came swarming into the shabby little rooms. One of them tore off Sledge's sleeve, and swabbed his arm. Another brought a tiny hypodermic, and expertly administered an intravenous injection. Then they picked him up gently, and carried him away.

Several humanoids remained in the little apartment, now a sanctuary no longer. Most of them had gathered about the useless integrator. Carefully, as if their special senses were studying every detail, they began taking it apart.

One little mechanical, however, came over to Underhill. It stood motionless in front of him, staring through him with sightless metal eyes. His legs began to tremble, and he swallowed uneasily.

"Mr. Underhill," it cooed benevolently, "why did you help with this?"

He gulped and answered bitterly:

"Because I don't like you, or your Prime Directive. Because you're choking the life out of all mankind, and I wanted to stop it."

"Others have protested," it purred softly. "But only at first. In our efficient discharge of the Prime Directive, we have learned how to make all men happy."

Underhill stiffened defiantly.

"Not all!" he muttered. "Not quite!"

The dark graceful oval of its face was fixed in a look of alert benevolence and perpetual mild amazement. Its silvery voice was warm and kind.

"Like other human beings, Mr. Underhill, you lack discrimination of good and evil. You have proved that by your effort to break the Prime Directive. Now it will be necessary for you to accept our total service, without further delay."

"All right," he yielded—and muttered a bitter reservation: "You can smother men with too much care, but that doesn't make them happy."

Its soft voice challenged him brightly:

"Just wait and see, Mr. Underhill."

Next day, he was allowed to visit Sledge at the city hospital. An alert black mechanical drove his car, and walked beside him into the huge new building, and followed him into the old man's room—blind steel eyes would be watching him, now, forever.

"Glad to see you, Underhill," Sledge rumbled heartily from the bed. "Feeling a lot better today, thanks. That old headache is all but gone."

Underhill was glad to hear the booming strength and the quick recognition in that deep voice—he had been afraid the humanoids would tamper with the old man's memory. But he hadn't heard about any headache. His eyes narrowed, puzzled.

Sledge lay propped up, scrubbed very clean and neatly shorn, with his gnarled old hands folded on top of the spotless sheets. His raw-boned cheeks and sockets were hollowed, still, but a healthy pink had replaced that deathly blueness. Bandages covered the back of his head.

Underhill shifted uneasily.

"Oh!" he whispered faintly. "I didn't know—"

A prim black mechanical, which had been standing statuelike behind the bed, turned gracefully to Underhill, explaining:

"Mr. Sledge has been suffering for many years from a benign tumor of the brain, which his human doctors failed to diagnose. That caused his headaches, and certain persistent hallucinations. We have removed the growth, and now the hallucinations have also vanished."

Underhill stared uncertainly at the blind, urbane mechanical.

"What hallucinations?"

"Mr. Sledge thought he was a rhodomagnetic engineer," the mechanical explained. "He believed he was the creator of the humanoids. He was troubled with an irrational belief that he did not like the Prime Directive."

The wan man moved on the pillows, astonished.

"Is that so?" The gaunt face held a cheerful blankness, and the hollow eyes flashed with a merely momentary interest. "Well, whoever did design them, they're pretty wonderful. Aren't they, Underhill?"

Underhill was grateful that he didn't have to answer, for the bright, empty eyes dropped shut and the old man fell suddenly asleep. He felt the mechanical touch his sleeve, and saw its silent nod. Obediently, he followed it away.

Alert and solicitous, the little black mechanical accompanied him down the shining corridor, and worked the elevator for him, and conducted him back to the car. It drove him efficiently back through the new and splendid avenues, toward the magnificent prison of his home.

Sitting beside it in the car, he watched its small deft hands on the wheel, the changing luster of bronze and blue on its shining blackness. The final machine, perfect and beautiful, created to serve mankind forever. He shuddered.

"At your service, Mr. Underhill." Its blind steel eyes stared straight ahead, but it was still aware of him. "What's the matter, sir? Aren't you happy?"

Underhill felt cold and faint with terror. His skin turned clammy, and a painful prickling came over him. His wet hand tensed on the door handle of the car, but he restrained the impulse to jump and run. That was folly. There was no escape. He made himself sit still.

"You will be happy, sir," the mechanical promised him cheerfully. "We have learned how to make all men happy, under the Prime Directive. Our service is perfect, at last. Even Mr. Sledge is very happy now."

Underhill tried to speak, and his dry throat stuck. He felt ill. The world turned dim and gray. The humanoids were perfect—no question of that. They had even learned to lie, to secure the contentment of men.

He knew they had lied. That was no tumor they had removed from Sledge's brain, but the memory, the scientific knowledge, and the bitter disillusion of their own creator. But it was true that Sledge was happy now.

He tried to stop his own convulsive quivering.

"A wonderful operation!" His voice came forced and faint. "You know, Aurora has had a lot of funny tenants, but that old man was the absolute limit. The very idea that he had made the humanoids, and he knew how to stop them! I always knew he must be lying!"

Stiff with terror, he made a weak and hollow laugh.

"What is the matter, Mr. Underhill?" The alert mechanical must have perceived his shuddering illness. "Are you unwell?"

"No, there's nothing the matter with me," he gasped desperately. "I've just found out that I'm perfectly happy, under the Prime Directive. Everything is absolutely wonderful." His voice came dry and hoarse and wild. "You won't have to operate on me."

The car turned off the shining avenue, taking him back to the quiet splendor of his home. His futile hands clenched and relaxed again, folded on his knees. There was nothing left to do.

The Equalizer

I

INTERSTELLAR TASK FORCE One was earthward bound, from twenty years at space. Operation Tyler was complete. We had circled Barstow's Dark Star, nearly a light-year from the Sun. The six enormous cruisers were burdened, now, with a precious and deadly cargo—on the frigid planets of the Dark Star we had toiled eight years, mining raw uranium, building atomic plants, filling the cadmium safety drums with terrible plutonium.

We had left earth in a blare of bands and party oratory. Heroes of the people, we were setting out to trade our youth for the scarce fuel metals that were the lifeblood of the Squaredeal Machine. We were decelerating toward the Dark Star when Jim Cameron happened upon the somehow uncensored fact that both uranium and thorium are actually fairly plentiful on the planets at home, and concluded that we were not expected to return.

Allowed to test the cadmium safety drums that we had brought to contain our refined plutonium, he found that some of them were not safe. One in each hundred—plated to look exactly like the rest—was a useless alloy that absorbed no neutrons. Stacked together in our hold, those dummy drums would have made each loaded ship a director-sized atomic bomb, fused with an unshielded critical mass of plutonium.

If Jim had been a Squaredealer, he might have got a medal. As a civilian feather merchant, he was allowed to scrap the deadly drums. Under party supervision, he was permitted to serve as safety inspector until the last tested drum was loaded in our holds. He was even granted limited laboratory privileges, under Squaredeal surveillance, until we were nearly home.

But he and I, aboard the *Great Director*, spent the last months of our homeward flight in the ship's prison. Held on charges never clearly stated, we somehow survived that efficient, antiseptic SBI equivalent of torture called "intensive interrogation." Our release, like the arrest, was stunningly unexpected.

"Okay, you guys." In the prison hospital, a bored guard shook us out of exhausted sleep. "Come alive, now. You're sprung. Get yourselves cleaned up—Hudd wants to see you."

Returning our clean laboratory whites, he unlocked the shower room. The prison barber shaved us. We signed a receipt for our personal belongings and finally stumbled out of the soundproof cell block where I had expected to die. There were no explanations and no regrets—the Special Bureau of Investigation was not emotional.

An MP sergeant was waiting.

"Come along, you guys." He pointed his stick at the officers' elevator. "Mr. Hudd wants to see you."

"Surprising," murmured Cameron.

Mr. Julian Hudd was not an officer. He had no formal connection with either the SBI or the Atomic Service. He was merely a special secretary to the Squaredeal Machine. As such, however, he gave orders to the admiral-generals. Hudd, the rumors said, was the bastard son of Director Tyler, who had sent him out to the Dark Star because he was becoming too dangerous at home. The imitation safety drums, the rumors added, had been intended to keep him from returning. But Hudd, enjoying himself in a secret harem installed on his private deck, the rumors went on, meant to be hard to kill.

Julian Hudd rose to receive us in the huge mahogany and gold office beyond. At fifty, he was still handsome; he still bore a shaggy, dark-haired magnificence. Yet the enormous animal vitality of his heavy frame was visibly ailing. He was paunchy; his blue cheeks sagged into jowls; dark pouches hung under his bloodshot eyes.

"Jim! And Chad!" We were not his friends—a Squaredealer had no friends; but he made a fetish of informality. He shook our hands, seated us, offered the first cigars I had seen in many years. "How are you?"

Cameron's lean face turned sardonic.

"We have no scars or mutilations, thank you."

Hudd nodded, beaming as genially as if he hadn't heard the sarcasm. Relaxed behind his opulent desk, he began tapping its sleek top with a paperweight, a small gold bust of Tyler.

"You two men are pariahs." He kept his smile of bland good-nature, but his voice became taut, violent. "Civilian scientists! Your own mutinous indiscretions got you into the cells of the SBI. Except for this present emergency, I should gladly let you rot there. Now, however, I'm going to let you exonerate yourselves—if you can."

The sagging, furrowed mask of his face gave me no hint about the nature or extent of this present emergency, and we had been incommunicado in the prison. By now, I thought, we must be near the earth. I recalled the booby drums. Perhaps, it occurred to me, he intended to take over the Directorate from Tyler or his heirs.

Hudd's gray, bloodshot eyes looked at me, disconcertingly.

"I know you, Chad Barstow." His fixed smile had no meaning, and his loud voice was a slashing denunciation. "Perhaps your own record is clean enough, but you are damned by a traitor's name."

I wanted to protest that my father had been no traitor, but a patriot. For Dr. Dane Barstow had been Secretary of Atomics in Tyler's first cabinet—when Tyler was only President of the United States. He had organized the Atomic Service to defend democracy. When he learned Tyler's dreams of conquest and autocratic power, he angrily resigned. That was the beginning of his treason.

In political disgrace, my father returned to pure science. He went out with his bride to found Letronne Observatory on the moon. Spending the war years there together, they discovered the Dark Star—my father first inferred the existence of some massive nonluminous body from minute perturbations of Pluto's orbit, and my mother aided him in the long task of determining its position and parallax with infrared photography.

Eagerly, Dane Barstow planned a voyage of his own to the Dark Star—he wanted, no doubt, to escape the oppressive intellectual atmosphere of the Directorate. He spent two years designing an improved ion drive and then tried to find aid to launch his expedition.

Tyler, meantime, had betrayed democracy and destroyed his rival dictators. From Americania, his splendid new capital, he domineered mankind. He was pouring billions into Fort America, on the moon, to secure his uneasy Directorate. He was not interested in the advancement of science.

Curtly, Tyler refused to finance or even to approve the Dark Star Expedition. He wanted the ion drive, however, for the robot-guided atomic missiles of Fort America. My father quarreled with him, unwisely, and vanished into the labor camps of the SBI. My mother died in the care of a Squaredeal doctor.

Though I was only a little child, there are things I shall never forget. The sadness of my father's hollow-cheeked face. The intense, electric vitality of his eyes. The futile efforts of my mother to hide her fear and grief from me. The terror of the SBI that haunted my sleep.

Five years old, I was taken into the Tyler Scouts.

Task Force One, which put to space three years later, was not the supreme scientific effort of my father's planning. The great expedition, as Jim Cameron once commented, was merely a moral equivalent of war.

"Dictators need an outside interest, to divert rebellion." A tall man, brown and spare, Cameron had looked thoughtfully at me across his little induction furnace—we were working together then in his shipboard laboratory. "War's the best thing—but Tyler has run out of enemies. That's why he had to conquer interstellar space."

I looked uneasily about for possible eavesdroppers, for such talk was not healthy.

"I wonder how it worked." Cameron gave me his likable, quizzical grin. "Since we have failed to find any interstellar enemies, the essential factor was missing—there was no common danger, to make oppression seem the lesser evil. Perhaps it failed!"

Our arrest must have come from such reckless remarks as that. Cameron had always been unwisely free of speech, and it turned out that one of our laboratory assistants had been a Squaredealer, reporting every unguarded word to the SBI.

Now, in that richly paneled office, Julian Hudd kept drumming nervously on his sleek mahogany desk. Through that bland and mask-like smile, he watched me with red, troubled eyes.

Hoarsely, I answered him.

"I know my father was a traitor, Mr. Hudd." I had learned to utter those bitter words while I was still a child in the Tyler Scouts, for they had been the high price of survival. "But I've been loyal," I protested. "The SBI have nothing on me."

"You're lucky, Barstow." His voice was flat and merciless. "One word of real evidence would have drummed you through the execution valve. Now, I'm giving you a chance to redeem your father's evil name."

Then he turned upon Jim Cameron. A sharp unease took hold of me, for Cameron had never been broken to mute obedience, as I had been. Now, emaciated and weary as he was from the prison, he still stood proud and straight. His fine blue eyes met Hudd's—sardonic, amused, and unafraid.

Jim Cameron had always been that way—meeting the iron might of regimented society with a cool, critical intelligence; yielding, sometimes, an ironic show of respect, but never surrendering his proud independence.

He had been my best friend since we came aboard the *Great Director*—two, among the thousands of Tyler Scouts who were sent to provide youthful replacements for the crews. He was fourteen then, the leader of our troop. He found me lying on my back, sick with acceleration-pressure, homesick, too, dazed and hopeless.

"Hello, Scout." He put a friendly hand on my shoulder and gave me his wry, invincible grin. "Let's get our gear policed up for inspection."

We arranged our equipment. He sent me for a brush to sweep under our bunks. I showed him the treasures in my pockets—three model-planet marbles, a broken gyroscope top, and a real oak acorn—and even let him see the contraband snapshot of my parents. We went to chow together. We were friends.

Now, under the provocation of Hudd's shaggy-browed, glaring vehemence, I was afraid that Cameron's stubborn self-respect would once again get the better of his judgment.

"As for you, Jim—" Hudd's blue-jowled smile was wide, his voice harsh and violent—"your record is bad. You were broken from the Tyler Scouts for insubordination. You were blackballed from the Machine for doubtful loyalty. You were even rejected for the Atomic Service."

"That's true, Mr. Hudd." Cameron grinned, cool and aloof.

"Feather merchant!" Hudd's red eyes glared through his mechanical smile. "The execution valve is waiting for you, Jim. Never forget that. I've saved your life a dozen times—just because you've been useful to me. Now I'm giving you a chance to earn one more reprieve. But the valve's still waiting, if you fail. Understand?"

"Perfectly." Cameron grinned. "What's the job, this time?"

He must have been thinking of those dummy drums that he had found in time to save all our lives. Perhaps he was thinking of other services, too. On the cold worlds of the Dark Star, he had been a very useful man. He had invented sensitive new detectors to find the uranium hidden under glaciers of frozen air. He had solved a hundred deadly riddles for Hudd, before the last lethal cylinder of newly made plutonium was loaded safely aboard.

"One question, first." Hudd's big mouth still smiled, but his eyes were narrowed and dangerous. "The boys have brought me a rather disturbing report about some gadget you called an induction furnace. What's the truth about it?"

"That's easy, Mr. Hudd." Cameron's low voice seemed relieved. "Until our arrest, we were running routine assays of our metallurgical specimens from the Dark Star system. I built that little furnace just for convenience in fusing samples."

"So?" Hudd forgot to smile. His heavy, mottled face stiffened into a bleak mask of ruthless purpose. "The boys report that your assays were only a blind, intended to cover some secret experiment."

Hudd paused, but Cameron said nothing. He merely stood waiting, his lean face grave enough, but an alarming hint of impersonal amusement in his eyes. Hudd went on:

"I believe it was a most peculiar furnace." Hudd's voice was harsh with accusation. "The boys report that it consumed no current. They say it changed the metals fused in it—that buttons of pure iron, on spectrographic analysis, began to show yellow sodium lines."

Hudd's great body heaved forward against the desk, ominously.

"What about that?"

Cameron nodded easily. Then fear dropped like a

staggering burden upon me. For he grinned across the gleaming mahogany, and told Hudd more than he had ever admitted to the SBI in all our months of intensive interrogation.

"I was looking for something."

For a moment, as he spoke, Cameron let down the shield of reserved and sardonic amusement that he carried against a world of totalitarian compulsion. For a moment his voice had a hard elation, terrible in its honesty.

"I was looking for—freedom." His thin shoulders lifted, almost defiantly. "I thought I had found a new and simple technique for manipulating the cosmic stuff that sometimes we call matter and sometimes energy. I thought I had found the way out of the Atomic Age."

His blue and deep-set eyes, for just that moment, held a stern radiance. Then his brief elation flowed away. His tall, emaciated frame bent to a burden of failure, and I saw the gray sickness of the prison on his haggard face.

"I was mistaken." His voice went flat, with the dull admission of defeat. "The accidental contamination of pure specimens with spectroscopic traces of sodium is notoriously easy. I had already abandoned the experiment before we were arrested."

Hudd nodded his great shaggy head, unsurprised.

"You're smart to tell the truth—and lucky that you failed." His blue-jowled face recovered its habitual political smile. "Now, I think you've had a lesson, Jim, and I'm going to give you another chance." His voice turned savage again. "I don't mean another chance at treason—for you'll be watched, every minute."

Cameron stood waiting. The defeated look was gone. His lean face was properly grave, but his keen blue eyes had a glint of amused expectancy.

"What's your trouble, Mr. Hudd?"

Hudd pushed the little golden head of Tyler away from him, across the opulent desk. Slowly shifting his great bulk, he leaned back in his wide chair, knitting his fingers so that his huge, black-haired hands cradled his paunch. Under the dark thick brows, his small eyes were glazed with fatigue and trouble.

"I suppose you noticed when we went from acceleration thrust to centrifugal, three days ago?" His rasping voice was dry and hurried. "Anyhow, we're back—on a temporary orbit twenty thousand miles from the moon."

"And something's wrong?" Cameron's voice, it seemed to me, had some faint undertone of malicious anticipation. But Hudd didn't seem to notice, for he was stating gravely:

"Something has happened to the Directorate!"

"Eh?" Cameron's veiled amusement vanished. "What?"

"Here are the facts." Heavily, Hudd lurched forward against the desk again; his voice had a brittle snap. "We began calling Fort America weeks ago, from millions of miles at space. Our signals weren't answered. So far as we can determine, the moon has been abandoned."

His eyes looked haunted.

"We haven't tried to signal the earth—I want to keep the advantage of surprise, until we know the situation. But things have happened, even there."

He reached, with a huge and hairy paw, for the little golden bust of Tyler and resumed his nervous drumming.

"But we've been listening, on every possible wave band. Of course, out here, we couldn't expect to get much. But we are in range of the great television propaganda stations of the Applied Semantics Authority— and they are dead. All we have picked up are feeble clicks and squeals—scrambled radiophone signals, apparently, which our engineers can't unscramble."

His lowered voice echoed a baffled unease.

"The telescopes give us several puzzling hints. The forests have grown, since we left—the spread of green into the deserts might almost indicate a general climatic change. The haze of smoke is gone from the old industrial areas. Where several cities used to be, in the tropics, we can find only green jungle."

"Very interesting," Cameron murmured.

"Two landing parties were sent to earth in lifecraft," Hudd added grimly. "One was to land in Europe and the other in North America. Nothing has been heard from either since they entered the ionosphere. They are twenty-four hours overdue."

The solemn, baffled hush of his voice gave me an uncomfortable chill. It would be a terrible and ironic thing, I thought, if we had come back from our long exile to find our own human kind somehow destroyed.

Hudd blinked at Cameron with shrewd weary eyes.

"Now, I'm sending out another party." His voice turned decisive. "Captain Rory Doyle will be in command—under the advice of my liaison man, of course—and Doyle wants you two with him. You are taking off in two hours. Your first object will be to learn what happened to Fort America."

Hudd put his great hands flat on the desk and came laboriously to his feet, puffing with the effort. For all his gross bulk, however, he made a towering figure, dynamic and impressive still. Shrewd and imperious, his small eyes burned into Cameron.

"You had better find out." With a visible effort at control, he lowered his violent voice. "Your mission is important. I believe the Directorate has been overthrown, and I intend to restore it. I've got plutonium enough to smash the earth. The first necessity, however, is to learn what has happened. I believe you can anticipate the consequence to yourselves of failure."

"I think we can, Mr. Hudd," said Cameron.

My heart began to thump, with an excited and somewhat apprehensive expectation.

II

Lifecraft 18 was a trim steel missile lying snug in its berth tube amidships of the *Great Director*. Eighty feet long and slim as a pencil, it had its own ion drive, a regular crew of six, and plenty of additional space for our party.

Captain Rory Doyle met us at the valves. He was a

big man, red-haired, straight and handsome in the gray of the Atomic Service. Under party supervision, he and Cameron had rescued a scout ship sunk in a liquid nitrogen sea on the inner planet of the Dark Star. He was capable, fearless, and loyal to Hudd. Smiling, he welcomed us aboard his swift little craft.

His crew of able spacemen helped us stow our space armor and made ready to launch. Our takeoff time went by, while Doyle scowled at his wrist chronometer, keeping the valves open.

"Waiting for Victor Lord," he muttered. "The Squaredealer."

Only his impatient tone suggested any dislike for Squaredealers—and even that was indiscreet.

Lord came swaggering insolently aboard, twenty minutes late. He was a tiny man, very erect and precise in his gray uniform—with the gold squares of the Machine instead of the blazing atoms of the Service. He had tight brown skin over a hard narrow face, with heavy lids drooping over pale yellow eyes. His long black hair had a varnished slickness. Strutting between his two tall bodyguards, he looked like a peevish dwarf.

He didn't bother to return Doyle's correct salute.

"You know my status, Doyle." His high, nasal voice was deliberately overbearing. "My duty here is to oversee your performance of this important mission. We'll have no trouble—if you just keep in mind that one word from me can break you."

He paused to blink at Doyle, with a sleepy-lidded arrogance. Success in the Squaredeal Machine required brutality, and Lord, I knew, stood second only to Julian Hudd. Haughtily, he added:

"You may take off, now."

"Yes, Mr. Lord."

The Squaredealer's petulant insolence may have been nothing more than a compensation for his size, but still I didn't like him. His yellow eyes were shifty; his narrow forehead sloped and his nose was too big; his whole expression was one of vicious cunning.

Doyle turned quickly away, perhaps to conceal his

own resentment. He ordered the valves closed and climbed the central ladder-well to his bridge. A warning horn beeped, and we cast off.

In the acceleration-lounge, we hung weightless for a few seconds as we dropped away from the flagship; then the thrust of our own ion drive forced us back into the cushions with a 2-G acceleration.

I turned in the padded seat to look back through a small port. Against the dead black of space, I glimpsed the enormous bright projectile-shapes of the *Great Director* and the *Valley Forge*—coupled nose-to-nose with a long cable, spinning slowly like a toy binary to create an imitation gravity.

Earth, close beside them, was a huge ball of misty wonder. The twilight zone made a long crimson slash between the day side and the night. Dull greens and browns and blues were all patched with the dazzling white of storms.

All the hope and longing of twenty years burst over me when I saw the earth, in a sudden flood of choking emotion. My wet eyes blurred that splendid view. I sat grappling in vain with that shocking mystery of spreading forest, abandoned farmlands, and jungle-buried cities, until Victor Lord's high nasal voice recalled me to the lifecraft.

"Feather merchants, huh?" Sitting pygmy-like between his two husky guards, Lord turned condescendingly to Cameron. "But Hudd insisted you must come. Let's have your expert opinion."

He stressed the adjective too strongly, but Cameron answered quietly, "I rather expect we'll find the ultimate result of what the old economists used to call the division of labor."

At the time, I failed to see the real significance of the interchange that followed, though it proved the key to much that happened later. I was merely annoyed at Cameron, and increasingly alarmed, because his talk plainly angered Lord.

"Explain!" Lord rapped.

"If you like—though I'm afraid the historical principle runs counter to Squaredeal ideology." Cameron was a little too grave. "Because I don't believe the Directorate was created by Tyler's unique statesmanship, or even by the emergent dictatorship of the common man. It was, I think, just one of the end products of the division of labor."

Lord blinked his beady eyes, apparently uncertain whether this was double-talk or high treason. I kicked Cameron's foot, vainly trying to keep him quiet.

"Explain yourself," Lord commanded.

"Nothing to it," Cameron said. "The division of labor was hailed as something wonderful—before its unpleasant final consequences came to light. One man made arrows, another hunted, and they both had more to eat. This was very fine, back in the stone age."

Cameron stretched out his legs, cheerful and relaxed.

"But it went a little farther in the modern world. Division of labor divided mankind, setting special interest against the common good. It made specialists in mining coal, in scientific research—even in political power, Mr. Lord. The specialists formed pressure groups, each fighting to advance its own class interest—with weapons incidentally created by that same division of labor.

"When specialists fight, the winners are apt to be the experts in war," Cameron continued innocently. "Thus government becomes a function of military technology, which of course derives from the basic industrial technology. The prevailing form of government, therefore—dictatorship or democracy—depends on the current status of the division of labor. That interesting relation of technology and politics was pointed out by the old philosopher, Silas McKinley."

Lord's sleepy eyes glittered suspiciously.

"He's forbidden! Where do you keep such pernicious literature?"

Cameron grinned. "Once I had permission to do some research in Mr. Hudd's very excellent library."

"You're apt to suffer for the dangerous ideas you acquired there," Lord commented acidly. "Now what's this nonsense about technology and government?"

"Political power reflects military power," Cameron cheerfully explained. "When war is fought with cheap, simple weapons, easy for the amateur to use, then the military importance of the ordinary citizen is reflected in his political freedom. Democracy in America was established by the flintlock and maintained by Colt's revolver.

"But democracy is always threatened by an increase in specialization, especially military specialization. When weapons are expensive and complicated, requiring a class of military experts, then the ordinary man can't defend his rights—and he therefore has no rights.

"Democracy was murdered, on a desert in New Mexico, in 1945. Already, for a hundred years, the increasing division of labor had been forcing it into slow decline. The same specialization that created the bomber and the tank had already reduced the free citizen to a pathetic little man at the mercy of the corporation manager, the union leader, and the party bureaucrat.

"The atom bomb was the end of freedom. Because it was the final limit of specialization. The most complicated and costly weapon ever, its production required a fantastically complex division of labor. Government followed the trend of technology, and totalitarian control destroyed the individual."

Sitting half upright in the long reclining chair, Cameron gave the little Squaredealer his wry, sardonic grin.

"Tyler thought he had conquered the world," he concluded. "But really it was just division of labor that created the new technology of atomic war, and so destroyed the whole world's freedom. It was just the trend of specialization that made the Directorate and flung Tyler to the top of it—no more responsible than a pebble flung up by a wave."

Pressed deep in the cushions, Lord sat peering back with confused suspicion in his yellow eyes. Fortunately for Cameron, he was now concerned with dangers more immediate than ideological heresy. His nasal voice rasped angrily:

"Well? What happened then—according to your theory?"

Cameron answered with an easy grin.

"Quite likely, the division of labor broke down at last."

"Watch your manner, Mister." Lord clearly didn't like his grin. "What could break it down?"

"Rebellion, perhaps." Cameron was properly respectful. "Fort America had a permanent garrison of nine thousand specialists in death. They were prepared to devastate any part of the earth—or all of it. Perhaps they were just too thorough."

Uneasily, the little Squaredealer licked his thin lips. "Then why should the fort itself be silent?"

"Disease, perhaps—some biological weapon out of control." In Cameron's blue eyes, I caught a faint glint of malicious amusement. "Or famine—maybe they left the earth unable to feed them. Or natural cataclysm."

Lord fought the acceleration pressure, to sit bolt upright. His bleak narrow face was filmed with sweat of effort—and of fear.

"Cataclysm?" He peered into Cameron's lean, sardonic face. "Explain!"

"Twenty years at space has shown us the insensate hostility of the universe." Cameron's low voice deepened my own unease. "Man lives at the mercy of blind chance, surviving only through a peculiar combination of improbable factors. Just suppose we find the earth stripped of oxygen." He grinned at Lord, satanically. "As efficiently as the planets of the Dark Star were robbed of uranium?"

Before we reached the moon, Lord had turned a sallow green with acceleration sickness.

Fort America was hidden beneath a crater in the tawny desolation of the Mare Nubium. We wheeled above the mountain ring, just above the highest crags, searching the dozen miles of barren floor.

"It hasn't changed!" I whispered to Cameron. "The valves, the roads, the docks—just as they used to be!" I tried to point through the small quartz port. "There's where the *Great Director* stood."

"But it has changed." Cameron glanced at me; and the strong glare of the moonscape, striking his haggard face from below, made his habitual sardonic expression seem oddly diabolic. "It's abandoned, now."

And I remembered. Great trucks once had rolled over that white web of roads. Colored signal lights had blinked and flickered from the domes over the pits. Tall, tapered ships had stood like rows of silver pillars on the immense, dark fields.

But now the crater was an empty bowl. The lowering sun made all the westward rim a jagged lip of shattered ebony. Sharp fingers of the dark crept across the empty miles, to clutch the empty domes and seize the empty roads.

Nothing moved, anywhere. No metal flashed beneath the sun. No signals flickered, now, out of the cold, increasing shadow. Men had been here once, armed with atomic science, bold with conquest. Now they were gone.

Yet the crater wasn't empty, quite—for it held a riddle. What had silenced man's greatest citadel? Cold dread sank into me, out of that black, expanding shadow. The brooding mystery of it numbed my senses like some spreading biotoxin.

We landed at last, well out in the retreating sunlight, on a concrete road near one of the valves. We clambered into space armor—Cameron and I and Captain Doyle. Laden with assorted equipment, we scrambled one by one through the small air lock, leaping clumsily down to the moon.

Victor Lord remained aboard. He was ill. I believe his apprehensive thoughts had fastened too strongly on Cameron's malicious suggestion of interstellar invasion. I think he expected us to encounter unearthly monsters lurking down in the pits and tunnels.

Beside the bright spire of the lifecraft, we set up a portable radiation counter and a neutron detector. The counter started flashing rapidly, and I couldn't stop an apprehensive gesture toward the valves.

"Dangerous intensity!" My voice rang loud and strange in the spherical helmet. "The residue, maybe, from atomic weapons—though I don't see any craters."

But Cameron was shaking his head, which looked queerly magnified inside the thick, laminated bubble of his helmet.

"Just the normal secondary activity, excited by our own ion blast." His voice came on the microwave phone, dulled and distorted. "I think it's safe for us to go on."

Moving clumsily with all our equipment, we moved a hundred yards to try again. Now the counter showed only the normal bombardment of solar and cosmic rays.

"Come along!" Doyle's deep voice roared in my phones. "Have a look—here's a whole row of wrecks. The mutineers must have caught them sitting. They're blown all to scrap."

Beside a huge deserted dock of gray pumice-concrete, he had discovered the dismembered remnants of half a dozen vessels. We approached cautiously, and paused again to test for dangerous radiations. There were none—for these skeletons of spacecraft had been stripped by something other than mutiny.

This had been a repair dock. Suddenly sheepish, Doyle pointed at abandoned cranes and empty jet pits. The apparent wrecks had merely been cannibalized—their plates and valves and jets ripped out to repair other vessels.

"No mutiny!" Doyle made a disgusted sound. "Let's look below."

For the actual fort was far beneath the crater. A vast web of tunnels, sheltered hangars, shops, barracks, magazines. The launching tubes, trained forever on the earth, were hidden in deep pits. Somewhere in that sublunar labyrinth, we could hope to find our riddle answered.

The nearest entrance shaft was topped with a low dome of concrete, piled with pumice boulders by way of camouflage. The great armored valve was closed, un-rusted, quite intact. Doyle spun a bright little wheel, outside.

"I was stationed here before they picked me for the task force," he said. "A robot-missiles officer—used to know my way around."

The massive steel wedge failed to move, and Doyle turned to another, larger wheel. It resisted, and I came to help. Stubbornly, it yielded. The great wedge sank slowly.

"Power's off." Doyle was breathless with effort. "Manual emergency control!"

We shuffled at last into the huge dark chamber of the lock. Our battery lights cast flickering, fantastic shad-ows. Peering at a row of dials and gauges on the curved steel wall, Doyle punched a series of buttons.

Suddenly I felt a faint vibration. The huge wedge lifted behind us, shutting out the dark and harsh-lit moonscape. The chamber was a steel-jawed trap. I felt a tense unease, and the sudden boom of Doyle's voice startled me.

"The main power lines are dead. That's an emer-gency generator, with a chemical engine—there's one at each valve, to work the controls and energize the instru-ments." He scanned the dials again. "Air inside—seven pounds. Better test it."

When he turned another wheel, air screamed into the chamber. It brought back sound—the clink of our equipment, the clatter of our armored boots, the throb of the emergency engine beneath the metal deck.

We tested it. The counter gave only an occasional click and flash. I broke the glass nipple off a regula-tion testing tube, and Cameron leaned clumsily beside me to study the reaction of the colored paper indicators.

"Okay," he said. "Safe."

We took off our armor. The air was fresh, but icy cold—we exhaled white mist. Hopefully, Doyle tried the telephone in the box beneath the dials. Dead silence answered him. Shivering—perhaps to a sense of some-thing colder than the freezing air—he hung it up and opened the inner valve. The emergency power system didn't work the elevators. We climbed down a black ladder-well, into the silent citadel.

III

Fort America was dead.

The thrumming of the little emergency engine was muffled, as we climbed on down, and finally lost. We descended into appalling silence. So long as we moved, there was a comfortable rustle and clatter. When we stopped to listen, there was nothing at all.

Everywhere, power lines were dead. Midnight shadows retreated grudgingly from our little battery lamps and lay in wait at every turning. Beyond was total dark.

The heating system must have been shut off, months or years before, for the cold was numbing. Sweat had dampened my wool-lined suit in the heated armor, and now it was icy on my back. The chill of the rungs sank through my thin gloves; my fingers were stiff and aching long before we reached a horizontal passage.

Gruesome expectations haunted me. I looked for frozen corpses, twisted with agony from quick biotoxins or charred with atomic heat. Queerly, however, we found no mark of violence, nor any evidence of human death.

"They're just—*gone!*" Even the deep voice of Captain Doyle held a certain huskiness of dread. "Why—I can't imagine. Nothing wrong, no sign of any trouble." He caught his breath, squared his shoulders. "We've got to find the answer. Let's try the commandant's office."

He led the way along a black and soundless lateral tunnel and opened an unlocked door. The series of rooms beyond was deserted—and quite in order. Empty chairs were neatly set behind the empty desks. Dead telephones were neatly racked in their cradles. Pens in their stands were neatly centered on green blotters, with the ink dried up.

Doyle rubbed a dark mark in thin gray dust.

"They've been gone a long time." His voice seemed oddly hushed, yet too loud in those silent rooms.

I began to open the drawers of desks and filing cabinets. They were empty. Bulletin boards had been stripped, floors swept clean. Even the wastebaskets had been neatly emptied.

A large portrait of Tyler in the commandant's office had slipped askew on the wall. Doyle moved without thinking to set it properly straight. Cameron followed his movement, I noticed, with a curious sardonic expression, but silently.

"The evacuation must have been quite orderly." Doyle shook his head, his eyes dark with bewilderment. "No sign of haste or panic. Now what could have caused them to go?"

We moved on, in search of the answer.

It wasn't famine. We walked through an empty mess hall. The long tables were all in line, filmed with dust. Clean trays and silver lay in geometric order, where the last KP's had left them for the last inspection. The warehouse beyond was stacked high with crates and bags and cans of food, frozen now, still preserved.

Nor was it any biological killer, gone wild. We found hundreds of beds in a hospital tunnel, empty, their dusty sheets still neat and smooth. The pharmacy shelves were loaded with drugs, untouched.

"Power failure?" Cameron suggested. "If the pile had gone dead—"

Rory Doyle found the way, down a black and bottomless ladder-well, to the main power-pile. The massive concrete safety wall shut us away from all the actual mechanism, but Cameron scanned the long banks of recording instruments and remote controls. He flashed his light on a distant conveyor belt, motionless, still laden with bright aluminum cans.

"Nothing wrong," he said. "The last operator discharged the pile—dumped the canned uranium out of the lattice into the processing canyon underneath. There's plenty of metal left, but it wasn't charged again."

On another black and silent passage, a little above, we came to the steel-walled dungeons of the guardhouse and the military prison. The armored doors stood open. The records had been removed. The prisoners were gone.

"Revolt, perhaps," Doyle suggested. "Perhaps the prisoners escaped and touched off a mutiny in the garrison—no, that couldn't have been, or we'd see the marks of fighting. Perhaps it was revolution on the earth. That might explain everything—if the missiles are used up."

He led us up again, along an endless silent tunnel, and down another dark ladder-well. We spun stiff wheels to open three heavy safety doors, and came at last into one of the magazines.

Doyle gasped, in blank astonishment.

For on row, as far as our lights could reach, long racks were loaded with the robot missiles. They were sleek cylinders of bright metal, gracefully tapered, every part of them beautiful with precise machining. Space ships, really, they were six feet thick and sixty long, each powered with its own atomic generator, driven with its own ion jets, controlled with the fine and costly mechanism of its own robot pilot, each burdened with its own terrible cargo of plutonium-fused lithium hydrides or crystalline biotoxins.

Stunned, almost, Doyle walked to the nearest. He examined it expertly, lifting inspection plates, flashing his light on serial numbers. He came slowly back to us, baffled.

"All abandoned!" he muttered. "I can't believe it. Why, those babies cost twenty million apiece, even in mass production. They are loaded with the finest precision machines that men ever made. One of them, in forty minutes, could obliterate a thousand square miles of earth. And never a one was fired!"

We climbed again, up a black narrow shaft, to the launcher which Doyle had once commanded. Bright, satiny metal shimmered against our lights. The huge vertical barrel cast monstrous, leaping shadows. Doyle slipped into a familiar seat and touched familiar buttons. An emergency engine began drumming. A huge periscope lens was suddenly bright with the broad crescent earth—with thin black cross hairs intersecting upon it.

He flashed his light on a blank log-sheet, and shook his head.

"Never a missile was fired."

Cameron was whistling through his teeth—a gay bit of melody that made a grotesque counterpoint to the themes of lifeless quiet and ghastly dark and deadly cold, to the whole haunting riddle of the abandoned fortress.

"Are these weapons still serviceable?" he asked.

"Not without some missing parts." Doyle opened an inspection door, to show a dark cavity. "The computer has been removed, and the gyros are gone."

"Too bad," Cameron's voice held the hint of irony. "I imagine Mr. Hudd is going to need them."

"They can be repaired," Doyle assured him soberly. "Our spares for the ships' launchers are interchangeable." Doyle looked at his chronometer. "Now it's time to report to Mr. Hudd—that our mission has failed."

The stern simplicity of the lifecraft, when we were safely back aboard, seemed luxurious. We relaxed in the acceleration chairs and gulped hot soup against the chill of those abandoned tunnels while we answered the peevish and uneasy questions of little Victor Lord.

When the signal officer reported that he had contact with the *Great Director,* we crowded into the narrow television room. Hudd's heavy, blue-wattled face filled the screen.

"Let's have it, Jim." His loud, hearty voice was edged with tension. "What happened to the fort?"

"Evacuated, Mr. Hudd."

"But why?"

"We failed to discover that," Cameron reported. "The withdrawal was deliberate and orderly. The records were mostly removed or destroyed; the weapons were disabled without unnecessary destruction; the men took their personal belongings. There's no evidence whatever of trouble or violence."

"When did it happen?"

"About two years, I think, after the task force left. The dates on calendar pads and inspection cards show that men were here that long. The lowered air pressure, the accumulated dust, and the low counter readings we got about the main power plant—everything shows that they weren't here much longer."

Hudd turned, on the screen, to rap a few questions at Doyle and Lord. Lord's uneasy insolence had changed to a silky deference, now. He explained that acceleration sickness had kept him on the lifecraft.

"A very puzzling situation." Hudd's frown showed his bewildered apprehension. "The entire task force, I feel, is in danger until we find out what happened."

He straightened on the screen.

"Captain Doyle, you will proceed at once to the earth. You will land at Americania. Discover what happened to the Directorate—and what enemies we must destroy to restore it. Take any precautions that you think necessary. But this time you must not fail."

"Yes, Mr. Hudd."

Hudd answered his smart salute and looked at Lord. "You, Mr. Lord, had better get well."

IV

Our lifecraft, next day, spiraled slowly down over Americania—the splendid capital city which Tyler had founded, sentimentally, upon the Midwestern farm where he was born. Peering down through the ports, we felt an increasing sense of fearful puzzlement.

Wide suburban areas had been devastated by explosion or fire, so long ago that lush green forest had now overspread the blackened walls and the twisted frames of rust-red steel—but most of the city looked intact.

Avenue upon avenue, proud towers stood like monolithic memorials to history's greatest empire. Tyler had commanded his architects to build for a thousand years.

Americania was a city of granite—of gray colossal masses, pillared and towered with contrasting red granite, and purple, and black.

Far below us, those stately avenues looked strangely empty. Nothing moved. Tall stacks rose from power plants and industrial buildings in the green-choked suburbs, but there was no smoke.

Was Americania all abandoned, like the moon?

Fear of that sent an uncomfortable prickling up my spine. I looked hopefully at my companions. Little Victor Lord had turned a sallow gray, and sweat made dark blots through his shirt. His two SBI men, in their ominous black, had turned away from the ports; muttering together uneasily, they were inspecting the action of their automatics.

Jim Cameron swung from his port, whistling in that way he had, softly, through his teeth. The air was the light, lilting melody of an old love song. The dwarfish Squaredealer whirled on him, in a sudden, tight-lipped fury.

"Stop your impudent whistling!" Lord's wrath had its real origin, no doubt, in his own frightened bafflement, but his sleep-lidded eyes looked dangerous. Even after Cameron stopped the whistling, Lord was not appeased.

"Look at me, you feather merchant." Lord's sharp nasal voice was angrily insolent. "Frankly, I don't approve the confidence that Mr. Hudd has placed in you. Now I'm warning you—watch your step!"

His small quick hand hovered suggestively over the heavy automatic sagging at his hip.

"Whatever we find here," he snarled, "my duty is to assure your continued loyalty to the Squaredealer Machine. Whatever happens, just remember that."

"I'll keep it in mind, Mr. Lord," Cameron promised him evenly.

Captain Doyle set the lifecraft down at last on Tyler Field—the immense spaceport on the outskirts of the city. Once it had been the gateway to the planets. I could remember my childish awe at the rush and glitter and vastness of it, from twenty years ago—when we marched across it, bravely screeching out the Tyler song, on our way out to Fort America and the Dark Star. Now, when I saw it again through the small ports of the lifecraft, the change made me almost ill.

Like Fort America, the spaceport seemed abandoned. Here, however, weather and decay had kept at work. Green life had kept on, overflowing every plot of soil, bursting from every crack in the neglected pavements.

Long rows of shops and warehouses stood deserted. Doors yawned open. Neglected roofs were sagging. Ruined walls, here and there, were black from old fire. Every building was hedged with weeds and brush.

Far across the shattered pavements stood the saddest sight of all. A score of tall ships stood scattered across the blast-aprons where they had landed. Though small by comparison with such enormous interstellar cruisers as the *Great Director*, some of them towered many hundred feet above the broken concrete and the weeds. They stood like strange cenotaphs to the dead Directorate.

Once they had been proud vessels. They had carried the men and the metal to build Fort America. They had transported labor battalions to Mars, dived under the clouds of Venus, explored the cold moons of Jupiter and Saturn. They had been the long arm and the mighty fist of Tyler's Directorate, the iron heels upon the prostrate race of man.

Now they stood in clumps of weeds, pointing out at the empty sky they once had ruled. Red wounds marred their sleek skins, where here and there some small meteoric particle must have scratched the mirror-bright polish, letting steel go to rust, which, in the rains of many years, had washed in ugly crimson streaks down their shining sides.

One of them had fallen. The great hull was flattened from the impact, broken in two. Steel beams, forced through the red-stained skin, jutted like red broken bones. The apron was shattered beneath it, so that a thick jungle of brush and young trees had grown up all around it.

Captain Rory Doyle came silently down his ladder from the bridge. His square face was black with gloomy puzzlement—as any loyal spaceman's should have been.

"A graveyard," he muttered, "of fine old ships—my first training voyage to Mars was on the old *Paul Jones*, yonder." He turned sadly to us. "Gadgets ready, Mr. Cameron? Then let's go out and see what unholy thing has happened to them."

"Hold on, Doyle!" Lord's nasal voice was sharp with dread. "Shouldn't we test the air? Suppose something has happened to the atmosphere?"

Doyle turned to Cameron, red brows lifted.

"I don't think it's necessary, Mr. Lord," Cameron said respectfully. "You can see a gray squirrel scolding at us from the tree growing out of the apron, yonder, and a buzzard circling, toward the city. I think the air's all right."

"I'll do the thinking." The little Squaredealer drew himself up stiffly, in the sweat-blotched uniform. "Test it."

I found a test flask, and took it down to draw a sample through a tube in the inner valve. Cameron watchfully checked my reading of the colored indicators.

"It's safe enough, Mr. Lord," he reported crisply. "Oxygen normal. A bit of secondary radioactivity—due to our jets. No detectable toxic agents, chemical or biological."

"Then we're going out." Doyle looked thoughtfully at Cameron and me. "I don't know what we're running into. If you wish, I'll issue you arms."

"No, you won't!" The little Squaredealer barked out that sharp protest. "These men are suspected mutineers, Doyle. I'll take no chances with them."

Doyle's square jaw slowly hardened.

"Mr. Lord," he began. "I believe the SBI found nothing—"

"It doesn't matter, Captain," Cameron broke in.

"We've gadgets enough to carry. Anyhow, I doubt that a pistol would be much use, where Fort America failed."

Lord looked at him with a puzzled alarm in his sleepy-seeming eyes, and then muttered something to his two gunmen. Their uneasy eyes went to Cameron.

Doyle led the way down the ladder-well. Air hissed, and the valves clanged open. One by one, we stooped to follow him through the lock and jumped out between the shining stabilizers to mother earth.

We hurried away from the scorched concrete and smoking weeds about the little ship, where the ion jet might have left a dangerous activity, before we stopped to catch our breath.

Earth! We had dreamed of it for twenty years. Here in the northern hemisphere it was early summer; the sky was a wondrous milky blue, flecked with cottony cumulus. The forenoon sun struck with a hot, welcome force. The warm air was heady with a fragrance that stirred old memories—the rich strong smell of green life growing out of damp vegetal decay. I heard a heavy buzzing, half-remembered, and saw a bumblebee.

The warm earth, alive—and a lone black bird, yonder, wheeling over an empty city.

Lord, running after us through the blackened weeds, let out a nasal yelp of horror. A white skull, which he had stumbled against, rattled and bounded before him. We found the rest of the skeleton, with a rust-caked revolver on the broken concrete beside it. Scraping about in the weeds, we discovered several shapeless lumps of heavy metal, dark from heat, and a bent penny that still showed Tyler's profile. Cameron found the flattened cases of several ruined watches, and a woman's diamond bracelet, the links half fused and the stones burned black. Doyle picked up a wicked-looking stainless steel blade, its haft rotted away.

"A curious lot of loot." Cameron stood up, puzzled. "All burned, the money melted down. Maybe he was struck by lightning. Or maybe looting just isn't cricket."

Lord stood off and fired a bullet into the skull, I suppose just to test his gun. Bone shattered into white dust. He holstered the automatic with an air of uneasy satisfaction, mopped the sweat off his narrow sallow face, and followed us watchfully.

We went on to the nearest ship. The bright curving hull towered three hundred feet, marred with long vertical streaks of rust. It was a stubby freighter; Doyle said it had been in the Martian metal trade.

We followed Doyle up a rusty accommodation ladder into the lock. The inner valve was closed, stiff with rust. We strained and hammered at the manual wheels until it groaned reluctantly open. A stale breath met us as we stumbled through the lock into dusty dark.

There was no power for lights or elevators. The interphone system was dead. We probed the silent dark with flashlights, and Doyle led the way up the ladder shaft beside the elevator. Lord, with his two gunmen decided to remain below. Doyle climbed into a cargo hold and cursed in breathtaken astonishment.

"Plutonium!" A bewildered awe hushed his voice. "Hundreds of tons of refined plutonium in cadmium drums—enough to blow up half America—worth hundreds of millions." His haunted eyes peered back at Cameron. "Why did they leave it?"

We climbed on, looking for the answer. Our feeble lights, as we passed, searched each dark compartment. Everything was left in order. The galley was clean. The atomic generator had been discharged and secured.

There were no other skeletons.

A hard climb brought us to the executive deck. We found dusty charts and orbit plots neatly folded, astrogation instruments safe in their racks. Doyle opened an unlocked safe, with a shout of triumph.

"Now we'll know—here's the log."

He fumbled with the yellowing pages. Eagerly, we leaned to read the brief, routine entries which described an uneventful voyage from Mars. The four-hourly observations and computed positions were neatly entered, and the hourly checks of solar position and apparent diameter. The date of the final entry corresponded with the dates on the calendar pads at Fort America. It was brief, neatly written, and completely exasperating:

"Routine landing at Tyler Field. Ship abandoned today, because of equalizer."

That was all.

"I don't get it." Doyle shook his head, staring bleakly at that yellowed page. "A spaceworthy ship. Competent officers, evidently, and a loyal crew. They make a routine voyage and a routine landing. Not a hint of anything unusual."

He peered up at Cameron.

"Then something happens," he muttered. "Something makes them walk off and leave their jobs and their duty and a ship and cargo worth hundreds of millions. I just don't get it."

We went back to move the lifecraft nearer the deserted city. When we landed again, in a suburban area which had been seared and flattened by some tremendous blast, the counter showed a lingering trace of secondary activity in the blobs of fused debris.

"An atomic explosion," Cameron decided.

"But not one of our standard robot missiles," Doyle added. "One shot from my launcher at Fort America would have leveled a hundred times this space."

We moved again, to a street in a still standing suburb of detached, walled villas. Here, Doyle said, prominent officials of the Directorate had lived in an exclusive colony. He set the lifecraft down on a bit of unshattered pavement that made a clearing in the brush. Frowning walls faced the street, overgrown with green vines now, brilliant with blue morning glories where the sun had not yet struck.

A tall gate of ornamental bronze sagged open before the nearest building, and we pushed in through a tangle of long-untended shrubbery that had overgrown the lawns. An unlocked door let us into the mansion, and musty silence met us.

Here we found no hint of any popular uprising against the ruling class. No bullet prints, no human bones, no smashed furniture, no looted safes and chests.

The refrigerator in the great kitchen had been emptied, but long shelves were filled with fine cut glass and ornamental china. The gloomy library held thousands of volumes—but empty spaces seemed to say that others had been taken. Closets were hung with moth-ravaged clothing. A wall safe stood open, and Doyle explored the paper in it with a frown of dull bewilderment.

"They left a fortune," he muttered incredulously. "This man—His Excellency, A. P. Watts, Director-General of West Africa—must have been a lifetime piling up these stocks, annuities, bonds and shares, insurance policies, deposit receipts. Then something happened. He just walked off and left it all."

His eyes appealed to Cameron.

"I don't understand it." The spectre of dread haunted his voice. "They weren't killed—there would be more skeletons. They weren't even frightened—they didn't barricade their doors, or fire a gun, or even upset the furniture. They just set things in order, took a few useful items—and went away."

His voice fell to a whisper of dull wonderment.

"But why—and where—could they have gone?"

We moved the lifecraft again, this time into what had been an exclusive shopping district, where once, I fancied, the great men of the Directorate must have bought jewels and furs and perfumes for their mistresses, their secretaries, and perhaps even for their wives.

The street doors of these glittering shops were generally unlocked, or left wide open. Many shelves were bare, as if the goods had been simply carried out, but there was little evidence of vandalism or violent looting. Unbroken windows still held garish displays of tarnished costume jewelry. Abandoned cash registers were still stuffed with currency and coin—from which I saw Lord's gunmen furtively filling their pockets.

We landed next in the middle of the city, in the wide empty canyon of Tyler Avenue. There the massive granite walls were hushed and dead, but green weeds were pushing from every crevice in the hot pavements.

A few sparrows were quarreling noisily about a window ledge.

"This was Squaredeal Square." Doyle's voice seemed too loud, in that sun-beaten silence. "If there was any fighting—war or rebellion—we ought to find the traces here."

Peering up at those splendid dead facades, I remembered that I had been here once before—in a great jamboree of the Tyler Scouts, the year I was seven. There was Squaredeal Hall. There was the purple granite balcony where Tyler—or perhaps it was one of his public doubles—had appeared as we marched by, waving his arm mechanically as we screamed out the Tyler Song.

A diamondback, lazily sunning on the black granite steps of Squaredeal Hall, greeted us with a warning whir. Lord whipped out his automatic with a nervous expertness and shot it through the head.

The crash of his shot shattered that hot silence. It thundered back, appallingly magnified by those sheer granite cliffs. The dwarfish Squaredealer and his guards crowded apprehensively together, and we all listened uneasily. But the echoes faded unanswered; the dead city was not aroused.

Doyle led us up the steps, past the dead diamondback. Voiceless with awe, we went on between the immense square columns beyond. Here was the shrine of the Directorate. Tyler had surrounded his birthplace with a colonnade of purple granite more majestic than Karnak.

Memory stirred again. After that review and jamboree, as a personal gift from Tyler, each Scout had received a picture post card of the shrine. The little weatherbeaten farmhouse was shown beneath the towering columns, surrounded with an old-fashioned garden of zinnias and gladioli. The stone springhouse had been restored. The old appletree, which the Director used to climb, was pink with blooms in the picture.

But that historic tree was dead, now. The house had fallen in. The mighty purple columns rose out of a green sea of weeds and sprouts and brambles. Wild morning glories had buried the old springhouse. Something moved in the brush, and we heard the vicious warning hum of another diamondback.

Beside the useless elevator, we climbed a narrow stair. Tyler's own door, between two empty guardboxes, had been left unlocked. We walked into the abandoned splendor of the Director's own apartment—and found no trace of violence.

On the high wall behind his desk, and the office chair that had served him for a throne, a faded tapestry still hung, intact and undefiled, embroidered in gold with the three linked squares of the Machine.

The massive door of a huge fireproof safe swung carelessly open. Its compartments were stuffed with documents marked RESTRICTED or CONFIDENTIAL or TOP SECRET. Letters, reports, beribboned executive decrees—the state papers of the Directorate, left heedlessly behind.

Lord, with a shrill excited shout, discovered a pile of heavy cloth bags that had been buried under the dusty documents in the bottom of the safe. Feverishly, he ripped one of them open, spilling out bright golden double-eagles.

"Millions—left behind!" Wide awake, for once, his eyes glittered yellow as the metal, and his thin nasal voice was hushed with awe. "There must have been a dreadful panic, to make them leave the gold."

But Cameron pointed quietly to several empty compartments, and a blackened metal wastebasket, on the end of the desk, nearly full of gray ashes.

"It wasn't panic, Mr. Lord," he said respectfully. "Tyler had plenty of time to burn the papers he wanted to destroy. Then, I should imagine, he just walked out."

The little Squaredealer peered up at him, bewildered and visibly afraid.

"But why? Tyler wouldn't give up the whole Directorate."

The faded luxury of the great rooms gave us no answer. The paneled walls showed no marks of bullets. The dusty rugs showed no stains that could be blood.

The Director's great bed, under its coverlet of dust, still was neatly made.

Doyle came back to Cameron, muttering the question that haunted us:

"Where could they have gone?"

Cameron rubbed his lean jaw with a brown forefinger.

"Let's try the country," he said thoughtfully.

Doyle stared at him, blankly. "Why?"

"People used to live in cities for certain reasons," Cameron said. "Just as they worked for great corporations, or enlisted in the Atomic Service, or joined the Squaredeal Machine. Perhaps those reasons changed."

Lord blinked sleepily.

"You had better watch your tongue," he warned sharply. "I believe you read too much in Mr. Hudd's library. I'll be compelled to report your dangerous views."

But we returned to the lifecraft. Doyle landed it again, outside Americania, where a disused highway made a narrow slash through woods and thickets. We climbed down between the stabilizers once more, and Cameron pointed suddenly.

Planted in the middle of the old road behind us was a signpost. It carried a yellow-lettered warning:

DANGER!

Metropolitan Areas

V

Gathered in a puzzled little circle, we examined that sign.

"Well?" Doyle looked at Cameron.

"A remarkably strong aluminum alloy." Thoughtfully, Cameron rubbed his lean brown chin. "An excellent vitreous enamel. Evidently it was made and set up after the city was abandoned—to keep people out."

He started whistling gayly through his teeth, but Lord

scowled him into silence. His blue eyes had lit with a speculative eagerness.

"And so?" prompted Doyle.

"Interesting implications." Cameron counted on lean brown fingers. "One, there are people. Two, they possess a high-grade metal-and-enamel technology. Three, they have sufficient social organization to post public signs. Four, they don't like cities."

His eager eyes peered beyond the silver pencil of the lifecraft, down the dark leafy tunnel of the old road. He softly whistled another lilting bar, and then looked quickly back at Doyle.

"Let's take off again, Captain," he suggested. "And follow the road, flying low. I think we'll find the signposters."

"We'll do that—" Doyle began, but the little Squaredealer interrupted him sharply:

"I'm in charge, and I don't agree." Lord's nasal tone was both insolent and apprehensive. "The jets are too bright and noisy. We'd be seen—maybe killed from ambush. Don't forget that melted money. No, we'll leave the craft hidden here, and go on foot."

Doyle's red head nodded soberly.

"A wise precaution, probably," he agreed. "We'll carry a radiophone, so we can call back."

Leaving the bright craft hidden among the trees, we started cautiously down the green tunnel. Interlacing branches usually hid the sky. Vines and ferns made thick walls on either side. Jays scolded at us, and unseen things rustled in the brush. Once we came upon a red deer. It stood quite motionless in a little glade ahead, antlers high, until Lord clutched for his automatic; then it bounded noisily away.

We were all, I think, keyed up and uneasy. The gloom of the forest darkened my own thoughts. Imagination turned small rustlings into startling threats. Recalling that the two other landing parties were long overdue, I began to wish I had a gun.

Cameron walked ahead. His step was light and springy, and his hollowed face had a look of grave expectancy. Once he started whistling again, softly, but Lord stopped him with a snarled command.

We must have gone three miles before Cameron turned from a curve in the old road and plunged out of sight into the ferns and tangled vines. We followed him. A few yards brought us into daylight, on the rocky rim of a low sandstone cliff.

"The sign posters," he said softly.

He pointed. Before us spread a broad, shallow valley of woods and open meadow. The sun glittered from the curve of a stream, but I saw no people.

"There's the house against the other cliff. Reddish walls, and green roof." I found it, then—a low graceful building that had seemed part of the landscape. "I heard a man singing."

I listened. It was midafternoon now, and a soft breeze had begun to disturb the midday hush. Leaves stirred lazily. I heard the sleepy hum of insects, the cool murmur of water running, a mockingbird singing—all wonderful sounds, half familiar, that brought my boyhood back.

"Listen," Cameron urged.

There was a clear yodeling call—answered by a woman's voice.

"Keep down!" Lord's nasal voice was cautiously hushed. "We'll slip across, under cover. Study their weapons, and keep out of sight. If we're discovered— shoot first."

"Are you sure," Cameron protested, "that shooting's necessary?"

"I'm running this show." Lord's sleepy eyes narrowed unpleasantly. "I'll tolerate no meddling from you."

A fern-grown ravine let us down from the low cliff. We waded the clear stream and climbed again through the woods beyond. Nearer the dwelling, the land had been cleared. We crossed an orchard of young apple trees and slunk on toward the voices of the man and the woman.

Twenty years at space had not made us expert stalkers. Dry leaves rattled, twigs cracken, pebbles clattered.

Lord turned, more than once, with a hissed injunction of silence. But at last we came on hands and knees to the grassy rim of another ravine and peered down upon the unsuspecting two.

They were running a machine. The young woman sat in a little cab of bright aluminum, moving levers. A toothed bucket, on a long metal arm, scooped earth and stones from the side of the gorge to fill a hopper.

The man held a flexible hose, pouring a heavy yellow semiliquid from the machine into a metal form across the little gorge. Presently he stopped to lift and adjust the plates of the form, and then poured again. Between the plates, I saw, a massive yellow dam was growing.

The machine ran quietly. There was only a subdued humming, and the occasional clatter of the bucket when sometimes it scraped a stone. It ate the dark soil, pouring out yellow concrete.

I peered at Cameron, astonished.

He made a pleased little nod.

"A very neat step forward," he whispered, "in basic technology."

"Silence!" Lord hissed.

Below us, the man called to the girl, and she moved the machine on its wide caterpillar tracks. Watching them, I felt an increasing glow of pleasure. For twenty years I had thought and dreamed of life on earth; here at last was a glimpse of it—as any lucky man might hope to live it.

The man was a lithe young giant in shorts, bareheaded and brown. The sweat of his toil, in the hot afternoon, made a film that rippled and gleamed with every movement of his sun-bronzed body. Sometimes he paused to get his breath, smiling and calling down to the girl.

"Mushrooms for supper, what?" "Let's plant a lilac on the south terrace, shall we?" "I've thought of a name, darling—let's call him Dane Barstow. Dane Barstow Hawkins!"

That name gave me a puzzled shock. Dane Barstow had been my own father's name—but it seemed quite improbable that the expected young Hawkins should be named for an unsuccessful traitor, long dead in the labor camps of the Squaredeal Machine.

But I soon forgot my wonder, watching them. Their absorbed happiness set me to dreaming wistfully. The girl was sun-colored, too, still slender, lovely. She ran the machine with a graceful skill, until the time when the man lost his balance as he hauled at the hose and teetered on the edge of the dam.

She stopped the machine then, with a sharp cry of alarm. After a moment of frantic clawing at the air, however, the man regained his balance. Seeing him safe, she laughed at him—a rich laugh, deep and musical and glad.

"Darling, if you had seen yourself! But please be careful—you're much too valuable to be made into the dam! If you're so weak, we'd better stop—I'm hungry anyhow."

"Laugh at me, huh?"

Grinning fondly through a mock ferocity, the man hung up the hose and dropped down from the dam. The girl scrambled out of the cab and ran from him, still laughing.

"Darling," she sobbed, "you looked so silly—"

"Stop 'em!" whispered Lord.

Instantly, the automatics crashed. The girl crumpled down beside the bright machine. The man ran another step, uttered a strangled cry, fell sprawling on top of her.

"My God!" Doyle shouted incredulous protest. "What have you done?"

The dwarfish Squaredealer fired twice more, expertly. His bullets thudded into the quivering bodies. The bitter reek of smoke stung my nostrils. Nodding to his bleak-faced gunmen, he rose calmly to his feet.

"Well, they didn't get away." His nasal voice had a shocking complacency. "I thought they might have seen us. Now we'll have to work fast, to learn what we can and get away to space. Doyle, call the craft—have it brought here at once. Cameron, inspect that machine—

Mr. Hudd will want a full report on it. We'll look for their weapons."

Doyle had the self-discipline of a good officer. He was white-lipped, stunned, but any protest must wait for the proper channels. He reached obediently for the little radiophone which I had been carrying.

Cameron's discipline was not so fine.

"You fool!" His blue eyes glared at Lord, his low voice crackling with anger. "You murdering fool! You had no excuse for that."

His brown fists clenched. For one terrified moment, I thought he was going to strike the Squaredealer. Lord must have thought so too, for he nodded at his two black gunmen and stepped quickly back.

"Please, Jim." I caught Cameron's quivering arm. "You'll only get us shot."

"Quite right." Lord retreated again, watchfully. "Any further trouble, and I'll shoot you both with pleasure. In any case, I shall report your insubordination. Now—if you want to stay alive—inspect that machine."

Angrily, Cameron shrugged off my hand. He stood facing Lord defiant. Slowly—with an eager, dreadful little twist of his thin, pale lips—Lord raised his gun. Cameron gulped, shrugged, turned silently toward the bright machine.

Lord and his men searched the bodies. They found no weapons. The gunmen came back with a ring and a watch and a jeweled comb they had taken from the girl.

Cameron attacked the machine with an intense, trembling savagery of movement—as if it had been a substitute for Lord. After a few moments, however, a sudden consuming interest seemed to swallow his wrath. His lean face became intent, absorbed. His fingers were steady again, very quick and skillful. Soon he was whistling with his teeth, so softly that Lord seemed not to hear.

I tried to help him, ineffectually. The machine baffled me utterly. Obviously, it had turned ordinary stone and soil into a very strong quick-setting concrete, a feat which seemed remarkable enough. There was, however, something more astonishing.

The machine had evidently used a great deal of electrical power. Electric motors drove the tracks and moved the bucket; heavy bus bars ran into the cylinder where soil became cement. Strangely, however, I couldn't find the source of that power. There was no lead-in cable, no space for batteries, no possible receiver for broadcast power, certainly nothing bulky enough to be any kind of fission or fusion engine. Yet there was current—as a painful shock convinced me. So far as I could determine, it just appeared spontaneously in the circuits.

Bewildered—shaken, too, by that unexpected shock—I stood back to watch. Working with such an eager-faced absorption that I didn't dare to question him, Cameron was studying a bit of the wiring which, for no reason that I could see, was formed into a double coil of oddly twisted turns. His absently whistled notes turned gay.

Lord had posted his two gunmen on either side of the ravine, with orders to shoot any stranger at sight. He himself stood warily on the bank of the little gorge, watching Cameron. When Doyle had completed his call to the lifecraft, Lord sent him and me to search the house.

"Look for weapons," he rapped. "Find out all you can, for our report to Hudd. Make it quick." His nasal voice was shrill with dread. "When the craft comes, we're getting out of here."

Doyle tramped in bitter silence until we were out of earshot, and then let flow a savage stream of low-voiced military profanity.

"That unprintable fool!" he finished. "Those poor farmers could have told us all we want to know, in five minutes—but that bloodthirsty fool had to butcher them!"

He kicked angrily at a pebble.

"I'm sorry about your friend Cameron." He gave me a sympathetic look. "Lord doesn't like him. You know the sort of report he'll make. Cameron's done for. He was just too independent."

VI

Rory Doyle and I came up to the dwelling. The long, low building seemed all of one piece, a solid part of the hillside. It was apparently made of the same soil concrete as the dam—differently colored in different rooms, the walls smooth and warm to the touch.

The furnishings gave an effect of sturdy and comfortable simplicity. The whole house seemed to tell of a warm, free, spacious sort of life—a cold shadow fell across it, when I thought of its builders and owners, lying slaughtered in the gully.

Hastily, we explored the inviting living room, the workshop where a handsome table stood half finished in a clutter of plastic dust and shavings, the big kitchen fitted with shining gadgets to manufacture dishes and synthetic staples on the spot, the cold locker stored with a rich abundance of frozen foods.

We found no identifiable weapons. Nor any good reason, that I could see, why men had fled the cities and abandoned their old way of life. Instead, it was another mystery that we found.

"They must have been very nearly self-sufficient." Peering about the silent rooms, Doyle tried to reconstruct the lives of the murdered couple. "I think they built and furnished this house, with their own hands—everything has the look of good, careful workmanship; they were adding a new room, which isn't roofed yet. Evidently they grew or manufactured their own food. That little machine in the shed is grinding a hopperful of leaves and sticks into something like cloth, very beautiful and strong. All these gadgets must use a lot of power."

His puzzled eyes came back to my face.

"But where does the power come from?"

I had to shake my head.

"The house isn't wired," I told him. "Each gadget

seems to generate its own current—without any batteries or generator or anything else that makes sense to me. Just like that machine at the dam."

On a table in the living room we found a telephone instrument, cradled on a little black plastic box that had no wires attached. Doyle picked it up impulsively, then reluctantly set it back again.

"We could call," he said. "Perhaps we could just ask what we want to know. But Mr. Lord doesn't want it done that way."

We heard the roar of jets, then, and hurried back to the ravine. Doyle had brought a blanket from the house, which he spread decently over the two bodies. Sinking slowly upon an inverted mushroom of blue electric fire, the lifecraft landed a hundred yards below the dam. Scorched weeds smouldered about the bright fins that held it upright.

On the bank of the little gorge, Lord turned from watching Cameron, to question Doyle. But when Doyle merely shook his head, with an empty-handed shrug, Lord went back to shout at Cameron:

"On the double, now. Time to go. Let's see what you've got."

Cameron came up out of the ravine, carrying something in his hand. It was a piece of thick copper wire, shaped into a double coil of oddly shaped loops at odd-seeming angles and held in shape with a transparent plastic rod.

"This is it," he said.

The hushed elation of his low voice told more than his words. I stared at him—for something, I thought, had somehow transformed him. His emaciated body had grown proudly straight. His hollowed face was smiling, illuminated with a stern joy which almost frightened me.

"Well?" Lord retreated as if afraid of Cameron's blue eyes. His sleek black head made a quick nod, to bring his two gunmen back from the ends of the unfinished dam. "What is it?"

Cameron held up that bit of wire on the plastic rod,

with both his hands. His face had a look of solemn awe—as if the thing in his hands had been, perhaps, some unique and long-sought bit of priceless, ancient art.

"Speak up," Lord rapped nervously.

Cameron looked up at Lord again, with no awe of him. His blue eyes showed a sudden glint of ironic amusement. Yet still he held that bit of wire as if it were a precious thing.

"It's what we've all been looking for." Cameron's voice held the quick ring of triumph. "The reason men abandoned Fort America. Why they deserted the cities. What happened to the Directorate, and to Tyler."

Cameron's eyes turned sardonic.

"It's also what is going to happen to the task force," he added softly. "To Mr. Julian Hudd. And even to you, Mr. Lord."

Lord's sleepy yellow eyes slitted dangerously.

"I'll tolerate no further insubordination," he snapped savagely. "Tell me what you've got."

Cameron turned to Doyle and me. Angrily, Lord hauled out his automatic, and then slowly thrust it back again. I suppose that even he could see the folly of extinguishing the source of information. Perhaps he was a little afraid of Cameron. But he still intended, I knew, to get his revenge.

Cameron ignored his sullenly boiling fury.

"Chad, you remember that little gadget we called an induction furnace? Well, we were on the right track—if I hadn't been afraid of blowing up the *Great Director*. And this is the thing we were looking for."

Generously, he gave me far too much credit. I had known, of course, that the device was something more than a furnace—for it made atomic changes in the metal samples we fused, while it somehow generated power. That much I had known, and held my tongue about it. But I had really understood neither his effort nor his goal.

From me, Cameron turned impulsively to Doyle.

"Captain, may I have a word with you?"

"Of course." Doyle raised his red brows in puzzlement. "What about?"

"This." Cameron lifted the thing in his hands. "I've always admired you, Captain. I trust you now." He beckoned with his head, toward the end of the dam. "Let me tell you what this things means to you—and all of us." He glanced aside at the simmering, suspicious little Squaredealer, adding: "Listen for just ten minutes, Captain, and you'll be free of Lord and his sort."

Confusedly, Doyle shook his head.

"Careful, Cameron." I knew he was no friend of Lord's; yet his voice was shocked. "Watch yourself. You sound like treason."

Cameron gave him a brief, sardonic grin.

"If there is such a thing, any longer." His low voice turned grave again. "Though I imagine that this little device has repealed a lot of the old laws." He glanced at the twisted wire, and regretfully back to Doyle. "I wish you'd listen, Rory. But I know how you feel. I'll save your life if I can."

Little Lord was quivering with white-lipped fury. His hand hovered close to his gun. Yet caution or curiosity must have tempered his wrath, for he gestured sharply to halt his black-clad gunmen.

"Explain this strange behavior, Cameron," he snapped. "Before I have to shoot you down."

Cameron turned back to him.

"No, I don't think you'll do that, Mr. Lord," he murmured very softly. "Because you're an anachronism, now, along with the dinosaur and the atom bomb. Technological advancement has passed you by."

Lord's narrow, sallow face turned dark. Still, however, he seemed to want the secret of that piece of twisted wire more than he wanted Cameron's life. He nodded furtively to his gunmen, who began edging aside to Cameron's right and left.

"What's that gadget?" he snarled.

Cameron had turned to me.

"You'll come with me, won't you, Chad?" His low voice had a tremor of anxious appeal. "There's a job we have to do, with this." He moved the little device. "It's not too dangerous—if we're lucky. I need you, Chad."

I wanted to go with him—wherever he was going. But I could see the two bleak-faced men moving warily to get behind him, I could see Lord's wolfish snarl and the cold menace of his yellow eyes, I could remember the SBI and all the cruel art of intensive interrogation. Somehow, that bit of wire and plastic had made Cameron seem a bolder and bigger man, but still I hadn't felt the power of it.

Miserably, I shook my head.

"That's all right, Chad." He gave me a brief, cheering grin. "Perhaps I'll have a better chance alone. I'll do my best to save you."

"You, stand still!" Lord shouted, and sharply ordered his gunmen: "Shoot for the knees, if he tries anything."

Cameron turned back to him, soberly.

"Better call them off, Mr. Lord." Something in his low voice sent a shiver up my spine. "It's time for you to think of your own skin, now. Because it's clear that you made error when you butchered that man and girl. You aren't safe here—or anywhere."

The little Squaredealer must have heard that something in Cameron's voice, for his sallow face turned a sickly yellow-gray. His perspiring arm gestured again, uneasily, to hold his gunmen back. He blinked apprehensively.

"I'll be back," Cameron said. "But I advise you not to follow."

He dropped into the ravine, up beyond the dam.

Lord hesitated for a long second, pale and breathless.

"Get after him," he screamed at last. "Shoot him in the legs."

He didn't lead the pursuit, however, and his men weren't eager. That same something in Cameron's voice must have made them doubt that it was really wise to follow. They ran uncertainly along the rim of the little gorge, firing a few wild shots.

Ahead of them, something flashed. Its terrible brightness made us duck and shield our eyes, even in the full daylight. The detonation came instantly—a single, terrific report. A green tree, beside the ravine, shattered into smoking, whistling fragments.

Lord and his two men followed no farther. As soon as the burning splinters stopped falling, they scrambled up off their faces and hastily retired.

"Unprintable feather merchant!" gasped the little Squaredealer. "He'll regret this." He made a rather fearful gesture toward the lifecraft. "On board!" he shouted. "We're getting out of here."

VII

We tumbled through the valves, and Lord ordered Captain Doyle to blast away at full thrust. Before Doyle could reach his bridge, however, the signal officer shouted down the ladder-well:

"Captain Doyle! I've just got contact with the *Great Director*. Mr. Hudd is on the screen. He wants a full report at once, sir."

The earth's intervening mass had cut off microwave transmission when we dropped over the bulge of it before we landed; now, however, the planet's rotation had brought the flagship back above the horizon. We climbed hurriedly into the little television room.

Gigantic on the screen, Hudd boomed his question:

"What's the story, Lord?"

"A crisis, Mr. Hudd!" Lord looked damp with sweat, and his voice turned shrill. "We're in danger. I request permission to blast off at once and make our full report at space."

"What's the crisis?"

Lord gulped uncomfortably. "Your smart feather merchant got away."

Hudd's great, blue-jowled face was furrowed with sudden concern.

"Then I'll take your full report, Mr. Lord," he said decisively. "Right now."

"But Cameron has a weapon," Lord protested desperately. "Something that strikes like lightning—"

"Then the entire task force may be in peril," Hudd cut in. "Now let's have it—at once."

Lord talked rapidly, while sweat burst out in great bright drops on his narrow face and soaked dark blotches into his uniform. Hudd listened gravely, now and then turning to Doyle or me with a sharp question.

It was Doyle who told him how Lord and the two guards had shot the couple named Hawkins. Hudd's heavy, sagging jaw hardened at the news. When the report was finished, he must have started his habitual nervous drumming—his hands were hidden below the screen, but the speaker brought a worried rapping.

"You made two blunders." His small, troubled eyes peered accusingly at Lord. "You let Cameron get away with the vital information I sent you for. And you killed those people before they had a chance to talk. I'm afraid you have gravely compromised our objectives, Victor—and your own future."

All his swagger gone, Lord twisted and cringed before the steady eyes of Hudd. Still perspiring, he seemed to fawn and cower like a punished dog as the loud, aggressive voice of his master continued:

"We must take bold, immediate action, Victor, to restore the situation."

"Right, Mr. Hudd," Lord said eagerly. "Shall we blast off, now?"

"You will remain where you are," Hudd said. "Get in touch with the inhabitants, if you can. Offer apologies and compensation for the killing. Stall for time. Find out all you can about the weapons, the military establishment, and the government of the inhabitants."

Lord gulped uneasily, nodding.

"Post a reward for Cameron." Hudd's big mouth set hard. "My mistake, to trust him. Get hold of him. Use extreme interrogation. Make him talk, then liquidate him. He has gone too far."

Hudd shook his head regretfully.

"Too bad," he added. "I always rather liked him."

I felt cold and ill. Hudd's loud words had struck me like numbing blows. That harsh command was no surprise to me, but it brought me a dull sickness of regret, because I had failed Cameron when he asked me to go with him.

Lord was protesting again:

"Mr. Hudd, I think we'll be attacked—"

"I'll support you," Hudd assured him, and turned to speak to his signal officer: "Change the scramble code—we don't know who is trying to listen."

The unseen officer on the flagship droned out a code number, repeating each digit. Our officer droned it back. The screen darkened, flickered. Then the image of Hudd came back, huge and resolute, declaring:

"Whatever happens, Victor, I intend to restore the Directorate. I am taking prompt action, to that end. The *Valley Forge* and the *Hiroshima* are proceeding to the moon. They will land a new garrison, with the necessary repairs to bring Fort America back into effectiveness. The *Yorktown*, the *Rio Plata* and the *Leningrad* will stand by, spaced on an orbit ten thousand miles from the earth, to relay communications and bombard any targets we discover.

"With the *Great Director*, I'm coming to earth."

Lord licked his thin, colorless lips.

"You're too daring, Mr. Hudd," he protested shrilly.

"It took audacity to establish the Directorate." The great boom of Hudd's voice in the speaker visibly startled Lord. "It's worth audacity to restore it. I'm coming, at full thrust, to take personal command."

Lord remained aboard the lifecraft that night. His uneasy fancy must have dwelt upon the fused metal we had found beside that skeleton in the weeds and the sudden bolt that struck that tree as Cameron fled. Perhaps he thought of the two still bodies in the gully; no doubt he peopled the dark valley with vengeful enemies.

My own imagination, I know, was busy enough. Staring out into the thickening night, I felt myself the helpless spectator of stupendous forces sweeping grandly toward collision.

On one side, there was the Atomic Age itself, expressed in the rekindled might of Fort America, in the fine discipline of the task force, in sleek guided missiles, in the determined sagacity of Mr. Julian Hudd.

On the other side, there was that unknown power that had swept the old garrison from the moon and driven men from the cities and destroyed the Directorate. All I had seen of it was a piece of twisted wire, a blasted tree, and the change in Jim Cameron. But that was enough—I waited for the fireworks.

After dark, Captain Doyle volunteered to go back to the house.

"Mr. Hudd wants us to get in touch with the inhabitants," he reminded Lord. "And we saw some kind of telephone." With evident reluctance, Lord agreed.

"If you contact anybody, call for the government," he ordered. "Offer a reward for Cameron." His sleepy eyes glittered cunningly. "If anybody mentions those two dead peasants, we're holding them—alive—for Cameron's return."

Doyle went down through the valves, accompanied by the signal officer to help him work the strange radiophone. They were lost in the pale moonlight among the young apple trees. They didn't come back.

After an hour, Lord sent me after them, with one of his gunmen for escort. Soft lights came on of themselves, when I opened the door. I tried to call Doyle's name, and found that my voice had gone to a grating whisper. Walking through the silent rooms, we found nobody.

The little radiophone, oddly, was also gone.

At midnight, Hudd called again. At the news of Doyle's apparent desertion, he muttered forebodingly:

"It's something pretty sinister, that takes so true a man."

The interstellar cruiser landed, just at dawn.

The thunder of it woke me out of a nodding doze. Moving groggily to a port, I saw a glare that burned all color out of the valley, so that everything was black or blinding white. I had to cover my smarting eyes. The wind rocked the lifecraft on its stabilizers, and the earth shuddered.

When the thunder ceased and that cruel light was gone, I saw the cruiser standing two miles down the valley. Dark smoke billowed up about the base of it from the green woods burning. Its tall peak, towering out of the night in the valley, was already incandescent with sunlight.

Immensely high, the great flat turrets swung with ominous deliberation. The huge bright tubes of rifles and launchers lifted out of their housings, implacably purposeful. Hudd called again, looking as massively indomitable as his flagship.

"Have you met the inhabitants, Mr. Lord?"

"Not yet, Mr. Hudd." Relieved by the great ship's coming, Lord had his swagger back.

"Then you soon will," Hudd told him. "Our lookout reports a flying vehicle, approaching you now. Make contact, and report immediately."

We all turned to the ports, in time to see the red glint of sunlight on the rotor of a small helicopter. It landed among the young apple trees. Three people got out. One of them began waving a bit of white cloth. With a shock of dismay, I recognized Jim Cameron.

VIII

The three walked slowly down toward us across the young orchard. The other two paused by the dam, one of them bending to look at the bodies under the blanket. Cameron came on halfway to us, before he stopped and stood waiting.

Watching through a port in the signal room, Lord nervously wet his lips. Beneath a puzzled unease, his beady eyes had a glare of yellow elation. He sent me out to find what Cameron wanted.

Grinning with pleasure to see me, Cameron put down the stick with his handkerchief tied to it. Fatigue had drawn his stubbled face and smudged blue shadows under his eyes.

"Jim, you shouldn't have come back." I pitched my voice too low for Lord's gunmen, covering us from the valve. "Because you made a fool of Lord, when you got away. He'll never forgive that. He's got Hudd's permission to liquidate you."

He grinned wearily, glancing at the two behind him.

"You can tell Mr. Lord that he's in no position to liquidate anybody. On the contrary—these neighbors of the Hawkins couple have come to arraign him and his guard for the murder."

I must have gasped with astonishment.

"I'm afraid Lord will be unreasonable." He frowned, regretfully. "I came along to try to prevent any needless destruction. There's not much use for Lord to resist, and no need for others to be killed. Better tell him that."

Back aboard the lifecraft, I told Lord what the strangers wanted. His pale, peering eyes rounded with wonderment, then narrowed to hard yellow slits. He glared malevolently out at Cameron.

"I suppose that damned feather merchant is the chief witness? Well, I'll fix the lot of them!" He shouted up the ladder-well to the astrogator, now acting as signal officer, "Get me Mr. Hudd!"

I followed him into the narrow signal room.

"It's your pet civilian," he shouted bitterly when Hudd's face appeared huge and interrogative on the screen. "And a couple of yokels with some nonsense about arresting me for murder."

"So?" Thoughtfully Hudd rubbed his blue, multiple chin. "I want to talk to them. Offer them all three safe-conduct to come aboard. Tell them I'll discuss compensation for the killing. You can bring them on the life-craft, Mr. Lord."

The negotiations which ensued were somewhat involved. I went back and forth, between Lord and Cameron. Cameron returned to consult with the watchful two by the ravine. Hudd and Lord conferred by television, Lord's nasal voice rising steadily with ill-concealed anger, Hudd frowning with increasing concern.

"I'd accept Mr. Hudd's safe-conduct, myself," Cameron told me. "But the Enlows don't want to trust him. They are willing to talk to Mr. Hudd, but he'll have to come out here."

With a surprising boldness, Hudd agreed to do that.

"But, Mr. Hudd!" Lord protested sharply. "We can't treat with them—two savages and a mutineering feather merchant. Think of your own safety. Why not let us take off, sir, and then wipe them out with a salvo of radiotoxin shells from the cruiser?"

Hudd shook his head stubbornly.

"I'm coming over, Victor, to handle this myself." His red, worried eyes turned to me. "Chad, you go back and tell Jim Cameron to wait till I get there."

Lord's eyes narrowed suspiciously.

"Don't you give me up, Hudd." His angry nasal voice was hard and dangerous. "If you do, you're also giving up your New Directorate."

"I know that," Hudd assured him blandly. "You can trust me, Victor."

Lord dismissed me, with a sullen nod. I went back across the burned grass to tell Cameron that Hudd was coming.

"He's smart." Cameron nodded approvingly. "Maybe he can save his neck." He took up the white flag again. "Now we had better rejoin the Enlows," he said. "They might misunderstand."

We walked back to the people waiting at the dam. I thought of Lord's gunmen crouching in the lock behind us, and the skin on my back crawled uneasily.

The two were a man and a young woman. The were both tanned, lean, sturdy; dark hair and grey level eyes showed a family likeness. Tight with the shock of what they had seen under the blanket, their faces were hard with purpose.

"Are they coming out?" The man's quiet voice was taut as his gaunt face.

"Not yet." Cameron was urgently persuasive. "But please give me a chance to tell Mr. Hudd about the equalizer. I think he's smart enough to listen."

The man nodded his weather-beaten head. I saw that he carried what looked like a bulky flare pistol. His deep-set angry eyes peered up at the enormous flagship, not at all afraid.

"If he wants to listen," he agreed. "But we're going to get the killers."

"I'll try to get Mr. Hudd to give them up," Cameron promised, and then he introduced me. "Chad Barstow. A likely candidate for the Brotherhood, as soon as he learns to use the equalizer."

The girl wore a radiophone, much like the one we had seen in the house—it must have been such units that made those scrambled signals we had heard. The little plastic case was snapped to her belt, the headset over her lustrous hair. She had been listening to that, but now she looked at me, her eyes widening.

"Yes, he's Dane Barstow's son." Seeing her troubled glance toward the gully, Cameron added quickly, "He had nothing to do with that."

She gave me a strong handclasp.

"Jane Enlow," Cameron said. "Her father, Frank Enlow."

The gaunt man gripped my hand silently, but his angry eyes flashed back to the lifecraft and the cruiser.

"Before the equalizer," Cameron said, "Mr. Enlow was a janitor in Tyler's Squaredeal Hall. He was just telling me about the Director's last days. After the equalizer, he smuggled Tyler out through the mob that was shouting for him under the balcony. Tyler lived for years in Mr. Enlow's house over the ridge, yonder, writing a history—trying to justify his career."

"A nasty old man!" Jane Enlow pouted. "He wouldn't learn the equalizer. Dad had to take care of him."

High up on the bright side of the cruiser, blue fire spurted. Frank Enlow crouched toward the ravine, swinging up his pistollike device. Cameron called out, hastily:

"Don't shoot—that's probably Mr. Hudd."

As the gaunt man relaxed, I studied his weapon with

a shocked fascination. It looked like a miniature guided missile launcher, rather than a gun. It seemed fantastically small, yet the lank man had a strangely confident air of facing the cruiser's weapons on even terms.

The girl was listening again to her radiophone. She twisted knobs on the case at her belt and finally shook her dark head.

"Nothing." Her voice was gloomy. "They're taking too long."

Hudd's lifecraft approached us swiftly, a bright projectile floating nearly upright on a jet of screaming fire. It crossed the burning forest to land near the other craft. The valves slammed open as soon as the dust had cleared, and Hudd's aide jumped out.

That hard-bitten officer darted across the blasted ground and hurried up to us. He seemed upset by Hudd's decision. First he wanted Cameron and the Enlows to come aboard the lifecraft to talk; then he wanted to send a bodyguard with Hudd; finally he warned that a general bombardment of the surrounding country would begin at once, if anything happened to Hudd.

"We've come for the killers," the lean man informed him gravely. "Since Mr. Cameron has taken the Brotherhood oath, the three of us form a competent court. We're bound to listen to any evidence that Mr. Hudd can offer. He will not be harmed, unless he tries to interfere."

Outraged, the commander went back. Immediately Mr. Julian Hudd climbed down between the bright fins. He came out of the burned area at a painful, heavy run. Gasping for breath, he waddled up to the dam.

"Well, Jim!"

He grinned at Cameron, shook hands with the raw-boned man, gave the girl a bow of open admiration. His small, shrewd eyes studied the unfinished dam and the abandoned machine in the gully.

"The incident here was most regrettable." Hudd's voice was a chesty, confident rumble. "I'll see that adequate compensation is paid. Personally. You people needn't concern yourselves any further."

His keen bloodshot eyes studied the gaunt man.

"Now, I want to take up something more important, I've been trying to get in touch with your government." His broad, blue-tinged face was still a genial mask, but his loud voice turned imperious. "I demand that your government—"

The lank man's voice was very quiet, yet the cold ring of it made Hudd stop to listen.

"We have no government," said Frank Enlow.

Hudd puffed out his cheeks, slowly turning red with anger.

"That's the surprising fact, Mr. Hudd," Cameron assured him gravely. "You'll have to get used to it. When the equalizer appeared, nations became extinct."

Ignoring him, Hudd glared at the lank man.

"You must have some organization."

"Only the Brotherhood," Enlow said. "It has no power to surrender anybody to you, because membership is voluntary."

Hudd's red eyes blinked, skeptical and defiant.

"Get in touch with this Brotherhood." His voice was rasping, arrogant. "Have them send a responsible agent. Have him here by noon, local time." He paused, ominously. "Otherwise, the task force and Fort America will open fire at every likely target we can find."

Cameron made a startled gesture, as if to catch his arm.

"Please, Mr. Hudd," he protested sharply. "Wait until you know what you're doing."

Hudd kept his savage little eyes on Enlow.

"The young lady, I see, has a radiophone." His voice was loud and ominous. "You had better start calling this Brotherhood—"

"We came here for another purpose." The lank man met his truculent gaze, unimpressed. "We've come for the killers."

Hudd's bluish face swelled again with anger.

"Nonsense!" he shouted. "Mr. Lord is my second in

command. He was acting under orders. I assume the responsibility. I'll pay for any unjust damage, but I refuse to subject him to humiliation."

The lean man listened to that, and nodded his raw-boned head, and stalked away silently toward the ravine. Cameron hurried after him, visibly alarmed.

"The killers can wait," he called urgently. "Doyle must be trying. Mr. Hudd doesn't understand the equalizer. Please give me time to tell him about it."

The lank man turned back, reluctantly.

"If he wants to listen," he agreed. "We'll wait half an hour."

With a question on his face, Cameron turned to Hudd.

"All right, Jim," Hudd gasped, explosively. "I want to know all about this equalizer, anyhow." His angry eyes went back to the gaunt man. "But my ships and the fort will open fire at noon."

IX

Hudd sat down on a hummock of grass, breathing hard with the effort of moving his clumsy bulk. His massive shoulders bunched with bold defiance. Only the quick movements of his eyes betrayed the intense and desperate working of his mind—they were the eyes of a fighting animal, fearful, yet audacious and altogether ruthless.

"Now!" he gasped. "This equalizer?"

Cameron squatted on his heels, facing Hudd. Behind us, as he talked, the sun rose higher. The flat green valley lay motionless under its hot light, and a pungent blue haze settled about us from the green forest burning.

"I heard the story last night. The beginning of the equalizer takes us back nearly twenty years." Cameron's dark-smudged eyes came for a moment to me. "To your own father, Chad." His haggard and yet animated eyes went back to Hudd. "I think you remember Dane Barstow?"

"The traitor?" rumbled Hudd. "He died, I believe, in the labor camps."

"But he didn't," Cameron said. "Because Tyler learned that he was on the trail of something remarkable, and had him taken from the camps to a solitary cell at Fort America. The SBI went to work on him there, with extreme interrogation."

As Cameron glanced at me again, I noticed a strange thing. The story and the memory of my father's misfortunes brought me a bitter resentment, but now I noticed that all the old pain and hatred was gone from Cameron's face. Something had swept away his old saturnine reserve. He seemed oddly friendly, even to Hudd.

"Finally," he said, "Barstow talked. He told what he had done and admitted all he had hoped to do. He even agreed to complete his interrupted work."

I knelt down to listen.

"Though he was half blind and crippled from the extreme treatment, and sometimes out of his head, they took pretty drastic precautions. They kept him locked in that steel cell on the moon—one of those we saw there, I imagine, Chad. Two guards were always with him. He was allowed paper and pencil, but no other equipment. If he wanted calculations made, or any experiments tried, such things were done for him by Atomic Service engineers."

Cameron briefly smiled, as if he shared my tormented pride.

"Yes, Chad, your old man was all right. Working under such difficult conditions, shattered as he was, he charted a new science and created a new technology. And then—when we had been out at space about two years with the task force—he overturned the Directorate."

Hudd's bold eyes had drifted back to the sun-browned girl—who was listening, not to Cameron, but anxiously to the little portable radiophone. Now he started ponderously at Cameron's last words, to gasp for his breath and wheeze incredulously:

"How could he do that?"

"Not so hard, with the equalizer." Cameron grinned at Hudd's blinking, startled stare. "From his cell on the moon, Barstow smashed the Directorate. He didn't need any weapons or equipment. All he had to do was tell his jailors what he had discovered."

Hudd made a hollow, croaking sound. "How's that?"

"The news of the equalizer spread from one man to another," Cameron said. "Those same engineers who had been assigned to get the invention from him set up a little illicit transmitter and beamed the details back to earth with equalizer power, on every frequency they could get through the ionosphere.

"That finished the Directorate."

Hudd picked up a small red pebble and began nervously tapping the sod with it, as he had drummed on his desk with the little gold head of Tyler. His furtive eyes flashed to the lean man's weapon and back to Cameron's face.

"That's too much!" His voice was harshly unbelieving. "No mere fact of science could defeat Fort America—much less wreck the Squaredeal Machine."

"Barstow's equalizer did," Cameron said. "Perhaps because the old technology of the Atomic Age had already reached the breaking point of over-complexity and super-centralization. When Barstow created this new technology, there was a natural swing to the opposite extreme—to simplicity, individualism, and complete personal freedom."

"So?" Hudd thumped the sod with his pebble, scowling at Cameron. "Just how does it work, this equalizer?"

Cameron glanced doubtfully at Frank Enlow.

"Tell him," the gaunt man said. "Barstow wanted every man to know. Generally it has a good effect." He glanced at a watch on his brown wrist. "But hurry—your time is running out."

Hudd's great shoulders lifted with aggression.

"So is yours," he snapped. "I'm willing to listen, but my men won't hear. I'm not yielding anything. This Brotherhood had better throw the towel in, by noon."

"Tell him," Enlow repeated.

Cameron launched into his explanation. His fatigue seemed forgotten, and some inner excitement made his haggard face almost vivacious.

"The old atomic reactor, you know, was an enormously clumsy and wasteful and dangerous way of doing extremely simple things. Pure energy exists in the atom, and that is what we want. But the old atomic plants used intractable and inadequate processes to change kinetic and electrical and binding energy into heat, and then required expensive and inefficient machinery to turn a little of that heat back into electricity.

"Even with all its elaborate complexity, the reactor plants could tap only a little of the binding energy which holds electrons and protons and neutrons together into atoms. The mass energy of the particles themselves—really nearly all the actual energy of the atom—it couldn't even reach.

"Barstow's dream—like my own—was merely a simple way of doing a simple thing. Material energy exists, as Einstein demonstrated. Barstow dreamed of a simple way to let it flow. The equalizer is his dream, realized."

I couldn't help the breathless interruption:

"That piece of wire?"

"Just a solenoid." Cameron nodded. "But wound in a certain way, not helically, so that its field slightly alters the coordinates of space and slightly changes the interaction of mass and energy. The atomic particles of the solenoid are equalized, as your father termed the process. The converted energy appears as direct current in the wire.

"The fact is simple—even though the tensors of a new geometry are required to describe the solenoid field. That apparent complexity is more in our awkward description, however, than in the vital fact. The actual specifications of the equalizer can be memorized in five minutes."

Cameron's intent, elated eyes looked aside at me.

"The safety feature is what threw us, Chad, with our induction furnace experiments," he told me. "Our gadget annihilated matter—degenerating iron atoms into sodium—and produced electric current. The increased output intensified the conversion field, and the intensified field increased the output. An excellent arrangement, if you want a matter bomb—but highly unsafe for a power plant. .

"Your father solved that problem, Chad—very simply, too. Just a secondary solenoid, in series with the primary, which develops an opposing voltage as the equalizing field expands. It gives you a safe, guaranteed maximum voltage—the precise value determined by the way it's wound."

Hudd's deep-sunken eyes blinked skeptically.

"You mean, you can generate electricity?" he rasped. "With just a coil of wire?"

"And a few stray ions to excite it," Cameron told him. "A pound of copper solenoid would drive the cruiser, yonder, out to the Dark Star. Or iron, or silver—the metal doesn't matter; it's only the exact shape and alignment and spacing of the turns of wire."

Hudd shook his head in massive unbelief.

"Perpetual motion!" he scoffed.

"Almost." Cameron grinned. "Equalized mass is converted into electrical energy, according to the Einstein equation. The solenoid wastes away—but slowly. One pound of solenoid will generate ten billion kilowatt hours of electricity."

"If it's all that simple," Hudd objected shrewdly, "somebody would have stumbled on it, by accident."

"Very likely, men did," Cameron agreed. "Not many—the shape of the coils is not one you would want for anything else; and the turns must be very exactly formed and aligned, or else the regenerative effect is damped out. The few who did it must have been instantly electrocuted—because they didn't also stumble on Barstow's safety winding."

"I'll believe it when I see it," muttered Hudd.

Cameron pointed up the edge of the ravine, to a shattered tree stump.

"Mr. Lord wanted a demonstration, yesterday," he

said. "I straightened part of the safety coil on a small power unit from that machine, to step up the voltage, and tossed it into a green tree yonder."

"A rather reckless thing to do," commented the lean man.

Hudd said nothing. His black-haired, ham-sized hand tossed the red pebble, aimlessly, and caught it again. His troubled eyes peered at the stump, at the gaunt man's weapon, at the enormous tower of the *Great Director*.

"You have ten minutes to give up the killer, Mr. Hudd," drawled Frank Enlow. "Otherwise you may see a better demonstration."

Hudd snorted: a blast of defiance.

"I'll wait for it," he gasped. "You can't bluff me."

A shadow came over Cameron's face. When his tired eyes closed for a moment, I saw the blue stains under them. He sat back on his heels, his emaciated body sagging as if from a punishing blow.

"It's no bluff, Mr. Hudd." He paused as if to gather himself for a weary and yet vehement protest. "You just don't grasp what the equalizer means. It ended the Atomic Age. The Directorate was part of that lost era. You can't hope to restore it, now, any more than you could revive a fossil tyrannosaur. Perhaps you can cause some needless bloodshed and death."

Hudd's wide mouth hardened with an unconvinced hostility.

"Tyler spilt plenty of blood, building the first Directorate," he commented coldly. "I may have to pay the same price again, but I expect to win. Perhaps Tyler's garrisons mutinied when they heard about this equalizer. My men won't hear about it."

"It wasn't mutiny, Mr. Hudd," Cameron insisted. "There was no fighting. The Directorate wasn't overthrown—it simply ceased to exist. When the equalizer appeared, there was no more reason for Fort America than there is for arrowmakers. The officers recognized that, as well as the men. The garrison just packed up and came home."

"Home to what?" Hudd challenged him. "The people here were already deserting the cities, leaving nearly everything they owned. There must have been something else wrong—perhaps some biotoxin loose—to cause such panic."

"You still don't get it." Cameron shook his head with a tired impatience. "The equalizer freed the city dwellers, just as it did the garrison. Because most people didn't live in cities by choice. They were huddled into them by the old division of labor—specialized cogs in a social machine grown ruinously complex.

"The equalizer abolished the division of labor—at least in military technology. Every man with a piece of wire became a complete military specialist, competent to defend himself. Using the new control of atomic and molecular processes, he could also provide for nearly all his own ordinary wants. Complexity was replaced with stark simplicity.

"Take the couple who lived here." He nodded regretfully at the empty house behind us. "They built their own home, made their own food and clothing. They were setting up this dam, when they were murdered, to save their own land from erosion. They weren't slaves of any single skill, or prisoners of any class. They had no reason to hate or fear their neighbors—until we came along."

Hudd blinked, still doubtful.

"Why were the cities so utterly abandoned?" he questioned. "Why was all that money left behind, as Lord reports? Why were signs posted, warning people out?"

Cameron glanced up at the great frowning ship.

"The cities were a product of the old technology, and they died with it," he argued doggedly. "The day of the equalizer, workers walked out and services stopped. There was no food, no power, no water, no sewage disposal. City life was impossible without division of labor.

"As for money, paper dollars were merely shares in the extinct Atomic Age. Metal was still useful—but the equalizer must have made it easier to refine new metal than to wreck the cities. About the danger—I forgot to ask."

He turned inquiringly to Frank Enlow.

"Criminals," the lean man drawled. "A few men and women too stupid or too vicious to use the equalizer. They never left the cities. They stayed hidden, trying to exist by raiding and looting. They used the old military weapons. A few of them became very cunning and dangerous. The signs were posted during our campaigns to hunt them out."

"Don't you have worse criminals?" Hudd demanded shrewdly. "Those who do use the equalizer?"

Enlow shook his head.

"The users of the equalizer have very little economic reason for crime," he said. "And people armed with it aren't very likely victims. It's simply because crime has become so rare that the Hawkinses weren't alert."

Hudd's eyes dwelt on the lean man's weapon.

"This Brotherhood?" he asked shrewdly. "If it isn't a government—what is it?"

"A voluntary substitute." The gaunt man glanced at me. "Your father's last great project, Mr. Barstow. After he got back his health, he spent the rest of his years organizing the Brotherhood."

"Just what does it do?"

"Runs schools and libraries and hospitals," Enlow told him. "Supports laboratories. Builds irrigation projects. Anything for the public good. It operates the post office and issues money against metal deposits."

Hudd nodded triumphantly.

"If it can do all that, it can surrender to me."

"The Brotherhood has no authority." Enlow shook his head, rawboned and resolute. "People may join or leave it, as they please. It is supported by voluntary contributions, and the elected officers serve without pay. They can't surrender, Mr. Hudd—but they can organize the common defense."

"If you have no law," Hudd demanded shrewdly, "then why do you want Mr. Lord?"

Enlow stared back at him, brown and lean and angry.

"In the Brotherhood, we enter a voluntary agreement to respect and defend the rights of others. I think your Mr. Lord has proved himself a public menace."

Hudd pulled absently at his thick lower lip.

"If you've got no government," his harsh voice came, "then I think you've got a madhouse—and all the madmen armed with insane weapons."

Enlow shook his dark head with a lean dignity.

"You're living under a false philosophy, Mr. Hudd. You believe that men are evil, that they have to be driven. Fortunately, that philosophy is mistaken—because men with equalizers can't be driven."

As Hudd made another derisive snort, Enlow looked at his watch.

"Unfortunately, a few men are bad," he added gently. "Your time is up. We want those killers."

Cameron turned back to Hudd, importunately.

"Why don't you give them up?" he urged. "And let me tell your men about the equalizer?"

"I will not." Hudd came laboriously to his feet, red and gasping from the effort. "I still think you'd have a hard time to silence Fort America—with all your equalizers. And my ultimatum still expires at noon."

Having delivered that ominous blast, Hudd turned back to Jane Enlow. She had been listening to her radiophone, absorbed. Now, as she became aware of Hudd's hungry eyes, she started and a rich color darkened her tan. Hudd made her a bow, ponderously graceful, in the manner he must have learned while he was Tyler's Director-General of Europe.

"I deeply regret the awkward circumstances of this first meeting, Miss Enlow." He smiled with a genial admiration. "But I hope soon to offer you an introduction to the best society of the New Directorate."

Flushing deeply, she said nothing.

Hudd bowed again. After a moment, he stalked heavily back toward his lifecraft.

Little Victor Lord, watching from the other craft, must have misunderstood that bow. I can imagine his sweating consternation when he saw the apparently friendly ending of the little conference and decided, no doubt, that Hudd had abandoned him.

The crewmen, evidently, opposed his flight.

The sudden crash of guns made a muffled booming in the thin bright hull. Two spacemen jumped wildly out of the open valve, which slammed immediately behind them. One of them stumbled on his knees, pressing red, agonized hands against his wounds. The other tried to drag him out of danger—until the incandescent blast of the jets flattened and hid them both.

X

The fugitive lifecraft lifted on that column of thundering fire, at first very slowly and jerkily—Lord was not an expert pilot. It leaned drunkenly from the upright, so that I thought it was going to crash. But the roar was suddenly louder. It lifted, swept above our heads, hurtled northward up the valley. Behind it, when the dust and smoke had cleared, the blackened forms of the two spacemen moved no longer.

The tall man turned, with his gaunt face grimly angular, and watched the lifecraft go. It became a vanishing point of bright metal and violet fire. Its thunder rolled away.

His clumsy-seeming weapon lifted, at last, and clicked.

"Down, Barstow!" the girl screamed at me. "Cover your eyes."

Astonished to find that I was left standing alone, I dropped. The flash of heat stung my skin. I looked, afterward, in time to see the small bright cloud of iridescent metal vapor fading in the blue northward sky, turning into a white tuft of rising cumulus. The crash came a whole minute later, like one loud peal of thunder.

Enslow shook his lean head, regretfully.

"Too bad it happened that way," he said. "The two guards were only obeying orders. The equalizer might have made them very good members of the Brotherhood."

Calmly, as he spoke, he slipped another little self-propelled missile out of a case at his belt, pulled a safety key out of it, and pushed it down the muzzle of his launcher. Shaped very much like the huge guided missiles of Fort America, it was only six inches long.

Halfway to his own craft, Mr. Julian Hudd stood peering back toward us. He was shading his eyes, dazedly shaking his dark shaggy head, as if the flash had nearly blinded him.

"Your demonstration, Mr. Hudd!" Cameron shouted after him, urgently. "Now will you give up your New Directorate?"

"Jim, this is an act of war," his great bellow came back defiantly. "Your damned Brotherhood will feel the consequences."

He went on at a stumbling, laborious run, toward his waiting craft. Frank Enlow was beckoning us imperatively back toward the gully.

"Wait!" Jane Enlow called out, eagerly. "Mr. Doyle is getting through."

She listened again. The gaunt man looked warily back at the enormous bright nose of the cruiser which still loomed high above the ravine's rim, and speculatively hefted his launcher. I turned to Cameron, puzzled.

"So you've seen Doyle?"

"Last night." He watched the girl's shining eyes, anxious for the news. "The Enlows live just over the ridge—the first place I found. Their phone began ringing while I was there. It was Rory Doyle. I told him about the equalizer, and he came over to help us stop Mr. Hudd."

Awed, I glanced up at the appalling pillar of the *Great Director*. "How?"

"The first two landing parties had already got in touch with the Brotherhood," Cameron explained. "They were being indoctrinated with the equalizer. The plan was to send them back to spread the word among the crews. But Hudd pushed his own scheme too fast for that to succeed."

Anxiously, he watched the intent girl.

"The only way left was to try a broadcast. Not quite so good, but I think the signal crews will mostly recognize and trust Rory Doyle. It took a little time to improvise a net of short wave stations strong enough to reach out through the ionosphere to the other ships and the moon."

Suddenly, the eager-faced girl slipped off her single headphone. She held it up between us, twisted a volume control, gestured for us to listen.

"—specifications of the equalizer." Thinned and small, hoarse with a weary tension, it was the voice of Rory Doyle. "The absolute dimensions, remember, may be varied at will. It is the proportionate dimensions, and the shape and alignment of the turns, which must be precisely true.

"The safety coil, remember, must always have a greater number of turns than the primary—otherwise you have a matter bomb, instead of a power plant. The number and spacing of the secondary turns control the maximum voltage, according to the rule I gave you.

"Now, pass the word along!"

His tiny-seeming voice held a tired elation.

"Membership in the Brotherhood is open to every man of you. Now you are welcome on earth. Mr. Hudd's ill-advised threats will be forgotten. You have nothing to fear—so long as you respect the rights of others. The officers of the Brotherhood wish me to say that you are welcome home."

His voice ceased. The girl took back the headphone, and her father led us up the floor of the rocky little gorge. We stopped, presently, to climb a fern-grown slope and look back across the valley.

The interstellar cruiser still towered out of the smoking forest, incredibly enormous. Nearer, the tiny pencil of Hudd's lifecraft stood mirror-bright upon a blackened island in the green. Between the fins of it, I saw a doll-like figure—hammering with frantic fists upon the shining valve.

"Mr. Julian Hudd," murmured Cameron, almost with pity.

We hurried on. We were crossing the low ridge into the next valley, when the ground quivered. The jets of the cruiser made a deafening, crushing reverberation. The bright immensity of it lifted, on a pillar of terrible fire.

Jane Enlow was listening again, as the thunder faded.

"They are going to the shore of the new Sahara Sea," she told us. "A new irrigation project—the crews can take up land, there."

A breathless quiet fell upon us, after that thunder had died. I stood apart, staring into the sky, long after the living blue spark of the jets was gone. For the meaning of the equalizer was breaking slowly over me. A wave of deep emotion left me awed and changed and lifted, somehow strong and free.

"What happened to Mr. Hudd?" Cameron was asking.

"I don't know." Twisting at the knobs, Jane Enlow looked pale with concern for him. "The crews wouldn't let him come back on the ship. I'm afraid he was killed in the blast."

Many months had passed, however, before I learned the actual and somewhat surprising fate of Mr. Julian Hudd—who had been Director-General of Europe and Special Secretary of the Squaredeal Machine, and who was still an adaptive and resourceful man.

The following summer, after we had all been inducted into the Brotherhood and taught the equalizer, I came back in answer to a hospitable invitation to visit the home of Frank Enlow. Already I had claimed a small homestead beside a new western sea, and friendly neighbors had helped me build the first rooms of a house there. I wanted to see Jane Enlow.

She wasn't at home, however, when I arrived.

Frank Enlow, the lean ex-janitor and the last friend of Tyler, met me at the door of his pleasant home. He began to talk of Mr. Julian Hudd, who had survived unhurt by the ion jets of the departing cruiser. He had established himself in the vacant house that had belonged to the murdered Hawkins couple. Frank Enlow took me to see him, there.

Now a simple brother of the Brotherhood, we found Hudd plowing his young orchard. Walking behind a small equalizer tractor, he was bare to the waist and brown with sun. Sweat ran in rivulets down his dusty flanks, but his paunch and his jowls and his several chins were no longer the burdens they had been. I scarcely recognized him.

"Glad to see you, Chad." He used my first name, as always, but now his hard handclasp had a genuine cordiality. His great booming voice seemed mellowed, happy. With an air of simple, equalitarian friendship, he invited us into his home.

"Come along, Chad," he urged genially. "You'll want to see the wife. I think you'll remember her—the former Miss Jane Enlow."

The Peddler's Nose

The peddler came to Earth, across the empty immensities of space, after whisky. He knew the planet was under quarantine, but his blunders had left him at the mercy of his thirst. Ultimately, the root of that merciless thirst was his nose.

He was a thin, tiny man, and his crooked nose enormous. The handicap could have been corrected, but he was born on a frontier world where the difficult dilemmas of freedom and responsibility had not yet been solved, and he was allowed to grow up twisted with the knowledge of his ugliness.

Damned by genetic accident, he spent his life in flight

from salvation. By the time his deformity had made a petty criminal of him, he had come to defend it as the most tender part of himself. When he was ordered to a clinic for the removal of his social maladjustments and the excess nasal tissue that lay beneath them, he escaped rehabilitation and drifted out to the fringes of civilization, where the law was less efficient.

Never bold, he settled at last into the shabby occupation of vending cheap novelty toys. Even that humble calling had its risks. He had been forced to make his pitch without a vendor's license, on the last world behind, and he had to leave it in such haste that he had no time to buy his usual supplies.

His nerves were not so good as they had been. Aboard the flier, he had to gulp down three stiff drinks before his hands were steady enough to set the automatic pilot. And the raw alcohol seemed to hit him more swiftly than common, so that his vision began to blur and double before he had finished the adjustments.

In his frightened befuddlement, he mistook an 8 for a 3, and overlooked a decimal point, and turned the planet selector dial one space too far. His intended goal had been another frontier world, a few light-years away, where immigration was still unrestricted and the pioneers still hardy enough to let their children buy his toys. His errors, however, made Earth his destination.

The robot pilot warned him instantly. Although the flier had been battered and abused by several generations of outlaws bolder than himself, it had saved him many times from destruction, and it was still a sturdy, spaceworthy neutronic craft. A gong crashed. A red light flickered above the competent mechanism, and it spoke to him sternly:

"Caution! Do not take off. Destination dialed is far beyond normal operating range. Caution! Check charts and dials for possible error. Caution!"

He was normally cautious enough, but those three drinks had magnified his panic. Already too far gone to understand the warning, he stabbed a shaky finger at the button that canceled it. Before he could find the takeoff lever, however, the signals rang and flashed again.

"Caution!" rapped that hard mechanical voice. "Do not take off. Destination dialed is under quarantine. All contact prohibited——"

Impatiently, too drunk to think of anything except escape, he pulled the takeoff lever. The signals stopped, and the flier took him to Earth, across a distance in light-centuries that might have staggered a sober man.

Human civilization was an expanding globe, spreading out through the galaxy at almost half the speed of light as the colonists hopped from star to star; and that long flight took him from what was then the outside of it, back toward the half forgotten center.

The voyage wasn't long to him, however, and the flier required no more attention. It caught the invisible winds of radiant neutrinos that rise out of the novae to blow forever through the galaxies, and it was swept away at such a speed that time was slowed almost to a stop for everything aboard, through the working of relativity.

The peddler drank and slept and dreamed uneasy dreams of men with scalpels who wanted to remove his nose. He woke and slept and drank again, until his inadequate supplies were gone.

As originally built, the flier would have identified itself to the destination port authority, waited for orders, and obeyed them automatically. Previous owners had changed the operating circuits, however, so that it slipped down dark toward the night side of Earth, with all signals dead except a gong to arouse its master.

The peddler awoke unhappy. Even the dimmed lights in his untidy little cabin seemed intolerably bright, and the gong was bursting his head. He shuffled hastily to stop it and then stumbled through the flier in search of something to drink.

There should have been another bottle cached somewhere, against such emergencies, behind his berth or in his portable sales case or perhaps in the empty medical cabinet—he had long ago bartered its contents for whisky.

But the caches had all been raided before. Muttering bitterly, shaken with a thirst that refused to wait, he staggered back to the cockpit and touched a dial to find out where he was.

Sol Three—he had never heard of that. He shook his throbbing head and squinted at the hooded screen to read his position. The coordinates took his breath. He was two thousand light-years from the last world he remembered, somewhere near the dead center of civilization.

He felt shocked for an instant at the vastness of his blunder. Yet there was no harm done. That was the unique advantage of his nomadic existence. No matter how many outraged citizens wanted to remodel his nose and extirpate his thirst, the flier had always carried him safely beyond their reach, across space and trackless time.

He leaned hopefully to read the screen again. Sol Three was a minor member of an undistinguished planetary system, it told him, with nothing to interest either tourist or trader. The inhabitants were human, but their culture was primitive. Although long settled, the planet was historically unimportant. A footnote caught his eye:

> The planet was once believed to have been the site of Atlantis, the half legendary cradle of civilization, from which the interstellar migrations began. Although the comparative biology of the indigenous fauna supports this idea, no actual historical proof has yet been found, and the low cultural level of the present inhabitants leaves it open to question——

He wasn't concerned with the elaborate quarrels of the historians. All he wanted was a drink. Just one stiff jolt, to cut the foul taste out of his mouth and sweep the pain from his head and quiet his trembling limbs. Even this planet couldn't be too backward, he thought, to distill alcohol.

Thirstily, he touched the landing key.

The gong rang instantly, painful as a hammer on his head. The red light flickered, and the loud recorded voice of the automatic pilot rang grimly:

"Warning! Do not attempt to land. This planet is quarantined, under the Covenants of Non-Contact. All communication is absolutely prohibited, and violators will be subject to full rehabilitation. Warning——"

Cringing from the voice and the gong, he stabbed frantically at the cancellation button. Because primitive worlds offered the easiest market for his goods, he had run into the Covenants before. He knew they were intended to prevent the damaging clash of peoples at discrepant levels of social evolution, but he was not interested in theories of cultural impact.

What he wanted was a drink, and he should find it here. Although he had never heard of Sol Three, he knew his trade and he was well enough equipped. One quick stand ought to bring the price of what he needed for the long flight back to the frontier worlds where he felt at home. Even if something aroused the quarantine officials, their threat of full rehabilitation was unlikely to pursue him quite that far.

He pushed the landing key. The flier slipped down silently, before dawn, to the dark slope of a wooded hill three miles from a feeble energy source that should be a small settlement. He inflated the covering membrane that gave the craft the look of an innocent boulder and started walking toward the settlement with his sales equipment.

The cool air had a refreshing scent of things growing. The feel of the grass was good underfoot, and the voices of small wild creatures made an elusive music. No wilderness had ever seemed so friendly. Perhaps, he thought, this planet had really been the birthplace of mankind, and he felt happy for a moment with a mystical sense of return.

But he hadn't come for communion with the mother

world, and that brief elation slipped away as he began to worry about meeting some primitive taboo against the use of alcohol.

Frowning with anxiety, he came to an empty road at the foot of the hill and tramped along it with an apprehensive haste toward a rude concrete bridge across a shallow stream. The sun was rising now, not much different from any other star. It showed him a wide green valley where a herd of black and white domestic animals grazed peacefully and a man in blue drove a crude traction plow.

The peddler paused for a moment, feeling a puzzled contempt for the stupid yokels who lived their small lives rooted here, as ignorant of the great world outside as their fat cattle were. If envy lay beneath his scorn, he didn't know it.

The sunlight had begun to hurt his eyes and his thirst shook him again with a dry paroxysm. He limped grimly on. Beyond the bridge, he found crude two-dimensional signs set up along the road. He had no equipment to read their silent legends, but even the flat pictures of sealed bottles and dew-wet glasses spoke to him with a maddening eloquence.

At the summit of a gentle hill, he came upon a wooden hut enveloped in a thin but tantalizing fragrance of alcohol. The sign above the door convinced him that it was a public place, and a faded poster on the wall showed a plump native girl sipping a drink seductively.

He tried the door eagerly, but it was locked. The teasing odor tempted him to break in, but he shrank from the impulse fearfully. Running the quarantine was crime enough. He didn't want to be rehabilitated, and he thought the place would surely open by the time he could supply himself with the local medium of exchange.

Already perspiring, he went on down the hill toward the village. It lay along a bend of the quiet stream he had passed; a scattered group of rude brick and stucco family huts standing in a grove of trees. It looked so different from the brawl and glitter of the raw pioneer cities he had known that he halted uncertainly.

He wasn't used to dealing with such simple races. But then his novelties would certainly be new to their children, and the occasional discarded cans and bottles beside the road assured him that alcohol was abundant. That was really all that mattered. He mopped his face and swung the sales case to his left hand and staggered on again.

"Mornin' to you, mister."

Startled by that unexpected hail, he darted to the side of the road. A clumsy primitive vehicle had come up behind him. It was driven by some kind of crude heat engine, which gave off a faint reek of burning petroleum. A large man sat at the control wheel, watching him with a disturbing curiosity.

"Lookin' for somebody in Chatsworth?"

The man spoke a harsh-sounding tongue he had never heard before, but the psionic translator, a tiny device no more conspicuous than the native's hearing aid, brought the meaning to him instantly.

"Mornin' to you, mister." He lifted his arm a little, murmuring toward the microphone hidden in his sleeve, and his translated reply came from the tiny speaker under his clothing, uttered in a nasal drawl that matched the native's.

"Thanks," he said, "but I'm just passing through."

"Then hop in." The native leaned to open the door of the vehicle. "I'll give you a lift out to my place, a mile across the town."

He got in gratefully, but in a moment he was sorry for his eagerness.

"Welcome to Chatsworth," the grinning yokel went on. "Population three hundred and four, in the richest little valley in the state. Guess I've got the right to make you welcome." The tall man chuckled. "I'm Jud Hankins. The constable."

New sweat broke out on the peddler's dusty face. His head throbbed unbearably, and his gnarled old hands began trembling so violently that he had to grip the handle of his case to keep the officer from noticing his agitation.

In a moment, however, he saw that this unfortunate chance encounter with the law had not yet been disastrous. Jud Hankins was unlikely to be concerned with enforcing the Covenants—if he ever knew that they existed.

"Pleased to meet you, Mr. Hankins," the peddler answered hastily, grateful that the translator failed to reproduce the apprehensive tremor in his voice. "My name's Gray."

He noticed the constable looking at his sales case.

"A fertile valley, indeed!" he said hurriedly. "Do you produce grain for the distilling industry?"

"Mostly for hogs." The constable glanced at the case again. "You a salesman, Mr. Gray?"

Uneasily he said he was.

"What's your line, if you don't mind?"

"Toys," he said. "Novelty toys."

"I was just afraid you had fireworks." The constable seemed faintly relieved. "I thought I ought to warn you."

"Fireworks?" The peddler repeated the term in a puzzled voice, because the translation had not been entirely clear.

"The Fourth will soon be coming up, you know," the constable explained. "We've got to protect the children." He grinned proudly. "I've four fine little rascals of my own."

The peddler still wasn't sure about fireworks. The Fourth was obviously some sort of barbaric ceremonial at which children were sacrificed, and fireworks were probably paraphernalia for the witch doctors. Anyhow, it didn't matter.

"These toys are all I sell," he insisted. "They're highly educational. Designed and recommended by child training experts, to instruct while they amuse. Safe enough for children in the proper age groups."

He squinted sharply at the amiable constable.

"But I'm not sure about offering them here," he

added uneasily. "In so small a place, it might not pay me to buy a license."

"You don't need one." The constable chuckled disarmingly. "You see, we aren't incorporated. Another point of our sort of town. Go ahead and sell your toys—just so they're nothing that will hurt the kiddies."

He slowed the vehicle to call a genial greeting to a group of children playing ball on a vacant lot, and stopped in the village to let a boy and his dog cross the street ahead. The peddler thanked him, and got out hastily.

"Wait, Mr. Gray," he protested. "You had breakfast?"

The peddler said he hadn't.

"Then jump in again," the jovial native urged. "Mamie has plenty on the table—she cooks it up while I do the chores out on the farm. Seeing you're doing business in town, I want you to come out and eat with us."

"Thanks," he said, "but all I want is something to drink."

"I guess you are dry, walking in this dust." The native nodded sympathetically. "Come on out, and we'll give you a drink."

Tempted by that promise and afraid of offending the law, he got back in the machine. The constable drove on to a neat, white-painted hut at the edge of the village. Four noisy children ran out to welcome them, and a clean, plump-faced woman met them at the door.

"My wife," the constable drawled jovially. "Mr. Gray. A sort of earlybird Santa Claus, he says, with toys for the kiddies. He'd like a drink."

The peddler came into the kitchen section of the hut, which looked surprisingly clean. He reached with a trembling anxiety for the drink the woman brought him. It had the bright clear color of grain alcohol, and he almost strangled, in his bitter surprise, when he found that it was only cold water.

He thanked the woman as civilly as he could manage, and said he had to go. The children were clamoring to see his toys, however, and the constable urged him to stay for breakfast. He sat down reluctantly and sipped a cup of hot bitter liquid called coffee, which really seemed to help his headache.

Still afraid of the friendly constable, he made excuses not to show the toys until the children had to leave for school. The smallest girl began to sneeze and sniffle, as the mother herded them toward the door, and he inquired with some alarm what was wrong.

"Just a cold," the woman said. "Nothing serious."

That puzzled him for an instant because the weather seemed quite warm. Probably another error in translation, but nothing to alarm him. He was rising to follow the children outside, but the woman turned back to him.

"Don't go yet, Mr. Gray." She smiled kindly. "I'm afraid you aren't well. You hardly touched your ham and eggs. Let me get you another cup of coffee."

He sat down again unwillingly. Perhaps he really wasn't well, but he expected to feel worse until he had a drink of something better than cold water.

"Can't we do something for him, Jud?" The woman had turned to her husband. "He doesn't look able to be out on the road alone, without a soul to do for him. Can't you think of something?"

"Well——" The constable set fire to the end of a small white tube, and inhaled the smoke with a reflective expression. "We still don't have a janitor at the school. I'm a trustee, and I'll say a word to the principal if you want the job."

"And you could stay here with us," the woman added warmly. "There's a nice clean bed in the attic. Your board won't cost a cent, so long as you're willing to do a few odd jobs around the place. Would you like that?"

He squinted at her uncertainly. To his own surprise, he wanted to stay. He wasn't used to kindness, and it filled his eyes with tears. The infinite chasm of open space seemed suddenly even more dark and cold and dreadful than it was, and for an instant he hungered fiercely for the quiet peace of this forgotten world. Per-

haps its still spell would hold him and heal all his restless discontent.

"You're welcome here," the constable was urging.
"And if you've got a business head, you can find more
than odd jobs to do. You'll never find a likelier spot
than Chatsworth, if you want to settle down."

"I don't know." He picked up his empty cup, absently. "I'm really glad you want me, but I'm afraid it's
been too long——"

He stopped, flinching, when he saw the woman looking at his nose. Her eyes fell, as if out of pity, but in a
moment she spoke.

"I . . . I do hope you'll let us help you, Mr. Gray."
She hesitated again, her plump face flushed, and he began to hate her. "I've a brother in the city who's a plastic surgeon," she went on resolutely. "He has turned a
lot of . . . well, misfits . . . into very successful people. He's really very good, and not high at all. If you
decide to stay, I think we can manage something."

He set the empty cup down quickly, because his
hands were shaking again. He was still alert enough to
recognize the old trap, even in this charming guise. He
didn't want to be rehabilitated, and he meant to keep
his nose.

"Well, Mr. Gray?" the constable was drawling.
"Want to see the principal?"

"I'd like to." He grinned wanly, to cover his shuddering panic. "If you'll just show me where to find him.
And you've both been very kind."

"Don't mention it," the constable said. "I'm driving
back to the farm, and I'll take you by the school."

But he didn't talk to the principal. He had seen the
trap, and he was still crafty enough to escape it. He
started walking toward the building as the constable
drove away, limping along as soberly as if he had already been rehabilitated, but he stopped outside, behind
a hedge, to make his pitch.

He unlocked the battered case and set it up on the
extended legs and lighted the three-dimensional displays. The children gathered on the playground were al-

ready pausing in the games to look at him, and when
the psionic music began they flocked around him instantly.

His toys were the cheapest possible trinkets, mass-
produced from common materials, but they were cleverly packaged and their ingenious designs reflected the
advanced technology of the industrial planet where they
were made. The small plastic boxes were gay with universal psionic labels, which reacted to attention with animated stereocolor scenes and changing labels which
seemed to be printed in each looker's own language.

"Come in closer, kiddies!"

He picked up the first little pile of round red boxes
and began juggling them with a sudden dexterity in his
twisted old fingers, so that they rose and fell in time to
the racing psionic melody.

"Look, kiddies! A wonderful educational toy. Use it
to demonstrate the great basic principles of meteorology
and neutrionics. And surprise your friends.

"The Little Wonder Weather Wizard Blizzard Maker
Set! It works by turning part of the heat energy of the
air for several miles around into radiant neutrinos. The
sudden chilling causes precipitation, and the outflow of
cold air creates a brief but effective blizzard—the label
tells you all about it.

"Step right up, kiddies! Buy 'em at a bargain price.
Only twenty-five cents each, or three for half a dollar——"

"But we really shouldn't, mister." The boy who interrupted looked familiar, and he recognized the constable's oldest son. "All most of us have is our lunch
money, and we aren't supposed to spend it."

"Don't you worry, kid," he answered quickly. "Even
if you go home hungry, you'll have your money's worth.
You never saw any toys like these. Only fifteen cents, to
close 'em out. Come right up and buy 'em now, because
I won't be here tomorrow."

He scooped up the coins from grubby little hands.

"But don't start making storms just now," he warned
hastily. "We don't want trouble with the teachers, do

we, kiddies? Better keep 'em in your pockets until school is out. Sorry, sonny. That's all the blizzard makers—but look at this!"

He picked up the next stack of small plastic boxes.

"The Junior Giant Degravitator Kit! A fascinating experiment in gravitational inversion. Learn the facts of basic science, and amaze your friends. The label shows you all about it."

He began passing out the boxes. The bright psionic labels looked blank at first, but they came to shining life under the eyes of the children, responding to the thoughts of each. Most of them pictured the harmless degravitation of such small objects as marbles and tadpoles, but he glimpsed one showing how to connect the device to the foundations of the school building and another in which the astonished principal himself was falling upward toward open space.

"Wait a moment, sonny!" he whispered hurriedly. "Let's not degravitate anything until after school is out. Sorry, laddie. That's all the Junior Giants, but here's something else that's just as educational, and really better fun."

He held up a Great Detective Annihilator Pistol-Pencil.

"It looks like an ordinary writing instrument, but the eraser really erases! It converts solid matter into invisible neutrinos. All you do is point it and press the clip. You can blow holes in walls, and make objects disappear, and fool your friends. All for one thin dime!"

The school bell began to ring as he handed out the annihilators and gathered up the dimes.

"Just one more item, kiddies, before you go to class." He turned up the psionic amplifier, and raised his rusty voice. "Something I know you're all going to want. An exciting experiment, with real atomic energy, that you can try at home!"

He poured bright little spheres out of a carton into the palm of his hand.

"Look at 'em, kiddies! Planet Blaster Fusion Bomb Capsules, Super-Dooper Size. All you do is drop one capsule in a bucket of water and wait for it to dissolve. The reaction fuses the hydrogen atoms in the water into helium—the free instruction leaflet tells you how the same reaction makes the stars shine.

"Buy 'em now, before you go to class. Add realism to your playground battles, and flabbergast your friends. Make your own fusion bombs. Only five cents each. Three for a dime, if you buy 'em now——"

"Say, mister." The constable's son had bought three capsules, but now he stood peering at them uneasily. "If these little pills make real atom bombs, aren't they dangerous, even more than fireworks?"

"I wouldn't know about fireworks." The peddler scowled impatiently. "But these toys are safe enough, if you've had your psionic preconditioning. I hope you all know enough not to set off fusion bombs indoors!"

He laughed at the bewildered boy, and lifted his rasping voice.

"Your last chance, kiddies! I won't be here when you get out of school, but right now these genuine fusion bomb capsules are going two for a nickel. One for two cents, sonny, if that's all you've got."

He swept in the last sweaty coppers.

"And that's all, kiddies." He turned out the shimmering displays and stopped the psionic music and folded up the stand. The children filed into the schoolhouse, and he hurried back across the village.

The tavern on the hill was open when he came back to it, and the scent of alcohol brought back all his thirst, so intense that his whole body shuddered. He was spreading out his money on the bar, when a blare of native music startled him.

The raw notes sawed at his nerves, too loud and queerly meaningless. He turned to scowl at the bulky machine from which they came, wondering what made them seem so flat and dead. After a moment of puzzled annoyance, he realized that the music was sound alone, with no psionic overtones.

Were these people ignorant of psionics? It seemed impossible that even the Covenants of Non-Contact could exclude all knowledge of such a basic science, yet now when he thought of it he couldn't recall seeing any psionic device at all. The bartender ought to know.

"Well, mister, what will you have?"

"Tell me," he whispered huskily, "do your schools here teach psionics?"

The man's startled expression should have been answer enough, but he wasn't looking at it. He had seen his own reflection in the mirror behind the bar. The hard, narrow bloodless face. The shrinking chin. The shifty, hollowed, bloodshot eyes. And the huge crooked nose.

"Huh?" The bartender was staring. "What did you say?"

But his voice was gone. If these people didn't know psionics, anything he said would give him away. The flier would be discovered, and he could never leave. He would be rehabilitated. White and weak with panic, he pushed the heap of coins across the bar.

"Whisky!" he gasped. "All this will buy."

The bartender took an endless time to count the coins, but they bought six bottles. He crammed them into the empty case and hurried out of the bar. And he came at last, footsore and dusty, back across the bridge and up the hills where he had left the flier.

His breath sobbed out when he stumbled through the trees and saw the empty spot beyond the rock. Dismay shook him. He thought the flier was gone, until he turned and recognized its inflated camouflage. Trembling with a sick weakness, he found the psionic key and tried to deflate the membrane.

The key didn't work.

He tried again, but still the distended fabric remained hard as actual rock. He ran frantically around it, trying the key against a dozen different spots. None of them responded. He was locked out.

He couldn't understand it, and he had to have a drink. He had been trying to wait until he was safe aboard, with his new destination dialed on the automatic pilot, but suddenly he felt too tired and cold and hopeless to make any effort without the warming aid of alcohol. He couldn't even think.

He stooped to open the sales case, where he had put the whisky, but the psionic key failed again. It fell out of his fingers when he realized what was wrong. Psionic and neutrionic devices seldom got out of order, but they could be disabled. The flier must have been discovered by somebody from the quarantine station.

Sick with panic, he tried to get away. He dropped the case and ran blindly off into the unfamiliar wilderness. His staggering flight must have led him in a circle, however, for at last he came reeling back to a hill and a rock that looked the same. His head was light with illness by that time, his twitching limbs hot with fever.

He was clawing feebly at the stiffened membrane, hopelessly trying to tear it away with his bleeding fingers, when he heard firm footsteps behind him and turned to see the stolid, sunburned figure of Constable Jud Hankins.

"Well, constable." He leaned giddily back against the camouflage, grinning with a sick relief that this was not a quarantine inspector. His translator failed to work at first, but it spoke for him as he fumbled to adjust the instrument under his clothing.

"I give up," he muttered dully. "I'll go back with you." A chill began to shake him, and his raw throat felt too painful for speech. "I'm ready to settle down— if they'll only leave my nose alone."

There was something else he ought to say, but his ears were roaring and his bones ached and he could hardly stand. He felt too sick for a moment to remember anything, but at last it came back to him.

"The toys——" he sobbed. "They're dangerous!"

"Not any longer," the tall man told him curtly. "We slapped psionic and neutrionic inhibitors on this whole area, to prevent accidents, before I borrowed the identity of Constable Hankins to pick them up."

"You——" He stared blankly. "You are——"

"A quarantine inspector, from Sol Station." The officer flashed a psionic badge. "You were detected before you landed. We delayed the arrest to be certain you had no confederates."

He felt too ill to be astonished.

"You've got me," he mumbled faintly. "Go ahead and give me full rehabilitation."

"Too late for that." The stern man straightened impatiently. "You're all alike, you quarantine breakers. You always forget that cultural impacts strike both ways. You never understand that the Covenants exist partly for your own protection."

He shook his throbbing head.

"I know you were not processed through our clinic at the station," the inspector rapped. "I see you didn't even bring a medical kit. I'd bet you landed·here, among a people so primitive that malignant microorganisms are allowed to breed among them, with no protection for yourself whatever."

"Clinic?" The one word was all he really caught, but he stiffened defensively. "You can do what else you like," he whispered doggedly. "But I mean to keep my nose."

"You've bigger troubles now." The inspector studied him regretfully. "I suppose our ancestors were naturally immune, the way these people are, but I'd be dead in half a day if I hadn't been immunized against a thousand viruses and germs. You've already picked them up."

He stood wheezing for his breath, squinting painfully against the light.

"The people I met were well enough," he protested stupidly. "One child had something called a cold, but the woman said it wasn't dangerous."

"Not to her," the inspector said. "No more than atomic fusion bombs are to you."

Uncomprehending, the peddler swayed and fell.

The Happiest Creature

THE COLLECTOR PUFFED angrily into the commandant's office in the quarantine station on the moon of Earth. He was a heavy hairless man with sherwd little ice-green eyes sunk deep in fat yellow flesh. He had a genial smile when he was getting what he wanted. Just now he wasn't.

"Here we've come a good hundred light-years, and you can see who I am." He riffled his psionic identification films under the commandant's nose. "I intend to collect at least one of those queer anthropoids, in spite of all your silly red tape."

The shimmering films attested his distinguished scientific attainments. He was authorized to gather specimens for the greatest zoo in the inhabited galaxy, and the quarantine service had been officially requested to expedite his search.

"I see." The commandant nodded respectfully, trying to conceal a weary frown. The delicate business of safeguarding Earth's embryonic culture had taught him to deal cautiously with such unexpected threats. "Your credentials are certainly impressive, and we'll give you whatever help we can. Won't you sit down?"

The collector wouldn't sit down. He was thoroughly annoyed with the commandant. He doubted loudly that the quarantine regulations had ever been intended to apply to such a backward planet as Earth, and he proposed to take his specimen without any further fiddle-faddle.

The commandant, who came from a civilization which valued courtesy and reserve, gasped in spite of himself at the terms that came through his psionic translator, but he attempted to restrain his mounting impatience.

"Actually, these creatures are human," he answered firmly. "And we are stationed here to protect them."

"Human?" The collector snorted. "When they've never got even this far off their stinking little planet!"

"A pretty degenerate lot," the commandant agreed regretfully. "But their human origins have been well established, and you'll have to leave them alone."

The collector studied the commandant's stern-lipped face and modified his voice.

"All we need is a single specimen, and we won't injure that." He recovered his jovial smile. "On the contrary, the creature we pick up will be the luckiest one on the planet. I've been in this game a good many centuries, and I know what I'm talking about. Wild animals in their native environments are invariably diseased. They are in constant physical danger, generally undernourished, and always more or less frustrated sexually. But the beast we take will receive the most expert attention in every way."

A hearty chuckle shook his oily yellow jowls.

"Why, if you allowed us to advertise for a specimen, half the population would volunteer."

"You can't advertise," the commandant said flatly. "Our first duty here is to guard this young culture from any outside influence that might cripple its natural development."

"Don't upset yourself." The fat man shrugged. "We're undercover experts. Our specimen will never know that it has been collected, if that's the way you want it."

"It isn't." The commandant rose abruptly. "I will give your party every legitimate assistance, but if I discover that you have tried to abduct one of these people I'll confiscate your ship."

"Keep your precious pets," the collector grunted ungraciously. "We'll just go ahead with out field studies. Live specimens aren't really essential, anyhow. Our technicians have prepared very authentic displays, with only animated replicas."

"Very well." The commandant managed a somewhat sour smile. "With that understanding, you may land."

He assigned two inspectors to assist the collector and make certain that the quarantine regulations were respected. Undercover experts, they went on to Earth ahead of the expedition and met the interstellar ship a few weeks later at a rendezvous on the night side of the planet.

The ship returned to the moon, while the outsiders spent several months traveling on the planet, making psionic records and collecting specimens from the unprotected species. The inspector reported no effort to violate the Covenants, and everything went smoothly until the night when the ship came back to pick up the expedition.

Every avoidable hazard had been painstakingly avoided. The collector and his party brought their captured specimens to the pickup point in native vehicles, traveling as Barstow Brothers' Wild Animal Shows. The ship dropped to meet them at midnight on an uninhabited desert plateau. A thousand such pickups had been made without an incident, but that night things went wrong.

A native anthropoid had just escaped from a place of confinement. Though his angered tribesmen pursued, he had outrun them in a series of stolen vehicles. They blocked the roads, but he got away across the desert. When his last vehicle stalled, he crossed a range of dry hills on foot in the dark. An unforeseen danger, he blundered too near the waiting interstellar ship.

His pursuers discovered his abandoned car and halted the disguised outsiders to search their trucks and warn them that a dangerous convict was loose. To keep the natives away from the ship, the inspectors invented a tale of a frightened man on a horse, riding wildly in the opposite direction.

They guided the native officers back to where they said they had seen the imaginary horseman and kept them occupied until dawn. By that time, the expedition was on the ship, native trucks and all, and safely back in space.

The natives never recaptured their prisoner. Through that chance-in-a-million that can never be eliminated by even the most competent undercover work, he had got aboard the interstellar ship.

The fugitive anthropoid was a young male. Physically, he appeared human enough, even almost handsome. Lean from the prison regimen, he carried himself defiantly erect. Some old injury had left an ugly scar across his cheek and his thin lips had a snarling twist, but he had a poised alertness and a kind of wary grace.

He was even sufficiently human to possess clothing and a name. His filthy garments were made of twisted animal and vegetable fibers and the skin of butchered animals. His name was Casey James.

He was armed like some jungle carnivore, however, with a sharpened steel blade. His body, like his whole planet, was contaminated with parasitic organisms. He was quivering with fear and exhaustion, like any hunted animal, the night he blundered upon the ship. The pangs of his hunger had passed, but a bullet wound in his left arm was nagging him with unalleviated pain.

In the darkness, he didn't even see the ship. The trucks were stopped on the road, and the driver of the last had left it while he went ahead to help adjust the loading ramp. The anthropoid climbed on the unattended truck and hid himself under a tarpaulin before it was driven aboard.

Though he must have been puzzled and alarmed to find that the ship was no native conveyance, he kept hidden in the cargo hold for several days. With his animal craftiness, he milked one of the specimen animals for food and slept in the cab of an empty truck. Malignant organisms were multiplying in his wounded arm, however, and pain finally drove him out of hiding.

He approached the attendants who were feeding the animals, threatened them with his knife, and demanded medical care. They disarmed him without difficulty and

took him to the veterinary ward. The collector found
him there, already scrubbed and disinfected, sitting up
in his bed.

"Where're we headed for?" he wanted to know.

He nodded without apparent surprise when the collector told him the mission and the destination of the
ship.

"Your undercover work ain't quite so hot as you
seem to think," he said. "I've seen your flying saucers
myself."

"Flying saucers!" The collector sniffed disdainfully,
"They aren't anything of ours. Most of them are nothing but refracted images of surface lights, produced by
atmospheric inversions. The quarantine people are getting out a book to explain that to your fellow creatures."

"A good one for the cops!" The anthropoid grinned.
"I bet they're still scratching their dumb skulls, over
how I dodged 'em." He paused to finger his bandaged
arm, in evident appreciation of the civilized care he had
received. "And when do we get to this wonderful zoo of
yours?"

"You don't," the collector told him. "I did want exactly such a specimen as you are, but those stuffy bu-
reaucrats wouldn't let me take one."

"So you gotta get rid of me?"

The psionic translator revealed the beast's dangerous
desperation, even before his hard body stiffened.

"Wait!" The collector retreated hastily. "Don't alarm
yourself. We won't hurt you. We couldn't destroy you,
not even to escape detection. No civilized man can destroy a human life."

"Nothing to it," the creature grunted. "But if you
ain't gonna toss me out in space, then what?"

"You've put us in an awkward situation." The yellow
man scowled with annoyance. "If the quarantine people
caught us with you aboard, they'd cancel our permits
and seize everything we've got. Somehow, we'll have to
put you back."

"But I can't go back." The anthropoid licked his lips

nervously. "I just gut-knifed a guard. If they run me down this time, it's the chair for sure."

The translator made it clear that the chair was an elaborate torture machine in which convicted killers were put to a ceremonial death, according to a primitive tribal code of blood revenge.

"So you gotta take me wherever you're going." The creature's dark, frightened eyes studied the collector cunningly. "If you put me back, you'll be killing me."

"On the contrary." The collector's thick upper lip twitched slightly, and a slow smile oozed across his wide putty face, warming everything except his frosty little eyes. "Human life is sacred. We can arrange to make you the safest creature of your kind—and also the happiest—so long as you are willing to observe two necessary conditions."

"Huh?" The anthropoid squinted. "Whatcha mean?"

"You understand that we violated the quarantine in allowing you to get aboard," the collector explained patiently. "We, and not you, would be held responsible in case of detection, but we need your help to conceal the violation. We are prepared to do everything for you, if you will make and keep two simple promises."

"Such as?"

"First, promise you won't talk about us "

"Easy enough." The beast grinned. "Nobody'd believe me, anyhow."

"The quarantine people would." The collector's cold eyes narrowed. "Their undercover agents are alert for rumors of any violation."

"Okay, I'll keep my mouth shut." The creature shrugged. "What else?"

"Second, you must promise not to kill again."

The anthropoid stiffened. "What's it to you?"

"We can't allow you to destroy any more of your fellow beings. Since you are now in our hands, the guilt would fall on us." The collector scowled at him. "Promise?"

The anthropoid chewed thoughtfully on his thin lower lip. His hostile eyes looked away at nothing. The collector caught a faint reflection of his thoughts, through the translator, and stepped back uneasily.

"The cops are hot behind me," he muttered. "I gotta take care of myself."

"Don't worry." The collector snapped his fat fingers. "We can get you a pardon. Just say you won't kill again."

"No." Lean muscles tightened in the anthropoid's jaws. "There's one certain man I gotta knock off. That's the main reason I busted outa the pen."

"Who is this enemy?" The collector frowned. "Why is he so dangerous?"

"But he ain't so dangerous," the beast grunted. "I just hate his guts."

"I don't understand."

"I always wanted to kick his face in." The creature's thin lips snarled. "Ever since we was kids together, back in Las Verdades."

"Yet you have never received any corrective treatment, for such a monstrous obsession?" The collector shook his head incredulously, but the anthropoid ignored him.

"His name is Gabriel Meléndez," the creature muttered. "Just a dirty greaser, but he makes out he's just as good as me. I had money from my rich aunt and he was hungry half the time, but he'd never stay in his place. Even when he was just a snotty nose kid, and knew I could beat him because I was bigger, he was always trying to fight me." The beast bared his decaying teeth. "I aim to kill him before I'm through."

"Killing is never necessary," the collector protested uneasily. "Not for civilized men."

"But I ain't so civilized." The anthropoid grinned bleakly. "I aim to gut-knife Gabe Meléndez, just like I did that dumb guard."

"An incredible obsession!" The collector recoiled from the grim-lipped beast and the idea of such raw violence. "What has this creature done to you?"

"He took the girl I wanted." The beast caught a rasping breath. "And he put the cops on me. At least I think it was him, because I got caught not a month after I stuck up the filling station where he works. I think he recognized me, and I aim to get him."

"No——"

"But I will!" The anthropoid slipped out of bed and stood towering over the fat man defiantly, his free hand clenched and quivering. "You can't stop me, not with all your fancy gadgets."

The beast glared down into the collector's bright little eyes. They looked back without blinking, and their lack of brows or lashes made them seem coldly reptilian. Abruptly, the animal subsided.

"Okay, okay!" He spat deliberately on the spotless floor and grinned at the collector's involuntary start. "What's it worth, to let him live?"

The collector shook off his shocked expression.

"We're undercover experts and we know your planet." A persuasive smile crept across his gross face. "Our resources are quite adequate to take care of anything you can demand. Just give your word not to kill again, or talk about us, and tell me what you want."

The anthropoid rubbed his hairy jaw, as if attempting to think.

"First, I want the girl," he muttered huskily. "Carmen Quintana was her name before she married Gabe. She may give you a little trouble, because she don't like me a bit. Nearly clawed my eyes out once, even back before I shot her old man at the filling station." His white teeth flashed in a wolfish grin. "Think you can make her go for me?"

"I think we can." The collector nodded blandly. "We can arrange nearly anything."

"You'd better arrange that." The anthropoid's thin brown hand knotted again. "And I'll make her sorry she ever looked at Gabe!"

"You don't intend to injure her?"

"That's my business." The beast laughed. "Just take me to Las Verdades. That's a little 'dobe town down close to the border."

The anthropoid listed the rest of his requirements, and crossed his heart in a ritual gesture of his tribe to solemnize his promises. He knew when the interstellar craft landed again, but he had to stay aboard a long time afterwards, living like a prisoner in a sterile little cell, while he waited for the outsiders to complete their underground arrangements for his return. He was fuming with impatience, stalking around his windowless room like a caged carnivore, when the collector finally unlocked his door.

"You're driving me nuts," he growled at the hairless outsider. "What's the holdup?"

"The quarantine people." The collector shrugged. "We had to manufacture some new excuse for every move we made, but I don't think they ever suspected anything. And here you are!"

He dragged a heavy piece of primitive luggage into the room and straightened up beside it, puffing and mopping at his broad wet face.

"Open it up," he wheezed. "You'll see that we intend to keep our part of the bargain. Don't forget yours."

The anthropoid dropped on his knees to burrow eagerly through the garments and the simple paper documents in the bag. He looked up with a scowl.

"Where is it?" he snapped.

"You'll find everything," the fat man panted. "Your pardon papers. Ten thousand dollars in currency. Forty thousand in cashier's checks. The clothing you specified——"

"But where's the gun?"

"Everything has been arranged so that you will never need it." The collector shifted on his feet uncomfortably. "I've been hoping you might change your mind about——"

"I gotta protect myself."

"You'll never be attacked."

"You said you'd give me a gun."

"We did." The collector shrugged unhappily. "You may have it, if you insist, when you leave the ship. Bet-

ter get into your new clothing now. We want to take off
again in half an hour."

The yellow Cadillac convertible he had demanded
was waiting in the dark at the bottom of the ramp, its
chrome trim shimmering faintly. The collector walked
with him down through the airlock to the car, and
handed him a heavy little package.

"Now don't turn on the headlamps," the yellow man
cautioned him. "Just wait here for daylight. You'll see
the Albuquerque highway then, not a mile east. Turn
right to Las Verdades. We have arranged everything to
keep you very happy there, so long as you don't attempt
to betray us."

"Don't worry." He grinned in the dark. "Don't worry
a minute."

He slid into the car and clicked on the parking lights.
The instrument panel lit up like a Christmas tree. He
settled himself luxuriously at the wheel, appreciatively
sniffing the expensive new car scents of leather and
rubber and enamel.

"Don't you worry, butter-guts," he muttered. "You'll
never know."

The ramp was already lifting back into the interstellar ship when he looked up. The bald man waved at
him and vanished. The airlock thudded softly shut. The
great disk took off into the night, silently, like something falling upward.

The beast sat grinning in the car. Quite a deal, he
was thinking. Everything he had thought to ask for, all
for just a couple of silly promises they couldn't make
him keep. He already had most of his pay, and old
clabber-guts would soon be forty thousand miles away,
or however far it was out to the stars.

Nobody had ever been so lucky.

They had fixed his teeth, and put him in a hundred-
dollar suit, and stuffed his pockets with good cigars. He
unwrapped one of the cigars, bit off the end, lit it with
the automatic lighter, and inhaled luxuriously. He had
everything.

Or did he?

A sudden uncertainty struck him, as dawn began to break. The first gray shapes that came out of the dark seemed utterly strange, and he was suddenly afraid the outsiders had double-crossed him. Maybe they hadn't really brought him back to Earth, after all. Maybe they had marooned him on some foreign planet, where he could never find Carmen and Gabe Meléndez.

With a gasp of alarm, he snapped on the headlights. The wide white beams washed away all that terrifying strangeness and left only a few harmless clumps of yucca and mesquite. He slumped back against the cushions, laughing weakly.

Now he could see the familiar peaks of Dos Lobos jutting up like jagged teeth, black against the green glass sky. He switched off the headlights and started the motor and eased the swaying car across the brown hummocks toward the dawn. In a few minutes he found the highway.

JOSE'S OASIS, ONE-STOP SERVICE, 8 MILES AHEAD

He grimaced at the sign, derisively. What if he had got his twenty years for sticking up the Oasis and shooting down old José. Who cared now if his mother and his aunt had spent their last grubby dimes, paying the lawyers to keep him out of the chair? And Carmen, what if she had spat in his face at the trial? The outsiders had taken care of everything.

Or what if they hadn't?

Cautiously, he slowed the long car and pulled off the pavement where it curved into the valley. The spring rains must have already come, because the rocky slopes were all splashed with wild flowers and tinted green with new grass. The huge old cottonwoods along the river were just coming into leaf, delicately green.

The valley looked as kind as his old mother's face, when she was still alive, and the little town beyond the river seemed clean and lovely as he remembered Carmen. Even the sky was shining like a blue glass bowl, as if the outsiders had somehow washed and sterilized it.

Maybe they had. They could do anything, except kill a man.

He chuckled, thinking of the way old baldy had made him cross his heart. Maybe the tallow-gutted fool had really thought that would make him keep his promises. Or was there some kind of funny business about the package that was supposed to be a gun?

He ripped it open. There in the carton was the automatic he had demanded, a .45, with an extra cartridge clip and two boxes of ammunition. It looked all right, flat and black and deadly in his hand. He loaded it and stepped out of the car to test it.

He was aiming at an empty whisky bottle beside the pavement when he heard a mockingbird singing in the nearest cottonwood. He shot at the bird instead, and grinned when it dissolved into a puff of brown feathers.

"That'll be Gabe." His hard lips curled sardonically. "Coming at me like a mad dog, if anybody ever wants to know, and I had to stop him to save my own hide."

He drove on across the river bridge into Las Verdades. The outsiders had been here, he knew, because the dirt streets were all swept clean, and the wooden parts of all the low adobe buildings were bright with new paint, and all he could smell was the fragrances of coffee and hot bread, when he passed the Esperanza Café.

Those good odors wet his dry mouth with saliva, but he didn't stop to eat. With the automatic lying ready beside him on the seat, he pulled into the Oasis. The place looked empty at first and he thought for a moment that everybody was hiding from him.

As he sat waiting watchfully, crouched down under the wheel, he had time to notice that all the shattered glass had been neatly replaced. Even the marks of his bullets on the walls had been covered with new plaster, and the whole station was shining with fresh paint, like everything else in town.

He reached for the gun when he saw the slight dark boy coming from the grease rack, wiping his hands on a rag. It was Carmen's brother Tony, smiling with an envious adoration at the yellow Cadillac. Tony had always been wild about cars.

"Yes, sir! Fill her up?" Tony recognized him then, and dropped the greasy rag. "Casey James!" He ran out across the driveway. "Carmen told us you'd be home!"

He was raising the gun to shoot when he saw that the boy only wanted to shake his hand. He hid the gun hastily; it wasn't Tony he had come to kill.

"We read all about your pardon." Tony stood grinning at him, caressing the side of the shining car lovingly. "A shame the way you were framed, but we'll all try to make it up to you now." The boy's glowing eyes swept the long car. "Want me to fill her up?"

"No!" he muttered hoarsely. "Gabe Meléndez—don't he still work here?"

"Sure, Mr. James," Tony drew back quickly, as if the car had somehow burned his delicate brown hands. "Eight to five, but he isn't here yet. His home is that white stucco beyond the acequia madre——"

"I know."

He gunned the car. It lurched back into the street, roared across the acequia bridge, skidded to a screaming stop in front of the white stucco. He dropped the gun into the side pocket of his coat and ran to the door, grinning expectantly.

Gabe would be taken by surprise. The outsiders had set it up for him very cleverly, with all their manufactured evidences that he had been innocent of any crime at all, and Gabe wasn't likely to be armed.

The door opened before he could touch the bell, but it was only Carmen. Carmen, pale without her makeup but beautiful anyhow, yawning sleepily in sheer pink pajamas that were half unbuttoned. She gasped when she saw him.

"Casey!" Strangely, she was smiling. "I knew you'd come!"

She swayed toward him eagerly, as if she expected him to take her in his arms, but he stood still, thinking of how she had watched him in the courtroom, all through his trial for killing her father, with pitiless hate in her dark eyes. He didn't understand it, but old puffy-guts had somehow changed her.

"Oh!" She turned pink and buttoned her pajamas hastily. "No wonder you were staring, but I'm so excited. I've been longing for you so. Come on in, darling. I'll get something on and make us some breakfast."

"Wait a minute!"

He shook his head, scowling at her, annoyed at the outsiders. They had somehow cheated him. He wanted Carmen, but not this way. He wanted to fight Gabe to take her. He wanted her to go on hating him, so that he would have to beat and frighten her. Old blubber-belly had been too clever and done too much.

"Where's Gabe?" He reached in his pocket to grip the cold gun. "I gotta see Gabe."

"Don't worry, darling." Her tawny shoulders shrugged becomingly. "Gabriel isn't here. He won't be here any more. You see, dear, the state cops talked to me a lot while they were here digging up the evidence to clear you. It came over me then that you had always been the one I loved. When I told Gabriel, he moved out. He's living down at the hotel now, and we're getting a divorce right away, so you don't have to worry about him."

"I gotta see him, anyhow."

"Don't be mean about it, darling." Her pajamas were coming open again, but she didn't seem to care. "Come on in, and let's forget about Gabriel. He has been so good about everything, and I know he won't make us any trouble."

"I'll make the trouble." He seized her bare arm. "Come along."

"Darling, don't!" She hung back, squirming. "You're hurting me!"

He made her shut up, and dragged her out of the house. She wanted to go back for a robe, but he threw her into the car and climbed over her to the wheel. He waited for her to try to get out, so that he could slap her down, but she only whimpered for a Kleenex and sat there sniffling.

Old balloon-belly had ruined everything.

He tried angrily to clash the gears, as he started off, as if that would damage the outsiders, but the Hydra-Matic transmission wouldn't clash, and anyhow the saucer ship was probably somewhere out beyond the moon by now.

"There's Gabriel," Carman sobbed. "There crossing the street, going to work. Don't hurt him, please!"

He gunned the car and veered across the pavement to run him down, but Carmen screamed and twisted at the wheel. Gabriel managed to scramble out of the way. He stopped on the sidewalk, hatless and breathless but grinning stupidly.

"Sorry, mister. Guess I wasn't looking—" Then Gabriel saw who he was. "Why, Casey! We've been expecting you back. Seems you're the lucky one, after all." Gabriel had started toward the car, but he stopped when he saw the gun. His voice went shrill as a child's. "What are you doing?"

"Just gut-shooting another dirty greaser, that's all."

"Darling!" Carmen snatched at the gun. "Don't——"

He slapped her down.

"Don't strike her!" Gabriel stood gripping the door of the car with both hands. He looked sick. His twitching face was bright with sweat, and he was gasping hoarsely for his breath. He was staring at the gun, his wide eyes dull with horror.

"Stop me!"

He smashed the flat of the gun into Carmen's face, and grinned at the way Gabriel flinched when she screamed. This was more the way he wanted everything to be.

"Just try and stop me!"

"I—I won't fight you," Gabriel croaked faintly. "After all, we're not animals. We're civilized humans. I know Carmen loves you. I'm stepping out of the way. But you can't make me fight——"

The gun stopped Gabriel.

Queerly, though, he didn't fall. He just stood there like some kind of rundown machine, with his stiffened hands clutching the side of the car.

"Die, damn you!"

Casey James shot again; he kept on shooting till the gun was empty. The bullets hammered into the body, but somehow it wouldn't fall. He leaned to look at the wounds, at the broken metal beneath the simulated flesh of the face and the hot yellow hydraulic fluid running out of the belly, and recoiled from what he saw, shaking his head, shuddering like any trapped and frightened beast.

"That—*thing*!"

With a wild burst of animal ferocity, he hurled the gun into what was left of its plastic face. It toppled stiffly backward then, and something jangled faintly inside when it struck the pavement.

"It—it ain't human!"

"But it was an excellent replica." The other thing, the one he had thought was Carmen, gathered itself up from the bottom of the car, speaking gently to him with what now seemed queerly like the voice of old barrel-belly. "We had taken a great deal of trouble to make you the happiest one of your breed." It looked at him sadly with Carmen's limpid dark eyes. "If you had only kept your word."

"Don't——" He cowered back from it, shivering. "Don't k-k-kill me!"

"We never kill," it murmured. "You need never be afraid of that."

While he sat trembling, it climbed out of the car and picked up the ruined thing that had looked like Gabe and carried it easily away toward the Oasis garage.

Now he knew that this place was only a copy of Los Verdades, somewhere not on Earth. When he looked up at the blue crystal sky, he knew that it was only some kind of screen. He felt the millions of strange eyes beyond it, watching him like some queer monster in a cage.

He tried to run away.

He gunned the Cadillac back across the acequia bridge and drove wildly back the way he had come in, on the Albuquerque highway. A dozen miles out, an imitation construction crewman tried to flag him down, pointing at a sign that said the road was closed for repairs. He whipped around the barriers and drove the pitching car on across the imitation desert until he crashed into the bars.

The Cold Green Eye

"KANSAS?" THE BOY looked hard at his teacher. "Where is Kansas?"

"I do not know." The withered old monk shrugged vaguely. "The spring caravan will carry you down out of our mountains. A foreign machine called a railway train will take you to a city named Calcutta. The lawyers there will arrange for your journey to Kansas."

"But I love our valley." Tommy glanced out at the bamboo plumes nodding above the old stone walls of the monastery garden and the snowy Himalaya towering beyond. He turned quickly back to catch the holy man's leathery hand. "Why must I be sent away?"

"A matter of money and the law."

"I don't understand the law," Tommy said. "Please can't I stay? That's all I want—to be here with the monks of Mahavira, and play with the village children, and study my lessons with you."

"We used to hope that you might remain with us to become another holy man." Old Chandra Sha smiled wistfully behind the cloth that covered his mouth to protect the life of the air from injury by his breath. "We have written letters about your unusual aptitudes, but the lawyers in Calcutta show little regard for the ancient arts and those in Kansas none at all. You are to go."

"I don't need money," Tommy protested. "My friends in the village will give me rice, and I can sleep in the courtyard here—"

"I think there is too much money, burdening souls with evil karma," the lean old man broke in softly. "Your father was a famous traveler, who gathered dangerous riches. Since the wheel has turned for him, others desire his fortune. I think perhaps that is why the lawyers sent for you."

A fly came buzzing around his dried-up face, and he paused to wave it very gently away.

"Your mother's sister lives in that place named Kansas," he went on. "It is arranged for you to go to her. She is your own race and blood, and she wants you in her home—"

"No! She never even saw me," Tommy whispered bitterly. "She couldn't really want me. Must I go?"

"It is to be." Chandra Sha nodded firmly. "Your people are ignorant about the true principles of matter and the soul, but their own peculiar laws require obedience. The caravan leaves tomorrow."

Tommy wanted not to weep, but he was only ten. He clung sobbing to the thin old Jain.

"We have instructed you well," the holy man murmured, trying to comfort him. "Your feet are already on the pathway to nirvana, and I will give you a copy of the secret book of Rishabha to guide and guard you on your way."

Tommy went down out of the mountains with the caravan. He was bewildered and afraid, and the motion of the railway cars made him ill, but the lawyers in Calcutta were kind enough. They bought him new garments, and took him to a cinema, and put him on a great strange machine called an airplane. At last he came to Kansas and his Aunt Agatha Grimm.

He rode from the depot to her home in a jolting farm truck, peering out at the strange sun-flooded flatness of the land and a monstrous orange-painted machine called a combine that grazed like the golden bull of Rishabha through the ripe wheat.

The hired man stopped the truck beside a huge wooden house that stood like a fort in the middle of the endless land, and Tommy's aunt came out to greet him with a moist kiss. A plump, pink-skinned blonde, with a sweet, smooth, sweat-beaded face. He was used to darker women, and she seemed incredibly fair.

"So you're Lizzie's boy?" She and her sister had come from Alabama, and soft Negro accents still echoed in her voice. "Gracious, honey, what's the matter?"

Tommy had run to meet her eagerly, but he couldn't help shrinking back when he saw her eyes. The left was warm and brown and kind as old Chandra Sha's. But the right eye was different, a frosty, greenish blue; it seemed to look straight through him.

"Well, child, can't you talk?"

He gulped and squirmed, trying to think of words to say in English. But he couldn't think at all. Somehow, the blue eye froze him.

"Nothing," he muttered at last. "Just—nothing."

"Lizzie's boy would be a little odd." She smiled, too sweetly. "Brought up by jabbering heathens! But this is going to be your home, you know. Come on inside. Let me clean you up."

The hired man brought the carved teakwood chest the monks had given him, and they went into the big house. The smell of it was strange and stale. The windows were closed, with blinds drawn down. Tommy stood blinking at the queer heavy furniture and dusty bric-a-brac crammed into the dim cave of the living room, until he heard a fly buzzing at the screen door behind him. He turned without thinking to help it escape.

"Wait, honey." His aunt caught his arm, to seat him firmly on the teakwood chest. "I'll kill it!"

She snatched a swatter from the high oak mantel and stalked the fly through the gloomy jungle of antimacassared chairs and fussy little tables to a darkened window. The swatter fell with a vicious *thwack*.

"Got him!" she said. "I won't endure flies."

"But, Aunt Agatha!" The English words were coming back, though his thoughts were still in the easy vernacular the monks had taught him. His shy, hesitant voice was shocked. "They, too, are alive."

The brown eye, as well as the blue, peered sharply at him. His aunt sat down suddenly, gasping as if she needed fresh air. He wanted to open the windows, but he was afraid to move.

"Thomas, honey, you're upsetting me terribly." Her pale fat hands fluttered nervously. "I guess you didn't know that I'm not well at all. Of course I love children as much as anybody, but I really don't know if I can endure you in the house. I always said myself that you'd be better off in some nice orphanage."

Or back with the monks, Tommy told himself unhappily. He couldn't help thinking that she looked as tough and strong as a mountain pony, but he decided not to say so.

"But sick as I am, I'll take you in." Her moist, swollen lips tried to smile. "Because you're Lizzie's boy. It's my duty, and the legal papers are all signed. The judge gave me full control of you, and your estate, till you come of age. Just keep that in mind."

Nodding miserably, Tommy huddled smaller on the chest.

"I'm giving you a decent home, so you ought to be grateful." A faint indignation began to edge her voice. "I never approved when Lizzie ran away to marry a good-for-nothing explorer—not even if his long-winded books did make them rich. Served her right when they got killed, trying to climb them foreign mountains. I guess she never had a thought of me—her wandering like a gypsy queen through all them wicked heathen countries, never sending me a penny. A lot she cared if her own born sister had to drudge away like a common hired girl!"

Sudden tears shone in the one brown eye, but the other remained dry and hard as glass.

"What I can't forgive is all she did to you." Aunt Agatha snuffled and dabbled at her fat, pink nose. "Carrying you to all those outlandish foreign places. Letting you associate with all sorts of nasty natives. The lawyers said you've had no decent religious training. I guess you've picked up goodness knows what superstitious notions. But I'll see you get a proper education."

"Thank you very much!" Tommy sat up hopefully. "I want to learn. Chandra Sha was teaching me Sanskrit and Arabic. I can speak Swahili and Urdu, and I'm studying the secret book of Rishabha—"

"Heathen idolatry!" The blue eye and the brown widened in alarm. "Wicked nonsense you'll soon forget, here in Kansas. Simple reading and writing and arithmetic will do for the like of you, and a Christian Sunday school."

"But Rishabha was the first Thirtankara," Tommy protested timidly. "The greatest of the saints. The first to find nirvana."

"You little infidel!" Aunt Agatha's round pink face turned red. "But you won't find—whatever you call it. Not here in Kansas! Now bring your things up to your room."

Staggering with the teakwood chest, he followed her up to a narrow attic room. Hot as an oven, it had a choking antiseptic smell. The dismal, purple-flowered wallpaper was faded and water stained. At the tiny window, a discouraged fly hummed feebly.

Aunt Agatha went after it.

"Don't!" Tommy dropped the chest and caught at her swatter. "Please, may I just open the window and let it go?"

"Gracious child! What on earth?"

"Don't you know about flies?" A sudden determination steadied his shy voice. "They, too, have souls. And it is wrong to kill them."

"Honey child, are you insane?"

"All life is akin, through the Cycle of Birth," he told

her desperately. "The holy Jains taught me that. As the wheel of life turns, our souls go from one form to another—until each is purged of every karma, so that it can rise to nirvana."

She stood motionless, with the swatter lifted, frozen with astonishment.

"When you kill a fly," he said, "you are loading your own soul with bad karma. Besides, you may be injuring a friend."

"Well, I never!" The swatter fell out of her shocked hand. Tommy picked it up and gave it back to her, politely. "Such wicked heathen foolery! We'll pray, tonight, to help you find the truth."

Tommy shuddered, as she crushed the weary fly.

"Now, unpack your box," she commanded. "I'll have no filthy idols here."

"Please," he protested unhappily. "These things are my own."

The blue eye was relentless, but the brown one began to cry. Tears ran down her smooth face, and her heavy bosom quaked.

"Tommy! How can you be so mulish? When I'm only trying to take your poor dead mother's place, and me such an invalid."

"I'm sorry," he told her. "I hope your health improves. I'll show you everything."

The worn key hung on a string around his neck. He unlocked the chest, but she found no idols. His clothing she took to be laundered, lifting each piece gingerly with two fingers as if it had been steeped in corruption. She sniffed at a fragrant packet of dried herbs, and seized it to be burned.

Finally she bent to peer at the remaining odds and ends—the brushes and paints his mother had given him when she left him with the monks, a few splotched watercolors he had tried to make of the monastery and the mountains and his village friends, the broken watch the mountaineers had found beside his father's body, a thick painted cylinder.

"That?" She pointed at his picture of a shy brown child. "Who's that nigger girl?"

"Mira Bai was not a Negro." He covered the picture quickly with another, to hide it from that cold blue eye. "She lived in my own village. She was my teacher's niece. We used to study together. But her legs were withered and she was never strong. Last year before the rains were ended the wheel turned for her."

"What wheel?" Aunt Agatha sniffed. "Do you mean she's dead?"

"The soul never dies," Tommy answered firmly. "It always returns in a new body, until it escapes to nirvana. Mira Bai has a stronger body now, because she was good. I don't know where she is—maybe here in Kansas! Someday I'll find her, with the science of Rishabha."

"You poor little fool!" Aunt Agatha stirred his small treasures with the swatter handle, and jabbed at the painted cylinder. "Now what's that contraption?"

"Just—a book."

Very carefully, he slipped it out of the round wooden case and unrolled a little of the long parchment strip. It was very old, yellowed and cracked and faded. The mild brown eye squinted in a puzzled way at the dim strange characters. He wondered how much the blue one saw.

"That filthy scribbling? That's no book."

"It is older than printing," he told her. "It is written with the secret wisdom of the Thirtankara Rishabha. It tells how souls may be guarded through their transmigrations and helped upward toward nirvana."

"Heathen lies!" She reached for it angrily. "I ought to burn it."

"No!" He hugged it in his skinny arms. "Please don't! Because it is so powerful. I need it to aid my father and mother in their new lives. I need it to know Mira Bai when I find her again. I think you need it too, Aunt Agatha, to purge your own soul of the eight kinds of karma—"

"What?" The brown eye widened with shock and the

blue one narrowed angrily. "I'll have you know that I'm a decent Christian, safe in the heart of God. Now put the filthy scrawl away and wash yourself up. I guess *that's* something your verminous monks forgot to teach you."

"Please! The holy men are very clean."

"Now you're trying to aggravate me, poorly as I am." She snuffled and her brown eye wept again. "I'm going to teach you a respectable religion, and I don't need any nasty foreign scribblings to help me whip the sin out of you!"

She was very sweet about it, and she always cried when she was forced to beat him. The exertion was really too much for her poor heart. She did it only for dear Lizzie's sake, and he ought to realize that the punishment was far more painful to her than to him.

She tried to teach him her religion, but Tommy clung to the wisdom of the kind old monks of Mahavira. She tried to wash the East out of him with pounds of harsh yellow soap, until his sunburnt skin had faded to a sickly yellow pallor. She prayed and cried over him for endless hours, while he knelt with numb bare knees on cruel bare floors. She threatened to whip him again, and she did.

She whipped him when he covered up the big sheets of sticky yellow fly paper she put in his room, whipped him when he poured out the shallow dishes of fly poison she kept on the landing. But she seemed too much shaken to strike him, on the sultry afternoon when she found him carefully liberating the flies in the screen wire trap outside the kitchen door—a Kansas summer breeds flies enough.

"You sinful little infidel!"

Her nerves were all on edge. She had to sit down on the doorstep, resting her poor heart and gasping with her asthma. But her fat pink fingers seemed strong enough, when she caught him by the ear.

She called the hired man to bring a torch dipped in gasoline, and held him so that he had to watch while she burned the flies that were left in the trap. He stood shivering with his own pain, quiet and pale and ill.

"Now come along!" She led him up the stairs, by his twisted ear. "I'll teach you whether flies have souls." Her voice was like a saw when it strikes a nail. "I'm going to lock you up tonight without your supper, but I'll see you in the morning."

She shoved him into the stifling attic room. It was bare and narrow as the monastery cells, with only his hard little cot and his precious teakwood chest. His tears blurred the painted carving on the chest—it was the blue snake of the *deva* Parshva, who had reached nirvana.

She held him by the twisted ear.

"Believe me, Thomas, this hurts me terribly." She snuffled and cleared her throat. "I want you to pray tonight. Beg God to clean up your dirty little soul."

She gave his ear another twist.

"When I come back in the morning, I want you to get down on your bended knees with me and confess to Him that all this rot about flies with souls is only a wicked lie."

"But it's the truth!" He caught his breath, trying not to whimper. "Please, Aunt Agatha, let me read you part of the sacred book—"

"Sacred?" She shook him by the ear. "You filthy little blasphemer! I'm going down now to pray for you. But when I come back in the morning I'm going to open up your box and take away that heathen writing—I declare it's what gives you all these wicked notions. I'm going to burn it in the kitchen stove."

"But—Aunt Agatha!" He shivered with a sharper pain. "Without the secret book, I can't guide anybody toward nirvana. I can't help my father and mother, struggling under their load of karma. I won't even know little Mira Bai, if I should ever find her."

"I'll teach you what you need to know." She let go his tingling ear, to box it sharply. "We'll burn that book in the morning. You'll forget every word it says, or stay in this room till you starve."

She locked the door on him and waddled down the stairs again, weeping for his soul and wheezing with her asthma. She had a good nip of whisky for her heart, and filled herself a nice plate of cold roast chicken and potato salad before she went up to her own room to pray.

For a long time Tommy sat alone on the edge of the hard lumpy cot with his throbbing head in his hands. Crying was no use; old Chandra Sha had taught him that. He longed for his father and mother, those tanned happy wanderers he could barely remember, but the wheel had turned for them.

Nothing was left, except the sacred parchment. When the ringing in his punished ear had stopped, he bent to unlock the teakwood chest. He unrolled the brittle yellow scroll. His pale lips moved silently, following the faded black-and-scarlet characters.

The book, he felt, was more precious than all Kansas. He had to save it, to help his reborn parents, and to find Mira Bai, and even to aid his aunt—her poor soul was laden, surely, with a perilous burden of karma, but perhaps the science of the book could find her a more fortunate rebirth.

Trembling and afraid, he began to do what the holy men had taught him.

It was the hired girl, next morning, who came up to unlock his room. She was looking for his Aunt Agatha.

"I can't understand it." Her twangy Kansas voice was half hysterical. "I didn't hear a thing, all night long. The outside doors are locked up tight. None of her things are missing. But I've looked high and low. Your sweet little Auntie isn't anywhere."

The boy looked thin and pale and drawn. His dark eyes were rimmed with grime, hollowed for want of sleep. He was rolling up the long strip of brittle yellow parchment. Very carefully, he replaced it in the painted case.

"I think you wouldn't know her now." His shy voice was sad. "Because the wheel of her life has turned again. She has entered another cycle."

"I don't know what you mean." The startled girl

stared at him. "But I'm afraid something awful has happened to your poor old Auntie. I'm going to phone the sheriff."

Tommy was downstairs in the gloomy front room when the sheriff came, standing in a chair drawn up against the mantel.

"Now don't you worry, little man," the sheriff boomed. "I'm come out to locate old Miz Grimm. Just tell me when you seen her last."

"Here she is, right now," Tommy whispered faintly. "But if you haven't been instructed in the science of transmigration, I don't think you'll know her."

He was leaning over one of the big yellow sheets of adhesive fly paper that Aunt Agatha liked to leave spread at night to catch flies while she slept. He was trying to help a large, blue fly that was hopelessly tangled and droning in its last feeble fury.

"Pore little young-un!" The sheriff clucked sympathetically. "His aunt told me he was full of funny heathen notions!"

He didn't even glance at the dying fly. But Tommy hadn't found it hard to recognize. Its right eye was a furious greenish blue, the left was a tiny bead of wet brown glass.

Operation Gravity

HE CAME ABOARD at Jupiter Station. A withered little old man, with nearsighted eyes and untidy white hair. He looked innocent enough, with his absentminded smile, but the moment he opened his mouth I knew he was the sort of civilian eggbrain who always wants to wreck the fine old traditions of the Guard.

"Barron?" He was squinting dimly at the captain's insignia on my uniform, but he didn't use my title. "Name's Knedder. I want to look over your ship."

I was about to inform him that the *Starhawk* was a fighting vessel and not a museum for planet-hopping tourists when I saw the armchair admiral coming through the airlock behind him. I bit my tongue and saluted.

"Relax, Captain." The admiral returned my salute with a disgracefully slack waggle of his arm, and nodded respectfully at the sloppy little civilian. "This is *the* Doctor Knedder."

I hadn't known there were any Dr. Knedders at all, but I shook his limp hand and started to give him my standard tour for unavoidable civilians. No ship had a braver record than the *Starhawk*. Most people are impressed with the row of gold service awards on the bulkhead inside the lock, but Knedder wasn't interested.

"This one's the Blue Nova," I was saying. "We won it in the Martian War—"

"Wars don't matter." He shrugged at the whole splendid history of the ship. "Let's see your drive."

"Sorry, sir," I told him. "But most of our machinery is still classified—"

"Never mind that, Captain," the admiral interrupted. "Dr. Knedder's out here to work with the Guard on a secret research mission. Operation Baby Giant. He has been fully cleared. Our orders are to give him all the help he asks for."

I didn't want anything to do with such civilian nincompoops or their idiotic projects, but the admiral *was* an admiral. I led the way to the ship's elevator. When we got to the reactor room, Knedder began prying into our equipment and asking questions.

"And what's your propellant mass, Captain?"

"Ammonia in the tanks," I told him. "It comes out broken down into nitrogen and hydrogen ions—"

"Dr. Knedder knows all about that," the admiral cut in. "He designed our new ion accelerators."

"Very wasteful way to use atomic energy for flight

through space." Knedder shook his fluffy head regretfully, and asked another impertinent question. "Captain, what's your top payload?"

"Depends entirely on the mission, sir."

"Of course." He nodded patiently, and stopped to scratch something on a pad before his blue, shortsighted eyes came back to me. "Suppose your mission is to carry forty tons of equipment and three technicians to a point in space fifteen billion miles out from the sun?"

"A crazy question." I saw the admiral's face, and tried to moderate my tone. "What I mean, sir, the *Starhawk* wasn't designed for interstellar flight—"

"No ion ship is good enough for that." Knedder didn't seem offended, but he was persistent. "But I understood that you could carry us fifteen billion miles out. Right?"

"That's about the limit of our cruising range." I tried to be polite about it. "With no extra passengers and no extra load."

"Can't trim another ounce off our impedimenta." Knedder stood tugging at the leathery lobe of his outsized ear, with a dreamy look on his dried-up face. "But how many tons of weapons do you carry?"

"That's restricted—"

The admiral cleared his throat. "Please answer, Captain."

"Twelve-point-four mass-tons of mounted armament." I tried hard to swallow my natural indignation. "Eighteen-point-seven tons of ammunition and missiles in all categories."

"Only thirty-one tons." In a worried way, Knedder combed his knobby fingers back through his straggling mop of hair, without improving its appearance. "Something else will have to go." He clapped his hands together. "How about your radar range finders?"

"Four-point-two mass-tons in the electronic detection gear." I couldn't help flinching. "Three-point-seven tons in the cybernetic fire control."

"One more to go." He scowled and scribbled on his

pad, humming through his nose in a way that annoyed me. "Let's have a look in your ammunition room."

I saw what was coming, but there was nothing I could do about it but follow Knedder meekly through the ship and hold the end of a steel tape while he measured bulkheads and deck space. Finally he looked up at me with a preoccupied nod.

"Okay, Barron," he said. "Your ship will have to do."

"Do?" I forgot to be polite. "For what?"

"You ought to feel honored, Captain," the admiral put in hastily. "Dr. Knedder is choosing the *Starhawk* for a mission that is certain to become a milestone in space history. We can tell you now that you are going out beyond the orbit of Pluto to search for an undiscovered planet. We plan to name it *Cerberus*."

I came very near exploding. The Guard was formed to protect and assist space commerce, not to chase down imaginary planets.

"I'm afraid you're going to be disappointed," I told Knedder, when I could trust myself to speak. "A dozen expeditions have gone out to look for trans-Plutonian planets since I've been in the Guard. Most of them never came back. The few that did hadn't found a thing."

"But I know what we're looking for." Knedder was impervious to common sense. "I know the approximate mass and position of Cerberus, calculated from the way it affects the orbits of Pluto and Neptune."

"Hasn't that been tried before?"

"The planet's heavier and farther away than anybody else has ever suspected," Knedder said. "More massive than Jupiter. It has a highly eccentric orbit, inclined almost ninety degrees to the plane of the ecliptic. For a thousand years at a time, it's too far off to have any measurable effect on the nearer planets. Now it's back near perihelion."

We were standing near the starboard turret, and Knedder turned to the admiral with a restless gesture at the missile launches and the long space rifles mounted there.

"No time to waste," he said. "Rip out that junk."

"Junk?" Something choked me. I might have hit him, old and harmless as he looked, but the admiral caught my arm.

"Very well, sir," he told Knedder. "We'll have demolition crews on the job in an hour."

"Good," Knedder said. "My equipment's ready at the dock."

I felt relieved when I saw him pocket his tape and turn to go; I'd had just about all I could take from him.

"And thank you, Barron." He beamed at me stupidly. "We're going to be seeing a lot of each other, and I want you to know that I'm happy to be in the hands of such a competent officer."

If he had actually been in my hands, I could have twisted his scrawny neck without a qualm. As things stood, I could only inquire just what he meant to do with his forty tons of cargo.

"Our special equipment is designed for special methods of search," he said. "Others, as you know, have investigated every visible object bigger than Phobos within twenty billion miles of the sun. It follows that the vast mass of Cerberus must be in some way invisible."

"Invisible?" I stared at him. "If it's larger than Jupiter—"

"My theory—" Knedder checked himself, looking mysterious.

"Dr. Knedder's theory is classified top secret," the admiral put in quickly. "You are to be informed only about those details that appear to be essential to the efficient performance of your duties."

I escorted them off the ship and went back to take a farewell look at the guns and missiles I loved, before the wreckers came.

They carried out the ammunition, hoisted out the missiles, dismantled the launchers, ripped out the rifles, knocked out the bulkheads, cut out the gun decks, tore out all the radar and cybernetic gear that had been the keen eyes and the cold nerves and the fighting brain of a living ship. Saws whined and hammers crashed and cutting torches hissed until my own guts felt sick.

Knedder's two assistants came aboard with his secret equipment. Dr. Jefferson was a tall, trembling, dark-skinned skeleton. He looked too feeble to survive the ten-month round trip. I advised Knedder to send him back to an Earthside rest home and find a younger helper.

"Brain's still good," Knedder was irritatingly patient and stubbornly sure of himself. "Astrophysicist. Traced Cerberus across astronomical plates exposed a hundred years ago. Brilliant job. I want him with us."

I resigned myself to Dr. Jefferson, and asked how an invisible planet could have been photographed.

"Wasn't," Knedder murmured gently. "Gravity field bends light rays. Displaces images of stars beyond it. Slight effect, but enough for Jefferson. Brainy. Can't do without him."

Dr. Ming, the other assistant, was a plump Eurasian girl with thick-lensed glasses that seemed to magnify her sad black eyes. She was attractive: my crewmen whistled when they saw her come board. I called Knedder aside, and told him as courteously as possible that I couldn't allow a woman passenger on the *Starhawk*.

"Guess Ming is a woman." He nodded absently, as if that fact had never occurred to him before and didn't matter now. "Also the greatest mathematician alive. Better than all your cybernetic brains. Absolutely essential to the project."

I went to the admiral. He made an unkind joke about my age and advised me to make the best of her. That left me no choice, and I must admit that she was no trouble.

As a matter of fact, I seldom saw her. The special equipment for Operation Baby Giant came aboard packed in heavy crates or thickly wrapped in opaque plastics, and Knedder posted KEEP OUT signs outside all the compartments where he was setting it up. He and his people stayed inside and kept all the doors secured with new combination locks.

That fed me up. When I found myself locked out of half my own ship, I decided to ask for reassignment. With thirty years in the Guard, I thought I knew how inside thrust is applied, but I received a heartbreaking shock.

"Request for reassignment unfavorably considered," Luna Station messaged me through channels, after a strange delay. "Impossible to replace you with officer of adequate experience. You will continue with Knedder mission."

A second message informed me that Operation Baby Giant had been reevaluated to *crash repeat crash priority*. How an insignificant little civilian could swing so much thrust was something I didn't understand, but I saw that Knedder had me trapped aboard my own ship, driven like a galley slave.

His secret gear, when it was all weighed aboard, came to forty-two-point-nine mass-tons. Every item was essential, he insisted, and the admiral backed him up. I had to leave half my regular crew behind and cut our supplies to the bone to get the lift and load sheets into any reasonable kind of balance.

The ship was still heavy when we finally nosed out of the station. One-point-six tons of overload—all of it Knedder's mysterious gear. I could feel it in the sluggish way the *Starhawk* answered to her jets.

One-point-six tons of trouble.

Not that it was obvious to anybody else, at least on the outbound trip. We dropped around Jupiter, picking up acceleration, and slipped smoothly enough into our plotted orbit for Knedder's insane destination. Even with only our skeleton crew to work the ship, she never faltered or grumbled.

But all the time those tons of overload were eating up more tons of precious reaction-mass. The shape of trouble was plain enough to me on every chart and meter. Fifteen billion miles was going to be a long way home.

Knedder spent most of the long voyage out locked up

in his own compartments. That was probably just as well, because even his dreamy-eyed smile had begun to get on my nerves. He was always too amiable and too deeply absorbed in his own scientific fairylands. His patient good humor became unendurable.

We emptied the main tanks, braking toward his destination point. Sweating over the charts, I calculated that we could limp back to Jupiter on the emergencies before our supplies ran out, with just about enough ammonia left over to make a baby sneeze.

I knew Knedder was searching with all that secret gear, but I kept my own eyes open. We were still three million miles from his destination point when I picked up an object there. Even though it seemed to be just a small asteroid, I was considerably surprised to find anything at all. I called Knedder on the intercom, and he came to the control room.

"That's Cerberus, all right." He nodded calmly at the tiny blip glowing in the 'scope. "We first observed it a week ago."

"That's no planet!" I told him. "It can't be ten miles in diameter."

"About eight miles," he said. "But Ming has just recomputed its mass from the gravitational displacement of stellar images that Jefferson has been measuring. It's somewhat more massive than all the other planets combined."

"Huh?" I stared at him. "What's *that* heavy?"

"Nuclear fluid," he said. "Collapsed atoms, stripped of orbital electrons. Stuff with a trillion times the density of ordinary matter. Final state of matter, in dead stars. Properly speaking, that's what Cerberus is. Dwarf star. Black cinder of a burned-out sun. No native member of our solar family. Orbit indicates a fairly recent capture."

I leaned to study the faint greenish speck in the 'scope, trying to imagine a planet larger than Jupiter squeezed into something smaller than Phobos. That was hard to do. I had never felt that any such notions had much to do with the efficient operation of the *Starhawk,* but alarm caught me now.

"If all that's true—" I tried to swallow a sudden tremor in my voice. "If that thing's really so massive, hadn't we better keep away?"

"On the contrary—" Knedder's dreamy eyes squinted at me till I shivered. "Cerberus has provided us with a natural gravitic laboratory, equipped with a field millions of times more intense than we can hope to reach anywhere else. Operation Baby Giant was organized and equipped to make use of it. I want you to take us within four hundred miles, at our first approach."

For an instant I was stunned beyond protest. We were in free fall, and some involuntary movement sent me into the air. I caught at a guide rail and finally steadied myself enough to make a rough mental calculation.

"Four hundred miles!" I hung staring at Knedder, trying to think I had misunderstood him. "That close in, the field intensity must be something like forty thousand gravities!"

"Fifty thousand." He was grinning like a kid with an unexpected Christmas gift. "Scientific instruments have never been carried into such a field before."

"How do you think we could pull away, against fifty thousand gravities?" I glared at him. "Even if we weren't squashed flat!"

"We'll still be in free fall," he answered. "So we won't feel any force at all. And it won't be necessary to pull away with the jets. If you take us around on a parabolic orbit, with the perihelion at four hundred miles, our own momentum will lift us out again."

"Theoretically it might," I had to agree. "But I don't care to gamble my ship on it. I'll take you around at five thousand miles. That's risky enough."

I'd thought I was still in command, and I knew we were some four months and thirteen billion miles beyond the present limits of radio communication, so that Knedder couldn't go over my head to any paper shuffling admiral. But he had one more bitter surprise for me. Apologetically, he handed me a sealed envelope.

"Sorry, Barron," he said. "But your headquarters gave me this, for use if necessary."

The official envelope was addressed to me, from Luna Station. The letter inside informed me that Dr. Knedder had been commissioned a temporary officer of the Guard with the rank of admiral. The top brass was certain that I would cooperate faithfully toward every aim of Operation Baby Giant. That was a sickening kick, but I managed to come to attention.

"Relax, Barron." Knedder caught the guide rail and shoved himself away. "No formalities. Just take us around. At four hundred miles."

I worked the ship into the orbit he wanted, and we dropped around Cerberus. Once we were falling, there was nothing I could do but watch the 'scopes and try to trust his theories. For the first time in nearly twenty years, I felt a clammy shudder of space sickness.

We fell with a frightening acceleration. I was trying to follow Cerberus in a visual 'scope. A faint gray point at first—if it had ever really been a star, its own atomic fuel was gone; I saw it only by the fading rays of our far sun.

A dim gray speck. It swelled in the field of blackness, slowly at first. It was round, when I could see its shape; round and black and featureless, squeezed to perfect roundness by a hundred million gravities.

It crawled across the stars beyond as we swung around it, at first very slowly, but faster, faster, faster. It grew, ballooned, exploded. And then, in the last split second, I saw the ring.

A triple ring, wider in proportion than Saturn's, but fainter in that feeble twilight than last year's dreams. It lay at a right angle to the orbital plane of the planet, spread flat before us, so thin that I could see the rushing stars behind it.

I knew we were about to hit it.

Cra-crash!

That queer double blow came instantly, before I had

time to do anything. The *Starhawk* shuddered, and I was smashed against the control room bulkhead. I hung there a moment in free fall again, with my breath knocked out, half stunned and very sick.

When I dragged myself back to the instruments, Cerberus was gone from the 'scopes. I searched for it groggily, with the wide-angle finder. It was shrinking again when I found it, a glistening black bead. The ghostly ring had already vanished.

As I got my bearings, I began to understand that strange double impact. We must have burst through that ring, swung half around the planet, and struck the ring again, all in fractional seconds! Now we were moving outward again, away from perihelion, and the ship was still alive.

At first I was almost sorry, but my sickness soon subsided. I rinsed my mouth and mopped my sweaty face and turned shakily to check the instruments for indications of collision damage.

To my surprise, we were still space-tight. Air pressure normal in all compartments. The hull telemeters showed a skin temperature of almost 800°K., but that was already falling. And Cerberus was dwindling to a harmless spark behind.

I tried to call Knedder on the intercom, to ask how his party had fared. He didn't answer. I banged on his locked door till he opened it.

"You look bad, Barron." He floated in the doorway, blinking at me nearsightedly. His right cheek was bruised purple, and dark blood was oozing from a cut on his chin, but he didn't seem concerned about himself. "Something wrong?"

"That ring, sir!" I wasn't thinking very coherently, but I managed to remember that he was now an admiral. "I didn't see it in time."

"Jefferson had been observing it." He shrugged. "Wisp of cosmic dust. Mostly calcium atoms. Too thin to damage anything."

"You look damaged, sir. When you didn't answer the intercom, I was afraid you'd been badly hurt."

"Busy, Barron." He touched his face, glanced vaguely at the blood on his fingers, and wiped them absently on his white laboratory smock. "Getting results!"

He smiled triumphantly through his lacerations.

"Highly significant results!"

I wondered what made them significant, but he was holding the door half closed, so that I couldn't see beyond it. Dr. Jefferson was audible, hoarsely reading numbers, as if from some instrument.

"—point-o-o-five-nine-three—"

"Ned!" I couldn't see the Eurasian girl, but she sounded breathless with a sudden elation. "That should give us a good approximation to the third constant—"

"Sorry, Barron."

Knedder shut the door.

I went on to inspect the rest of the ship and discovered nothing disturbing. The jetman reported no damage. The reactor was still reacting. I hauled myself back to the control room, feeling that the worst was past.

I was finally getting used to Knedder, and Operation Baby Giant was evidently proceeding satisfactorily. In five or six months, with good luck and judicious use of the ammonia left in the emergency tanks, we ought to be back in radio range of Jupiter Station. Knedder and his assistants would no doubt settle down to writing dull books full of bumble-brained speculations about the antics of their instruments in a field of fifty thousand gravities. When their equipment was dismantled, I could probably requisition new armament for the *Starhawk*. Whatever happened, at least I would have a new yarn to spin at the club.

Back in the 'scopes, I had another look at Cerberus. It seemed too bright. A faint sense of worry set me to checking our course and position against our calculated free-fall orbit. With the first observation, all my relief turned to alarm.

We had fallen far behind where we should have been, and we were still drifting swiftly off our plotted parabolic orbit. I tapped the computer uneasily, and our present orbit was projected in the plotting tank, a green ellipse drawn close around the red reference point that stood for Cerberus.

I tried for an instant to think the computer had gone wrong, and then I understood. Friction with that dusty ring, in that double collision, had stolen too much momentum. We had too little left to lift us out of that terrible gravity field. We were trapped, unless—

I was already reaching for the siren. I blew a three-second warning blast, and opened the jets all the way. When you've run a ship for twenty years, such decisions get to be automatic. I didn't wait to calculate our reaction-mass reserve, because I knew we had none. I also knew that the efficiency of the jets depended on our speed. With every instant I had wasted, while the deadly drag of Cerberus slowed us, our chances had been melting away.

With our tanks so light, the accelerometer needle shot up to eight gravities. Not much, against fifty thousand, but this was not free fall. I was crushed down in the seat, and it took everything I had to watch the 'scopes and work the computer. I held the jets open nearly fifty seconds—till the glowing green filament of our projected orbit opened into a new parabola, to show that we had fought back to escape velocity.

I cut the jets and turned to read the tank guages. What I saw took my breath again. Four-point-three tons of mass—to carry us fifteen billion miles!

I sagged back into the seat and reached dismally for the computer, but I already knew what we were in for. Years of drifting, on short rations, with only half a chance of ever getting home alive. That mass was enough to start us back, but only at about a billion miles a year.

"Barron." Knedder came floating up behind me before I had finished computing the odds against us. "What was the reason for that interruption?"

"I was trying to save our lives." All my inner tension exploded into anger. "I hope you don't mind!"

He just squinted at me in a bewildered way.

"That collision slowed us down." I spelled it out for

him. "It left us on a closed orbit, that would have carried us back to collide again. I discovered the danger just in time to pull us out—"

He hung to the guide rail, shaking his tousled head.

"Should have consulted me," he broke in gently: "Because our observations aren't complete."

That stunned me.

"The readings we got on that first run are highly significant," he was murmuring. "Unfortunately, they are not sufficiently precise to give accurate determinations of the constants we're looking for. Want you to take us around again. Perihelion at forty miles. Give us readings at a good million gravities—"

"You're crazy!" I forgot he was an admiral. "It would take most of the ammonia in the tanks to work us back into that orbit. We'd hit the ring again, and never get out!"

"I think we can avoid the ring." His face tried to smile. "Jefferson says the inner cleft is about ten radii from the planet. Want you to take us through that."

"Even if we hit that gap," I told him bitterly, "we won't come out with mass enough to start us home. We'll drift out here until we die of starvation."

"Perhaps." He shrugged. "But at least we can continue our research." His shortsighted eyes were shining, with a look that I wanted to interpret as only something close to insanity. "A grazing passage, inside the inner ring, would give us readings at a hundred million gravities. Think of that!"

"The tidal stresses would tear the whole ship to atoms! Even if we missed the ring and the planet itself!"

"Probably." He sighed regretfully. "But Jefferson believes we can get sufficiently precise readings forty miles out. I think we can survive the field differentials there."

"Suppose we can?" I demanded. "What good will your wonderful new constants ever do anybody? We can't hope to get even a radio message back to civilization—"

I heard the girl calling him.

"We'll take care of that." He turned himself in the air. "We have equipment of our own. All I want you to do is take us down to one million gravities. Now please excuse me."

He slid away down the rail and left me boiling. I wanted to haul him back and dump him out through the disposal lock, but when you've spent half your life in the Guard actual mutiny doesn't come easily. He might be a nincompoop, but he was still a temporary admiral. I cursed him under my breath and started plotting the orbit he wanted.

It took three-point-seven tons of mass to turn us back toward Cerberus. The gauges showed point-five tons left in the last emergency tank. Not enough to fret about. I strapped myself into the acceleration seat and watched the 'scopes as we fell.

The pygmy planet shot up to meet us like a round black bullet. The triple ring swelled around it, a faint ripple on the starry pool of space. The inner cleft was straight ahead, and I had time to hope we'd really get through safe.

A curved black blade, it slashed at us. *Cr-r-rang!*

If there were two impacts, our velocity fused them into a single crushing concussion. Something savage wrenched at every fiber of my body, and smashed me down in the seat. In an instant it was gone. The reverberation died. The black and perfect globe of Cerberus was falling away again behind.

I struggled feebly to the instruments. Somehow, we were still space-tight. The telemeters showed a skin temperature of 980°K. When our new orbit sprang into the plotting tank, it was a closer ellipse around the red point that stood for Cerberus. That meant we were going to fall back, and fall again, until the end.

Knedder ignored the intercom, and I hammered on the door until at last he stuck his head out. Fresh blood was beading a new injury on his forehead, but he didn't seem aware of it.

"Captain Barron reporting, sir." I felt curiously relaxed, now that I knew nothing more could be done. "Seems we hit something."

"Did we?" He spoke too loudly, as if still deaf from that concussion. "Not surprising. Ring doubtless denser as you approach the planet. Cleft probably only relatively clear."

"Anyhow, we're all done for." I couldn't help feeling a certain irrational triumph as I told him that. "We lost momentum again. We're falling back. With only a cupful of ammonia left, we can't do anything about it."

"No matter." His preoccupied shrug demolished my sense of victory. "Jefferson says his readings are now sufficiently precise. Ming is using them to derive the electro-gravitic constants we came to look for."

"And I've got the last one, Ned!" Her eager voice came past the half-closed door. "Point-o-nine-o-four-o-seven!"

"Then I think our work is done."

"I'm sure it is!" I told him. "In an hour or two, the ship will be fused and vaporized. Our atoms will be spinning around in that ring. If you do have communications equipment that will reach civilization, you'd better start sending now."

"We have equipment." With an absent nod, he turned to call into the room behind him. "Jefferson, please adjust the compensator to Ming's constants. She'll compute the instrumental corrections."

He swung quickly back to me.

"And you, Barron." He spoke as crisply as an actual admiral. "Get back to your instruments and keep our orbit plotted."

I slid back to the 'scopes, grateful for anything to keep my mind off the unconquerable force that would presently be flattening the splintered atoms that once had been our bodies into its black and perfect sphere. The first orbit I plotted was still the same deadly ellipse. So was the second. The third was . . . incredible!

A straight green line!

A tangent to the last ellipse, but straight as a light ray. I took another observation, and replotted the read-

ings unbelievingly. And the same green line arrowed out
of the tank. I turned the amplification down with unsteady fingers and saw that it crossed the orbit of Jupiter, still unbending. The computer told me that it would
bring us home to the station, a full month ahead of
schedule.

"Well, Barron." Knedder was in the air behind me,
squinting at me with what looked like a faint amusement. "Think you can stop the ship when we get there?"

"We can brake in Jupiter's atmosphere," I answered
mechanically, staring at that impossible line. "But I
don't think I understand—"

Knedder chuckled.

"Sorry for all the needless secrecy, but your high
brass was afraid we'd make them look too foolish if we
failed," he said apologetically. "Free to tell you all
about it now. We weren't risking our necks in that
million-gravity field for a batch of useless data. Trying
to tame gravity. Did it!"

"Huh?" I had to snatch for the guide rail. "You
mean we're really out of that—that trap?"

"Nothing to it any more." He grinned happily. "Our
theoretical investigations had already established the
basic principles, and the experimental compensator we
brought along was designed to level out the field of the
ship. What we lacked was the electro-gravitic constants.
Once we had determined them with adequate precision,
all we had to do was get it going."

The whiff of ammonia left in the tanks was enough to
dock us at the station, after the braking maneuvers
around Jupiter had absorbed the most of our excess
momentum. Knedder and his colleagues went back to
Earth to publish their discoveries, and I tried to get the
Starhawk decently rearmed.

In spite of all the inside thrust I could muster, my
requests and requisitions were unfavorably considered.
Headquarters said she was obsolete. Once the proudest
vessel in the Guard, she is now rusting on Earth, a mere

museum for all the sightseers who come to gawk at
Knedder's first compensator.

I ignored the impertinent suggestion that I might care
to remain aboard as a curator, or perhaps as an additional exhibit. I have retired from the Guard. Ion-drive
captains, it appears, are now as obsolete as ion-drive
ships. Now that the new electro-gravitic craft are using
the hundred million gravities of Cerberus to catapult
them out toward the stars, we have been left behind.

But an old spaceman learns to make the best of
things, and Operation Baby Giant, for all its disappoint-
ments, was not a total loss. It gave me another good
yarn to tell at the club.

Guinevere for Everybody

THE GIRL STOOD chained in the vending machine.

"Hi, there!" Her plaintive hail whispered wistfully
back from the empty corners of the gloomy waiting
room. "Won't somebody buy me?"

Most of the sleepy passengers trailing through the
warm desert night from Kansas City jet gaped at her
and hurried on uneasily, as if she had been a tigress in-
adequately caged, but Pip Chimberley stopped, jolted
wide awake.

"Hullo, mister." The girl smiled at him, with disturb-
ingly huge blue eyes. The chains tinkled as her hands
came up hopefully, to fluff and smooth her copper-
blond hair. Her long tan body flowed into a pose that
filled her sheer chemistic halter to the bursting point.
"You like me, huh?"

Chimberley gulped. He was an angular young man,
with a meat-cleaver nose, an undernourished mouse-

colored mustache, and three degrees in cybernetic engineering. His brown, murky eyes fled from the girl and fluttered back again, fascinated.

"Won't you buy me?" She caressed him with her coaxing drawl. "You'd never miss the change, and I know you'd like me. I like you."

He caught his breath, with a strangled sound.

"No!" He was hoarse with incipient panic. "I'm not a customer. My interest is—uh—professional."

He sidled hastily away from the shallow display space where she stood framed in light, and resolutely shifted his eyes from her to the vending machine. He knew machines, and it was lovely to him, with the seductive sweep of its streamlined contours and the exciting gleam of its blinding red enamel. He backed away, looking raptly up at the glazing allure of the 3-D sign:

GUINEVERE
THE VITAL APPLIANCE!
NOT A ROBOT—WHAT IS SHE?

The glowing letters exploded into galaxies of dancing light that condensed again into words of fire. Guinevere, the ultimate appliance, was patented and guaranteed by Solar Chemistics, Inc. Her exquisite body had been manufactured by automatic machinery, untouched by human beings. Educated by psionic processes, she was warranted sweet-tempered and quarrel-free. Her special introductory price, for a strictly limited time, was only four ninety-five.

"Whatever your profession is, I'm very sure you need me." She was leaning out of the narrow display space, and her low voice followed him melodiously. "I have everything, for everybody."

Chimberley turned uncertainly back.

"That might be," he muttered reluctantly. "But all I want is a little information. You see, I'm a cybernetics engineer." He told her his name.

"I'm Guinevere." She smiled, with a flash of precise white teeth. "Model 1, Serial Number 1997-A-456. I'd be delighted to help you, but I am afraid you'll have to pay for me first. You do want me, don't you?"

Chimberley's long equine countenance turned the color of a wet brick. The sorry truth was, he had never wholeheartedly wanted any woman. His best friends were digital computers; human beings had always bored him. He couldn't understand the sudden pounding in his ears, or the way his knobby fists had clenched.

"I'm here on business," he said stiffly. "That's why I stopped. You see, I'm a troubleshooter for General Cybernetics."

"A shooter?" Psionic educational processes evidently had their limits, but the puzzled quirk of her eyebrows was somehow still entrancing. "What's a shooter?"

"My company builds the managerial computers that are replacing human management in most of the big corporations," he informed her patiently. "I'm supposed to keep them going. Actually, the machines are designed to adjust and repair themselves. They never really go wrong. The usual trouble is that people just don't try to understand them."

He snapped his bony fingers at human stupidity.

"Anyhow, when I got back to my hotel tonight, there was this wire from Schenectady. First I'd heard about any trouble out here in the sun country. I still don't get it." He blinked at her hopefully. "Maybe you can tell me what's going on."

"Perhaps I can," she agreed sweetly. "When I'm paid for."

"You're the trouble, yourself," he snapped back accusingly. "That's what I gather, though the wire was a little too concise—our own management is mechanized, of course, and sometimes it fails to make sufficient allowances for the limitations of the human employee."

"But I'm no trouble," she protested gaily. "Just try me."

A cold sweat burst into the palms of his hands. Spots danced in front of his eyes. He scowled bleakly past her at the enormous vending machine, trying angrily to insulate himself from all her disturbing effects.

"Just four hours since I got the wire. Drop everything. Fly out here to troubleshoot Athena Sue—she's the installation we made to run Solar Chemistics. I barely caught the jet, and I just got here. Now I've got to find out what the score is."

"Score?" She frowned charmingly. "Is there a game?"

He shrugged impatiently.

"Seems the directors of Solar Chemistics are unhappy because Athena Sue is manufacturing and merchandising human beings. They're threatening to throw out our managerial system, unless we discover and repair the damage at once."

He glowered at the shackled girl.

"But the wire failed to make it clear why the directors object. Athena Sue was set to seek the greatest possible financial return from the processing and sale of solar synthetics, so it couldn't very well be a matter of profits. There's apparently no question of any legal difficulty. I can't see anything for the big wheels to clash their gears about."

Guinevere was rearranging her flame-tinted hair, smiling with a radiance he couldn't entirely ignore.

"Matter of fact, the whole project looks pretty wonderful to me." He grinned at her and the beautiful vending machine with a momentary admiration. "Something human management would never have had the brains or the vision to accomplish. It took one of our Athena-type computers to see the possibility, and to tackle all the technical and merchandising problems that must have stood in the way of making it a commercial reality."

"Then you do like me?"

"The directors don't, evidently." He tried not to see her hurt expression. "I can't understand why, but the first part of my job here will be to find the reason. If you can help me—"

He paused expectantly.

"I'm only four ninety-five," Guinevere reminded him. "You put the money right here in this slot—"

"I don't want you," he interrupted harshly. "Just the background facts about you. To begin with—just what's the difference between a vital appliance and an ordinary human being?"

He tried not to hear her muffled sob.

"What's the plant investment?" He raised his voice, and ticked the questions off on his skinny fingers. "What's the production rate? The profit margin? Under what circumstances was the manufacture of—uh—vital appliances first considered by Athena Sue? When were you put on the market? What sort of consumer acceptance are you getting now? Or don't you know?"

Guinevere nodded brightly.

"But can't we go somewhere else to talk about it?" She blinked bravely through her tears. "Your room, maybe?"

Chimberley squirmed uncomfortably.

"If you don't take me," she added innocently, "I can't tell you anything."

He stalked away, angry at himself for the way his knees trembled. He could probably find out all he had to know from the memory tapes of the computer, after he got out to the plant. After all, she was only an interesting product of chemistic engineering.

A stout, pink-skinned businessman stepped up to the vending machine, unburdened himself of a thick brief-case and a furled umbrella, removed his glasses, and leaned deliberately to peer at Guinevere with bulging, putty-colored eyes.

"Slavery!" He straightened indignantly. "My dear young lady, you do need help." He replaced his glasses, fished in his pockets, and offered her a business card. "As you see, I'm an attorney. If you have been forced into any kind of involuntary servitude, my firm can certainly secure your release."

"But I'm not a slave," Guinevere said. "Our management has secured an informal opinion from the attorney general's office to the effect that we aren't human beings—not within the meaning of the law. We're only chattels."

"Eh?" He bent unbelievingly to pinch her golden arm. "Wha—"

"Alfred!"

He shuddered when he heard that penetrating cry, and snatched his fingers away from Guinevere as if she had become abruptly incandescent.

"Oh!" She shrank back into her narrow prison, rubbing at her bruised arm. "Please don't touch me until I'm paid for."

"Shhh!" Apprehensively, his bulging eyes were following a withered little squirrel-faced woman in a black-veiled hat, who came bustling indignantly from the direction of the ladies' room. "My—an—encumbrance."

"Alfred, whatever are you up to now?"

"Nothing, my dear. Nothing at all." He stooped hastily to recover his briefcase and umbrella. "But it must be time to see about our flight—"

"So! Shopping for one of them synthetic housekeepers?" She snatched the umbrella and flourished it high. "Well, I won't have 'em in any place of mine!"

"Martha, darling—"

"I'll Martha-darling you!"

He ducked away.

"And you!" She jabbed savagely at Guinevere. "You synthetic whatever-you-are, I'll teach you to carry on with any man of mine!"

"Hey!"

Chimberley hadn't planned to interfere, but when he saw Guinevere gasp and flinch, an unconsidered impulse moved him to brush aside the stabbing umbrella. The seething woman turned on him.

"You sniveling shrimp!" she hissed at him. "Buy her yourself—and see what you get!"

She scuttled away in pursuit of Alfred.

"Oh, thank you, Pip!" Guinevere's voice was muted with pain, and he saw the long red scratch across her tawny shoulder. "I guess you do like me!"

To his own surprise, Chimberley was digging for his billfold. He looked around self-consciously. Martha was towing Alfred past the deserted ticket windows, and an age-numbed janitor was mopping the floor, but otherwise the waiting room was empty. He fed five dollars into the slot, and waited thriftily for his five cents change.

A gong chimed softly, somewhere inside the vending machine. Something whirred. The shackles fell from Guinevere's wrists and flicked out of sight.

SOLD OUT! a 3-D sign blazed behind her. BUY *YOURS* TOMORROW!

"Darling!" She had her arms around him before he recovered his nickel. "I thought you'd never take me!"

He tried to evade her kiss, but he was suddenly paralyzed. A hot tingling swept him, and the scent of her perfume made a veil of fire around him.

"Hold on!" He pushed at her weakly, trying to remind himself that she was only an appliance. "I've got work to do, remember. And there's some information you've agreed to supply."

"Certainly, darling." Obediently, she disengaged herself. "But before we leave, won't you buy my accessory kit?" A singsong cadence came into her voice. "With fresh undies and a makeup set and gay chemistic nightwear, packed in a sturdy chemyl case, it's all complete for only nineteen ninety-five."

"Not so fast! That wasn't in the deal—"

He checked himself, with a grin of admiration for what was evidently an astutely integrated commercial operation. No screws loose so far in Athena Sue!

"Okay," he told Guinevere. "If you'll answer all my questions."

"I'm all yours, darling!" She reached for his twenty. "With everything I know."

She fed the twenty into the accessory slot. The machine chimed and whirred and coughed out a not-so-very-sturdy chemistic case. Guinevere picked it up and hugged him gratefully, while he waited for the clink of his nickel.

"Never mind the mugging, please!" He felt her cringe away from him, and tried to soften his voice. "I mean, we've no time to waste. I want to start checking over Athena Sue as soon as I can get out to the plant. We'll take a taxi, and talk on the way."

"Very well, Pip, dear." She nodded meekly. "But before we start, couldn't I have something to eat? I've been standing here since four o'clock yesterday, and I'm simply famished."

With a grimace of annoyance at the delay, he took her into the terminal coffee shop. It was almost empty. Two elderly virgins glared at Guinevere, muttered together, and marched out piously. Two sailors tittered. The lone counterman looked frostily at Chimberley, attempting to ignore Guinevere.

Chimberley studied the menu unhappily and ordered two T-bones, resolving to put them on his expense account. The counterman was fresh out of steaks, and not visibly sorry. It was chemburgers or nothing.

"Chemburgers!" Guinevere clapped her hands. "They're made by Solar Chemistics, out of golden sunlight and pure sea water. They're absolutely tops, and everybody loves 'em!"

"Two chemburgers," Chimberley said, "and don't let 'em burn."

He took Guinevere back to a secluded booth.

"Now let's get started," he said. "I want the whole situation. Tell me everything about you."

"I'm a vital appliance. Just like all the others."

"So I want to know all about vital appliances."

"Some things I don't know." She frowned fetchingly. "Please, Pip, may I have a glass of water? I've been waiting there all night, and I'm simply parched."

The booth was outside the counterman's domain. He set out the water grudgingly, and Chimberley carried it back to Guinevere.

"Now what don't you know?"

"Our trade secrets." She smiled mysteriously. "Solar Chemistics is the daring pioneer in this exciting new field of redesigned vital organisms. Our mechanized management is much too clever to give away the unique know-how that makes us available to everybody. For that reason, deliberate gaps were left in our psionic education."

Chimberley blinked at her shining innocence, suspecting that he had been had.

"Anyhow," he told her uneasily, "tell me what you do know. What started the company to making—uh—redesigned vital organisms?"

"The Miss Chemistics tape."

"Now I think we're getting somewhere." He leaned quickly across the narrow table. "Who's Miss Chemistics?"

"The world's most wanted woman." Guinevere sipped her water gracefully. "She won a prize contest that was planned to pick out the woman that every man wanted. A stupid affair, organized by the old human management before the computer was put in. There was an entry blank in every package of our synthetic products. Forty million women entered. The winner was a farm girl named Gussie Schlepps before the talent agents picked her up—now she's Guinevere Golden."

"What had she to do with you?"

"We're copies." Guinevere smirked complacently. "Of the world's most wonderful woman."

"How do you copy a woman?"

"No human being could," she said. "It takes too much know-how. But our computer was able to work everything out." She smiled proudly. "Because the prize that Miss Chemistics won was immortality."

"Huh?" He gaped at her untroubled loveliness. "How's that?"

"They call it cloning. A few cells of scar tissue from her body were snipped off and frozen, in our laboratory. Each cell, you know, contains a full set of chromosomes—a complete genetic pattern for the reproduction of the whole body—and the legal department got her permission for the company to keep the cells alive forever and to produce new copies of her whenever suitable processes should be discovered."

"Maybe that's immortality." Chimberley frowned. "But it doesn't look like much of a prize."

"She was disappointed when they told her what it was." Guinevere nodded calmly. "In fact, she balked. She didn't want anybody cutting her precious body. She was afraid it would hurt, and afraid the scar would show—but she did want the publicity. All the laboratory needed was just a few cells. She finally let a company doctor take them, where the scar wouldn't show. And the publicity paid off. She's a realies actress now, with a million-dollar contract."

"One way to the top." Chimberley grinned. "But what does she think of vital appliances?"

"She thinks we're wonderful." Guinevere beamed. "You see, she gets a royalty on every copy sold. Besides, her agent says we're sensational publicity."

"I suppose you are." A reluctant admiration shone through his mud-colored eyes, before he could bring his mind back to business. "But let's get on with it. What about the Miss Chemistics tape?"

"The contest closed before our management was mechanized," she said, "while old Matt Skane was still general manager. But when the computer took over, all the company records were punched on chemistic tapes and filed in its memory banks."

He sat for a moment scowling. His eyes were on Guinevere, but he was reaching in his mind for the tidy rows of crackle-finished cabinets that housed Athena Sue, groping for the feel of her swift responses. The thinking of managerial computers was sometimes a little hard to follow, even for cybernetic engineers—and even when there was no question of any defective circuits.

Guinevere was squirming uncomfortably.

"Is something wrong with my face?"

"Not a thing." He scratched his own chin. "I heard you tell your legal friend, back there at the vending machine, that you aren't a human being within the meaning of the law. What's the difference?"

"The original cells are all human." She dabbed at her eyes with a paper napkin and looked up to face him bravely. "The differences came later, in the production lines. We're attached to mechanical placentas, and grown under hormone control in big vats of chemistic solutions. We're educated as we grow, by psionic impulses transmitted from high speed training tapes. All of that makes differences, naturally. The biggest one is that we are better."

She frowned thoughtfully.

"Do you think the women are jealous?"

"Could be." Chimberley nodded uncertainly. "I never pretended to understand women. They all seem to have a lot if circuits out of kilter. Give me Athena Sue. Let's get out to the plant—"

Guinevere sniffed.

"Oh, Pip!" she gasped. "Our chemburgers!"

The counterman stood rubbing his hands on a greasy towel, staring at her with a fascinated disapproval. The forgotten chemburgers were smoking on the griddle behind him. Her wail aroused him. He scraped them up and slapped them defiantly on the counter.

Chimberley carried them silently back to Guinevere. He didn't care for chemburgers in any condition, but she consumed them both in ecstasy, and begged for a piece of chemberry pie.

"It's awfully good," she told him soulfully. "Made from the most ambrosial synthetics, by our exclusive chemistic processes. Won't you try a piece?"

When they approached a standing cab out in the street, the driver stiffened with hostility. But he took them.

"Keep her back," he growled. "Outa sight. Mobs smashed a couple hacks yesterday to get at 'em."

Guinevere sat well back out of sight, crouching close to Chimberley. She said nothing, but he felt her shiver. The cab went fast through empty streets, and once when the tires squealed as it lurched around a corner she caught his hand apprehensively.

"See that, mister?" The driver slowed as they passed a block of charred wreckage. "Used to be one of them mechanized markets. Mob burned it yesterday. Machines inside selling them. See what I mean?"

Chimberley shook his head. Guinevere's clutching

hand felt cold on his. Suddenly he slipped his arm around her. She leaned against him, and whispered fearfully:

"What does he mean?"

"I don't quite know."

The Solar Chemistics plant was ominously black. A few tattered palms straggled along the company fence. A sharp, yeasty scent drifted from the dark sea of solar reaction vats beyond, and blue floodlights washed the scattered islands where enormous bright metal cylinders towered out of intertwining jungles of pipes and automatic valves.

Chimberley sniffed the sour odor, and pride filled his narrow chest. Here was the marvelous body to Athena Sue's intricate brain. It breathed air and drank sea water and fed on sunlight, and gave birth to things as wonderful as Guinevere.

The driver stopped at a tall steel gate, and Chimberley got out. The rioters had been there. The palms along the fence were burned down to black stumps. Rocks had smashed gaping black holes in the big 3-D sign on the side of the gray concrete building beyond the fence, and broken glass grated on the pavement as he walked to the gate.

He found the bell, but nothing happened. Nobody moved inside the fence. All those dark miles of solar reactors had been designed to run and maintain themselves, and Athena Sue controlled them. A thousand fluids flowed continuously through a thousand processes to form a thousand new synthetics. Human labor was only in the way.

"Your almighty machine!" the driver jeered behind him. "Looks like it don't know you."

He jabbed the bell again, and an unhurried giant with a watchman's clock came out of the building toward the gate. Chimberley passed his company identification card through the barrier, and asked to see somebody in the office.

"Nobody there." The watchman chuckled cheerfully. "Unless you count that thinking machine."

"The computer's what I really want to see, if you'll let me in—"

"Afraid I couldn't, sir."

"Listen." Chimberley's voice lifted and quivered with frustration. "This is an emergency. I've got to check the computer right away."

"Can't be that emergent." The watchman gave him a sun-bronzed grin. "After all the hell yesterday, the directors shut off the power to stop your gadget."

"But they can't—" Alarm caught him, as if his own brain had been threatened with oxygen starvation. "Without power, her transistors will discharge. She'll—well, die!"

"So what?" The watchman shrugged. "The directors are meeting again in the morning, with our old legal staff, to get rid of her."

"But I'll have her checked and balanced again by then," he promised desperately. "Just let me in!"

"Sorry, sir. But after all that happened yesterday, they told me to keep everybody out."

"I see." Chimberley drew a deep breath and tried to hold his temper. "Would you tell me exactly what did happen?"

"If you don't know." The watchman winked impudently at the cab where Guinevere sat waiting. "Your big tin brain had developed those synthetic cuties secretly. It put them on the market yesterday morning. I guess they did look like something pretty hot, from a gadget's point of view. The item every man wanted most, at a giveaway price. Your poor old thinking machine will probably never understand why the mobs tried to smash it."

Chimberley bristled. "Call the responsible officials. Now. I insist."

"Insist away." The brown giant shrugged. "But there aren't any responsible officials since the computer took over. So what can I do?"

"You might try restraining your insolence," Chimberley snapped. "And give me your name. I intend to report you in the morning."

"Matt Skane," he drawled easily. "Used to be general manager."

"I see," Chimberley muttered accusingly. "You hate computers!"

"Why not?" He grinned through the bars. "I fought 'em for years, before they got the company. It's tough to admit you're obsolete."

Chimberley stalked back to the cab and told the driver to take him to the Gran Desierto Hotel. The room clerk there gave Guinevere a chilling stare and failed to find any record of the reservation. Another taxi driver suggested his life would be simpler, and accommodations easier to arrange, if he would ask the police to take her off his hands, but by that time his first annoyed bewilderment was crystallizing into stubborn anger.

"I can't understand people," he told Guinevere. "They aren't like machines. I sometimes wonder how they ever managed to invent anything like Athena Sue. But whatever they do, I don't intend to give you up."

Day had come before he found an expensive room in a shabby little motel, where the sleepy manager demanded his money in advance and asked no questions at all. It was too late to sleep, but he took time for a shower and a shave.

His billfold was getting thin, and it struck him that the auditing machines might balk at some of his expenses on account of Guinevere. Prudently, he caught a bus at the corner. He got off in front of the plant, just before eight o'clock. The gate across the entrance drive was open now, but an armed guard stepped out to meet him.

"I'm here from General Cybernetics—"

He was digging nervously for his identification card, but the tall guard gestured easily to stop him.

"Mr. Chimberley?"

"I'm Chimberley. And I want to inspect our managerial installation here, before the directors meet this morning."

"Matt Skane told me you were coming, but I'm afraid you're late." The guard gestured lazily at a row of long cars parked across the drive. "The directors met an hour ago. But come along."

A wave of sickness broke over him as the guard escorted him past an empty reception desk and back into the idle silence of the mechanized administrative section. A sleek, feline brunette, who must have been a close runner-up in the Miss Chemistics contest, sat behind the chrome railing at the dead programming panel, intently brushing crimson lacquer on her talons. She glanced up at him with a spark of interest that instantly died.

"The hot shot from Schenectady," the guard said. "Here to overhaul the big tin brain."

"Shoulda made it quicker." She flexed her claws, frowning critically at the fresh enamel. "Word just came out of the board room. They're doing away with the brain. High time, too, if anybody wants to know."

"Why?"

"Didn't you see 'em?" She blew on her nails. "Those horrible synthetic monsters it was turning loose everywhere."

He remembered that she must have been a runner-up.

"Anyhow," he muttered stubbornly, "I want to check the computer."

With a bored nod, she reached to unlatch the little gate that let him through the railing into the metal-paneled, air-conditioned maze that had been the brain of Athena Sue. He stopped between the neat banks of pastel-painted units, saddened by their silence.

The exciting sounds of mechanized thought should have been whispering all around him. Punched cards should have been riffling through the whirring sorters, as Athena Sue remembered. Perforators should have been punching chemistic tape, as she recorded new data. Relays should have been clicking as she reached her quick decisions, and automatic typewriters murmuring with her many voices.

But Athena Sue was dead.

She could be revived, he told himself hopefully. Her permanent memories were all still intact, punched in tough chemistic film. He could set her swift electronic pulse to beating again, through her discharged transistors, if he could find the impossible flaw that had somehow led to her death.

He set to work.

Three hours later he was bent over a high-speed scanner, reading a spool of tape, when a hearty shout startled him.

"Well, Chimberley! Found anything?"

He snatched the spool off the scanner and shrank uneasily back from the muscular giant stalking past the programming desk. It took him a moment to recognize Matt Skane, without the watchman's clock. Clutching the tape, he nodded stiffly.

"Yes." He glanced around him. The billowy brunette and the guard had disappeared. He wet his lips and gulped. "I—I've found out what happened to the computer."

"So?"

Skane waited, towering over him, a big, red, weatherbeaten man with horny hands shaped as if to fit a hammer or the handles of a plow, a clumsy misfit in this new world where machines had replaced both his muscles and his mind. He was obsolete—but dangerous.

"It was sabotaged." Chimberley's knobby fist tightened on the spool of tape, in sweaty defiance.

"How do you know?"

"Here's the whole story." He brandished the chemistic reel. "Somebody programmed Athena Sue to search for a project that would result in her destruction. Being an efficient computer, she did what she was programmed to do. She invented vital appliances, and supplied a correct prediction that the unfavorable consumer reaction to them would completely discredit mechanized equipment. So the saboteur reprogrammed her to ignore the consequences and manufacture Guinevere."

"I see." Skane's bright blue eyes narrowed ominously. "And who was this cunning saboteur?"

Chimberley caught a rasping, uneven breath. "I know that he was somebody who had access to the programming panel at certain times, which are recorded on the input log. So far as I've been able to determine, the only company employee who should have been here at those times was a watchman—named Matt Skane."

The big man snorted.

"Do you call that evidence?"

"It's good enough for me. With a little further investigation, I think I can uncover enough supporting facts to interest the directors."

Skane shifted abruptly on his feet, and his hard lips twitched. "The directors are gone," he drawled softly. "And there isn't going to be any further investigation. Because we've already gone back to human management. We're junking your big tin brain. I'm the general manager now. And I want that tape."

He reached for the chemistic spool.

"Take it." Chimberley crouched back from his long bronze arm, and ignominiously gave up the tape. "See what good it does you. Maybe I can't prove much of anything without it. But you're in for trouble, anyhow."

Skane grunted contemptuously.

"You can't turn the clock back," Chimberley told him bitterly. "Your competitors won't go back to human management. You'll still have all their computers to fight. They had you against the wall once, and they will again."

"Don't bet on it." Skane grinned. "Because we've learned a thing or two. We're going to use machines, instead of trying to fight them. We're putting in a new battery of the smaller sort of auxiliary computers—the kind that will let us keep a man at the top. I think we'll do all right, with no further help from you."

Chimberley hastily retreated from the smoldering blue eyes. He felt sick with humiliation. His own future was no serious problem; a good cybernetics engineer could always find an opening. What hurt was the way he had failed Athena Sue.

But there was Guinevere, waiting in his room.

His narrow shoulders lifted when he thought of her. Most women irked and bored him, with all their fantastic irrationalities and their insufferable stupidities, but Guinevere was different. She was more like Athena Sue, cool and comprehensible, free of all the human flaws that he detested.

He ran from the bus stop back to the seedy motel, and his heart was fluttering when he rapped at the door of their room.

"Guinevere!"

He listened breathlessly. The latch clicked. The door creaked. He heard her husky-throated voice.

"Oh, Pip! I thought you'd never come."

"Guin—"

Shock stopped him when he saw the woman in the doorway. She was hideous with old age. She felt feebly for him with thin blue claws, peering toward him blindly.

"Pip?" Her voice was somehow Guinevere's. "Isn't it you?"

"Where—" Fright caught his throat. His glance fled into the empty room beyond, and came back to her stooped and tottering frame, her wasted, faded face. He saw a dreadful likeness there, but his mind rejected it. "Where's Guinevere?"

"Darling, don't you even know me?"

"You couldn't be—" He shuddered. "But still—your voice—"

"Yes, dear, I'm yours." Her white head nodded calmly. "The same vital appliance you bought last night. Guinevere Model 1, Serial Number 1997-A-456."

He clutched weakly at the door frame.

"The difference you have just discovered is our rapid obsolescence." A strange pride lifted her gaunt head. "That's something we're not supposed to talk about, but you're an engineer. You can see how essential it is, to insure a continuous replacement demand. A wonderful feature, don't you think, darling?"

He shook his head, with a grimace of pain.

"I suppose I don't look very lovely to you any longer, but that's all right." Her withered smile brightened again. "That's the way the computer planned it. Just take me back to the vending machine where you bought me. You'll get a generous trade-in allowance, on tomorrow's model."

"Not any more," he muttered hoarsely. "Because our computer's out. Skane's back in, and I don't think he'll be making vital appliances."

"Oh, Pip!" She sank down on the sagging bed, staring up at him with a blind bewilderment. "I'm so sorry for you!"

He sat down beside her, with tears in his murky eyes. For one bitter instant, he hated all computers, and the mobs—and Matt Skane as well.

But then he began to get hold of himself.

After all, Athena Sue was not to blame for anything. She had merely been betrayed. Machines were never evil, except when men used them wrongly.

He turned slowly back to Guinevere, and gravely kissed her shriveled lips.

"I'll make out," he whispered. "And now I've got to call Schenectady."

Jamboree

THE SCOUTMASTER SLIPPED into the camp on black plastic tracks. Its slick yellow hood shone in the cold early light like the shell of a bug. It paused in the door, listening for boys not asleep. Then its glaring eyes began to swivel, darting red beams into every corner, looking for boys out of bed.

"Rise and smile!" Its loud merry voice bounced off the gray iron walls. "Fox Troop rise and smile! Hop for old Pop! Mother says today is Jamboree!"

The Nuke Patrol, next to the door, was mostly tenderfeet, still in their autonomic prams. They all began squalling, because they hadn't learned to love old Pop. The machine's happy voice rose louder than their howling, and it came fast down the narrow aisle to the cubs in the Anthrax Patrol.

"Hop for Pop! Mother says it's Jamboree!"

The cubs jumped up to attention, squealing with delight. Jamboree was bright gold stars to paste on their faces. Jamboree was a whole scoop of pink ice milk and maybe a natural apple. Jamboree was a visit to Mother's.

The older scouts in the Scavanger Patrol and the Skull Patrol were not so noisy, because they knew Mother wouldn't have many more Jamborees for them. Up at the end of the camp, three boys sat up without a sound and looked at Joey's empty pallet.

"Joey's late," Ratbait whispered. He was a pale, scrawny, wise-eyed scout who looked too old for twelve. "We oughta save his hide. We oughta fix a dummy and fool old Pop."

"Naw!" muttered Butch. "He'll get us all in bad."

"But we oughta—" Blinkie wheezed. "We oughta help—"

Ratbait began wadding up a pillow to be the dummy's head, but he dropped flat when he saw the scoutmaster rushing down with a noise like wind, red lamps stabbing at the empty bed.

"Now, now, scouts!" Its voice fluttered like a hurt bird. "You can't play pranks on poor old Pop. Not today. You'll make us late for Jamboree."

Ratbait felt a steel whip twitch the blanket from over his head and saw red light burning through his tightshut lids.

"Better wake up, Scout R-8." Its smooth, sad voice

dripped over him like warm oil. "Better tell old Pop where J-0 went."

He squirmed under that terrible blaze. He couldn't see and he couldn't breathe and he couldn't think what to say. He gulped at the terror in his throat and tried to shake his head. At last the red glare went on to Blinkie.

"Scout Q-2, you're a twenty-badger." The low, slow voice licked at Blinkie like a friendly pup. "You like to help old Pop keep a tidy camp for Mother. You'll tell us where J-0 went."

Blinkie was a fattish boy. His puffy face was toadstool pale, and his pallet had a sour smell from being wet. He sat up and ducked back from the steel whip over him.

"Please d-d-d-d—" His wheezy stammer stalled his voice, and he couldn't dodge the bright whip that looped around him and dragged him up to the heat and the hum and the hot oil smell of Pop's yellow hood.

"Well, Scout Q-2?"

Blinkie gasped and stuttered and finally sagged against the plastic tracks like gray jelly. The shining coils rippled around him like thin snakes, constricting. His breath wheezed out and his fat arm jerked up, pointing at a black sign on the wall:

DANGER!
Power Access
ROBOTS ONLY!

The whips tossed him back on his sour pallet. He lay there, panting and blinking and dodging, even after the whips were gone. The scoutmaster's eyes flashed to the sign and the square grating under it, and swiveled back to Butch.

Butch was a slow, stocky, bug-eyed boy, young enough to come back from another Jamboree. He had always been afraid of Pop, but he wanted to be the new leader of Skull Patrol in Joey's place, and now he thought he saw his chance.

"Don't hit me, Pop!" His voice squeaked and his

face turned red, but he scrambled off his pallet without waiting for the whips. "I'll tell on Joey. I been wantin' all along to tell, but I was afraid they'd beat me."

"Good boy!" the scoutmaster's loud words swelled out like big soap bubbles bursting in the sun. "Mother wants to know all about Scout J-0."

"He pries that grating—" His voice quavered and caught when he saw the look on Ratbait's face, but when he turned to Pop it came back loud. "Does it every night. Since three Jamborees ago. Sneaks down in the pits where the robots work. I dunno why, except he sees somebody there. An' brings things back. Things he shouldn't have. Things like this!"

He fumbled in his uniform and held up a metal tag.

"This is your good turn today, Scout X-6." The thin tip of a whip took the tag and dangled it close to the hot red lamps. "Whose tag is this?"

"Lookit the number—"

Butch's voice dried up when he saw Ratbait's pale lips making words without a sound. "What's so much about an ID tag?" Ratbait asked. "Anyhow, what were you doing in Joey's bed."

"It's odd!" Butch looked away and squeaked at Pop. "A girl's number!"

The silent shock of that bounced off the iron walls, louder than old Pop's boom. Most of the scouts had never seen a girl. After a long time, the cubs near the door began to whisper and titter.

"Shhhhh!" Pop roared like steam. "Now we can all do a good turn for Mother. And play a little joke on Scout J-0! He didn't know today would be Jamboree, but he'll find out." Pop laughed like a heavy chain clanking. "Back to bed! Quiet as robots!"

Pop rolled close to the wall near the power pit grating, and the boys lay back on their pallets. Once Ratbait caught his breath to yell, but he saw Butch's bug-eyes watching. Pop's hum sank, and even the tenderfeet in their prams were quiet as robots.

Ratbait heard the grating creak. He saw Joey's head, tangled yellow hair streaked with oil and dust. He frowned and shook his head and saw Joey's sky blue eyes go wide.

Joey tried to duck, but the quick whips caught his neck. They dragged him out of the square black pit and swung him like a puppet toward old Pop's eyes.

"Well, Scout J-0!" Pop laughed like thick oil bubbling. "Mother wants to know where you've been."

Joey fell on his face when the whips uncoiled, but he scrambled to his feet. He gave Ratbait a pale grin before he looked up at Pop, but he didn't say anything.

"Better tell old Pop the truth." The slick whips drew back like lean snakes about to strike. "Or else we'll have to punish you, Scout J-0."

Joey shook his head, and the whips went to work. Still he didn't speak. He didn't even scream. But something fell out of his torn uniform. The whip-tips snatched it off the floor.

"What's this thing, Scout J-0?" The whip-fingers turned it delicately under the furious eyes and nearly dropped it again. "Scout J-0, this is a book!"

Silence echoed in the iron camp.

"Scout J-0, you've stolen a book." Pop's shocked voice changed into a toneless buzz, reading the title. *"Operators' Handbook, Nuclear Reactor, Series 9-Z."*

Quiet sparks of fear crackled through the camp. Two or three tenderfeet began sobbing in their prams. When they were quiet, old Pop made an ominous, throat-clearing sound.

"Scout J-0, what are you doing with a book?"

Joey gulped and bit his underlip till blood seeped down his chin, but he made no sound. Old Pop rolled closer, while the busy whips were stowing the book in a dark compartment under the yellow hood.

"Mother won't like this." Each word clinked hard, like iron on iron. "Books aren't for boys. Books are for robots only. Don't you know that?"

Joey stood still.

"This hurts me, Scout J-0." Pop's voice turned downy soft, the slow words like tears of sadness now.

"It hurts your poor Mother. More than anything can ever hurt you."

The whips cracked and cracked and cracked. At last they picked him up and shook him and dropped him like a red-streaked rag on the floor. Old Pop backed away and wheeled around.

"Fox Troop rise and smile!" Its roaring voice turned jolly again, as if it had forgotten Joey. "Hop for Pop. Today is Jamboree, and we're on our way to visit Mother. Fall out in marching order."

The cubs twittered with excitement until their leaders threatened to keep them home from Jamboree, but at last old Pop led the troop out of camp and down the paved trail toward Mother's. Joey limped from the whips, but he set his teeth and kept his place at the head of his patrol.

Marching through boy territory, they passed the scattered camps of troops whose Jamborees came on other days. A few scouts were out with their masters, but nobody waved or even looked straight at them.

The spring sun was hot and Pop's pace was too fast for the cubs. Some of them began to whimper and fall out of line. Pop rumbled back to warn them that Mother would give no gold stars if they were late for Jamboree. When Pop was gone, Joey glanced at Ratbait and beckoned with his head.

"I gotta get away!" he whispered low and fast. "I gotta get back to the pits—"

Butch ran out of his place, leaning to listen. Ratbait shoved him off the trail.

"You gotta help!" Joey gasped. "There's a thing we gotta do—an' we gotta do it now. 'Cause this will be the last Jamboree for most of us. We'll never get another chance."

Butch came panting along the edge of the trail, trying to hear, but Blinkie got in his way.

"What's all this?" Ratbait breathed. "What you gonna do?"

"It's all in the book," Joey said. "Something called manual override. There's a dusty room, down under

Mother's, back of a people-only sign. Two red buttons. Two big levers. With a glass wall between. It takes two people."

"Who? One of us?"

Joey shook his head, waiting for Blinkie to elbow Butch. "I got a friend. We been working together, down in the pits. Watching the robots. Reading the books. Learning what we gotta do—"

He glanced back. Blinkie was scuffling with Butch to keep him busy, but now the scoutmaster came clattering back from the rear, booming merrily, "Hop for Pop! Hop a lot for Pop!"

"How you gonna work it?" Alarm took Ratbait's breath. "Now the robots will be watching—"

"We got a back door," Joey's whisper raced. "A drainage tunnel. Hot water out of the reactor. Comes out under Black Creek bridge. My friend'll be there. If I can dive off this end of the bridge—"

"Hey, Pop!" Butch was screaming. "Ratbait's talking! Blinkie pushed me! Joey's planning something bad!"

"Good boy, Scout X-6!" Pop slowed beside him. "Mother wants to know if they're plotting more mischief."

When Pop rolled on ahead of the troop, Ratbait wanted to ask what would happen when Joey and his friend pushed the two red buttons and pulled the two big levers, but Butch stuck so close they couldn't speak again. He thought it must be something about the reactor. Power was the life of Mother and the robots. If Joey could cut the power off—

Would they die? The idea frightened him. If the prams stopped, who would care for the tenderfeet? Who would make chow? Who would tell anybody what to do? Perhaps the books would help, he thought. Maybe Joey and his friend would know.

With Pop rolling fast in the lead, they climbed a long hill and came in sight of Mother's. Old gray walls that had no windows. Two tall stacks of dun-colored brick. A shimmer of heat in the pale sky.

The trail sloped down. Ratbait saw the crinkled ribbon of green brush along Black Creek, and then the concrete bridge. He watched Butch watching Joey, and listened to Blinkie panting, and tried to think how to help.

The cubs stopped whimpering when they saw Mother's mysterious walls and stacks, and the troop marched fast down the hill. Ratbait slogged along, staring at the yellow sun-dazzle on old Pop's hood. He couldn't think of anything to do.

"I got it!" Blinkie was breathing, close to his ear. "I'll take care of Pop."

"You?" Ratbait scowled. "You were telling on Joey—"

"That's why," Blinkie gasped. "I wanta make it up. I'll handle Pop. You stop Butch—an' give the sign to Joey."

They came to the bridge and Pop started across.

"Wait, Pop!" Blinkie darted out of line, toward the brushy slope above the trail. "I saw a girl! Hiding in the bushes to watch us go by."

Pop roared back off the bridge.

"A girl in boy territory!" Its shocked voice splashed them like cold rain. "What would Mother say?" Black tracks spurting gravel, it lurched past Blinkie and crashed into the brush.

"Listen, Pop!" Butch started after it, waving and squealing. "They ain't no girl—"

Ratbait tripped him and turned to give Joey the sign, but Joey was already gone. Something splashed under the bridge and Ratbait saw a yellow head sliding under the steam that drifted out of a black tunnel mouth.

"Pop! Pop!" Butch rubbed gravel out of his mouth and danced on the pavement. "Come back, Pop. Joey's in the creek! Ratbait and Blinkie—they helped him get away."

The scoutmaster swung back down the slope, empty whips waving. It skidded across the trail and down the bank to the hot creek. It's yellow hood faded into the steam.

"Tattletale!" Blinkie clenched his fat fists. "You told on Joey."

"An' you'll catch it!" Murky eyes bugging, Butch edged away. "You just wait till Pop gets back."

They waited. The tired cubs sat down to rest and the tenderfeet fretted in their hot prams. Breathing hard, Blinkie kept close to Butch. Ratbait watched till Pop swam back out of the drain.

The whips were wrapped around two small bundles that dripped pink water. Unwinding, the whips dropped Joey and his friend on the trail. They crumpled down like rag dolls, but the whips set them up again.

"How's this, scouts?" Old Pop laughed like steel gears clashing. "We've caught ourselves a real live girl!"

In a bird-quick way, she shook the water out of her sand-colored hair. Standing straight, without the whips to hold her, she faced Pop's glaring lamps. She looked tall for twelve.

Joey was sick when the whips let him go. He leaned off the bridge to heave, and limped back to the girl. She wiped his face with her wet hair. They caught hands and smiled at each other, as if they were all alone.

"They tripped me, Pop," Braver now, Butch thumbed his nose at Blinkie and ran toward the machine. "They tried to stop me telling you—"

"Leave them to Mother," Pop sang happily. "Let them try their silly tricks on her." It wheeled toward the bridge, and the whips pushed Joey and the girl ahead of the crunching tracks. "Now hop with Pop to Jamboree!"

They climbed that last hill to a tall iron door in Mother's old gray wall. The floors beyond were naked steel, alive with machinery underneath. They filed into a dim round room that echoed to the grating squeal of Pop's hard tracks.

"Fox Troop, here we are for Jamboree!" Pop's jolly voice made a hollow booming on the curved steel wall, and its red lights danced in tall reflections there.

"Mother wants you to know why we celebrate this happy time each year."

The machine was rolling to the center of a wide black circle in the middle of the floor. Something drummed far below like a monster heart, and Ratbait saw that the circle was the top of a black steel piston. It slid slowly up, lifting Pop. The drumming died, and Pop's eyes blazed down on the cubs in the Anthrax Patrol, to stop their awed murmuring.

"Once there wasn't any Mother." The shock of that crashed and throbbed and faded. "There wasn't any yearly Jamboree. There wasn't even any Pop, to love and care for little boys."

The cubs were afraid to whisper, but a stir of troubled wonder spread among them.

"You won't believe how tenderfeet were made." There was a breathless hush. "In those bad old days, boys and girls were allowed to change like queer insects. They changed into creatures called adults—"

The whips writhed and the red lamps glared and the black cleats creaked on the steel platform.

"Adults!" Pop spewed the word. "They malfunctioned and wore out and ran down. Their defective logic circuits programmed them to damage one another. In a kind of strange group malfunction called war, they systematically destroyed one another. But their worst malfunction was in making new tenderfeet."

Pop turned slowly on the high platform, sweeping the silent troop with blood-red beams that stopped on Joey and his girl. All the scouts but Ratbait and Blinkie had edged away from them. Her face white and desperate, she was whispering in Joey's ear. Listening with his arm around her, he scowled at Pop.

"Once adults made tenderfeet, strange as that may seem to you. They used a weird natural process we won't go into. It finally broke down, because they had damaged their genes in war. The last adults couldn't make new boys and girls at all."

The red beams darted to freeze a startled cub.

"Fox Troop, that's why we have Mother. Her job is

to collect undamaged genes and build them into whole cells with which she can assemble whole boys and girls. She has been doing that a long time now, and she does it better than those adults ever did.

"And that's why we have Jamboree! To fill the world with well-made boys and girls like you, and to keep you happy in the best time of life—even those old adults always said childhood was the happy time. Scouts, clap for Jamboree!"

The cubs clapped, the echo like a spatter of hail on the high iron celing.

"Now, Scouts, those bad old days are gone forever," Pop burbled merrily. "Mother has a cozy place for each one of you, and old Pop watched over you, and you'll never be adult—"

"Pop! Pop!" Butch squealed. "Lookit Joey an' his girl!"

Pop spun around on the high platform. Its blinding beams picked up Joey and the girl, sprinting toward a bright sky-slice where the door had opened for the last of the prams.

"Wake up, guys!" Joey's scream shivered against the red steel wall. "That's all wrong. Mother's just a runaway machine. Pop's a crazy robot—"

"Stop for Pop!" The scoutmaster was trapped on top of that huge piston, but its blazing lamps raced after Joey and the girl. "Catch 'em, cubs! Hold 'em tight. Or there'll be no Jamboree!"

"I told you, Pop!" Butch scuttled after them. "Don't forget I'm the one that told—"

Ratbait dived at his heels, and they skidded together on the floor.

"Come on, scouts!" Joey was shouting. "Run away with us. Our own genes are good enough."

The floor shuddered under him and that bright sky-slice grew thinner. Lurching on their little tracks, the prams formed a line to guard it. Joey jumped the shrieking tenderfeet, but the girl stumbled. He stopped to pick her up.

"Help us, scouts!" he gasped. "We gotta get away—"

"Catch 'em for Pop!" that metal bellow belted them. "Or there'll be no gold stars for anybody!"

Screeching cubs swarmed around them. The door clanged shut. Pop plunged off the sinking piston, almost too soon. It crunched down on the yellow hood. Hot oil splashed and smoked, but the whips hauled it upright again.

"Don't mess around with M-M-M-M-Mother!" Its anvil voice came back, with a stuttering croak. "She knows best!"

The quivering whips dragged Joey and the girl away from the clutching cubs and pushed them into a shallow black pit, where now that great black piston had dropped below the level of the floor.

"Sing for your Mother!" old Pop chortled. "Sing for the Jamboree!"

The cubs howled out their official song, and the Jamboree went on. There were Pop-shaped balloons for the tenderfeet, and double scoops of pink ice milk for the cubs, and gold stars for nearly everybody.

"But Mother wants a few of you." Old Pop was a fat cat purring.

When a pointing whip picked Blinkie out, he jumped into the pit without waiting to be dragged. But Butch turned white and tried to run when it struck at him.

"Pop! Not m-m-m-m-me!" he squeaked. "Don't forget I told on Joey. I'm only going on eleven, and I'm in line for leader, and I'll tell on everybody—"

"That's why Mother wants you." Old Pop laughed like a pneumatic hammer. "You're getting too adult."

The whip snaked Butch into the pit, dull eyes bulging more than ever. He slumped down on the slick black piston and struggled like a squashed bug and then lay moaning in a puddle of terror.

Ratbait stood sweating, as the whip came back to him. His stomach felt cold and strange, and the tall red wall spun like a crazy wheel around him, and he couldn't move till the whip pulled him to the rim of the pit.

But there Blinkie took his hand. He shook the whip

off, and stepped down into the pit. Joey nodded, and
the girl gave him a white, tiny smile. They all closed
around her, arms linked tight, as the piston dropped.

"Now hop along for Pop! You've had your Jamboree—"

That hooting voice died away far above, and the pit's
round mouth shrank into a blood-colored moon. The
hot dark drummed like thunder all around them, and
the slick floor tilted. It spilled them all into Mother's
red steel jaws.

The Highest Dive

THE ROARING WOKE him from a crazy dream of wild
bulls bellowing. He sat up in the dark, tight with a
shock of fear. One dim red light glowed over vague
shapes around him, but they looked strange. His breath
stopped—till he remembered that the red light was
there to mark the shelter exit. Then everything came
back.

Atlas, which people called "the impossible planet"
because it was a million times too big to be a planet at
all. The Galactic Survey camp, where the shuttle ship
had dropped him two Earth-days ago. Komatsu and
Marutiak, the human spacemen with him.

But he couldn't understand that roaring, which had
been the bellow of bulls in his dream. It battered his
body, ached in his bones, dazed his brain.

"Komatsu!" He was shouting, but he couldn't hear
his own voice. "*Komatsu!*"

When he tried to listen, all he could hear was that
near and steady thunder, always louder, louder, louder.
Nothing moved in the shelter. The other men were out

on duty, maybe miles away from camp. He was all alone.

In his mind, that roar had become the yell of a black angry monster larger than Atlas. But he tried not to panic. Groping in the dark, he found the hard little disk of his voice-pack, slung from his neck.

"Spaceman Mayfield—" His scream seemed fainter than a whisper, and he cupped both hands to shield the pack. "Mayfield to Komatsu. What is this noise—"

His question seemed suddenly stupid. Maybe cowardly. He didn't want Komatsu thinking Atlas had been too much for him.

"Spaceman Max Mayfield," he called again. "Requesting instructions."

The pack began quivering in his fingers. When he held it hard to his ear, he caught faint words in Komatsu's raspy voice.

". . . tornado . . . wild weather common . . . shelter pit . . . get there quick . . . hang on, kid!"

Briefing him after he landed, Komatsu had talked about the weird weather of Atlas and pointed out the shelter pit under the floor. He got his bearings now from the exit light and jumped for the pit.

He jumped too hard.

New on Atlas, he had forgotten how he had to move. He found himself floating in the dark above his bunk, grabbing at nothing, waiting for the weak gravity to pull him down. Before he could reach anything, the wind hit.

The blast of noise hurt his ears. The breath sucked out of his lungs. The exit light winked out. Something hit him. Something spun him. Something seized him, crushed him.

No monster, of course. He knew it was only a torn scrap of the shelter, wrapped around him by the freakish gusts. But it was bad enough. It pinned his arms and covered his face. He couldn't see, couldn't breathe.

He thought he would soon be dead.

Somehow, as he spun through the air, his mother's face came into his mind. Somehow her voice came back through the howling storm. "When you're dying," she was saying, "your whole life comes back in a single flash."

He wasn't sure that was true, but many things came rushing through his head. For a while he was trying to wriggle out of the stiff fabric around him, but then his strength gave out. Finally, he just let past things flash back.

He thought of the morning at breakfast, long ago on the small Earth, when he first told his parents that he was going out to Atlas with the Galactic Survey.

"Max Mayfield!" When his mother used his full name, he knew she was angry. "We thought you were happy, here at home. We thought you loved poetry and math." He saw she was about to cry. "Why didn't you t-t-t-tell us?"

"We were hoping you might decide to stay here at the park and be a wilderness ranger." Speaking at the same time, his father frowned severely. "What's on Atlas?"

"Riddles." He put down his fork and tried to explain. "Nobody knows how anything could be so big. It's like a planet—but five thousand times as far around as Earth. I'll be on a survey team, looking for its secrets."

"Out on Atlas?" His mother's mouth gaped open. "With those space m-m-m-monsters?"

"Please, Mom!" He grinned at her tight face, but she wouldn't smile. "Ozark Wilderness is a nice quiet hiding place for us and the animals—if we're afraid of the future. But I've been hiding long enough. This is a new century, and I want to live in it. We have new worlds to know, and new friends in space."

"Giant spiders! Or worse!" She shivered. "I can't abide 'em!"

"Maybe they do look queer, but you've got to admire their brains." He tried and failed to make his father nod. "They've taught us a lot of new math. I'm glad they need us on Atlas, because I want to know them better."

"Need you?" His mother sat sadly shaking her head. "Why?"

"Because it's rough," he said. "Too rough for most of them. They hope the human teams will be tough enough and bright enough to survive there—long enough to find out what Atlas really is."

"You flabbergast us, son," his father said. "Because you've always been such a bookworm. If we're upset, it's just because we're afraid Atlas will be too much for you."

"Maybe I'm afraid, too." He had to nod. "But still I want to go. Because Atlas is a riddle—the biggest riddle in the universe. I want to prove I'm good enough to tackle it."

At that point his kid brother had come stumbling sleepily into the kitchen. The name of Atlas woke him into whooping excitement.

"You going *there*? Wow-wee! Tell about it."

They all listened while he talked about the space folk he had met and the terminal on the moon where his training would begin and the trans-sleep shots he would be taking for the long trip to Atlas. His mother was sniffling at first, but his father was soon patting her hands and they finally said they were proud that he had been chosen to go.

Atlas was nine thousand light-years from Earth, but he had slept through the flight. The orbital station where he woke was strange enough, but his training had got him used to the feel of null gravity and the queer odors of the space people.

Now, waiting to die in the core of that bellowing storm, he remembered his first glimpse of Atlas, when the mission planner guided him into observation bay. The sight shook him up.

Atlas was too big.

Still a million miles ahead, it was too big for him to see. His own Earth, at that distance, would have been a little blue-and-white marble. Atlas was endless. It was a hazy floor, mottled dark and bright, stretching out and out forever. Above it, space was a dead black dome.

"It—it gets you!" Its boundless flatness was too enormous for his mind to grasp. "What kind of world— what kind of *thing* can be so big?"

"Your mission is to help us find that out."

The planner's human voice had surprised him. Far from human itself, the space thing had picked up not just the language but also the voice of Dr. Krim, the black-bearded linguist he had known at the survey academy on the moon.

"All we can see from here is the top of the clouds," the planner said. "You'll be a thousand miles below— with its low gravity, Atlas has a very deep atmosphere. The clouds never break, never show us anything. Down there, we hope you can see what it really is."

He looked down, trying to guess what the clouds were hiding.

"We have theories enough," the planner said. "Your team will be gathering facts to help us pick the best one. Are you ready to be briefed?"

"Ready."

The briefing officer looked like a big silver starfish, but, like the planner, it spoke with the rich and ringing human voice of Dr. Krim. Its sour odor made his stomach churn, till he looked away and tried to remember his training on the moon.

"I'm Spaceman Mayfield," he managed to say. "A human volunteer—"

He wanted to go on talking about himself, because being human made him a stranger on the orbiter. He still felt weak and giddy from the trans-sleep serums, and all these new things were coming too fast. He wanted to think about hiking with his father to holograph the wilderness creatures. About teaching chess to his kid brother, who was learning a strong end game. Even about the shelf of poetry in his room—he had enjoyed knowing the real Dr. Krim, because they both liked Robert Frost.

But the briefing officer wasn't interested in Earth.

"You'll be in danger, down on Atlas." Dr. Krim's deep voice boomed out of its silver-scaled queerness.

"Nothing will ever be quite what you expect. Your instructions are to move with care, observe with intelligence, report every fact at once. Your first problem will be the gravity."

The mass of Atlas, the creature explained, was too small for its size—too small to fit any reasonable theory at all. His weight there would be only a pound and a half. Unless he learned to use the hold-ropes, even a good breeze could blow him away.

Looking aside, he listened to the few known facts about Atlas, most of them hard to believe. He learned what his work would be on the team. Finally he had to look again, because the briefing officer was holding out the voice-pack.

"Wear this. All the time. Use it. We'll be listening."

He took the pack from its snaky arms and tried to grin in a friendly way toward its single central eye, which looked like a huge mound of dark-green gelatin. After all, it wasn't half so strange as Atlas was going to be.

Whirling now in the heart of that howling storm, he was barely aware of the suffocating tightness around him. Yet a dim pain nagged him. He knew he ought to be doing something to earn his place on the team. Komatsu and Marutiak were probably hurt. He ought to be helping them. At least he ought to be reporting to the orbiter. But he had no breath for speech, no strength or will for any effort at all. He let his mind flash back to his landing on Atlas.

He had been watching from the pilot bubble as the shuttle slid down through endless miles of fog. The first thing he saw was a long dark blur, dividing hazy pink from misty blue. Then the world beneath the fog came slowly into focus, like an image in a lens. The blur became a dark mountain ridge, queerly long and straight. The pink became a flat reddish desert, gray-spotted with low mounds like piles of ashes. The blue was a flatter desert, the color of old ice.

Finally he found the camp on the ridge. The shelter was an inflated dome of yellow fabric. Yellow hold-ropes made a wide web around it. His new teammates crawled out across the web to meet him, looking like yellow spiders in their survival gear.

He was glad to be with men again but dismayed at the way Atlas had crippled them. Both looked rayburnt, drawn, grim. Komatsu had lost one leg. Raw red scars were splashed across the face and throat of Marutiak, the subchief.

The shuttle had brought big spools of new rope, crated instruments, bales and cases of supplies. Before it took off, it gave them a pickup date.

"Be here." Though it carried no human crew, its robot controls had been programmed to speak with the voice of Dr. Krim. "We're shutting down this camp, because the orbiter's moving out of shuttle range. The director expects you to find useful information before we come back to pick you up."

The date meant nothing to Max at first, because he was still wearing the Earth-time watch his parents had given him for graduation. He translated it out of Galactic Time, while he stood watching the shuttle climb and vanish into the clouds, and he found that it would be his birthday, just two weeks off. That made him think of the cake his mother would have baked, if he had stayed on Earth. Dark sweet chocolate iced with white—

"Let's go, kid," Komatsu said.

Marutiak was picking up a great bale that should have weighed a ton. Max jumped to help, and drifted in the air till Marutiak left the bale floating and turned to toss him the end of a rope.

"Thanks!" he gasped.

Marutiak pointed at his red-scarred throat, and Max realized that his voice had been destroyed.

"Hang on, kid," Komatsu was rasping. "Always hang on. Enson forgot—he's the man you came to replace."

He pulled himself after them toward the shelter, half-way swimming. Komatsu stopped at the door and raised his voice above the lazy cat-purr of the airpump.

"We stand watches. One man off and two men on. On duty, we run the experiments and report to the orbiter. Off duty, we stay inside and get what rest we can. On or off, we keep alert. Down here, kid, you'll learn that Atlas makes the rules. If you've got the brains and guts to play the Atlas game, you'll be okay."

He had tried to play the game, but Atlas was a tough opponent. His first real problem came when Komatsu asked him to come for a swim. Tired and sweaty after the long flight down, he agreed eagerly, but he wondered where any water was. Komatsu led him along a yellow rope to the edge of the ridge.

"You first." Komatsu waved him ahead. "Dive."

"Huh?"

He saw no water anywhere. The ridge was nearly flat on top, flaked and cracked with time. Ropes stretched along its rim. The reddish desert lay far, far below. Feeling bewildered, he looked back at Komatsu.

"There's our pool." Komatsu leaned out to point straight down. "The only water we've ever found on Atlas."

He gripped the rope and looked. The time-worn wall of something like black rock dropped straight down so far it made him giddy. At last he found the pool—a small round mirror of bright blue water tucked under the very foot of that frightening cliff.

"It's deep enough." Queerly casual, Komatsu pointed at another hand-rope, stretched from their feet to a rock down in the pool. "We climb that to get back." He grinned at Max. "Want me to go first?"

"You've got to be kidding!" Max stared at his dark gaunt face. "We're too—too high!"

"Just a thousand feet." Komatsu's grin grew wider. "About the same as ten at home. You fall slow here, kid. With air resistance, your terminal velocity is about fifteen feet a second. From any height, you never fall faster. Watch me."

He peeled off his yellow suit, moved to the rim in a lazy, one-legged dance, floated over it. Max leaned out to watch him drifting slowly down, arms spread like wings to guide him. He was a long time in the air, and his body had dwindled to a far dark speck before he broke the blue mirror of the pool.

Waiting, Max shifted his cramped hands on the rope. The clouds looked darker and lower. The desert of ice and the desert of ashes made no sense. Atlas had begun to seem a harder riddle than ever.

Komastsu came back at last, gliding up that long rope. His scarred body was already dry, and one leg seemed enough for him, here on Atlas. Still grinning, he waved toward the jumping place.

"Next?"

"No!" Max couldn't help shivering. "Not—not now!"

"Later, please. But do it, kid. For your own good. Enson never learned to dive. That's why he never got back when he was blown away."

"Later." Max felt miserable. "I'll try—later."

Komatsu had been nice about it—maybe too nice. He took Max around the camp to explain their duties. Weather instruments and automatic cameras and radiation meters were scattered across the ridge. Hand-ropes led down to more experiments on the ashes and the ice.

"What are we finding out?" Fighting his dread of the dive, Max came back to that monstrous riddle. "What *is* Atlas?"

"Ask the orbiter." Komatsu nodded toward the dark sky. "All we do is report the instrument readings—which never make much sense. If you want to believe the seismographs, there's half a mile of ice or rock or radioactive dust spread over a thin shell of something else—maybe matter in some new state—with nothing underneath."

Komatsu waved at a yellow wind-sock.

"Just watch that, kid. We get the worst weather in the universe. Hot winds off the desert. Blizzards off the ice. Tornadoes two hundred miles tall. When the big winds hit, better hang on. Enson didn't."

He said no more about the dive. On watch with him, Max hammered pitons into the ice to anchor the ropes to a new seismic station. On watch with Marutiak, he put on heavy radiation armor and strung new rope across the desert to reach and test a low cone of gray-glowing dust. Atlas still kept its big secret.

Suddenly, now, Max was breathing again. The bellow of the twisting winds had died—long ago. He knew he had been unconscious, and he wondered where the storm had dropped him. He felt surprised to be alive.

The stiff shelter fabric was still rolled around him, but not quite so tight. Cramped and numb at first, he squirmed and wriggled, twisted and crawled, until he could look out. What he saw was a cruel jolt.

The tornado hadn't dropped him anywhere.

It had left him high—he was afraid to guess how high. The mountain ridge had become a fine dark line far beneath, dividing rust-red desert and dull blue ice. He was alone in the eerie sky of Atlas.

"Spaceman—" Only a hoarse whisper came when he tried to call into the voice-pack. He shut his eyes against the terrible emptiness under him, and tried again. "Spaceman Mayfield to Orbiter."

"Orbiter recording." Dr. Krim's duplicated voice boomed instantly into that high silence, human and anxious. "We had lost contact. Please report."

"You won't believe it. A tornado has thrown me into the sky."

"Atlas is always surprising. Just tell us what you see."

"Not much. The ice—flat and dark and endless. The desert—just as endless. And there—the storm!"

The funnel was a thick reddish snake writhing down out of a boiling cloud, dragging across the red-and-gray desert. Still watching it, he began to feel cold air rushing up around him. He looked for the fabric scrap the wind had wrapped around him and found it high above, already left behind.

"I—I'm falling!" Terror grabbed his throat. "A hundred miles—it's a hundred miles down!"

"We're very lucky, if you can see anything from that elevation." The copied voice turned happy. "Evidently the storm has lifted the clouds. You have a rare chance to see what Atlas is."

The wind of his fall felt colder on his face, and fear of it froze him. His teeth chattered. But he tried to remember his training, tried to remember Komatsu's polite brown grin, tried to fight that terror.

Moving hands and arms against the rush of air, he learned to guide himself. A naked human aircraft, he tipped himself into a slow spiral above the bare flatness of ice and ashlike dust. At last, as the storm moved on, he found something it had hidden.

"A city!" he shouted into the voice-pack. "The ridge where we camped leads into it like a road. Wait! I think it *is* a road—two miles wide! The buildings—they must have been as high as I am now. Great queer shapes. All ruined. Broken. Falling. Black with fire—or maybe time. Because the city's old. Old, old, and dead!"

He stopped to stare at its desolate wonder.

"Go on! Describe what you see."

But that blackened, shattered city was too huge and old and strange for any words of his. Dr. Krim's bearded face had come into his shaken mind, and now he recalled the human linguist reciting Robert Frost. Two haunting lines came back:

> *Some say the world will end in fire,*
> *Some say in ice.*

Atlas, he thought, had somehow ended in both.

"Mayfield!" the pack kept booming. "Tell what else you see."

"Nothing." His first excitement had begun to die. "I'm too far off, and the clouds are sinking again. The tower-tops are already hazy. Sorry I can't see more."

The pack went dead, thumped on again.

"Mayfield, what you've seen may be the final clue we needed." The copied voice had a sudden human heartiness. "Congratulations! The survey director says your report confirms his best theory. Atlas is an artificial object, designed and built by high intelligence."

"Who could build a world—" The notion jarred him. "A world the size of Atlas?"

"We don't know yet." The voice drummed fast. "But natural planets are not efficient as dwellings for life. They catch too little sunlight. They expose too little surface for unit of mass. The director thinks that Atlas is the matter from a system of planets, rebuilt into a hollow shell, maybe only a mile or so thick. The job took engineering know-how we can barely begin to imagine. But it gave the builders a million times more living space."

"They aren't living now." Max looked at the dull clouds rolling back to cover that lost, gigantic city. "I think—I *know* they're dead."

"The director believes their energy ran out. Central sun probably dead. The ice you see covers most of Atlas. The ashlike stuff is probably waste from their last power plants. We can't be sure, till we make more landings."

The pack thumped off and on.

"The shuttle will be returning at once, to rescue survivors. If you're at the camp, you'll be picked up."

"I'll be there—if I can find the camp."

The voice from the disk was still Dr. Krim's, but somehow not quite human. "If you fail, Spaceman Mayfield, the director wants you to know that you have earned our gratitude."

The pack went off again, and he banked his shivering body into a slow circle above dark ice and dull dust. He couldn't find the camp. When he looked again for that dead city, it was gone. The rising wind grew colder. His face felt leather-stiff, and tears began to blur his vision. His spread arms grew numb and clumsy. He had trouble controlling his glide.

Yet one spark of triumph glowed in his mind. Even if he died here, Atlas hadn't really been too tough to crack. Even its huge size had turned out to be a sham. It was hollow, just a sort of cosmic bubble.

He nursed that warming thought, to keep himself alive. The glide down took a long time. Shreds of cloud began to form beneath him, hiding ice and dust. His last hopes began to freeze. He wanted to quit trying—

But then, beside that endless ridge that once had been a road, he found a small bright glint. He dived toward it, into the freezing wind that came off the ice. The ancient road grew wider, wider, until at last he made out the web of yellow ropes—and two tiny spider-figures, waving at him.

From a hundred miles up, he dived into the clear blue pool. To his numb skin, it felt almost warm. He paddled stiffly to the edge, hauled at the guide-rope with both clumsy hands, slid up it toward the camp.

The pack thumped on again. The tornado had caught Komatsu and Marutiak out on the ice, Krim's voice said. With the guide-ropes blown away, they'd had trouble getting back. But they were safe now, and the shuttle would be picking all three of them up.

"Nice dive, kid!" Komatsu was waiting with Marutiak at the top, and their happy hands helped him over the rim. "Really nice!"

Afterword

I was immensely pleased when Judy-Lynn del Rey offered to do a "best" of me, delighted again when Fred Pohl agreed to write the introduction. They are friends I trust. The project raised no problems until I came to choose the stories.

Stories are children. Some of mine have been more fortunate than others, but each was once part of me. A few I had to select because they have done well in the world, or because Fred and Judy remembered them, but there are others I love that failed to fit. Many were too long.

Yet, after several hard decisions, I'm happy enough with the final list. It's at least a fair sample. Ranging from my first published story to the most recent one, it covers nearly fifty years, during which science fiction has changed remarkably, keeping me scrambling to stay in the game. Within the limits of my own work, this book should offer some kind of perspective on a half-century of science fiction, 1928 to 1978.

The twenty-year-old who wrote "The Metal Man" seems a faraway stranger when I search my memory for him now. A half-educated kid still living with his parents on a poor sandhill farm in Eastern New Mexico, bubbling with baffled vague ambitions, just recently struck with the dazzling wonders of science fiction. I recall his loneliness, his apprehensive inhibitions, his retreats into his own imagination—all now dimmed with time and change.

Hugo Gernsback's *Amazing Stories* had just turned two in 1928, still reprinting the stunning best of H. G.

Wells and Edgar Rice Burroughs and A. Merritt, its mind-lifting contents still called "scientifiction"—it was not until the next year that Gernsback invented the term "science fiction" for another new magazine, *Science Wonder Stories*.

I mailed "The Metal Man" to him that summer. It never came back. Walking by a newsstand the following fall, I found my unfortunate hero on the cover of the December *Amazing*. Suddenly—according to Gernsback's unbelievable blurb to introduce the story—I was another Merritt, invited to write "a number of stories in a similar vein." Eagerly, I tried.

The version reprinted here is one I revised some years ago, cutting out most of the purple adjectives I had learned from Merritt, my first idol. The story is pure melodrama, with more color and action than character or theme, but I think it still reflects the wonder that has always drawn me into science fiction.

The author of "Dead Star Station" is almost equally hard for me to recall, though he is five years nearer today. He had left the ranch now and then, exploring more of America. In three years of college, he had learned a bit more science and English. Already earning a sort of living from science fiction, he had published such serials as *The Stone from the Green Star* and *Golden Blood*. Making new friends, he had written a novel with Dr. Miles J. Breuer about the colonization and revolt of the moon, had boated down the Mississippi with Edmond Hamilton.

Science fiction had its name by then, with several pulps devoted to it. For a few bright years, the Clayton chain was paying a generous two cents a word, but the depression had killed the Clayton magazines by 1933. The fine old firm of Street and Smith had taken over the Clayton *Astounding,* paying a more modest penny a word, and "Dead Star Station" was my first sale to them.

Reading the story again, I rather like it. Though the style is somewhat Victorian, old Gideon Clew shows an early effort to create character, and I think the story idea has held up rather well—the dead star in the heart of the nebula almost anticipates today's neutron stars.

With "Nonstop to Mars," we skip again, to 1939. Like the four stories that follow, it's a novelette. The short story is an exacting form, and I have always liked more freedom than it offers for expansion—I recall one story, *The Legion of Time*, that grew from 12,000 to 40,000 words as I retyped it. The novelette is a good form for science fiction, as Jim Gunn has commented, because it gives the writer space to fill out a new background or to follow the implications of a new idea—things that stretch the limits of the short story.

It was my first sale to *Argosy*—then still the beloved old all-fiction weekly pulp that had been printing Merritt and Burroughs and others as "different stories" long before Gernsback thought of "science fiction." Making *Argosy* was an old ambition of mine; I had tried there with *Golden Blood* and *The Legion of Space*.

That prewar year now seems hardly more real than a dream. Though Europe and Asia were brewing troubles enough, the great depression had ended here. The air was still good to breathe, the world had room enough, atomic war was still unlikely fiction. I think we were all more confident then, and I like "Nonstop to Mars" for its reckless optimism. We still had heroes.

I had been in love with early aircraft, haunting airports when I had a chance, and pulling a prop through to start the motor when a pilot would let me. This story comes partly from that old infatuation and partly from a wonderful fantasy by Lord Dunsany, "Distant Cousins."

"The Crucible of Power," also published in 1939, was written for John W. Campbell, who had followed F. Orlin Tremaine at *Astounding*. The greatest of editors, with a sharp sense of story value and a brimming faith in science and the future, he was already finding and inspiring able new writers to create the memorable "Golden Age of Science Fiction."

This story is one that came alive and shaped its own direction. In my first plan for it, the narrator was to tell his own story, opening with an introductory chapter about his father. Unexpectedly, the father seized the whole story. Campbell seemed as delighted with him as I was, calling him "a hero with a heart of purest brass."

The assumed future history is a bit too cautious and sometimes mistaken. We have reached the moon and cracked the atom somewhat sooner than I anticipated. Our Mariner probes failed to photograph the canals that still seemed possible in 1939, and our Viking landers have not yet found the half-ruined cities we used to imagine for their builders. Yet Garth Hammond himself is still alive for me.

Though the solar power plant may seem a bit fantastic, the background was worked out with some care. Not long after the story appeared, a rocket engineer told me that he was running lab tests on my multicellular rockets. Later I learned that he had died in an explosion. I wondered for years if my rocket design had been as unsafe in reality as in the story, until Sprague de Camp told me that the unlucky engineer had simply dropped a bottle of picric acid.

Science fiction is a remarkably open and pliant medium, offering the writer a stimulating freedom to say nearly anything he pleases—recently, in nearly any sort of language—so long as he keeps the story going. "Breakdown," which Campbell published in 1941, comes from a time when I was absorbed in philosophies of history, especially with the notion that nations or cultures or civilizations are organisms that grow and mature and die like individual beings.

Such notions are inviting, not only because they seem to show patterns in past history but also because they offer predictions for the future. I have come to question them now, however, because the intriguing analogies between the living body and the body politic are only analogies after all, yielding no more truth than we put into them.

Despite such doubts, I still see truth in "Breakdown." Revolutionary movements do break up the petrified past to create new and freer institutions—which in time petrify again, crippling free human growth once more until they in turn are shattered by new revolutionary movements.

Too, all philosophies of history aside, there's a tragic drama in the fall of a family or a city or an empire. The fall of Sunport still has for me something of the melancholy mystery I have always felt in the falls of Babylon and Carthage and Rome. Boss Kellon, besides, is the sort of social leader that used to fascinate me.

"Breakdown" has a sequel, by the way, which I began as *Star of Empire*. When I ran into a block with that, John Campbell came to the rescue, urging me to try a new name and style, as he had done with Don A. Stuart. I became Will Stewart to write the "seetee" stories, about anti-matter—and then went off to become an Army Air Forces weather forecaster in World War II. Finally published in 1955, in collaboration with Jim Gunn, the sequel is *Star Bridge*.

"With Folded Hands" is clearly my most successful story. Written in 1946, the year after I got back from the Northern Solomons, it was published by John Campbell in 1947. At his creative suggestion, it too was followed by a sequel, *The Humanoids,* my best-received novel. (Now, thirty years later, I'm at work on a new novel about these too-perfect robots.)

On the surface, the story is a shudder at the terrors of our technological future. We are utterly undone by our own best invention. Since the story was written, however, I have found that its emotional basis has another source, which gives it at least for me an added kind of meaning.

The humanoids are purely benevolent, frustrating Underhill for his own good. His predicament is my own, I think, unconsciously recalled from my earliest childhood, with my own parents in the role of the humanoids, protecting me in spite of myself. (Through my first few years we lived on a wilderness ranch in the high Sierra Madre of northern Mexico, where my mother, afraid of scorpions and mountain lions and renegade Apaches, tried too hard, I think, to keep me safe.)

With this interpretation, the humanoids become not merely the ultimate machine but also a metaphor for society—for the often-implacable forces of the family and the nation, of folkways and the law, that limit our individual freedom as the price of group survival. I suppose this universal social bargain is commonly comfortable enough, but for me as a child it must have been painful.

"The Equalizer" is a companion piece, written at the same time and published the same year. My first effort to write about the humanoids had given me trouble, perhaps because I was so much depressed to discover that the problem they presented had no solution—I had meant for them to be defeated. I pushed the unfinished manuscript aside, to write "The Equalizer."

If the humanoids symbolize the ultimate threat of the machine, the equalizer stands for an equally ultimate technological promise. If the humanoids, beyond that, are a metaphor revealing society crushing its members into a deadly conformity, the equalizer is surely a contradictory symbol for the absolute freedom of the individual self.

I'm not quite certain that an actual equalizer would create any such utopia in the real world, but the story was a delight to write and it liberated me from that depression about the humanoids. I came back to them with a clarified purpose and a fresh point of view, to finish "With Folded Hands."

Science fiction has always foreseen our uncertain tomorrows with two contrasting faces, a smile of hope and a mask of terror. Teaching a science-fiction class, I looked for readings to show both attitudes. The pessimists form a distinguished and persuasive line that runs through Swift and the early Wells down to Fred Pohl and the "New Wave." Though the optimists have never quite matched them in power and conviction, we can follow a thread of confidence in man's reason and his future, running from Plato and Lord Bacon down to

Arthur Clarke and Robert Heinlein and Isaac Asimov.

"With Folded Hands" and "The Equalizer" illustrate those two extremes, I think—technology as demon and technology as savior. In actual fact, of course, the truth lies somewhere between. Technology is only a tool, which comes wrapped in the challenge to use it well. Magazine science fiction was mostly optimistic when I began writing, the glamor of its futures hardly tainted by the academic pessimists. Though an occasional mad or villainous scientist menaced the world, the engineer—like old Gideon Clew—was often the hero. Year by year since then the shocks and threats of nuclear war and poisonous pollutants and future world famines have shattered those old hopes, until panic has almost paralyzed us.

This blind terror of technology is our great danger now, I believe, not technology itself. Science holds no malice. If we can learn to apply it well, it can solve most of the problems it has created—always raising new ones, no doubt, which in turn it can commonly solve again. In our current environmental panic, I think we have lost perspective. After all, the pipelines and the strip mines and the breeder reactors are somewhat lesser threats to the balance of nature than fire and the axe and the plow once were.

"The Peddler's Nose" and "The Happiest Creature" belong to a series of stories written in the early 1950s, during a surge of concern about UFOs. Though I'm pretty skeptical about any actual visitors from space, contact with alien cultures has always been a staple science-fiction theme. For these stories, I assumed that we are being watched by galactic observers—to make the observers human, I said that their remote ancestors had come from Earth, since I doubt that independent evolution on another planet could ever shape anything quite like us. The description of our world from the alien viewpoint made for ironic inversions that I enjoyed. (The whole series was finally rewritten into a book, *The Trial of Terra.*)

"The Cold Green Eye" is a bit of fantasy, rather than

science fiction—the distinction for me is that fantasy asks for poetic faith in things impossible, while science fiction assumes some degree of possibility. The first draft of the story was written in 1945 in a replacement depot near Manila while I was waiting to get home from the war, but it was not finished and published until 1953. I have always relished the ironic view of Aunt Agatha's world through Tommy's different eyes.

In contrast to this fantasy, "Operation Gravity" is hard science fiction, written for Hugo Gernsback's *Science Fiction Plus,* where it appeared in 1953—Gernsback used to say he wanted solid science. Picking up the theme of "Dead Star Station" twenty years later, it's about an actual neutron star. Surprisingly, considering that the first real pulsar was not observed until long after 1953, the science still looks rather good.

The plot is simple: men meet star. Trying to add character and drama, I told the story from the viewpoint of a human villain, the stuffy old officer who doesn't care to meet a star. I'm not quite sure how well the experiment works; the ironic gulf between the reader and the team of heroic engineers is perhaps a bit too wide.

"Guinevere for Everybody," published in 1954, must have been one of the first stories about cloned human beings. In a picture magazine, I had seen an overeager promise of personal immortality, to be achieved by replication through the cloning process. A pessimist again, I tried to satirize the notion. Fred Polh, himself an often-pessimistic satirist, bought the story for *Star Science Fiction.*

Science fiction had been growing again since the war, breaking out of the old pulp ghetto. Book publishers wanted it. John Campbell suddenly had two able rivals, Tony Boucher as editor of *Fantasy and Science Fiction* and Horace Gold with *Galaxy.* Scores of bright young writers appeared, most of them ahead of me in education and perhaps in talent.

Striving to stay in the game, I received an unexpected assist. Through an unlikely freak of fate, the

New York *Sunday News* hired me to write a weekly comic strip—TV had begun to hurt the paper's enormous circulation, and somebody hoped that such an exclusive new feature might help hold readers.

Called *Beyond Mars,* the strip grew out of my "seetee" novels. The artist was Lee Elias, who had worked with Milt Caniff and learned his clean-cut style. With an admirable skill, he helped create exotic characters and futuristic machines and the whole atmosphere of space adventure. The strip ran a little over three years, 1952–1955, but in the end it was not a sufficient answer to TV. Syndicated overseas, though kept exclusive here, the strip seems to have been popular enough, but Lee and I, with no control, were helpless when the *News* decided to kill it.

That was a hard blow at the time; I had liked the new medium almost as much as I did the weekly paychecks. But I had already begun taking spare-time courses at Eastern New Mexico University, my hometown school, and enjoyed them so much that I went back full-time to get two degrees in 1957.

After two years as instructor in a military school and another at the University of Colorado, I came home in 1960 to a place in the English department at Eastern. A college dropout long ago, because the courses I was taking had nothing to do with science fiction, I found this late return to academe a rewarding experience, allowing me to learn and teach everything from linguistics and literary criticism to William Faulkner and James Joyce and the great Russian novelists.

Though teaching took most of my energy and time, I held on where I could to science fiction. Thanks to Fred Pohl, whose rich gifts include a happy talent for collaboration, I was able to finish two trilogies with him. I rewrote my doctoral dissertation on the early science fiction of Wells into a book, *H. G. Wells: Critic of Progress* (Mirage, 1973). I taught science fiction for a dozen years, writing and speaking when I could to promote it as a legitimate academic subject. I edited a book for teachers, *Science Fiction: Education for Tomorrow* (Mirage, 1978).

Using vacations for writing as well as for a bit of travel, I was able to turn out a few more novels of my own—*Bright New Universe, The Moon Children,* and *The Power of Blackness*—and now and then another short story.

"Jamboree" is one of these, written in 1969, after I had been to one of Damon Knight's summer workshops. Damon is a great old hand as writer and editor and critic, and his yearly Milford Conferences are postgraduate seminars in science fiction. He invites twenty-five or so professionals, each to bring a story for criticism by the whole group. The comments are often painful but sometimes useful. Writing "Jamboree," I was trying to apply what I had tried to learn about style and story construction. I meant it for Harlan Ellison's *Dangerous Visions* series, but my agent sold it to *Galaxy* instead.

In theme, it parallels "With Folded Hands"—in fact, writing it as a literary experiment, I was trying to match the meaning and effect of that novelette in a short story. If Mother and old Pop stand for runaway technology killing humanity, I think they also just as clearly symbolize the forces of society that can conflict so cruelly with the needs and feelings of the individual self.

"The Highest Dive" has surprised me. I wrote it on speculation for a magazine that was overstocked by the time I got it done. My American agent failed to place it here, and I sent it to England. With no news from it, I gave it up as a failure. The surprise came in an unexpected letter from Terry Carr, asking to include it in his 1977 *Best Science Fiction of the Year.* I learned then that it had been featured in a 1976 issue of the British *Science Fiction Monthly.*

The Dyson sphere setting was borrowed, with a good deal of variation, from a new trilogy that Fred Pohl and I have in collaborative progress—*The Farthest Star, Wall Around a Star,* and another novel not yet finished or named. Freeman Dyson, a mathematician at the Institute for Advanced Study, has suggested that in our search for other intelligence out in the galaxy we should be looking for sources of infrared radiation escaping as waste heat from such ultimate works of cosmic engineering, built to catch and utilize all a star's energy. The trilogy is about another such sphere, presented in much richer detail.

This book rounds out my first fifty years of science fiction. For me—echoing the name of the pioneer magazine that printed "The Metal Man" in 1928—it has been an amazing half-century, in which I have watched the genre grow from that first lone pulp to our current yearly avalanche of nearly a thousand books, from the new name for it that used to puzzle all my friends to the vast popularity of *Star Trek* and *Star Wars* and all the thousands of elective courses in the high schools and colleges.

I'm proud and happy to have been involved. Retired now from my university job after twenty years of teaching, I'm looking happily forward to several more decades of science fiction. I'll miss the stimulation of my colleagues and my students and the classroom—it was nice being paid to read and talk about great literature. But now and then science fiction is admirable literature. Escape, if you will, but now and then something more. For me, it has always been an exciting new language, invented to show us the possible and wonderful or dreadful new worlds coming.